Praise for

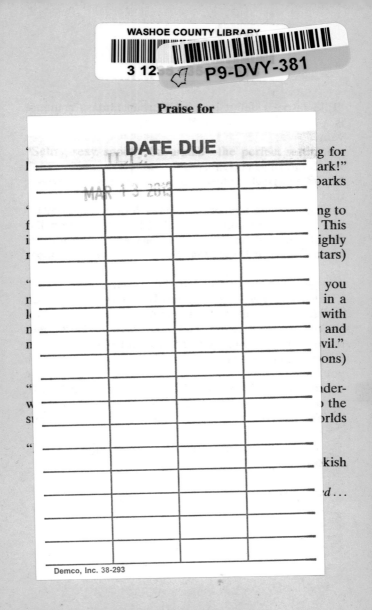

"Setr... esy... the perfect ...ing for
... ...ark!"
... ...parks

"... ...ng to
f... . This
i... ...ighly
r... ...tars)

"... ...you
n... ...in a
le... ...with
n... ...r and
n... ...vil."
... ...ons)

"... ...der-
w... ...o the
su... ...rlds

"... ...kish

... d . . .

"Elle Jasper's debut into light urban fantasy romance is a quick and fun romp into the underground of Savannah's warm nights . . . in this seductive, witty drama where the story flows like magic and the characters are very exciting. Mixing pop culture and occult references, Ms. Jasper brings to the table a sizzling new adventure that will leave you panting for more."

—Paperback Dolls

"Bravo to Ms. Jasper for giving readers a vampire/urban fantasy series they can sink their teeth into."

—The Romance Dish

"The first book in the Dark Ink Chronicles starts out with a bang. The protagonist, Riley Poe, grabs you by the throat and doesn't let go. Instead of slowly building, the characters and steamy setting of Savannah pull the reader right into their world and have their way with you. It's a superb beginning to an unusual and addictive series and Jasper is destined to become a fan favorite."

—*Romantic Times* (4½ stars)

The Dark Ink Chronicles
by Elle Jasper

Afterlight

Everdark

THE DARK INK CHRONICLES

ELLE JASPER

A SIGNET ECLIPSE BOOK

SIGNET ECLIPSE
Published by New American Library, a division of
Penguin Group (USA) Inc., 375 Hudson Street,
New York, New York 10014, USA
Penguin Group (Canada), 90 Eglinton Avenue East, Suite 700, Toronto,
Ontario M4P 2Y3, Canada (a division of Pearson Penguin Canada Inc.)
Penguin Books Ltd., 80 Strand, London WC2R 0RL, England
Penguin Ireland, 25 St. Stephen's Green, Dublin 2,
Ireland (a division of Penguin Books Ltd.)
Penguin Group (Australia), 250 Camberwell Road, Camberwell, Victoria 3124,
Australia (a division of Pearson Australia Group Pty. Ltd.)
Penguin Books India Pvt. Ltd., 11 Community Centre, Panchsheel Park,
New Delhi - 110 017, India
Penguin Group (NZ), 67 Apollo Drive, Rosedale, Auckland 0632,
New Zealand (a division of Pearson New Zealand Ltd.)
Penguin Books (South Africa) (Pty.) Ltd., 24 Sturdee Avenue,
Rosebank, Johannesburg 2196, South Africa

Penguin Books Ltd., Registered Offices:
80 Strand, London WC2R 0RL, England

First published by Signet Eclipse, an imprint of New American Library,
a division of Penguin Group (USA) Inc.

First Printing, June 2011
10 9 8 7 6 5 4 3 2 1

For the girls at Coffee Buy the Book in Pulaski, Virginia: Tracey, Jill, Steph, Pennie, Ally, Holly, Jill (there're two!), Janie, Tawana, and the only nongirl, Dan the Man—this one's yours, guys. Thanks so much for your support, hospitality, and the big freaking production you make for the fan-freaking-tastic book signings you invite me to! It's the most fun I've had as an author yet! For the super readers and fans who show up to support and buy my books, for the food and wine, and for an always-memorable stay at the gorgeous Rockwood Manor—and for the friendship. I thank you. Totally. You make me feel like a rock star!

ACKNOWLEDGMENTS

The following people *rock* at motivating, supporting, and encouraging me throughout the sometimes-grueling (self-inflicted!) and rewarding process of writing a novel. They give that certain special and influential kick in the ass I am so deserving of at times, and for that, I'm eternally grateful. They are my sisters, my best pals—my she-wolf pack! Kim Lenox, Leah Marie Brown, Betsy Kane, Eveline Chapman, Karol Miles, Molly Hammond, Allison Bunton, Valerie Morton, Bhing Dequito, Tyler Homberger, Sheri Dotson, Tracy Pierce, the Denmark Sisterhood, and, as always, my best friend of all—my mom, Dale Nease. You guys freakin' rock-a-dilly! Thanks for being in my life.

Part One

TAINTED

"Life and death appeared to me ideal bounds, which I should first break through, and pour a torrent of light into our dark world."

—Mary Shelley, *Frankenstein*

"There's a part of me that knows Eli wants me forever—as in it's unacceptable for him to even consider my death, no matter how far into the future it may be. Okay—I like that. Who wouldn't? Never have I wanted someone so badly, and never has anyone wanted me the way Eli does. But I think he wants to turn me, and that sort of freaks me out. I don't want to live forever. It's not . . . natural. I'm not scared of him or anything, but let's just say I sleep with one eye open."

—Riley Poe

Da Island, Gullah
Off the coast of Savannah, Georgia
mid-September

"Hold her down!"

Fire ripped through my insides, through my veins, under my skin, deep into my muscles, and I thrashed against the three pairs of strong arms trying to hold me still—I didn't know why or who they were. I didn't know where I was. I saw nothing but blood behind my eyes, streaks of crimson blurring my vision, and my head pounded with each sluggish thump of my exaggerated heartbeat. I knew only pain, and I wanted to get the freaking hell away from it, out of the tangled arms trying to restrain me. "Get the fuck off me!" I gritted through my teeth. Their grips tightened. The air was smoldering hot all around me as if it poured from a five-hundred-degree oven. It made the burning inside my body even more intense, and the heavy scent of salt and rotted sea life wafted to me. I wanted to puke.

"I liked it better when she couldn't move," a voice I knew but couldn't place said sarcastically. It had a slight French accent.

I kicked out hard and caught someone on the jaw with my heel. A muffled curse and laughter reached my ears. I didn't care. I was in friggin' agony, and getting out of it was all that mattered. I fought harder, growling and spitting. An all-consuming hate filled me. I felt it through my skin, all the way to my bones. Finally, I broke free. I scrambled on all fours but didn't make it far. Someone's full body slammed me into the scorching sand, and I lay there, trapped, under the crushing weight—in anguish. I swore, but the sound came out muffled as coarse grains pushed into my open mouth. Whatever was on top of me was squeezing the breath out of me. I coughed. Air had a hard time getting back into my lungs. I wheezed.

"Ease up, Zetty," another familiar voice said. "You're pushing her face into the sand. She can't breathe."

Zetty? What the hell? An unfamiliar, guttural sound came from the weight trapping me. I bucked, or tried to, anyway.

"Here, give this to her," another voice said. "Fast."

"You give it to her, Bro."

I heard a muttered curse, then felt a sharp pinprick in my ass. I bucked again, hard. I screamed, but it was no use. I lay there in the sand, with a big, heavy-ass Zetty stretched out on top of me as I cursed and wailed, until a drugging, calming haze swept over me, pulling me down. The pain eased, my lids grew heavy, and, finally, shadows crowded me, claiming me. I knew nothing else, and that was freaking fine by me. For however long, I slept.

A breeze drifted over my skin and across my face, and I cracked open my eyes. I anticipated pain, and that unbearable burning, but thankfully, there was none. My vision was blurry, but long shadows fell over me, accompanied by the cooler temperature of the afterlight, making everything around me hazy.

"Hey, you."

Only then did I notice strong fingers interlaced with mine, and I turned my head and blinked several times until Eli's face, lit by a kerosene lamp, came into focus. Dark shadows melded against perfect, pale skin, and the contrast made my breath catch. Had I ever feared him? Even now, it was hard for me to imagine his face contorted into the monster I knew he could become. He bent closer, and I inhaled his unique, drugging scent. "Hey," I said, my voice scratchy, sore, and broken. "What happened? I feel as if a train hit me." I did, too. My whole body ached, down to the bone—almost to the cellular level. Grinding my teeth together, I noticed grit. Sand?

"Yeah, sand," Eli said, brushing my hair back from my forehead. "And your body aches because Zetty threw his full weight onto you. Damn, he's one big Tibetan." I found a bottle of water pressed to my lips. "Rinse and drink." I did. Eli then leaned down and pressed his mouth to mine. A thrill shot through me, and my insides fluttered as the pressure of Eli's lips settled, moved, tasted, caressed.

Possessed.

The pressure eased, and Eli pulled back, his darkening gaze fastened on mine. The small silver hoop still adorned his brow, and I decided I seriously liked it. "You fight like a wildcat." The corner of his mouth tipped upward into the sexiest grin I'd ever seen. He nuzzled my neck. "Turns me on," he whispered.

"Yeah, I bet it does, freak," I said lightly. I laughed, shaking off the erotic shiver that coursed through my body at his seductive words. A powerful surge of desire for Eli gripped me, and, to be frank, it sort of took me off guard. It was strong. And not just midtwenties, hot-blooded American girl, horny strong. It was powerful as hell.

Eli's striking blue eyes darkened even more, turning almost stormy in color as he stared down at me. "It's one of your tendencies," he said, and he stroked my bottom lip with his thumb.

"What is?" I asked, shivering.

"Your extreme horniness," he answered proudly. "Definitely a perk, not that you had any problem before—"

My hand over his mouth stopped his words, and I grinned. "You're in big trouble now, Dupré," I said, my voice raspy, deeper than usual, and I slipped my hand around his neck, pulling his mouth to mine.

"Promise?" Eli whispered against me.

"Oh yeah," I said, and parted his lips with my tongue, kissing him deeply. A thousand sensations blasted through me at once as an intense, almost unbearable heat pooled between my legs. In the next second, a burst of power exploded from my body as I grabbed Eli, flipped him over, off the makeshift bed of pillows and quilts, and onto the hard-packed sand. A small grunt escaped his throat, and for some reason, I liked that. I pinned him beneath me, my legs straddling his waist, my crotch grinding against him, my knees digging into the coarse sand and my hands trapping his above his head. All in under three seconds. Swear to God.

Eli Dupré did nothing more than smile. And it was a wicked, wicked smile.

With such speed I surprised myself, I gathered both of his hands in one, and before my brain even registered my actions, I was reaching for his button fly. I wanted him, and I meant to have him—yesterday.

The dark glimmer in Eli's eyes meant he was going to let me.

I had three buttons undone, my hand inside his jeans, and a low moan emitting from Eli's throat when a voice interrupted.

"Whoa, girl," Phin said, way too close. "Not in front of the children, huh?"

"Yeah, dude. Get a room."

Laughter erupted around me, deep male chuckles mixed with squeaky adolescent ones.

In the next instant, my body left Eli's, and I was lifted and settled hard on my feet, outside the open-air tent in which I'd been attacking Eli. I turned, and a small flickering campfire cast amber light into laughing green eyes filled with mischief. "Yeah, Sis. Especially not in front of the children. That's just . . . gross."

I leapt and threw my arms around my brother. "Seth!" I said, burying my face against the strong column of his neck. It was the first time I'd seen him since, well, before. When he'd been in transition, before his almost-quickening. "Oh my God, I've missed you!" My heart literally pounded with sheer joy. I had my brother back! I squeezed tighter, and happiness shot through me.

Seth's long arms hugged me tightly, and he lifted me off the ground. "I missed you, too, Ri." A small crack in his voice let me know just how emotional my little brother really was.

I hugged him for a long, long time and, finally, after drawing in his familiar scent, I pulled back and looked at him—really looked at him. Bare-chested, barefoot, and wearing only a pair of low-slung black board shorts that hung to his knees, he seemed . . . different. Way different—not the teenage brother I'd known a month before. Without even thinking, I touched his face, then his jaw. Pushing aside the dark sweep of hair from his forehead, I felt the growing muscles in his chest, the rocks carved into his stomach. I turned him around and checked out his lean back. His normally pale skin was tanned from the sun, and, just below the board shorts, I saw a strip of colorless skin where his tan ended and his white butt began. Just as fast, I turned him back around to face me. I blinked. He hardly looked like my baby brother. It wasn't that he looked older or anything. Just . . . different. Can someone look wiser? I stared at him. "You've changed, Bro."

"Right?" he said proudly, and gave himself a quick glance. "I've been working out with Zetty and the guys." Then, his face grew serious, his eyes somber, and worry lines gathered between his brows. "Are you gonna be all right?"

For whatever reason, his concern worried me. I glanced at Phin, Luc, then Eli, before turning back to Seth. "Of course," I assured him, and punched his arm. "No prob. I feel better already, just seeing you." I did, too. It seemed like forever since I'd seen him. Normal, that is. If you could call what we'd become normal. I stared at my brother a little more. Something struck me, deep inside—a twinge. My gaze moved from his face to his throat, and there it lingered. The pulse of his heart barely lifted the skin there, keeping in sync with the beat as the blood pulsed through his veins. I became transfixed, staring at that spot. Inside my body, seemingly just beneath the surface, I quivered.

Seth studied me a few seconds more, grinned, and draped an arm over my shoulders. "Good. So, you wanna hang?"

"Probably not a good idea," Eli said, glancing at me before meeting Seth's gaze. "Not alone, anyway. At least, not for a while." He gave me a slight smile. "Still working out a few kinks." He pulled my arm. What was wrong with me?

"Yeah," Luc said with a laugh, giving me a twinkling-eyed look. "Kinks. That's what they call it now. Kinks."

It was only then I noticed the others. Phin, Luc, and Josie stood behind Seth, along with several of the teens who'd been on the verge of become newling vamps.

"Smokin' hot as usual, babe," Riggs Parker said from the small crowd. He pushed closer, his shaggy dark hair hanging across his eyes. With a quick flip of his head, he whipped his hair aside. "I'll work the kinks out with you, Riley."

Luc smacked Riggs on the back of the head. Everyone laughed. Riggs merely shrugged and grinned. "Can't blame a dude for tryin'."

So Riggs had made it. Still a freaking little pervert, and cocky as always, but he'd made it. I noticed the same pulsing point at his throat that I'd noticed on Seth, but

I shook my head and forced myself not to fixate on it. I glanced around at the familiar faces, and some new ones, and then looked at Eli. "So, what is this? Some weird vampy version of *Lord of the Flies*? Or *Vamp Camp*?" Then, it hit me, and I scowled. "What kinks?"

"Whoa, time to go," Luc said, and gave Riggs a push. "I think Eli can handle this. Come on, guys. Ricky's got some 'splainin' to do. Estelle has dinner ready, anyway." With a series of shrill whoops, the *Lord of the Flies* boys, all bare to the waist and wearing various colors of board shorts, took off with Luc. I couldn't help but wonder exactly what dinner was going to be. I glanced around. Zetty stood, arms crossed over his big chest and his eyes trained on me. I'd never seen Zetty dressed in anything except his traditional Tibetan clothes—a long red yak wool wrap and baggy black pants tucked into short leather boots. He now wore, like the others, a pair of baggy board shorts. His were red. The handwoven, multicolored sheath crossed his bare chest, encasing the traditional Nepali knife he never went anywhere without. He didn't say a word. He, too, had a pulse point that drew my attention. His hand slipped up and covered the spot; then he glared at me. His shiny black brows were furrowed, and the unique red and yellow tattooed squares and dots that marked him as a once-Shiva follower sat stark against his tanned forehead. They made him look unapproachable; scary. And I'd apparently done something to piss him off.

Seth pulled me out of thought and into a tight hug. "I love you, Ri," he said against my ear. "Swear to God, I'll never leave you again."

That boy always could melt my heart. I hugged him fiercely back. "You won't have to," I assured him, even though his concern really concerned me. I pulled back and studied him. "Now go. Eat. I'll be right behind you."

Seth held my gaze for several seconds. "You probably won't be, but it's okay. I'll be there when you're ready." He smiled, presenting a sincere, winsome look that made him seem mature beyond his fifteen years. Then he turned to Zetty. "Let's go, Zet-Man." The two took off up the beach, Seth's tanned body alongside Zetty's, well, huge one, melding into the afterlight. I stared after my brother, my jaw dropping in wonder at the speed at which Seth ran—and how Zetty could almost keep up. The mystical man from Nepal had a long black braid that whipped from side to side as he ran. I stared until my vision blurred. "Whoa," I muttered, and shook my head. "Weird." In the distance, I saw another campfire, larger, close to the shore, its orange hues and blue sparks reaching toward the darkening sky. A small figure huddled close to the flames. Squinting, I made out the colorful fabric patches of Estelle's familiar billowy skirt.

A nervous twinge gripped me. Something was up. I was purposely being kept apart from everyone. I wanted to spend time with my brother, and I missed my Gullah grandparents. "What's wrong with me?" I asked Eli. The look in Seth's eyes had disturbed me.

Strong arms slid around my waist from behind, and Eli pulled me against him tightly. He rested his chin on my shoulder, his lips close to my ear. I shuddered and leaned my head against his chest. "Tell me," I said. "Everything. I can't remember anything except waking up on Da Island, unable to move. And I don't even know how long ago that was."

Eli sighed and held me tighter. "Your body is going through d.t.'s, sort of," he said. "Your recovery is going a little slower than we'd hoped. "You've been here almost two weeks."

Damn. I'd lost two weeks out of my life. "D.t's? From what?" I asked.

"The Arcoses' venom. It has tainted your blood."

"Seriously?" I asked, and, swear to God, my blood at that moment suddenly felt several degrees colder.

"Yeah, I'm serious," he said. He cocked his head and studied me. "You don't remember me taking you to Da Island, after Bonaventure?"

I thought, then shook my head. "I guess I don't."

Eli nodded. "I'm glad. You were not in a good way, Riley. We had to contain you and the others, and staying in the city would have been risky. So we brought the almost-newlings—you, Seth, the others—to Da Island for rehab. You got the worst of it since both Arcoses infected you. Although your blood and their venom were mixed for only a short time, it was long enough for you to become addicted to it—intensely addicted, from the moment they bit you. Your body craves it now, and there's no way to tell how long it will last. You've been in d.t.'s the whole time with only short periods of lucidity. Like now."

"Is that what was wrong with me a few minutes ago?" I asked, my throat tightening at the thought. "I . . . was staring at the pulses in Seth's throat, in Zetty's, Riggs'. As if I wanted it. Wanted their blood." With the pads of my fingers, I pushed against my closed eyes, then looked up at him. "So you're telling me I could snap at any second like some animal? Attack Seth? That's what I'd felt a second ago. As if I wanted to jump on him." I shook my head. "No freaking way, Eli. I want it out of me."

Eli gripped my shoulders and stared sternly at me.

"Preacher has been working crazy hours to flush your system safely. The side effects are . . . extreme. Out of control." He turned me around and stared down at me. With his thumb, he grazed my jaw. "Riley, you will always carry some of their DNA. And that makes you more than a little unpredictable. But I can handle you. We will work through this. Together. I won't leave you alone for a second. Understand?"

I watched the play of firelight dance across his features, noticing how it threw parts of his face into dark shades and jagged planes. I would always have a little Arcos in me? That bothered the hell out of me. At least the d.t.'s would eventually go away. I didn't like eyeballing my brother's arteries. "The pain?" I asked, remembering the torturous feeling that had gripped me into a feral insanity. "Will it come back?"

Eli nodded. "Yes, it will. It's not over yet," he said, and I could plainly see how much he hated telling me, or rather, how much he hated that it would happen. "I hate it way more than you can imagine," he said, reading my thoughts. "It kills me to see you in agony, and that I can't do a goddamn thing about it pisses me off even more." In the firelight, his eyes darkened dangerously, and I knew then that to be on Eli Dupré's bad side could be a frightening thing. Luckily, he liked me.

I pushed aside my mounting fear and braved a big fake smile. "Don't worry, Dupré. I can handle it," I said, and slipped my arms around his waist. "Easy peasy. No prob. Just make sure I don't hurt anyone."

With a muttered French curse, Eli shook his head. "Always a badass, huh, Poe?" he said, then cocked his head at me and smiled. "I truly dig that about you."

"I know you do," I answered, and grazed his lips

slowly with mine. Then, Eli kissed me—the kiss possessive, hard, erotic—and for so long I lost my breath. At
some point, I lost consciousness—as in totally passed
out. I'd like to say Eli's intense, passionate kissing/mak-
ing out rocked my world so hard that I fainted, but only
later did I realize what had really happened, and for
how long.

Nightmares plagued me; hunger plagued me worse. I
crawled around on all fours, lunging and gnashing at
anything that happened by. Heartbeats thumped all
around me, and I could hear blood rushing through ves-
sels. I wanted it. I needed it.

I fought to get it. I didn't care whose it was.

The big one had to have a lot; I could smell it, almost
taste it on my tongue. Like a cat, I waited; he grew close.
I leapt, wrapped my legs around his waist, and used all
my strength to hold him still. I wanted what pumped
through his veins. Hands grasped me; voices yelled. I
was pulled off. I thrashed; my body writhed; on all fours
I scrambled away. My senses alerted me to another—a
smaller one—but the resonating whoosh-whoosh of the
substance I craved pumping through his body beckoned
me. I crouched, then lunged, wrapping my whole body
around him to prevent escape. Something coldcocked
me in the head—in the fucking head! I flew back, my
prize released, and I hit the ground hard. Air left my
lungs. My head throbbed. I lay there, seeing nothing
but darkness and stars. My chest rose and fell. My heart
barely beat. Stillness washed over me. I was unsure
whether I was sleeping or dead.

I wasn't dead; I'd learned a lesson. Pretending to be
asleep, I waited for another to come to me; the hun-

ger inside me roared as I sensed his approach. Why wasn't anyone giving it to me? I'd fucking get it myself. I waited. He drew closer. His breath brushed over me, leaning close. Quickly, I wrapped my legs around him, grabbed his head, and found his throat with my mouth. I held fast, with my teeth and body. Something was wrong, though. There was no rush of blood; no thump-thump as it beat through his body. Weakened, I allowed him to shake me off. I hit the ground, and he landed on top of me. He held me down; at first I thrashed. He allowed me to. Drained as I was, slumber claimed me and pulled me into darkness.

A cold sweat awakened me, and I bolted up out of my sleep. Vague flashes of horrifying dreams crossed my memory, but not in full. As if I were watching an old reel of film on fast-forward, bits and pieces of scenes broke into my vision. They came so fast, I couldn't tell if I was even in them. I couldn't even tell whether they were dreams I was remembering, or reality. My breath came fast, as though I'd been running; yet my heart pumped slowly, sluggishly, almost inhumanly, and I could hear it echo inside my head like a deep, bellowing gong. I glanced down at myself. Only a pair of panties and a tank covered my body. All else was bare. My inked dragons burned, as though literally searing into my skin, my back, my arms, as if they were alive. It was nighttime. The sky was an eerie blue hue, darkness surrounded me, and a slight breeze wafted through the gaping front of my tent. It grazed my skin, and it cooled the burning. I craved . . . something. To eat? I wanted it badly, with the same intensity of having the freaking munchies after a toke party. But I didn't want corn chips and soda. I wanted . . . steak—very, very rare steak. I moved to get up but was stopped.

A strong arm snaked around my middle, and only then did I realize Eli sat behind me on the makeshift quilted bed. We were still on Da Island, I supposed. With his legs on either side of me, he cradled my body and pulled me against him. After a few seconds of trying to figure out where the hell I was and what was happening, I relaxed and rested my head against his chest. The craving was still there, but it eased.

"What'd I miss?" I asked, vaguely thinking how odd it was not to feel his heartbeat at my back. Eli Dupré was a creature of the afterlight. He didn't have a heartbeat. But he did have heart. I snuggled into his warmth—well, as much warmth as a vampire could have, anyway. I snuggled into his lukewarmness.

"About another week," he admitted, grasping my hands, pulling them to my waist, and lacing his fingers through mine. "You had me seriously worried this time, Riley."

"I don't remember," I said, and turned my head to the side, looking up at him. His face was lost in shadows. "The last I recall, you were kissing me, then . . . nothing. And I don't like having chunks of my life missing. So tell me."

Eli let out a deep sigh—funny, since he didn't need lungs or air to breathe—and tightened his arms around me. "You did pass out, but not for long. When you came around, you were wild. Bad withdrawals, Riley. Crazy-bad, as in mad-dog, foaming-at-the-mouth, rabies-type withdrawals. I could barely restrain you. You had night sweats, day sweats, chills, and you pretty much tore up Estelle's camp. That pain caused you to make sounds

I've never heard a human make before." He brushed his scruffy jaw against my cheek. "You were like a new-ling, having the strigoi blood inside you. It was torturous, Riley, and I never, ever want to hear it come from you again. I felt . . . as if it were happening to me." His lips grazed my skin, and I shuddered at the intimacy. "I felt hopeless. Never again, baby."

"I remember flashes of weird dreams, as if I were at-tacking someone," I said, struck by his endearing name for me. It was the first time he'd used it. I stared into the darkness. "Jesus, tell me I didn't attack someone. What else?"

"You kicked my ass—that's what else," he said, and I could feel his grin, his teeth, against the skin of my neck.

That should have caused me a little fear—especially since I had flavor-of-the-month-for-vampires blood. But, it didn't. "Strong as a freaking horse, you are, woman," he continued. "Phin, Luc, and I had to take you to an-other island, just to keep the others safe."

I turned in his lap and stared in the vicinity of his face. "What?"

Eli's low, soft chuckle filled the night air. "We had to leave Da Island before you hurt someone else. We're close by—just another barrier isle. We had to put a little water between you and the others."

"Someone else?" I asked, almost shrieking. "I can't believe I attacked anybody. Who did I hurt? Are they okay? Oh my God, tell me it wasn't Estelle."

"Shh," he said, tugging me backward. "Lie still and relax, and stop squirming all over the place. Everyone's okay, and no, it wasn't Preacher or Estelle."

"Who?" I demanded, but allowed Eli to settle me against him. "I need to know, Eligius. Tell me. Now."

Again, he chuckled, so it must've not been that bad. "Let's just say Zetty won't cross you again for a while. At least, not without a few more protective charms from Estelle. Neither will Riggs." He laughed. "Jack and Tuba won't come near you without a blade. And I think the Romanian swear words were enough to damage all of them for life. Nasty language, Riley. Seriously—freaky-filthy." He nuzzled my neck. "Good thing no one else knows Romanian. I know it, though. At least the curse words. And I like it." He nipped my skin. "I got the worst of it, though. I guess because I stayed by you."

I sat up again and turned toward him. "God, you're a perv. Come on. What did I do to you? A two-hundred-year-old wicked-tempered vampire?"

In one quick move, Eli picked me up and turned my whole body around, then settled me in his lap, face-to-face. "Besides beating the holy hell out of me," he said, resting his hands on my hips, "you tried to drain my blood. Not that I have any—but that didn't stop you." He rubbed a hand over his throat. "Damn, my neck is still sore."

I closed my eyes, mortified. "I'm sorry," I said, and looked at him. "I can't believe I did that."

"Freaking weird, huh?" Luc suddenly said, ducking into the tent. Phin followed. "You were like, on vamp crack or something. Went after throats as if there were no tomorrow."

"Yeah, Ri," Phin said. "Wrapping those long legs around your prey. Like some weird spider monkey or something. You'd make one badass strigoi, that's for sure. Eyes all wide and scary, teeth gnashing." He shuddered dramatically. "Scary."

"Like, Underworld badass," Luc said, then studied me. "Pretty hot, though."

"Too bad I didn't turn on you," I said, thinking it vaguely funny that they, vampires themselves, thought it was all, well, funny. I narrowed my gaze. "Watch your neck."

Luc laughed. "Don't worry."

Phin squatted down and looked at me with a grin. "If you ever get tired of being with an old man"—he inclined his head to Eli—"you know where to find me. I dig kick-ass chicks with long legs and tats."

I shook my head. "You'll be the first to know."

I was silent for a moment, then cleared my throat. "Okay, so here we are, on another barrier island, isolated, with unpredictable teeth-gnashing scary me in my freaking panties, straddling your brother. How 'bout a little privacy, huh?" I said, then turned to Eli. I couldn't see his features—just his silhouette; his very beautiful silhouette. "Is it safe yet?" I asked him.

"You mean, are you safe yet?" Luc corrected.

"We won't know for sure for a while," Eli said, "but I think I can handle it. Luc, Phin—get out of here." Eli's hands slid around my waist, pulling me closer. Fire shot through me.

"Are you sure, Bro—"

"Now," I said. It was more of a growl.

Eli's brothers laughed and, just as fast as they had appeared, they disappeared into the darkness. I didn't stare after them; I didn't wait to see if they'd actually gone. Fact was, I didn't care. They could stay and watch for all that it mattered. What I wanted—desperately needed—was right in front of me; rather, beneath me. Obsession to take him claimed me.

I eased down, shoved my fingers through Eli's hair, and pulled his mouth to mine with more force than I'd

meant. The desperation to have him crushed me, frightened me, made me breathless, reckless, and, thank God,
his craving matched mine. As if we were starved, our
mouths met hungrily, taking whatever was being offered. Eli's hands eased up my side, palming my breasts
through the thin cotton tank I wore. Unsatisfied, I slung
his hands away, yanked the thing over my head, and
threw it aside. Thankfully, Eli wasn't wearing a shirt. His
hands were on me again, skimming my bare skin, my
ribs, my back, caressing my breasts, and I savored his
mouth as though tasting an exotic flavor for the very
first time. Hot and sweet, our tongues and mouths slid
against one another, the slick friction an aphrodisiac
that nearly made me lose my mind. I lifted a hand to our
melded mouths, slipped a finger between our lips, and
felt his tongue tangle with mine. I groaned at the sensation, then felt Eli's hands skim my spine, cup my buttocks, and pull me hard against him. Again, I groaned.

"I want you inside me," I whispered hoarsely, breathless, running my palm over the hard ridges of his abs,
lower, groping. I dragged my lips across his neck, to his
ear. "Us. One. Now."

I quickly found myself hard on my back. A whoosh
of air escaped my lungs, and, before I could catch my
breath, his nimble fingers had grasped my panties and
ripped them right off me. The sound of ragged material
cracked the still night air, and the roughness excited me.
Filtered moonlight reflected off Eli's eyes; a dangerous
gleam that sent a thrill through my body. I wrapped my
legs around his waist, grabbed him by the neck, and
pulled his mouth down to mine.

I don't know when Eli lost the board shorts he was
wearing, but I was damn glad for it. Skin to skin, his just

a fraction cooler in temperature than mine, we melded. As he pushed into me, I groaned, dug my heels into his ass, and gasped as he moved, seductive, possessive, wild and out of control.

A slow, tumultuous orgasm built from somewhere deep within me, growing in strength, making me struggle for breath as it peaked, and crashing over me in shuddering waves until my body shook. I wanted to sink straight into Eli—into his soul. I buried my face in his neck as he wrapped his arms around me; total bodies embraced, limbs entwined, and his shudders rocked me as an orgasm wracked him, too. With his mouth at my ear, his full lips dragging seductively across my skin, he whispered, gasped, spoke unknown words in French, muttered my name, and clung to me as though our lives depended on it. I felt him so deeply, I couldn't tell where he ended and I began. Eli made me feel more vulnerable than I'd ever care to admit. And it scared the hell out of me.

Without words, Eli pulled me up, cradled me in his arms as he lay back, and together we drifted, content; I couldn't remember ever having felt so thoroughly absolute. To the feel of his strong fingers dragging softly against my skin, I allowed exhaustion to claim me, and it pulled me under in a swift, shadowy, slumbering wave. I hoped that if this was an isolated moment of lucidity, I'd remember it later. I mean, damn.

In the dark recesses of my subconscious, I cherished Eli Dupré as though we were spending our very last moment together.

* * *

Three days later . . .

"We're not stopping until you get it right."

I glared first at Eli, then at my opponents: Jack and Tuba, two young, healthy, very large Gullah guys—both heavily muscled and bare to the waist. Tuba gave me a closed-mouth smile. Jack's face remained unreadable. "I am freaking doing it right," I said, the words coming out between clenched teeth. I bent over at the waist, grasped both knees with my hands, and breathed—hard. We'd been at it for hours. The sun blasted down, not a single cloud in the sky to filter its strength. Sand gnats buzzed around my head. I swatted at them irritably, stomped my feet, then rose and pushed the sweaty bangs that had escaped my ponytail off my face. Maybe I was PMSing. I was irritable as hell and just felt . . . bitchy. "How much more right does it have to be, Eli?"

"Blades seized and bodies down."

"You're freaking crazy," I muttered under my breath. He smiled.

I swore loudly in Romanian—a nasty habit I'd unwillingly and inadvertently picked up after having been bitten by those two strigoi Arcos assholes. "Are you freaking kidding me, Dupré?" I kicked the sand, said a few more choice expletives (one day I'd have to learn what they exactly meant—for now I just knew they were bad, and that made me feel better), then walked toward the surf, hands on hips. The salt water licked my bare feet, the crushed shells and coarse sand abrasive between my toes and against my soles. The low-rise board shorts I wore were navy and black, as was the string bikini top—too damn dark for midday, that was for sure. The material sucked in the sun's sweltering rays, literally frying my hineisca and boobs. No lie, my ass was on fire. I rushed into the water, dunked under, and emerged. Water rolled off my skin. I may have even seen steam.

"Are you going to spend the rest of the afternoon whining, or are you going to get it right? They both have their weapons, Riley. You have to do more than jump over them," Eli said, now standing in the water, arms crossed over his bare chest, and with a look so smug I wanted to throw him into the surf. One dark brow—the one with the silver hoop—lifted. He'd read my thoughts again. "Really?" He chuckled. "Come on, Poe, if you think you can take me."

I turned, rushed, dropped to a crouch, shot my leg out, and swept Eli's ankles, leaving behind an arc of water. Without looking, I knew I'd gotten him; I'd heard the splash and curse as he'd landed. I ran directly at Jack and Tuba, who, for the most part, stood, stunned at what I'd done to Eli. I grabbed Jack's blade, leapt, pushed off his shoulder with one bare foot, and as I flipped over Tuba, I relieved him of his blade, too. I landed on my hands and feet in a kick-ass, impressive crouching-dragon position—all in under five seconds. I flipped my head cockily, swinging my sopping wet ponytail out of my face, and found Eli's gaze penetrating mine. We stared for a handful of seconds. A burst of pride filled me at my conquered tendencies. God—I'd felt so . . . *Matrix*-y. And it felt good. Maybe being tainted by strigoi DNA wasn't so bad after all.

"Again," Eli said, still sitting in the water. "You didn't take them down."

"Screw you," I replied with a grin. "I took you down. That counts for both of them."

Jack and Tuba laughed.

With lightning speed I kicked out and swept both of their ankles. Two very large Gullah guys hit the sand. Still crouching, I flung their blades hard. Each stuck in the sand no more than an inch from their crotches. They both made a noise that highly resembled a tire with an air leak. I rose, brushed my hands off on my ass, and turned toward Eli. I grinned.

He stood, sunlight reflecting off his bare wet skin, and swaggered toward me. He bent down to pick up a shell, and I caught a glimpse of the family crest I'd inked between his shoulder blades, just before all hell broke loose. Not only was it sexy schmexy as hell, but his brothers now wanted one, too. I'd created a gang—a vampire gang. How exciting.

Eli made his way toward me. I was surprised that his shades had stayed on after I'd knocked him down. Wet board shorts clung low on his hips, those sexy lines of muscle on his sides and abdomen that disappeared beneath the waistline; I noticed every detail, appreciating them all. And he knew it. With long fingers, he shoved the loose wet hanks of dark hair from his face, put his hands on his hips in a total cocky-guy manner, and, his shades still on, stared down at me. I waited; I didn't have to wait long.

The corner of his mouth tipped upward. "I'm impressed."

I nodded and pushed his shades up onto his forehead. Pale blue eyes regarded me. "Turns you on, doesn't it?" I said.

"Hell yeah," he answered in a quiet, seductive voice meant only for my ears. In a possessive grasp, he draped his hands over my hips and pulled me close. "But Jack and Tuba are mere mortals. Estelle could take them, with the right training. I want to see"—he shook his head—"I want to know you can handle yourself against a vampire, or a handful of them, if I'm not around, Riley." His eyes turned serious. "So, from now on, you train with me, my parents, my brothers and sister." He tapped the end of my nose. "And maybe with Zetty."

With the palms of my hands firmly pressed against the hard muscles of Eli's chest, I pushed. "If you think for a second I'm going to seize blades and kick to the ground your sweet, elderly parents, you are insane," I said. "Your siblings, sure. Zetty? Absolutely. I owe him, anyway. You? Any day of the week. But your parents? No way."

Eli grazed my jaw with a knuckle. "Oh, you will, *chérie*. I promise you. You're ready. And tomorrow, we go back to Da Island." He grinned, making himself seem more like just a regular hot guy at the beach than a nearly two-hundred-year-old strigoi vampire who had the capability of snapping someone's spine in half with barely a flick of his wrist. "And I'd pay good money to see you call my parents elderly to their faces. Neo."

I couldn't help but return the cocky grin at Eli's reference to my new *Matrix*-y capabilities. I had no idea what I'd ever do with them, but one thing I did know. Seth and I, while changed with supertendencies, couldn't stay on Da Island forever. I had a business to run. Seth had to finish school. We had lives to return to—and the sooner, in my opinion, the better, even if it did mean kicking some old, sweet-looking Dupré strigoi vampire ass.

A few days later . . .

It's strange to think of all that's happened over the past month; to grasp how much I've changed. Stranger still, that I've accepted it. I'm not a huge fan of change. Once I'm used to something, I like to stick with it. Not that I had any choice. I was damn lucky to leave Bonaventure that night with my life, instead of a new unlife. Seriously. Having both Arcoses sink their fangs into my flesh, squirt their disgusting venom into my blood, and still walk away alive? Eli had saved me; he'd killed Valerian, and nearly Victorian, as well. Preacher told Eli that half a minute longer and I would have either died from blood loss or turned completely strigoi, neither of which I had a hankering for. The screams of those innocents who'd been attacked that night still resound inside my head. Visions; flashes of bodies twisted, distorted; blood; the sound of bone snapping—I wish like hell I could forget about it, forget the sound, forget them. But I can't. I don't think I ever will. I'll hear those screams inside my head until I die. And now even that would be a very long time.

So much of what happened after Bonaventure is still a blur. You know, after I was two bites to the wind and lying in a pile of graveyard dust. Once I'd been taken to Da Island (and after I'd briefly awakened), I fell into the throes of strigoi venom d.t.'s for much of the time and was, according to Estelle, one crazy-eyed white girl. She wasn't referring to my Caucasian race. Eli had told me I'd turned white, as in literally opaque white. Weird white. *Night of the Living Dead* white. Zetty's exact words, in his unique Nepal accent, had been *You was one scary crazy white bitch*. I believe them, too. Ole Zetty, to be such a big, frightening, knife-wielding Tibetan, was as superstitious as they came, and he gladly carried the pouch of graveyard dust and crushed black cat bones Estelle had given him. He even wore it around his big thick neck, tied to a leather cord. I guess he thought throwing the mixture at me, pouch and all, would keep him safe. He'd done it more than once, after I'd attacked him. Estelle had told him she wouldn't give him any more if he couldn't use it right. I still laugh when I think about it. Can't say I blame him, though. I'd have been scared shitless, too.

A breeze blew in off the water, rustled the canvas of our tent, and brushed over my bare body. I turned to stare outside, into the varying shades of gray and black as darkness hung over the small barrier isle, and Eli's arms tightened around me and pulled me close. I knew he wasn't asleep; he pretended, though, just for me I guess. There were times I just lay awake, my thoughts rambling around in my head, and Eli simply let me. No interference, no smothering—just let me have my thoughts, allowed me to ponder the changes in my life, my brother's, without interruption. He was there if I needed him, or if I grew frightened, and I have to admit it was something I could get used to real fast. After Mom's death, I'd always had Preacher and Estelle, but never had I allowed a man inside my heart, and I damn sure never depended on one to comfort me. I can't say for sure that I've let Eli; but it was definitely worth considering. Commitment of one's heart and soul—literally—required a lot of deep thought. The problem was I'd had so much to think about and consider lately that my brain was on total overload, and, to be frank, I was a little intimidated to commit myself to a man who would most definitely outlive me. Sure—it'd take a lot longer, now that I had tendencies. Still, it was a lot to ponder.

The sounds of the tide's ebb and flow blended with the bubbling oyster shoals close by, and the crackle of palm fronds split the night air as the storm that had been threatening since midnight picked up strength. No rain—just wind, thunder, and streaky lightning that occasionally flashed the dark sky. I lay in the semiwarmth of a vampire's embrace, his hard, perfectly shaped body wrapped possessively around mine, and I couldn't think of any other place I'd rather be right now. Sharp, salty air assaulted my senses; a scent I loved and drew fully into my lungs. I picked up another scent—faint, farther away, and I smiled as I recognized Preacher's tobacco. It was weird how one of my vampiric tendencies was a caninelike sense of smell. Gilles had said it was because somewhere along the Arcos vampire family tree a loup-garou had come into play. So I not only had strigoi venom floating around inside me and permanently attaching itself to my friggin' DNA, but werewolf slobber, too. I hoped to God I didn't start lifting my leg and peeing on bushes, or worse—humping legs. Christ Almighty damn.

The pipe tobacco drifted to my senses again, and I smiled. No doubt Preacher had sneaked outside to smoke, out of reach of his wife's broomstick. Estelle would whack him for sure if she caught him. Root doctor, conjurer, or not—Preacher was still susceptible to mortal diseases. I thought so, anyway.

See? My thoughts rambled from vampire venom to Gullah tobacco smoke to wives smacking husbands with broomsticks to werewolves humping legs to cancer, all in the matter of minutes. I was brain fried. Or, I suppose, some would call it Southern fried. Whatever that meant.

I needed a walk, a breath of storm-salty air—a good lung-burning run—to clear my thoughts. I shifted, eased off the quilts, but Eli's strong arm stopped me.

"What's wrong?" he asked, nuzzling my neck with his scruffy chin. "Can't sleep?"

I turned my head and pressed my lips against the strong, corded column of his throat. "You know I can't, faker. I just want to go for a run along the beach." I slid my palm along his bare hip, then over his chest. "I'll be back in a few, okay?"

Eli groaned—a sexually frustrated noise that stirred my insides. "Hurry."

I kissed his Adam's apple. "You're a prince. I'll be right back." I rolled off the quilts, blindly grabbed the short cotton dress I wore over my swimsuit, and pulled it over my head and bare body.

"Thought you weren't modest," Eli said. "No one on this island but us. You could run naked."

At the tent's open doorway, I turned and looked at him. Arm bent, head propped on the heel of his hand, Eli watched me like a hungry wolf. I grinned. "I trust your brothers about as much as I trust Riggs. They're all pervs. I'll be right back."

Eli's laughter followed me out into the night.

I ran, and I ran hard—no warm-up jog, no stretching—I didn't need a warm-up; just a full-out, haul-ass run from the moment I stepped out of the tent. Sand and shell bits, and probably an unfortunate fiddler or ghost crab or two crunched beneath my bare feet as I tore up the shoreline, and the faster I ran, the more invigorated I felt. It took a lot for my lungs to burn any more, so I ran on as if I could literally run forever, fast, furious, my thighs and calves pumping, my arms swinging fiercely. It was . . . freeing—well, almost freeing. My mind still ran rampant, and my heart, well . . . It still chugged sluggishly along, in complete contrast with my body's motion. I'm not sure it would ever pump fast again. Weird. I felt adrenaline, but you'd never have known it with my body's response. Preacher and Gilles said it was the strigoi venom—a side effect that would never leave me; just one of many, so they said. I'm still discovering them. Right now? I didn't feel like attacking anyone. I didn't seem to have a craving digging at me from the inside out. I wasn't sure if that was because I was on this barrier isle alone, with just Eli, or if it meant I finally had run the d.t.'s course. Still, the discovery of each and every strange tendency was sort of like opening presents at Christmas. There was always something you didn't expect. Sort of like how I was involved with a family of guardian vampires whose own DNA had been altered by centuries of hoodoo herbs and magic; it still boggled my brain to see Eli out in the sun, in the middle of the day, looking like the rest of the world. Well, minus the fact that he was painfully beautiful. You know what I mean, though—Hollywood's concept of vampire's doesn't quite cover what's really out there. I hadn't once seen Eli rise slowly from a coffin, or even wear a black cape with a red lining. My vampire needed only a good nap during the day to function. His skin didn't catch on fire in the sunlight and he not only ate food, but peed—if he drank a lot of beer. Weird.

I wasn't sure exactly how big the barrier island was that we were on, but I ran around it three times before I stopped. I walked into the surf, the water lukewarm as it lapped at my thighs, and I stared out across the darkness, toward the open sound. There was the tiniest sliver of moon; everything was in shadows except the white, bleached-out sand. Heat lightning (I'm not sure if that's the scientific term for it, but it's what Seth and I called it growing up) followed the rumbling thunder and snaked across the black sky in thin silver web threads, and it would throw just enough of a surreal glow over the area to let me know what was out there, beyond the sand, water, palms. Inside my head, my mind whirled.

Victorian Arcos concerned me. I hadn't heard his voice in my head since that one time, when I'd first awakened on Da Island after being rescued from Bonaventure. I'd not mentioned it to anyone—not even to Eli. Just knowing Victorian was alive and free scared me. I wasn't scared of him—not physically, anyway. Not anymore. It was a different type of fear; maybe even fear of myself, and my response to him. I didn't even like to think of it, or him. Unavoidably, I did. He was obsessed with me, and his last words to me were a solid promise to come for me. He might not be in the vicinity, but he was still here. I could feel him. And that freaked me out. He possessed a mind control over me in the dreams that made me respond to him in a way that I loathed. Swear to God, I couldn't help myself. And one thing I hated was not being in control of my actions and thoughts.

As I dug my toes into the wet sand, I thought of everyone else in my life, and how my changes would affect them. Nyx was beside herself with worry, for me and Seth. As far as she knew, I was fine; it was Seth who'd needed me, after his supposed drug addiction. It was the only thing we could tell her. Seth hated it because he was so adamant about never being on drugs; we'd had no choice. I'd left Inksomnia in Nyx's very capable hands while Seth and I both spent time recovering. I hated lying to her; she was my best friend. But no way in hell could she ever handle the truth. And even if she did ever dare to believe in vampires, I could almost imagine her running around, hugging them all and thinking a little love would cure their barbaric sickness. If anyone could hug a vampire into being nice, it'd be Master Hugger Nyxinnia Foster. But I trusted only the Duprés in regard to creatures of the afterlight, and receiving Nyx's hugs. God, I missed her. She missed us, too, and wanted us home. Hopefully, that'd be soon. I suppose since I hadn't tried to suck anyone else's blood out that my withdrawals had finally come to an end. Thank God. I was freaking sick of all the ups and downs. It was like going through the midlife change, only with vampirism.

Strong arms encircled my waist, breaking my rambling thoughts, and, unlike my old, prevampiric-tendencied self, I didn't even flinch.

"Yeah, so why is that?" Eli said, his lips close to my ear. "Why don't you flinch?"

I rested my weight against him. "Because, you nerd," I said teasingly, "not only can I smell your scent two miles away, but I can hear you coming. I also heard you lay that quilt on the sand over there."

"Hmm," he said, his voice low, seductive, one hand leaving my waist to skim over my hip. "Hearing me come is quite a unique vampiric tendency." Slowly, erotically, he slipped his hand lower, beneath the hem of my short cotton beach dress, and dragged his palm up my hip. His body tightened behind me, and he buried his mouth into the crook of my neck. "Christ, Riley," he said, his hand skimming my bare skin, his voice deepening. "Running commando these days?" Both hands found their way beneath my dress, and my head fell against Eli's chest as the sensation of his palms gliding over first my thighs, hips, abdomen, then lower, came over me. He pulled me against him, held me tightly, and his hardness throbbed, pressing into my lower back. Vampires had to be, hands down, the horniest creatures of any light. Fine by me. As his mouth moved over the sensitive skin of my neck, then my ear, I lifted my hands, grasped his jaw, and threaded my fingers through his hair. The soft, wet brush of his lips caressing my skin turned me on almost as much as his palm cupping my bare, pantiless bottom. Aching for him, I squirmed a bit against his hand so that the sensitive nub would touch the right callused spot, and sensations raced through me as I succeeded. Before I came, he pulled away, lifted my dress over my head, flung it somewhere behind us, then turned me in his arms, and lowered his head until his mouth covered mine. With both hands holding my head in place, he kissed me, tasted my tongue with his, and slowly, he began walking me backward, deeper into the water. We stopped moving when it reached our waist, and although I couldn't see Eli's face in detail, I saw the silhouette. He watched me, silent, his hands moving softly over my jaw, chin, cheekbones, grazing my lips. The heat lightning overhead crept across the sky like the fine strands of a spiderweb, and, in the brief second it flashed, I saw Eli's eyes. They were fixed on me, dark, filled with a craving that caused me to shiver with eagerness.

"I've never wanted another as much as I want you," he mouthed against my lips before tasting them. "I've waited for you my whole existence, and I never thought for a second that I'd get so lucky." He kissed me, his full lips dragging over mine, our tongues brushing. His hands grasped my hips; his fingers dug into my flesh, I gasped, and he lifted me.

I wrapped my legs around him, the water making our

bodies slick, and I slid down his abdomen until his rigid hardness nudged me, entered me, completely filled me. His hands splayed over my buttocks, pulling me tightly against him, preventing all thoughts of escape, and he kissed me again. Hard. Demanding. Possessive. I nearly came again.

Without any more words, Eli moved through the water, back to the shore. At the quilt he'd laid on the sand, he followed me down and kissed me as slowly as he made love to me. The only time I could see him was when the lightning flashed, and even then for only a split second or two. But I felt him, inside me, surrounding me, and I knew then that making love with Eli was unlike any other experience I'd ever had, or would ever have. He reached a place so deep and hidden within me, that it frightened me, and I wasn't prepared to name it yet. I clung to him as we climaxed together, beneath an almost-moonless September night in the sand on a random Gullah barrier island. When our movement slowed, Eli's hands searched first my body, then my face, and he held me close, pressing his lips to my ear.

"You're mine forever, *chérie*," he said, his accent thicker than usual. "I want only you."

Before I could respond, his lips claimed mine, settled, tasted slowly. With his knuckles he grazed my jaw, traced my lips, then wrapped his arms and legs around me, pulling me close. I accepted the fact that while Eli had the courage to say the words out loud, I didn't. But I felt them just as strongly as I'd felt anything. One day, hopefully, I'd be able to tell him. Nestled against his chest, I hugged him and closed my eyes.

He kissed me again, whispered something French in my ear—I had no clue what it meant. I figured he'd just read my endearing thoughts and that my unspoken words were enough for him right now. Finally, exhaustion claimed me.

I confess, love—it pains me to know you've had another inside you. That you seem to enjoy it so fully excites me, though, and as I promised, one day you shall be no longer his, but mine. You will have me inside you over and over until you beg me to stop; and after, you'll never want another. There is no escape—you are meant for me. He may be inside you for a while—as long as it takes him to fuck you—but I live inside you. My blood is mixed with yours, and no amount of hoodoo magic can change it. We are one and I promise, I will come for you. Until then, I drown in thoughts of you, of touching you, of your mouth sliding over me. Soon, love. Very soon . . .

I bolted up from the quilts and gasped. I glanced around; I was alone. A hazy light filled the canvas tent, the sun not yet risen but still light enough outside to see. The pungent brine of low tide wafted through and rustled my hair, and I inhaled deeply. Oh Christ Almighty. Another dream.

Another message, rather. From Victorian. He was close. I could feel him.

"Eli?" I called out, and crawled on hands and knees to the tent opening.

The man I sometimes had a difficult time remembering was a vampire sat hunched down at the shore, watching the sun rise and picking at some random shell in the sand. The slightly tanned skin of his muscular back looked shiny in the peaking sunlight, the black-inked Dupré crest standing stark between his blades. He was buck naked. He turned and waved. "Come here, you," he said, and gave me a grin.

Pushing the fear of Victorian aside, I, also buck naked, left the tent and joined him at the water's edge. And as he took me in his arms, I flushed my mind of the other. He'd not ruin this. I simply wouldn't let him.

And I'd die making sure of it.

Part Two

VOICES

"There are such beings as vampires, some of us have evidence that they exist. Even had we not the proof of our own unhappy experience, the teachings and the records of the past give proof enough for some people."

—Bram Stoker, *Dracula*

"Swear to God, I thought I could handle this. Truly. I mean, the power of my tendencies is freaking amazing. I can do some outlandish shit. Even Gilles is impressed. But in becoming fearless, I've become reckless, and that's not so good. While Victorian looks deceiving—I mean, he's absolutely beautiful—I know the depth of his desires. He freaking tells me all the time—inside my head. He wants me as badly as Eli does, and I'm scared it's going to come down to an all-out war. The thing is, what am I willing to risk to stop it?"

—Riley Poe

My back hit the sand as I dropped to the ground, avoiding the blade Eli's mother had freaking flung at me. Before I could blink, Elise was over me, her tiny bare foot to my throat. As my eyes met hers, she shook her head and sighed.

"Riley, sweetheart," Elise said, her voice even, sweet, her heavier French accent enticing. "Never drop to your back. Crouch, *oui*. Jump, *oui*. But as you can see, being on your back leaves you vulnerable." She wiggled her toes against the sensitive part of my throat, then removed her foot and extended a hand to me. I took it and, with amazing strength, she helped me up. "In any situation."

"Yes, ma'am," I said, mortified that a very proper lady in her late fifties with delicately painted pink toes and weighing no more than a hundred and ten pounds could kick my ass. I brushed the sand off my skin. "Crouch. Don't drop."

She smiled. "One hundred and four pounds," she clarified, reading my thoughts as the Duprés frequently and freely did. "Seth," she called out.

"Yes, ma'am," he replied, leaving the gathered group, including all of the Dupré siblings, by the surf and running up to us.

"Join your sister."

Seth glanced at me and wagged his dark brows. "Yes, ma'am," he repeated.

I scowled at him. *Suck up*, I mouthed. He merely grinned.

Elise, dressed in a pair of knee-length white Bermuda shorts, a pale pink tank top to match her toes, and her hair pulled back into her signature stylish ponytail, studied us. The late-afternoon sunlight winked off the various rubber practice blades (we didn't want to get stuck) sheathed around her slim waist, her thighs, and over both shoulders. She looked too petite to have the ability to carry such a load, but I knew she had the strength to toss me two hundred feet into the sound if she wanted. She was wicked strong, wicked fast, and wicked lethal, despite her sweet looks.

"Phin, Luc," she called, grinning at me. "Come here."

My eyes met Eli's briefly as his brothers jogged across the sand. He offered no smile, no cocky grin—only that profuse stare that seemed to pierce my insides, clear to my soul. It made me shiver.

Phin and Luc circled Seth and me, as Elise barely seemed to shift in the sand. Their eyes bored heavily into us, like hunters stalking prey. The boys were just as armed as their mother, and this was nothing more than a test of reflexes. Seth and I had no blades—just our wits and superfast tendencies. Hopefully, they were superfast enough; neither of us wanted to get nailed on the noggin with a rubber blade. With our backs pressed together, Seth turned his head.

"No dropping," he whispered. "I got Phin and Mrs. Dupré. You take Luc."

"And now they know our master plan," I hissed. "Clear your mind, Bro. They freaking cheat."

All the Duprés on the beach laughed, and in the next breath, Phin and Luc lunged.

Seth leapt; I crouched. After that, I could keep track only of what I did and hoped my brother could handle himself. Luc got too close; I relieved him of three lower body blades before he realized it. I heard the whir of another rubber blade through the air and I turned, gauged the weight and distance of the sound, then raised my hand and caught the blade Elise had thrown by the hilt. Three more followed, rapid-fire, and with a speed that amazed even me, I caught each one and flung it into the sand before the next one reached me. Luc lunged again. I leapt over him, grabbed the blade sheathed at his shoulder, and landed in the sand behind him. A dull pain in my thigh made me drop. Luc had thrown the one remaining blade at his hip at me. Prick. I winced, and he grinned. Good thing I healed fast these days. Whatever bruise appeared would be gone within an hour. And because of my mixed Arcos blood, my own wasn't quite as potent as it was before. In other words, the Duprés didn't continuously want to latch on to a major artery as much as before. Lucky me. I turned to watch my brother.

Seth jumped over Phin and had both his shouldered

blades flung into the sand. Phin already had the rest of his blades removed. Seth landed, swept Phin's shins with blinding speed, and had those blades out of their sheaths, too. I blinked, and by the time my eyes focused again on my brother, he was circling Elise. The intense look of concentration, determination, and intimidation on his face was more than shocking. Seth was a guy raised to respect not only his elders, but all women. Presently, he looked as though he wanted to take down little Elise Dupré in her pressed white Bermudas and pink toenails.

By now, the crowd gathered at the surf had come closer, and the boys who had once been almost-new-lings cheered and whistled as Seth and Elise circled each other. Jack and Tuba, Zetty, Estelle and Preacher, as well as Eli, Gilles, and Josie, drew close. Elise still had two blades—one on her hip, the other on her shoulder. With wicked speed, she whipped the hip blade at my brother. He crouched, reached up, and grabbed it, in midair. The boys hollered.

In the next instant, Elise threw the last blade, and this time, Seth wasn't as lucky. It nailed his shoulder, and I winced as he did. Then, so fast, swear to God, he lunged at Elise, grabbed the blade before it landed on the ground, and hit her full force, taking her to the sand and flat onto her back. He had the blade in his hand, the tip at her throat.

Wow. Freaking, wow.

The *Lord of the Flies* boys cheered, and I glanced at Eli. He gave an approving nod. I couldn't see his eyes—they were covered by his shades—but I'd be willing to bet they shined with pride for my brother.

"Hey, punk," Luc said, pulling my thoughts back. "Get your ass off my mother."

"Sorry, Mrs. Dupré," Seth said, jumping off Elise and extending a hand to help her up. She took it, and his cheeks turned red.

"Well done, sweetheart," she said, brushing off her sandy backside. She put a hand on his bare shoulder. "You sincerely impress me."

Phin propped an elbow on top of my shoulder and leaned close. "Your brother has serious gifts," he said. "Not many can best my mother."

I smiled. "It's his extreme Southern mannerisms that make him so deceiving. I bet Elise wouldn't allow it to happen again."

Phin grinned. "You're probably right." He glanced down at my thigh. "How's the leg?"

I followed his gaze to the place where Luc's blade had hit my thigh. I shrugged it off. "Barely hurts at all." The red splotch had started to turn purple. It wouldn't last long.

Had I been there, I'd never have allowed that blade, rubber or not, to reach your beautiful body.

I jerked my head around. So profound was Victorian's voice, it'd sounded as though he was standing right beside me. He, of course, wasn't. I'd known from his last message that he'd be back. I pushed my thoughts, and his voice, out of my head—for now, anyway. My eyes cast around the gathering. No one looked concerned. No one but I heard the voice inside my head. I wondered why Eli couldn't. He and the other Duprés could read my thoughts. How was it they couldn't hear Victorian?

Because, love. It is I injecting your mind with my thoughts. They're mine alone, meant only for you. See the power I possess?

"Go for a walk with me?" Eli said, suddenly behind

me, his arms snaking around my waist. He pulled me close. "I'm a little tired of sharing you with the whole Dupré family."

"Some would call that stingy," Phin said.

Eli led me away. "I've been called worse."

I glanced over my shoulder as we walked, shrugging off Victorian's voice in my head. My vision caught my brother. Seth waved. "See ya, Ri." I smiled back. "Later, Bro." I'd been a little clingy with him, once I'd awakened this last time. The impact of what could have truly happened to Seth hit me hard, and I was petrified that I'd lose him. Estelle had been the one to tell me to back off a bit, and with only a little resistance, I had. God, I just loved him so much. The pain and fear I'd gone through when the Arcos brothers had taken him almost did me in. I'd worried until I was sick from it. Damn, I couldn't help it. He was my brother. But I'd chillaxed a bit since, and I trusted him. I mean, Jesus. He could fight like something out of a movie. It was amazing to watch.

"Are you going to make me interact with you through your thoughts," Eli said, his mouth brushing my ear, "or what?"

I stared at him.

"Supper in thirty minutes, da both of you," Estelle called after us. I glanced over my shoulder at her and the setting sun gleamed off her flawless dark skin. "I mean dat, girl." She grinned.

"Yes, ma'am," I answered, and threw her a smile. "We'll be back."

"Hmm, you'd better. Naughty child," she answered, then turned and headed up the beach with the rest.

"Do you know what I can do to you in thirty minutes?" Eli whispered against the skin of my throat as we walked. His hands caressed the bare skin of my exposed stomach, grazed my belly button, slipped below the waist of my board shorts, then skimmed upward and gently tugged at the string tie holding my bikini top together. His lips moved down my neck and over my shoulder, and I shivered.

"All talk and no action, Dupré?" Completely turned on and burning at his touch, I egged him on, bending my head to the side as Eli's mouth moved against my skin. I grabbed his ass. "God, do you seriously need thirty minutes—"

So fast, my head spun, Eli whipped me around to face him. The waning afternoon sun behind him, he looked down at me, a small shift in breeze rustling his tousled hair. Blue eyes, dark with desire, stared so hard at me, I thought he would devour me, right there. "Trust me," he said, his voice low. "I want to." He slipped his hands over my waist, my buttocks, and pulled me against him. He was already hard, and he throbbed against me, the seam of my board shorts grazing just the right spot. I gasped. "Come." He grabbed my hand and pulled.

"Oh, don't worry," I promised, allowing Eli to drag me fast up the beach, putting distance between us and the others. "I will."

There really was nowhere else for us to go but the water; the small barrier island was void of most maritime forest, and what little of it there was housed Preacher and Estelle, and the rest of the camp. That left either the wide-open beach, or the water.

Eli read my thoughts; he pulled me into the warm surf, let my hand loose, and dove under. I did the same, and we both broke the surface. Eli glided to me, gathered me, and lifted my hips, pulling me onto his lap. Beneath the water, his fingers kneaded my lower back, and I draped my arms around his neck. For several seconds, we simply stared, the rising tide lapping at our skin, and he studied me with such intensity, I nearly looked away.

"Don't," he said, grasping my jaw to make sure my gaze remained on his. "Look at me, Riley."

I did, and my heart skipped a beat. It was almost a painful act to accomplish, fully looking upon him. Eli's beauty was so great; it literally stunned me every time my eyes raked over his features and his body. With his hair wet and sideswept, and water glistening off his lean frame, my breath involuntarily hitched.

"Yeah," he said so softly, I barely heard him. "That's what you do to me, too." He tucked a loose wet strand of hair behind my ear. "I can't get you off my mind. Ever. You're all I think about."

I smiled. "You're a horny vampire. I get it," I said.

"No," he replied fast. "It's not that. Well, not only that," he said. Then, those surreal blue eyes locked tightly on to mine, and I couldn't have looked away if I'd wanted to.

"It's that whole danger aspect, right?" I asked, trying for some reason not to be serious. "You know—you have to be extra careful with me because I'm still human and you can't let yourself fully go—" His fingers over my mouth hushed any more ridiculous words I might have spewed.

"No, Riley," he answered. "I've had a lot of sex, with a lot of willing partners," he said matter-of-factly. "But none of them reached me here." He drew my hand from around his shoulders to rest against his heart—rather, the area where it should have been. His gaze grew darker, more intense. "Not one. Only you. Nothing, or no one, will ever hurt you again, I promise." His knuckles grazed my jaw. "I thought I'd be alone forever. Now, I have you." He shook his head. "It's like a miracle or something."

My heart leapt. No one has ever made me feel the way Eli does. I know that our relationship is way more than based on just sex. Way more. This is probably why I joke around and try to make light of the serious stuff. I admit—I'm scared. Of what exactly, I'm not sure yet. What I do know is that I feel the same way toward Eli as he does toward me. As corny and obsessed as it sounds, I can't stand to be away from him for long. I want him close all the time.

"Oh yeah?" he said, pulling me closer, his smile wide. Then he moved his mouth to my ear. "That's what I'd hoped to hear," he whispered, then kissed my lobe. "Part of me never wants to leave here." He pulled back, meeting my gaze with one that was hooded, filled with a hunger that I'd never, ever seen in the eyes of a human male. It was . . . different. I can't explain it other than it made you feel wanted. Desired. Craved. Not just like . . . an object of sex for the moment, but more like . . . like a necessity.

Eli shook his head, moved his hand to the back of my neck, and lowered his mouth to mine. The sun had dropped now, and the breeze hitting my wet skin felt a bit cooler. But with Eli wrapped around me, I hardly noticed or cared. His lips grazed mine, his tongue slowly caressed, and I lost myself in his powerful, seductive kiss. And just as I lowered my hand, pressed against his chest, and trailed my fingers over the ridges of his stomach, he stopped and raised his head.

A smile—pained though it might be—tipped his sexy

mouth. "And to prove I'm not just some horny vampire who only wants in your pants, we're heading back to camp. Now."

With a lot less grace than I'd imagined, Eligius Dupré dumped me right into the Atlantic and walked back to the beach.

"Wait!" I said, sitting in the water. "It's totally cool if you only want in my pants!"

Eli laughed. "No."

I slapped the water and swore something filthy-nasty in Romanian. After Eli turned and stared at me in shock, he laughed again, so loudly it resounded off the palms of Da Island. I ducked underwater to cool my heated, raging, hormones.

Sitting around a roaring campfire on a Georgia barrier island at night with a handful of centuries-old vampires, Gullah conjurers, and adolescent boys with vampiric tendencies made for a way more interesting crowd than any other I'd ever hung with in my wild teenage years, or in my adult years, truth be known. No lie—it was surreal. Bizarre. Oh, and Zetty—can't forget the big Tibetan. The fact that he sat across from me with a pouch of ground-up black cat bone (I pray the poor thing was dead before its bones were harvested, but I have my doubts), graveyard dust, and God knows what else Estelle mixed up made me want to write to Zetty's mother in Kathmandu and tell on him. He was one seriously superstitious dude who no longer trusted me, and it'd probably be a long time before he did. I'd really freaked him out when I was detoxing on the vampire venom.

I looked around at my other fireside companions. Of course, the Duprés were their same charming, French selves. Phin and Luc sat in conversation, and Luc was peeling a piece of saw grass and throwing little slivers of it into the sand as they spoke. Strangely enough, they both looked serious, and it made me wonder what they were talking about. Gilles and Elise, next to them, were totally into each other, which I found pretty cool, given the number of years they'd been together. Gilles held Elise's hand, and her eyes lit up when looking at him. I'm guessing that's one of a vampire's greatest perks: When they love you, they really love you—obsessively, faithfully, and forever. I liked it.

Josie sat next to Seth; their heads bent together in conversation. Every handful of seconds, one or the other—or both—would laugh at some private joke they were sharing. They'd grown pretty close since the night the humans had been saved and brought to Da Island, and as long as she kept her fangs out of my brother's arteries, I was totally cool with all that.

The *Lord of the Flies* gang, all wearing T-shirts and board shorts, sat huddled together, their bare feet dug into the sand. Riggs had a stick that he kept jabbing into the fire, sending a spray of red sparks flying above their heads. Having' caught my eye twice already, he raised one eyebrow and grinned. I shook my head. Just what a juvenile guy needed—the sensual tendency of a vampire. He'd been bad enough when he was just plain teenage pubescent Riggs. Now? Good God. I couldn't help but like the kid, though. I'd watched him spar with a boy named Jacoby—both about the same size, same height. Riggs was fast, and he moved with such grace, he'd seemed to be floating. Like Seth, he'd matured physically, and he was damn fast. Mentally, as well—to a certain extent. I'd witnessed his intense concentration while he was sparring. Gone was the awkward gangliness of a fifteen-year-old. I was seriously impressed. I felt sorry for all parents of young available girls in Savannah.

Estelle and Preacher sat on one side of me, Jack and Tuba on the other side of them. Every once in a while Tuba would slip me a glance, then grin, his wide white smile seemingly glowing in the dark.

Gilles cleared his throat, and we all turned our heads toward him. The firelight played against the age lines grooved into his face by life, prior to becoming a vampire. His eyes, that same shocking Dupré blue, looked like glass as the amber light from the flames reflected in their depths. He glanced around. "You've all done well and have worked hard at honing your new skills. I remember, way back when, after I'd gained my own talents. Not an easy accomplishment." He gave a short nod. "I am proud."

A low murmur ran through the boys, pride evident on their faces.

"As you have acquired vampiric tendencies, there are things we will expect of you. You are all custodians of the city." Gilles' gaze searched the group of boys, and he smiled. "*Non*. That does not mean you must clean up, although if the notion strikes you, it would be an admirable thing to do."

The crowd chuckled, and Gilles continued.

"That means you are now like us—guardians. And things will be expected of you as such. You will watch over the city and keep the humans safe. If you use your tendencies against the humans, you will first be brought to trial, here. With Preacher and his dark ones."

The boys all looked around.

"And if they deem it necessary, we will relinquish your skills from you," he said.

Understanding lit the boys' eyes but fear quickly replaced it. That meant the Duprés would have no choice but to kill them. I prayed it never came to that.

"Now," Gilles continued, "we leave here in two days. You'll return to your homes, to school, and you will set examples for others your age." The smile he gave did two things: It warmed and chilled at the same time. Weird. "We'll be watching."

The boys got up and headed to their tents. Their silence meant they were thinking about all that—hard. Good. They needed to. I didn't want to have to make any more trips to the police station to bail their asses out for doing stupid stuff.

"Gilles, stop," said Elise softly, playfully smacking Gilles on his thigh. He wore a pair of plaid Bermuda shorts and a white Da Plat Eye T-shirt and flip-flops. He cracked my ass up. Gilles rose, pulling his wife up with him. He eyed me, grinned, then turned back to the small crowd. "You boys will no longer require as much sleep as before. Don't sit around idly. Read. Study. Make your mind sharp. Play sports." He thought for a moment. "I always fancied football. Rather, soccer." With a nod, he pulled his wife along. "Adieu."

The rest of the crowd dispersed. Preacher leaned over and patted my head. "You be good, child," he said, his satiny skin shining in the firelight. "Don't forget your tea." He grinned, Estelle giggled, and they disappeared toward the tents.

"We're gonna go for a walk," Seth said, Josie at his side. "See ya in the morning."

"Night," I said, and followed them with my eyes until the shadows swallowed them. Eli and I were left alone by the fire.

"Were you making fun of my father?" Eli whispered. I sat between his thighs, and his arms slipped around my waist. "Shame, shame, Riley Poe."

I tilted my head upward to look at him. The glow from the fire flicked shadows against his face, and I swear, I'd never seen a more beautiful soul in my life. "I'm not. It's just . . . funny. I'm used to seeing him dress so formal. Those flip-flops are a kick in the ass."

Eli's arms tightened around me, pulling me close. "Yeah, I know." He settled me in a way that I didn't have to crank my neck at such an awkward angle to see him. "How do you feel?" he asked seriously. "Ready to go home?"

I thought about it. I'd experienced short bursts of weird feelings, and I couldn't describe them if I tried. They were almost like little electric jolts. But I didn't want to attack anyone anymore, so that was a good thing. "Yeah, I am. Ready to see Nyx and my dog—so ready to get back to work," I said. I twined my fingers through his. "I miss my artwork. The smell of the ink. My music." I laughed. "I even miss the hum of the Widow." I met his gaze. "Just keep an eye on me for a while, huh? I don't wanna slip up and accidentally hurt someone."

"I guess I can do that," he said with a grin. He nuzzled my neck, and his mouth brushing my skin gave me goose bumps. "I'll be glad to have solid walls, a solid bed to take you in," he whispered, his gaze locking with mine. "Water sex is great, but I'm ready for a soft bed." He shrugged. "Or a hard brick wall."

Memories of Eli taking me against the wall in my bedroom rushed through me, followed by a thrill that made my skin flush. "All that nasty sex will have to be tuned down a bit, Romeo," I said. "My brother lives with me. Remember? Don't wanna gross him out and scar him forever."

His fingers splayed against my bare stomach, caressing my hip. "I guess we'll have to go to my place."

I studied his face for several moments, enjoying the rush of sensation that came with his fingers dragging across my skin. "You don't feel the urge to drain my blood anymore?" I asked. "Like before?"

Eli shook his head. "It's still there, just not as compelling as before," he answered. "Your DNA has changed, Riley. Your blood type is still unique, but it doesn't make me crazy like before." His eyes grew dark as they searched mine. "You make me crazy now. Insane-crazy. And I crave you instead of your blood."

I leaned into him. "I think I dig that, Dupré," I said, and slipped my hand up to grasp the back of his neck, pulling his mouth closer to mine. I grazed my lips against his, and it caused an immediate reaction in Eli. His tongue swept over mine, caressed, and he kissed me long. An acorn popped in the fire, breaking our trance. I pulled back and looked at Eli.

"Hey," I said, scooting back and smiling. "Make the face."

"What?" Eli said, then rolled his eyes. "Come on, Riley. Jesus."

"Make it," I egged. "Please?"

Eli studied me for a few seconds, grinned, then shook his head. "God, you're a freak—you know that, right?"

I smiled and tucked a long fuchsia red strand of hair behind my ear. "Yeah, and proud of it, too. Now, come on, do it."

Eli's face contorted in the blink of an eye; jaw unhinged, fangs long and exaggerated, eyes pure white with a red pinpoint pupil. I jumped, then stared in fascination.

"Whoa," I said in a low voice, completely enthralled. "Wicked."

Just that fast, his features relaxed and transformed back into the beauty of Eli. He again shook his head. "You are one cheap date, Poe. A freakishly cool, cheap date." He leaned down and kissed me breathless. "I like that about you."

I have to admit—I had no complaints. And the way Eli made me feel? It was indescribable. He literally made my heart soar, as if my heart had a motor on it and were flying up an empty highway. As I leaned back against his chest, his steely arms wrapped completely around me and his chin propped on my shoulder, I closed my eyes. Pretending was easy enough—I was a young girl in the prime of my life, with a hot, devoted boyfriend, a rockin' tattoo shop, booming business, a loving, extended Gullah family, and an adorable brother whom I loved with all my heart. I could pretend everything was normal and the world at my fingertips. I could actually almost forget that two strigoi vamps had bitten me, introduced their wicked-strong venom into my body, and left me with unpredictable tendencies—and that one of the vamps wanted me. Badly. And that he would not stop until he had me.

At some point, I fell asleep; so relaxed and exhausted that I didn't remember Eli carrying me to our tent. I don't know how long I slept. But I damn sure remember being awakened. . . .

Riley? Wake up, love. I know you are wrapped in the arms of a Dupré, and as much as I despise it, for now, I can do nothing more than accept it. Only because I cannot

*be there myself and I wouldn't dare think of restraining
your powerful sexual desires. It causes me physical pain
to be away from you, so the only thing I can do to relieve
some of the anguish is to connect our thoughts. Imagine
me instead of him, Riley, and us blessedly alone. Imagine my arms holding you, my hands touching you, our
bodies pressed together. Imagine right now my mouth on
yours, our tongues entwined, and my fingers sliding over
your soft, bare skin until they reach a place that makes
you lose your mind with desire for me. I promise, you'd
never long for another again. So powerful my memory is
of our short physical time together, I can actually inhale
and smell your scent, taste you on my tongue—*

"Riley, wake up."

I darted straight up and looked around. "What?"

Eli laughed. "Sorry—I didn't mean to scare you."
He pushed my disheveled hair off my face. "Father and
Mother are up. Pacing." He grinned. "Time to train."

Putting on my best poker face, I shrugged off the
heady dream-conversation—one-sided though it may
have been—with Victorian Arcos, pulled on a clean bikini top and board shorts, and ducked out of the tent for
two more days of training. I wasn't positive how long I
could hide the messages I'd been receiving from Victorian, and I wasn't sure how it was that Eli hadn't detected
them yet. He often slipped, uninvited, into my thoughts.
To be frank, I usually didn't mind. It was kind of . . . a
turn-on. Kinky, I know, but I'd never been accused of
being prim and proper. This was one time, though, I was
glad Eli had stayed out of my head. When the time was
right, and if I thought he proved a real threat, I'd let
Eli and his family know of Victorian's torment of my
private thoughts. For now, though, I could handle it. I'd

dealt with horny pervs nearly my entire adult life, and while Victorian Arcos was a bit . . . stronger, when all was broken down, he proved to be nothing more than a horny twenty-one-year-old dude. Add in the strigoi aspect of it and, okay—you had an extremely powerful, horny twenty-one-year-old dude. But I was no longer a mere mortal. I had strigoi tendencies. And I could damn well handle my own freaking self. I knew if I told Eli, he'd go ballistic, and there was no telling what he'd do. I wanted this right now. Peace; the newness of our relationship and all that it entailed. In other words, I was selfish. I wanted Eli to myself for at least a little while, and minus the stress and anger of dealing with Victorian. I knew it wouldn't last long, anyway. All in all, though, I felt a little down. I knew the past few weeks had been unrealistic and idyllic, living on a barrier island far away from the reality of strigoi, Arcoses, newlings, and a world where human life meant nothing, their blood consumed in the most gruesome of ways. I had a gut feeling nasty changes were upon us. A fresh batch of newlings had suffered and survived a strigoi quickening; they'd be hungry and out of control. They'd feed, kill, as well as change other humans. It was time to step back into reality, and this time, I'd go in with my eyes wide-open. I had tendencies. And I was freaking ready to use them.

Two days later . . .

It felt funny being back on the mainland. This was maybe because I knew I had emerged a different sort of human, or maybe because I was keeping a big-ass secret from the mortals of Savannah. I knew what Seth and I were, what Preacher and his family were, and what the Duprés were. I knew Riggs and the other boys were no longer regular teenage guys. I knew Zetty was more than a big Tibetan bouncer from Kathmandu with wicked tats on his forehead. We'd all changed. Maybe just knowing that made things seem so . . . weird. I hoped like hell I'd get used to it.

Seth rode with Gilles and Elise (yes, vamps drive and they have a kick-ass liquid silver Lexus) while I rode on the back of Eli's bike. Phin and Luc drove the boys all home, and, as far as their parents were concerned, they'd all been away at a special camp. At Gilles' request, they'd all—Seth included—continued their schoolwork so they wouldn't fall behind. A little mind control had to be issued, to the parents, principal, and teachers, but hey—the job was now done. It was the weekend, and school started back on Monday. No sweat.

Gilles dropped Seth and Josie off at Inksomnia, and Eli pulled next to the curb. Before my ass even cleared the bike's seat, the front door of my ink shop flew open and Nyx bounced out like some crazed Jack Russell on crack, an excited, barking Chaz on her heels. My heart nearly popped, I was so excited to see my friend and my dog.

We all prepared for hugs and licks.

"Riley! Seth! Oh my God, you're finally home!" Nyx said. Even with a pair of chunky Goth Mary-Janes, striped stockings, and black leather miniskirt, she was freaking fast. She launched herself first at Seth, and hugged him so tightly, I thought my brother wouldn't breathe for a week. But Seth wrapped his lanky arms around her just as tightly. In theory, they hadn't truly seen each other in almost two months—ever since Seth began the early stages of quickening.

"Wow—look at you," Nyx said, physically turning

Seth around. He good-naturedly allowed her to spin him several times. Finally, she stopped and stared at him in awe. "You're . . . buff, dude. And tanned."

Seth grinned. "Right? Crazy, huh?" He flexed his biceps. "Check this out."

Nyx grasped it and squeezed. Her eyes widened. "Gullah magic did you good, boy."

Seth glanced at me, then grinned widely. "Absolutely. And Nyx"—he wrapped his arms around her again and buried his face in her neck—"I missed you."

Nyx's big blue eyes, always full of every emotion she was feeling, misted with tears. She hugged him tightly, then pulled back; she pushed his hair off his forehead. "I missed you, too, Bro. It's great to have you home again." She grasped his face gently and peered into his eyes. "I don't ever want you to leave again."

Seth's cheeks turned red. "I won't, Nyx. Promise." He pulled away and knelt down. "Hey, boy!" he said to Chaz, and scrubbed him hard between the ears. Chaz licked his face and wagged his tailless rump.

My brother always could melt a heart—even a dog's heart.

"And look at you!" Nyx said, turning to me. Her eyes widened again as she checked me out. She pulled me into a big tight hug. "I don't think I've ever seen you tanned!" She pulled back and held her pale arm next to my now-browned one. She grinned. "It looks good on you, Ri." She gave me another hug. "Gosh, I missed you guys! It's been so lonely here without you." She immediately turned to Josie and gave her a squeeze; then she turned to Eli and hugged him, too. "Hey, Eli, it's good to see you again." She gave him a broad smile. "Thanks for returning my family to me."

Eli returned the smile and nodded. "My pleasure."

Nyx's face suddenly froze; then she turned. "Oh my God—I have a guy in the chair!"

We all watched Nyx hurry inside Inksomnia.

"She's a great friend," I said, really to no one.

"You're lucky to have her," Eli said, then touched my elbow to lead me inside. I whistled for Chaz, who hurried in ahead of us. The moment the scent of my ink shop hit my nose, I inhaled. It truly was great to be home.

For three straight days, all was perfect; quiet, without the first dream, or further trespassing of my thoughts by Victorian Arcos. Ned Gillespie (the guy with tendencies who'd been bitten by Josie many years before) had nothing to report in regard to any vampiric activity in the Savannah area. Seth and the guys started back to school, and not surprisingly, Seth did so with enthusiasm. He'd always liked school, loved learning, and was a freaking wizard at science. For all of three solid days and nights, my world was settled. God Almighty, I wished it could have lasted. Deep down inside, I'd known better.

Standing at my station, I cracked my neck, rotated it a few times back and forth to loosen up the muscles, and patted the bench. "Hop on," I instructed an older ranger, maybe late thirties and already adorned with several pieces of art. "And lose the shirt, sunshine, unless you think I can ink you through all that camo."

The man laughed, unbuttoned his work shirt, and shrugged out of it. "Yes, ma'am."

I'd felt like having a classics day, and to me nothing was better than a hoppin' day at Inksomnia, with lots of good-natured customers and old rock blasting through the speakers. Heart's "Barracuda" pulled me into that groove I loved being in when inking someone—

especially someone who was not a tat virgin, like this guy.

"Nice boots," he said, climbing onto the bench and lying facedown.

I glanced down at my thigh-high black boots that ended just where the hem of my black leather miniskirt began. I'd picked out a Blondie T-shirt, along with a pair of pink plaid suspenders to wear with the skirt—pretty kick-ass if you asked me. "Thanks," I said, giving him a broad smile. "Ready?"

"I deploy tomorrow," he replied, in a heavy smoker's voice. "I'm always ready, honey."

Rangers kicked ass. I gave him a smile and punched his arm. "Hurry home."

I transferred the image I'd sketched and printed out from my computer onto his left flank—just about the only place left on his back. It was a wicked-cool skeleton soldier's head, cigarette clenched between its teeth, wearing a World War II helmet with the words "Fuck Off" across the front of it. Gotta love it. Once the transfer dried, I lined up my ink pots, grasped the needle, and let the Widow's hum mix with Heart's lyrics, and together they pulled me into my work. I'd preferred to have stayed there, uninterrupted, in my "Barracuda" zone until the job was done. No such freaking luck. I'd just finished the helmet's chin strap and was blotting blood when the interruption occurred.

I fed last night, Riley. I've never enjoyed it—not like my brother. But it's necessary for me to live. I promise—I show mercy, and I feed only when I begin to grow weak, and I take only enough to sustain me. I do not butcher those I take from. I hope you believe me. It hurts to think you believe me a monster.

I froze, needle poised over skin, and felt my insides grow cold. Victorian's voice was so . . . inside me, I could almost feel the tenor of his voice reverberating off my bones. Now he was sharing his kills with me? The thought made my blood chill. And, he wanted my sympathy? What kind of freak-vamp was he? Wide-ass awake and his voice was just as strong, just as real as if he were in the room, standing right beside me. I glanced around, just to make sure.

"What's wrong?" Nyx said from her station.

Mentally, I could do nothing but shake it off. I damn sure couldn't tell Nyx what had happened. I sighed, stretched my back, and cracked my neck. "Nothing. Just a little stiff." I grinned at her. "I'm fine."

Nyx eyed me for a second or two longer, shrugged, and went back to work. For once, I felt sort of glad that Eli wasn't around. He would have zeroed right in on my thoughts and all hell would've broken loose for damn sure. Eli Dupré had a short fuse and would go off like a wild man, had he known Victorian Arcos was tormenting me in my thoughts. Good thing I was a big girl and could take care of myself.

For the rest of the day, the voices continued. All Victorian's voice, of course, but just when I'd think he was finished, he'd whisper something else, something unsettling, terrifying, inside my head. It was getting harder and harder to mask it.

Nyx had just left, my last customer was out the door, and I was on my way up the steps to my apartment to wait for Eli when Victorian interrupted once more.

Does it bother you to know I think of you when I feed? I feel you must know the truth, for it's thoughts of you, your body bare and slick with the sweat of our lovemaking, and my cock buried deep inside you, your legs wrapped around me, begging me for more, that keep me merciful. They . . . settle me. Does that make sense? I confess, it's a unique characteristic I didn't have before tasting your blood. Before part of you entered me, before we were . . . connected.

"Leave me alone!" I yelled out loud. "I swear to God—I'll kill you myself!" My heart, although uncharacteristically slow nowadays, beat hard, loud, and my breath hitched as I took the steps two at a time. Just as I kicked off my thigh-high boots and skirt, I heard the back door slam shut.

"I'm home!" Seth yelled.

"Okay," I answered, not wanting him to know how upset I truly was.

My mind reeling, I peeled out of the rest of my clothes, grabbed a pair of black yoga pants and a sports bra, stretched, and took my frustrations out on my workout bag. I don't know how long I was at it, but I never did hear Eli enter the apartment, or my room, and God knows how long he'd been standing there, reading my freaking thoughts.

"You've been dreaming of him again," Eli said, his eyes hard, his voice low, and uncharacteristically accusing. "Haven't you?"

I ignored him, my emotions on edge, extended my leg fully and, with a quick snap, kicked the workout bag hanging in my bedroom. I followed it with three sharp jabs. Anger and a little hurt built inside me, and after a few more kicks and rounds of punches, I broke a decent sweat.

Eli's strong hands grasped my shoulders and spun me around. "Don't ignore me, Riley." He drew his face close to mine. "Don't."

I frowned, totally pissed. "Then don't accuse me, Eli." I shook his hands off. "You know I can't help those dreams. You know it."

Eli stared at me several long seconds, then shoved his fingers through his hair, muttered some French expletive, and walked to the window. He looked at some distant point across the river. "You desire him."

Anger flashed inside me, and I crossed my arms over my chest. "How freaking old are you, Eli?" I asked. "Sixteen? Oh, no—that's right. You're over two hundred." I walked up behind him, grabbed him by the arm, and turned him around to face me. Brilliant blue eyes searched mine, and I knew he was reading my thoughts; digging through them like a madman was more like it. "You're acting like a jealous high school boyfriend," I said, a little more gently. I grazed his jaw with my index finger. "Seriously, Eli."

Another handful of seconds dragged by before his face went emotionless, his eyes dulled, those beautiful full lips that worked magic against my body thinned. "You don't deny it, do you Riley?" His voice held an edge, tinged with a heavier-than-usual bit of French. I'd learned fast that the heavier the accent, the more pissed off Eli Dupré was.

"Victorian forces the dreams on me," I said harshly. "Just as he forces the emotions within them." I stepped closer. "I. Can't. Help. It."

Anger pulled his features tighter. "Do you think this is some game? He is deadly, Riley. Do you think he has feelings for you? Other than obsession? He will drain every ounce of your blood in seconds. Regrets might come after it's too late." His eyes grew somber. "I think you enjoy the dreams a little too much," he said, moving past me. At the door, he stopped, staring straight ahead. "You could have come to me."

"What would you have done, Eli?" I said. "You can't go into my subconscious and change anything. You can't make him stop."

"You don't know what I can do," he said angrily. "You didn't give me a fucking chance."

He moved so fast, I didn't see him actually turn and leave. Only the sound of the back door closing alerted me to his absence.

I walked to the window overlooking River Street, propped a hip against the ledge, and stared out into the growing darkness. Soon, it would be pitch-black outside—everdark (the Gullah pronounced it evah-dock). It meant, pretty much, everlasting darkness. That was what it felt like, too—an endless night. Leaning forward, I pressed my forehead against the cool pane. Eli wasn't right, not by far. I did not enjoy the dreams; rather, the internal conversations I'd reluctantly had with the younger Arcos. Nor did I desire Victorian. In the dreams, I wanted two things: to continue the turn-on, then nothing more than for him to stop, to leave me the hell alone; he never did. He returned to me, time after time, with the most erotic, out-of-control dreams that make me respond to him in ways that mortified me. I loathed him. He made me excited. Yet I got a rush when his voice sounded inside my head.

Worse still, Victorian had begun speaking to me during my waking hours. Somehow, he'd gotten inside my head outside of the dreams. The only cause I could assume to be the reason for this was that we shared the strigoi DNA. I thought I could handle it. I wanted the bastard dead. I was the only one who could get close enough to do it. Dammit.

"What was that all about? You okay?"

I turned and met Seth's concerned gaze. I was a balled-up bundle of hot electrical wires, and I needed to burn off a little energy. It was either that or bang my head against a brick wall. "It's nothing, Bro. Seriously. You wanna go for a run?"

My brother gave me a crooked grin. "I'll pass. I'm meeting Josie for a little roof jumping." He wiggled his brows at me.

Seth Poe was definitely enjoying his vampiric tendencies. The kid had serious free-running talent. I'd been watching him closely, just to see if anything else, possibly weird, popped up. So far, it hadn't. I grinned. "Gotcha. I'll catch ya later."

Those fathomless green eyes stared at me for a moment; then Seth pulled me into a tight hug. "Love ya, Sis." Then he disappeared out the door.

I shook my head, yanked on my sneakers, and headed out into the early-September night air, crossed the merchant's drive, climbed the metal steps to Bay Street, and took off.

Savannah in September was still warm and humid, and the brine from the river clung heavily to the air. I drew it in fully as I ran, the muscles in my legs stretching with each long stride. I could go faster—much faster— but that would seriously draw attention. I mean, I can haul ass. Instead, though, I kept it to a typical human's pace, crossed Bay behind a group of ghost walkers, and headed up Bryan Street. Finally, I found myself alone. Full darkness had fallen, and I increased my speed, stretching my legs. Long shadows fell from the lampposts, parking meters, and the massive oaks that lined nearly every side street in the historic district. Everything looked distorted. I turned the corner and glanced over my shoulder.

An arm shot out of the shadows, clotheslined me, and knocked me flat on my back. I'd barely felt the sidewalk beneath me before I leapt up, adrenaline rushing, body rigid, poised, crouched, and ready to fight. I stared hard into the shadows.

I knew who awaited me before he emerged.

"My apologies for using such force to stop you," Victorian Arcos said in a low, seductive voice, "but you're amazingly fast."

"Thanks to you and your brother," I answered. "What are you doing here? They'll kill you if they find you." I met his gaze with a hard one. "Maybe I'll kill you."

Victorian stepped fully into the lamplight, and again I was stunned by his beauty. He looked older than twenty-one. Gone was the eighteenth-century clothing from before. Although he still kept his sleek black hair long and pulled into a queue, he was now dressed in a loose white button-down shirt hanging untucked from a pair of worn jeans and scuffed boots. It was difficult to believe he was so young. Well, that plus several hundred years. Apparently, my death threat fazed him nada.

He closed his eyes and drew in a lungful of air, then looked at me. "I can barely smell your blood," he said, stepping closer and inhaling deeply again. "Your dark brothers must have changed the drugs they use to mask your scent." Light reflected in his deep brown eyes, and they studied me closely, intensely. "I'm glad. I had to see you."

A car turned up the street, and the headlights flashed toward us. In the blink of an eye, Victorian stepped in front of me, pushing me backward through the thick, damp grass, and into the shadows of an aged brick historic house that dominated nearly an entire block. The car passed; the headlight beams swept above our heads, and then left us in total darkness. Victorian, who stood at least six feet tall, moved slowly, crowding me and forcing me to back up. I stopped when the brick pressed into my back. I felt completely powerless, as though I possessed zero control of my actions, my thoughts, my new tendencies—almost as if I'd had a stroke. The younger Arcos took full advantage.

He stared down at me, desire radiating off his body in heady waves. "You torture me, Riley," he said, his Romanian accent making his words seductive, erotic. "I think of nothing else but you"—he leaned close, his mouth brushing my jaw—"and of what I want to do to you." His soft lips grazed the skin at my neck, where he lingered, and a flash of fear mixed with an uncontrolled shiver rushed through me. "Of what I dream of you doing to me," he said at my ear. "It causes me physical pain to stay away, Riley Poe." His mouth moved to my jaw, dragging his lips to my chin, close to my mouth. "I want you now," he whispered. "I want to keep you forever."

I was shaking, my mind numb, my limbs paralyzed, and sensations tingled across the skin where his lips moved so erotically. I didn't want this, or his touch. I couldn't help but crave it. I breathed, squeezed my eyes shut, opened them, gathered my strength—God only knew where it came from—lifted my hands to his chest and pushed. Hard. Victorian flew backward and landed on his back several feet away. He lay there, staring at me and smiling.

When next I blinked, he stood in front of me, close,

crowding me once more, his hands grasping my wrists and grating my knuckles against the brick wall at my back. He lowered his head, his lips whispering against mine.

"Your tendencies do nothing more than fascinate me"—his mouth moved against mine—"and excite me even more." He pulled back and looked at me. "What other tricks do you possess that I might enjoy?" His alluring scent surrounded me as his mouth covered mine—

"Riley?" A hand grasped my shoulder and shook—hard. "Riley, wake up, dammit."

I gasped; my eyes fluttered open and I stared, confused, into Eli's questioning gaze. Behind him, early-morning sun streamed in through my bedroom window, casting a hazy glow on his face. He frowned. "You've been dreaming of him again," he said, his eyes hard and accusing. "Haven't you?"

I glanced down. I still wore the same black yoga pants and sports bra I'd gone for a run in the night before. I'd encountered Victorian on that run. Hadn't I? Or had it all really been a dream? I looked at my knuckles; the skin across them was scraped raw.

Inside my head, Victorian's seductive laugh resonated.

Now, either that little fucker was messing with me, or I was losing my goddamn mind.

Part Three

—━━◆━━◆━━—

TERRORS

"Death is when the monsters get you."

—Stephen King, *Salem's Lot*

"I've started having . . . visions. Night terrors. Day terrors. And they're not of Victorian. It's something—or someone—else; I get the sick feeling they're weirdly familiar. I'm seeing innocents die horrible deaths at the hands of a vicious monster; watching it happen through my own eyes as though it's me doing the killing; as if I'm the monster. I even feel what the monster is experiencing, and it's . . . disgusting. I'm not kidding—something's gotta give because I can't freaking take it anymore."

—Riley Poe

By the time I'd closed Inksomnia's doors a few nights later, I'd realized with complete lucidity that our lives—all of our lives—would never be the same again. There were no rose-colored glasses here. Nope. My goggles were scratch free and squeaky-clean, and, to be honest, I suppose I'd rather it be that way. Better to know what's coming than to ignorantly stand around with your thumb up your butt, waiting for junk to happen.

For instance, Preacher and Estelle no longer had to what the Gullah referred to as "fix" me. Let's face it. My DNA was royally screwed up, so I no longer needed that particular concoction of God-Knows-What from Preacher's special behind-the-haint-blue-curtain herb collection. I still had to have something—I mean, I was still human after all—but not such a heavy dose, and my

Gullah grandparents no longer had to trick me daily into drinking my protective tea. I willingly did so and kept a mammoth canister of it on my kitchen counter. Gilles said that because I had the venom of two strigoi vampires' mixed with my DNA, my blood would slowly start morphing into something unique, and soon I wouldn't even need the tea. I'm not sure if I should have been happy or freaked about that. Lucky for my brother, he had the venom of only one strigoi mixed with his DNA. We're both pretty messed up, though, I guess you could say. Messed up, but not stupid.

Another thing I've noticed, and this just since getting back home, is my senses. They're changing. I mean, I'd known about the whole werewolf/Arcos bit, but damn—I didn't realize it'd get so intense. Or that it'd continue to alter as it has. My hearing is ridiculously acute. I'm starting to hear the most insane sounds, like the nuns over at the Cathedral of St. John the Baptist (aka Cinderella's Castle by Seth and me), and that's all the way over on East Harris Street. I can literally hear them praying. At first, it was nothing more than a cluster of hushed murmuring whispers; but, by the second day, the whispers were totally clear and I could understand every word being muttered—every single word. It made me feel like some freaky eavesdropping voyeur or something. Weird. Even weirder was that I could now pick up heartbeats, and only God knew how far away they were. I heard them everywhere, and after a while it began to seriously grate on the nerves. Thump thump thump thump thump thump. Thump freaking thump. Eli promised to teach me how to channel it, tune it out, or make use of it. I was looking forward to learning those tricks and hopefully soon, because I felt as if I' were constantly holed up in a crowded bar with some drunken idiot banging a set of drums. The softer the sound, the louder it was inside my head. It was driving me frickin' nuts.

And my sense of smell was almost just as crazy. I could detect everything from a joint being toked three blocks away in an upstairs apartment, to some nasty drunk dude farting batter-fried onion rings in the corner booth at Spanky's.

I was standing in my kitchen, steeping strong Gullah tea, when the first terror-vision hit me. I wished to God it was my last. It wasn't. I remember glancing at the time on my Kit-Cat Klock—8:44 a.m.

A paralyzing grip suddenly snatched control of my body; I dropped the spoon I was using to stir sugar into my tea, and it clattered against the granite countertop, then hit the floor. I couldn't feel my fingers or toes, and, at first, I couldn't breathe. The insides of my eyes, behind the sockets, turned boiling hot, then frigidly cold. A loud ringing in my ears drowned out any and all noises, including the ones I heard blocks away. Then everything went pitch-black. I tried to speak, but my vocal cords were paralyzed, too. Panic, mixed with anger, seized me.

All at once, a live scene flashed behind my lids. It was nightfall, and I was following a girl out of the mall. I wasn't completely unfamiliar with the place, but it definitely wasn't Savannah. Young, petite, and blond, looking to be in her early twenties, wearing red flip-flops, holey jeans, and a purple tank top, she swung her hips as she made her way toward the covered parking garage. She happily chatted to someone on her cell and didn't seem to notice me. A horn blew from somewhere in the garage, and the girl squealed, then giggled to her phone companion. I grew closer. In the distance, sounds of traffic filled the night air.

Long shadows, birthed from low light cast from the overhead lamps bracketed onto concrete pillars, fell over the row of sparsely parked cars. Not many people were about on a weeknight; no one was in the direct vicinity of the girl. She turned down the row with a white metal sign marked by a black capital *B*. I watched her closely. She dug through her purse and retrieved a set of keys. At the same time, she stopped at a white Camry and pushed the key release. The horn gave one short blast as it unlocked the doors. With her chin she held her cell, and she reached for the door handle.

Hands not my own grabbed her, whipped her around, and slammed her back against the car. Large blue eyes widened in fear and confusion as they stared, horrified, into mine. Tremors of fear wracked her body; I could feel them. Adrenaline rushed through her veins; I could hear the swooshing sound it made as though magnified, only to my ears. Her heart slammed rapidly against her ribs, faster, harder. At the indention in her throat, her pulse beckoned me. The moment she filled her lungs with air to scream, I lunged at her neck and sank my teeth into her flesh. The scream died in her throat as I ripped through her larynx and her vocal cords, until the vessel I sought popped; a rush of wet warmth, sweet, erotic, and heady, saturated the inside of my mouth. I suckled her blood, excitement rushing through me as I felt the liquid slide down my throat. The girl's body jerked, involuntarily, as life left her. The jerks were hard at first, then weaker. The instant she sagged against me, her heart having stilled and her eyes dull and lifeless, I dropped her body. It crumpled into a heap at my feet, and I wiped my mouth with the back of my hand.

"Riley!"

Strong hands gripped my shoulders and shook me until my blurred vision cleared, and Seth's worried face came into view. He shook me again and shouted so loud my ears rang. "Ri, wake up!"

"Whoa, back off, Bro," I said, and shook his hands off me. I squeezed my eyes shut, opened them, and looked around. Slowly, my surroundings came into focus. I glanced at the Kit-Cat Klock on the wall. It was 8:50 a.m. Six minutes had passed.

What the fu—

"Your eyes were blank, but your face . . . ," he said, and it was then I noticed for the first time his voice had deepened.

"What about my face?" I asked. I moved to the sink, flipped the faucet on, and splashed myself with cold water.

Seth passed me the hand towel. "You looked, I don't know," he said, then looked at me with his expressive green eyes. "Mean. You looked mean, Ri. Scary-mean. Not yourself."

I dried my face and thought about that. "Did I say anything?"

Seth shook his head, a hank of dark hair falling into his eyes. He pushed it back. "No. You just stood there, staring, and looking . . . hateful."

The memory of the vision struck me, rushing back full force. I met my brother's worried gaze. "I saw something, Seth. Like a daydream, only it was so freaking real. It was"—I searched for the right word—"sickening."

"What was it?" he asked, and I noticed then how

worried he truly was. His brows pulled into a frown, his mouth thin. "Tell me."

I closed my eyes and dug my fingers into the sockets, rubbing hard. I looked at my brother. "I saw a kill. I saw a vampire feed."

Seth's face grew pale, and his eyes widened. "What?"

My mouth went dry as the memory of the vision, so clear and realistic, pushed to the very forefront of my mind. "It was as though I were him; I saw everything as if I were the killer, only when my hands reached out, they were not mine. They were his." I shook my head. "I felt everything, Seth. The girl's terror. The rush of excitement as my teeth sank into her artery. The blood as it pumped into my throat. Every freaking thing." Suddenly, my stomach rolled, every detail returning in vivid recall, and I felt the color drain from my face. My skin grew clammy. I covered my mouth with my hand. "I'm gonna be sick."

Seth grabbed my arm and pulled me down the hall and into the bathroom with such speed, my head spun just as violently as my stomach. Even then, we barely made it. I stumbled, kicked the lid open with my foot, and retched into the toilet. Seth held my hair back while I lost last night's lo mein noodles.

A cold, wet washcloth was suddenly resting on the back of my neck. Seth flushed the toilet, closed the lid, turned me around, and pushed me down onto it. I rested my forearms on my knees and breathed, and my baby brother, who seemed so grown up lately, squatted down to look at me. Green eyes just like mine met me with intensity.

"You gotta tell Eli," Seth said.

I thought about it. "Maybe. But I'm not. It's probably just my mind effing with me, you know? That night at

Bonaventure still haunts me. Seriously. It's just a lot of crap to take in. We've been through hell, little brother. Nasty-hell."

The frown still on Seth's face proved he didn't really believe me. "Yeah, I know, he said. He ducked his head. "You okay, Ri?"

I wasn't. Not at all. "Yeah. I'm totally fine. Let's get out of here, okay? And," I said, playfully punching his arm, "thanks. Not many dudes would hold a girl's hair while she puked her guts up."

Seth's eyes softened. "Well, I'm not just any ole dude, and you're my sister. I love you."

My heart was melting.

"I love you, too," I said. "I'd hug you, but—"

"Yeah, gross," he finished, taking a step back. He held up his hands in defense. "No postpuke hugging, please. That's just nasty." He shuddered.

We both laughed, and I did my very best for the rest of the day to forget the horror of the daydream. Good thing it was Sunday and Inksomnia was closed. I'm not positive I could have kept it to myself.

Eli had gone with his brothers and Gilles to some monthly guardian meeting at Bethesda with Preacher and his people, and while I missed being with Eli, I'd craved time alone with my little brother. So I spent the early part of the day with just Seth. It seemed like forever since we'd done that, and even in spite of the awful, realistic daydream, we had fun. We had breakfast with Estelle and took Chaz to Forsythe Park for a long walk. Then later we hit Cleary's for lunch. We both had the Reuben, and, swear to God, they make the best ones in Savannah. I could have eaten two and had to literally stop myself from ordering a second.

One of the tendencies Seth and I shared: voracious appetites. We both ate like friggin' hogs. Luckily our metabolisms kept up with the amount of food we dumped in.

On the way home, we hit the Pig (that's the ever-popular southern grocery chain store Piggly Wiggly, aka Hoggly Woggly, aka the PW), picked up some milk, dog food, a twelve-pack of Cherry Coke, a pack of T-bones, another twelve-pack of Octoberfest, some junk food, and a few things for Estelle, then headed home. As we cruised the city streets with the top off the Jeep, the sun pelted me through the sporadic holes in the overhead canopy of oaks and pines. As my skin warmed, and the briny breeze wafted from the Savannah River to my nostrils, I could almost put behind me the horribleness of that damn daydream, and the way that girl had died; the way I'd felt it, tasted it, experienced it, and how wicked-sick real it had been. I mean, I'd tasted her blood. I'd felt it slide down my throat. How the hell could that be?

The girl's face kept randomly flashing behind my lids, and it was disturbing as holy freaking hell. Her facial features, right down to the small gap in her front teeth, seemed so exact. It was almost as if I'd met her before. Maybe she was a past client I'd inked? That could definitely be a possibility. I'd inked a lot of people. Overall, though—why her?

The afternoon sun waned, and weak early-evening shadows now fell from lampposts, live oaks, and parking meters as we crossed Bay, pulled onto the merchant's drive and parked the Jeep behind Inksomnia.

"Hey, there's Eli," Seth said, and pointed.

Eli was there, waiting for me, and, I confess, he had the sole capability to take my breath away. His bike was almost as hot as he was. The liquid silverback chopper sat propped on its kickstand, half helmet hanging off a handlebar, the whole package looking kick-ass. Eli leaned casually against the seat; legs crossed at the ankles, arms folded over his chest, he was wearing nothing but a pair of low-slung worn jeans, boots, and a white T-shirt, and the silver hoop at his brow. I couldn't see his eyes—they were masked by his shades—but I knew he stared at me. He studied every inch of me. My sex drive kicked me mule-hard, and I wanted him. Just knowing he watched me behind the privacy of his sunglasses shot a thrill through me. A sexier man did not exist, I swear it.

A small smile tilted the corner of his mouth. Freaking ego. Of course, he'd been listening and had joyfully heard every word I'd thought.

"Hey, Eli," Seth said cheerfully, grabbing nearly all the bags from the back of the Jeep. He had a twenty-five-pound bag of Chaz's dog food slung over one shoulder as he passed what no one would ever guess to be a nearly two-hundred-year-old vampire.

"What's up, Seth?" Eli answered, but he didn't move. Behind those shades his gaze remained fixed on me.

"Nothin' much. Hangin' with the sister," Seth said with a grin, and disappeared inside. Chaz's excited bark met my ears, and in seconds, Seth emerged with the Australian shepherd on a leash. "Be back in a bit," he said, his smile wide. "We've got training at your folk's place at eight. I can't wait." He waved and disappeared around the corner.

Eli didn't move. He mouthed, *Come here*, and, oh hell yeah, I did just that. I stepped out of the Jeep and swaggered over to him, hoping I was half as distracting to him as he was to me. I was wearing my faded low-rise jeans and the fuchsia floral cami I knew he liked—

mainly because it skimmed just above my belly button. I stopped when I was directly in front of him and placed one leg on either side of his. I leaned forward, bracing my weight with the heel of my palms on the sides of his hips. I drew so close, our noses nearly touched. I could see my reflection in his shades.

Neither of us said a word.

Eli's hands slipped around my waist, grazing the bare skin of my lower back, and moved his mouth over mine in a kiss that had me wet and burning for him within five seconds. My hands slid up his back and around his neck; I kissed him back. The slightest pressure pulled my body against his, and I briefly thought how well we fit together. His hands moved over my ass; his hard bulge let me know I affected him just as much, and I groaned against his mouth. "I'm not above taking you right here, right now," I whispered, and licked his tongue. I felt his smile beneath my lips.

"Another thing I love about you," he said in a low voice. "You're not shy." His fingers threaded through my hair and he pulled me tight against his mouth. His kiss drugged me.

Finally, breathless, and just a shade under being pornographic in public, I leaned back and took off his shades. His profound stare never ceased to stun me; the weight of it froze me. Fathomless and ancient at once, his eyes locked on to mine. It was then I knew with complete certainty that I'd never be satisfied with anyone else except Eli—a pretty scary thought, actually.

The sexiest grin I'd ever seen crossed his face. "Ah, my evil plan has succeeded. Come here, mostly mortal woman. There is nothing to be scared of. Let me ravish you," he drawled in heavy French. I laughed, and

he pushed a loose strand of fuchsia hair out of my eyes
and tucked it behind my ear. Then he stopped, studying me; his gaze narrowed, and a slight early-evening
breeze rustled his already-tousled hair. All playfulness
had vanished, replaced by uncanny perception. "What's
wrong?"

I shrugged. "Nothing. A dream I had earlier shook
me up a little." I sighed. "Freaking vampires."

Eli pulled me close and buried his face in my hair. He
inhaled deeply. "Must've shaken you more than a little."
He leaned back and frowned. "You're making goofy
jokes and you didn't drink your tea."

That he could smell my unprotected blood amazed
me; it also knocked me a notch or two back to reality.

"It should," he said, taking more liberties with my
thoughts. "You might think you're invincible with your
new tendencies, but trust me—you're not. Your blood
may have changed some; I don't zone in on it rushing
through your veins like I used to. But it's still tempting,
addicting." He frowned. "Drink the damn tea, Riley. I
don't care if you eat the stuff. Just get it into your system." He grazed my jaw with a finger. "Please?"

"Okay, okay," I answered. "I really didn't mean to
forget it, even though your dad told me that because of
the strigoi factor in my DNA, I may be able to stop the
tea altogether."

"That's not now, so humor me. Drink the tea." With
his index finger, Eli traced the dragon inked into my
skin; all the way up my arm. He followed it until it disappeared beneath my shirt; then Eli grasped my chin. The
look he gave me sent two kinds of chills up my spine—
one of fear; one of pure sexual heat. "I don't want to
have to work so hard not to hurt you."

"Point taken, Dupré," I said, and I reminded myself I was crazy about a vampire who could kill me in seconds if he lost control. "Getting tea now."

"Oh—my parents want us to have dinner with them Saturday night," Eli said as we made our way into my ink shop. "Formal wear. You and Seth." He grinned down at me as we walked. "Every once in a while they like to dress up, like in the old days when, you know—that's the way it was done. Old music and stuff. It's kinda fun. You up for it?"

My mind mentally scanned my closet, then scanned Seth's. "When you say 'dress up like in the old days,' do you mean corsets and funny hoops beneath my dress, or what?"

Eli laughed. "No, just modern formal wear."

At the door I stopped, rose up on my toes, and kissed him. "I'm not your typical debutante, you know."

"Yeah, I know," he answered, eyes locked on mine. "It's one of your charms."

I grinned. "Yep. We're up for it. What time?"

"Seven."

Seth rounded the corner alley with Chaz just as we were stepping inside. "Sounds good. I'll ask Nyx to take my appointments after five."

"What's up?" Seth asked as we walked through the doorway. Chaz ran ahead, his nails clicking on the wood plank floor.

"Dinner with Dracula and Company," I answered, shooting Eli a smart-ass grin. "Saturday night. Seven. And no Vans and baggy shorts with the crotch at the knees and your drawers hanging out. Formal wear."

"Sweet," Seth said.

Eli just smiled and shook his head.

We spent the rest of Sunday pretending everything was normal. I guess for us, it was, although my mind never fully let loose the events that led me to where I'm at right now. Part of me was glad; Eli was in my life. For how long, I didn't know. The other part hated it. The Arcoses had nearly claimed my baby brother, and I don't know if I could have survived that.

We walked Estelle's stuff over and visited with her and Preacher for a bit. Their back kitchen seemed like a mystical, unearthly place now, dimmed lights and shadows, where the unique African herbs and concoctions from Da Plat Eye wafted in like some crazy aromatic air infusion. Estelle's sausage, shrimp, and red rice stewed on the stovetop, and she sat in the corner, surrounded by sweetgrass strands, weaving a basket and wearing her hair wrapped in one of her colorful traditional Gullah cloths. Preacher sat, wearing his usual long-sleeved plaid shirt and denims (he called them dungarees, and that totally cracked me up), scolding me (after Eli ratted me out) about forgetting my tea.

"Don' get too complacent, girl," Preacher had said, his ebony skin a beautiful contrast to his snow-white hair. He reminded me of an older Danny Glover. "I mean dat, right. You git too big for your britches, you might get hurt." He'd reached over and grasped my hands with his. "I ain't puttin' up wit dat, now."

Capote, Preacher's cousin, had stopped by, and I swear, he was one funny-ass old man. He never, never went without a big, blinding smile, and he always had some sort of hysterical story to tell about him and Preacher from their childhood. He sat at the table with us, a bag of boiled peanuts in his lap, eating and shelling just as fast as his fingers and mouth would work. He'd looked at me and shaken his head. "Girl, you done fell in wit some crazy folk, right?" he'd said, jerking his head toward Eli. "Dem Duprés—wooo, now, you done fell in wit dem for sure." He laughed and shook his head again. "Dey good folk doh, dat's right. Always have been. Dey treat you good. You do da same."

Once we left Preacher's (with a big Tupperware filled with Estelle's gumbo and a bag of boiled peanuts—I swear I could live off them), we headed to Monterey Square. Seth was already there with Josie; Phin and Luc had just returned from Tybee (they'd been checking out some new gaming software Ned Gillespie had developed); the *Lord of the Flies* boys, along with Zetty, walked in behind Eli and me. We'd all agreed on group training twice a week at the Dupré House, where the complete top floor had been renovated into a wicked-awesome, upgraded donjon. It'd been pretty cool as a gym before, but now? Damn. I walked in for the first time and stared.

"Wow," I muttered, and looked around at the punching bags, table of blades, the vamp dummies, and the various-sized surfaces—pretty much synthetic rock—for leaping and jumping. I glanced at Elise and Gilles, who'd followed us upstairs. "You've been busy."

"Yeah, sweet Mr. and Mrs. D.," Riggs said, pushing past me. "Awesome."

I glanced at Riggs; at his baggy shorts, his Eminem T-shirt, and his Nike Airs, and then, his shaggy hair held in place by a red bandanna. "Nice headband, Riggs," I said, noticing he had one holding back his bangs.

"I wore it just for you, babe," he said, grinning. He inclined his head. "Wanna spar?"

I grinned back. The little turd knew I hated being called babe. "Oh yeah," I said. "Let's go."

Luc let out a whistle, clapped, and smiled, the hoop in his lip silver and, in my biased opinion, so him. "Yeah, baby—some action! Step back, folks—kids, wannabes"—he glanced at his parents—"and the elderly." He grinned and backed toward the wall. "Poe's got the floor."

I rolled my eyes at him—what a nerd. I pointed at him. "You're next."

A round of oooh's went through the donjon.

Elise Dupré smiled broadly at me. "That I'll be looking forward to, darling." She turned to Gilles. "We've got that auction on eBay, darling."

"*Oui*," he answered, and, grinning, the two left the donjon.

I felt pretty certain she hadn't particularly appreciated being called elderly. It was one thing to think it, but to say it? Eesh. I did think it hilarious that the matriarch and patriarch of the family raced to eBay auctions.

Riggs sauntered to the center of the mat, whipped his Emenem shirt over his head, and tossed it aside, leaving a pretty impressive six-pack (for a kid) exposed. Good God, that boy thought his boat rocked. Before he had tendencies, he was just a smart-ass adolescent with a cocky attitude. Now he had . . . powers. And while his experience had matured him some, he was still, well, pervy, cocky Riggs. Now he and his ego would be impossible to live with. He needed an attitude adjustment.

I was going to kick his ass.

With a quick glance at Eli, whose wicked grin told me he'd just read my thoughts, I met Riggs on the mat. The others watching clapped, Phin whistled again, and Riggs began to circle me. I let him—for a few. You know, he had to show off a little, for the other Flies, and I gave him that. He did some pretty amazing wall jumps (where he ran toward the wall, then sort of ran up it, then flipped over me), some sick leaps directly over my head, and a few cool roundhouse kicks. Yep. He was one impressive little shit-with-tendencies.

The moment he landed from his roundhouse, I crouched and swept his legs with one kick. Riggs hit the mat, back down with a smack. Everyone laughed, clapped—whatever.

Riggs stared up at me from the floor, grinning, as I extended my hand. He took it, and I pulled him up. He leaned close. "See? I knew I'd get you to touch me," he said in my ear. "Babe."

Then, all at once, several things, none of which I had any control over, hit me hard.

Quick as lightning, Riggs grasped my forearm and whole-body flipped me. As I went airborne, that same sick sensation I'd experienced with Seth came over me; I knew another awful image was about to fill my brain. My body went limp, and shadows fell behind my eyelids. I saw nothing, heard nothing—couldn't speak, and I don't remember even hitting the mat. I remained weightless in some dark, cloudy fog, where nothing else existed, as if I'd totally left the donjon. Finally, a sound—a heartbeat. I can't tell you if it was mine or someone else's. At first, it was muffled, but it grew in tone and intensity.

Then, slowly, my vision returned. Blurred at first, it went in and out of tune like an old TV set, and finally, it focused on . . . I blinked several times. A girl. In a bar. No, a club. In a booth. Music banging. Punk music banging. Surroundings unfamiliar. Girl unfamiliar. Girl totally wasted. She was a partier, midtwenties, heavy black eye makeup, Marilyn Monroe–ish, white-bleached bobbed hair with orange streaks. Her black leather strapless bustier barely contained her heavy breasts. She leaned over the table, picked up the glass of her mixed drink, and licked first the rim, then her dark red lips. Her brown eyes were hazed, and her pheromones were so pungent, I could smell them. She was horny and wanted me, only . . . I wasn't me. Of course I wasn't me. I wasn't into girls. She saw him; not me. I could hear her heart beating erratically. She reached out for my hand, grasped it, and I looked down. The hand wasn't mine. It was male; older, rough-skinned, not Victorian's smooth pale skin. I knew that, though.

She stood and led me out of the booth. The leather miniskirt she was wearing hardly covered her ass, and the bustier was laced in back, revealing bare skin. I noticed a tattoo on her lower back. It was Death's fingers, his long skeletal bones spread out across her, beckoning; it was my work. I had inked her before. She was laughing, stumbling as she made her way to the exit. She was pulling me, and I could feel her hand in mine; yet . . . it wasn't me. But I could feel whoever it was. I knew what was going to happen; I could feel the anticipation of the kill inside me. I tried to move my lips, vibrated my vocal cords, and tried to warn her. I tried to scream, and deep inside me, I felt immense anxiety to warn her. It was no use. I was speechless, useless, not really even here. I could do nothing but watch—watch and be horrified.

The girl pushed out into the night, and the air was muggy, heavy; the faint scent of salt clung to my tongue. She hung on me as we walked, and she half stumbled, half pulled me along the sidewalk, drunkenly laughing, until the lights from the club, the thumping music from within, became dull and barely there. I heard only her heartbeat. I tried to yank back, but my body wasn't really my own. Long shadows fell across her, and she pulled me into an alley. The scent of mingled mold and urine and brine reached my nostrils, and she fell against the brick wall, staring at me with her wide, drug-hazed, lust-filled eyes. How stupid she was; how utterly freaking ignorantly stupid.

A zipper closed the front of her leather bustier. She grasped the metal tab and pulled it down to her waist. Her breasts spilled out, and she grabbed my hands, pressing them to her skin. Inwardly, I resisted. Again, it was no use. Her head fell back, and she moaned.

It was the very last sound she ever voluntarily made.

The heartbeat I felt wasn't mine, but hers, and it reso- nated within my head, strong, heady, and I lunged at her bared chest. Her moan died in a liquid curdling sound as her body fell hard to the cobbled ground; I followed her down. Blood, bone, and flesh flashed before my eyes, a vicious carnage that nauseated me. I couldn't pull away, I couldn't look away. Yet the need, the hunger—the horror—roared within me. Liquid warmth flowed down my throat, sweet, intoxicating, and my throat constricted as I sucked.

"Riley!"

My head snapped, hitting something hard, and my cheek stung as a hand smacked it. My eyes fluttered open, and I stared up—into the widened eyes of Riggs. He was straddling me, I was flat on my back on the don- jon mat, and his hand was raised to give me another smack. His hand never reached my skin.

"Don't do that again, kid," Eli said, his voice edged with threat, a death grip on Riggs' hand. "Get off her."

Riggs moved—fast, and then I was looking into Eli's eyes as he bent down on one knee and hovered over me.

He stared, hard, for several seconds, and I knew he was digging in my brain. With a stern look, his gaze traveled over my body, then searched my face. "Yeah, I am digging. What the hell's going on, Riley?"

Seth squatted down beside me and leaned over. "Ri? You okay?"

"I'm okay, Seth." I sat up. "Seriously. No worries."

Behind my brother stood Phin, Luc, and Josie; behind them, Zetty, Riggs, and the others. They all looked at me as if I'd grown another freaking head. "What?" I asked, glancing at all of them, then back to Eli. I stared silently, frustration and a little anger growing faster by the second. Tucking my foot under my ass, I moved to stand. Eli pushed me back down. In the next second Zetty was standing there, pinching dust from his protective pouch and sprinkling it over me.

He muttered something in Tibetan.

"Zetty, stop it!" I said, waving my hand in front of my face. "What the hell?"

"You got some bad stuff in you, Riley," he said in his heavy Nepali accent. "It needs to come out."

I glared at him. "Well thanks, Zet-Man. I'll see what I can do."

Zetty glared back, then moved away. Eli was there, doing his share of glaring.

"Tell me," he said, his frown deepening and his blue eyes growing dark. "Now."

I frowned back. "Jesus, Eli. Chill."

He continued to stare, waiting for an answer.

I sighed. "It was another daydream. Very realistic—"

"How realistic?" he asked.

I looked at him, blocking out everyone else from the room. I focused solely on Eli. "Very. I see a kill. Feel it. As if I'm the killer." With my thumb and forefinger, I rubbed my closed eyes, digging hard into the sockets, trying to erase the images, the feelings. "I . . . feel his emotions, his desires, and they're so gross—"

"Is it Victorian Arcos?" Eli asked.

The fury in his face was almost frightening. "No," I answered. "But he's male. In the daydream, when I reach out, it's not my hand but his." I shook my head and looked at him. "It's freaky, and I hate it." I inhaled. "Can I get up now?"

Eli didn't answer me, but he grasped my hand and pulled me up.

"So what's causing it, Eli?" asked Phin. He ran a hand over his short blond hair and stared at his brother. "I don't like it, Bro. Something's up."

Eli kept silent, his gaze trained on me. "Yeah." He inclined his head. "Let's go."

"Where?" I asked. "You know I don't like to be bossed—"

"Now, Riley," Eli said, his stern expression edgy. "I mean it. To my parents' study. They' have to know."

Phin and Luc were already halfway across the donjon floor. My gaze lit on Seth', and then on Josie, who stood right next to him. She looked at me, eyes fixed and reading me as though she could see straight through me. She picked up on my apprehension. "It'll be cool," she said with encouragement. "Eli's right. Mother and Papa can help."

With Eli's hand on my elbow, I made my way to the Duprés' study. Phin and Luc had waited. Eli reached around me, caught my gaze and held it, then turned the antique cut-glass knob and pushed open the door. I walked through a mixture of jasmine and the scent of a sweet cigar kicked up by a whirling ceiling fan as I entered the room. In the next second, a breeze grazed my cheek; Phin and Luc were across the room. I hadn't even seen them move. My gaze lit on Eli's parents, seated at a large mahogany desk near the window. Elise studied something on the computer's flat-screen monitor. Gilles leaned over her shoulder, obviously interested.

"Take the bid up to twenty-five pounds, love," Gilles said to Elise.

"Ah, and then we'll wait and snipe," Elise said, typing in her request. Gilles looked up and smiled at me. "On eBay. I've a penchant for antique pocket watches."

"Papa," Eli said, his slight French accent catching my attention. "Riley has ... an issue. We need your counsel."

Gilles rose and walked to me, stopping no more than a few feet away. His profound stare struck me. "What is the matter, *ma chérie*?" He cocked his head. "Dreams, I see," he said, nodding, before I could answer. "Of kills? Tell me."

I glanced at Eli, and he nodded. I continued. "It's as if ... I'm him. The killer. And it's not Victorian Arcos. It's another male, and I'm seeing through his eyes. I can feel him. He attacks and feeds, but I can't stop what he does." I shook my head. "I try, but I can't speak, move, or control his actions. It's as if I'm ... behind his eyelids." I looked at Eli's dad. "I recognized the last victim by her tattoo. It was my work."

Gilles stroked his smoothly shaven chin; clear blue eyes the same shocking color as Eli's regarded me. "You've a vampire's venom inside you, Riley," he said. "Yet you say it is not Victorian." His gaze, curious, sought mine. "How do you know?"

It wasn't that Gilles frightened me; he didn't. I trusted

him, just as I did Eli. But whenever I was around him, the feeling that I'd snuck and done something wrong and had just been busted overcame me. I'd been caught with Mary Jane stuffed in my locker in eighth grade once, and the school security guard had walked right up and caught me stuffing the plastic baggy in my backpack. He'd dragged me to the principal's office, and it was that feeling. Gilles Dupré was an extremely profound soul.

Gilles smiled, clearly amused. He truly loved to read my thoughts. "Again, *chérie*. How do you know that it is not Victorian? It can be no other, *oui*?"

"I ripped Valerian's heart out myself," Eli said quietly.

"I helped Phin burn the rest of his body," said Luc. "No way can it be him."

"That leaves Victorian," said Phin. He moved to stand next to me, folding his arms over his chest. "You have only the venom of the Arcoses. Like Papa said, there can be no other."

I shook my head and looked first at Phin, then at Gilles. "I've seen his hand—it's . . . rougher in texture, older skin, leathery. Definitely not Victorian's young pale skin."

Gilles glanced at Elise, then directly at Eli. "This concerns me, then. My only other guess is that another is projecting himself into you." He regarded me closely. "You've obviously captured another's attention."

"Pissed them off is probably more accurate," said Luc, and he looked at me. With a flip of his head, his shaggy dark blond hair swept out of his eyes. "Could've been any of the newlings," he said. "Or possibly someone they've since turned."

I closed my eyes, grasped the bridge of my nose, and swore in Romanian under my breath. "So what am I

supposed to do? Watch innocent people die? Deal?"
It's what I'd done my whole damn life, right? Why stop
now?

The room fell silent for all of five seconds; everyone
stared at me. I figured the whole Dupré family had read
my inner rant. At this point, I didn't care anymore. Let
'em read.

"We find him," Eli said, that deadly edge back in his
voice, his hand going protectively to the small of my
back. I shivered. "And we kill him."

Part Four

✦━✦━✦

MINDLESS

"Everyone knows the phenomenon of trying to hold your breath underwater—how at first it's all right and you can handle it, and then as it gets closer and closer to the time you must breathe, how urgent the need becomes, the lust and hunger to breathe. And then the panic sets in when you begin to think that you won't be able to breathe—and finally, when you take in air and the anxiety subsides . . . that's what it's like to be a vampire and need blood."

—Francis Ford Coppola's journal in
*Bram Stoker's Dracula:
The Film and the Legend*

"I gotta tell ya—I've always thought of myself as a pretty tough Betty. A badass in my own right and proud of it. I'm not afraid of much, and if I am scared, I damn sure won't announce it—to anyone. Unfortunately, my boyfriend and his entire family take privileges inside my private thoughts and know with certainty what scares me, what turns me on—and what pisses me off. All three of those emotions exist in heavy, intoxicating doses where this mystery bloodsucker is concerned, and the biggest fear I have is not that we won't be able to stop him, but what it's doing to Eli. He has become crazy-insane about what it's doing to me. Heads are gonna roll—and I mean that literally."

—Riley Poe

I thought I'd done a pretty fab job of holding it together after the terrors began. I mean, damn—I'd always fallen out in the throes of the terrors in front of someone, surrounded by, well, everyone. Yeah, they bothered me. Yeah, they were awful. And fuck-yeah, I wanted them to stop. The thing is I don't sleep as much as I used to. Tendencies, you see. So that means my waking hours, when the terrors hit? There're more of them—more opportunities for me to experience them. They do weird things to a mortal body, those terrors. I'm starting to feel different in a way I can't explain. Just . . . not myself. And when I do sleep, I fall hard, as in coma-sleep. Eli is usually right there. Snooping in my brain.

He's been on a wicked-dark edge lately that part of me totally digs, and yet part of me totally worries about. I could feel the tension in him; Eli isn't known for his patience. I mean talk about a friggin' stick of vampiric dynamite. So unlike his brothers who I know have the same frightening power; they just . . . contain it. Luc was so easygoing and laid-back, and Phin? I guess he was pretty much the same way. They had a good grip on their anger, their power. Eli? Ka-pow! All week at the shop, I felt his anger building. He'd done pretty well keeping it contained, but every once in a while, I'd see it; he'd extinguish it quickly. Today, though, he'd had enough. He'd parked his agitated ass right in the waiting area at Inksomnia and glared half the day while pretending to thumb through the tat design albums. Flip a page, glare. Flip a page, glare. Every freaking time I looked over at him. Glaring. At me. WTF? Nyx even noticed, but she thought we were just having a lover's spat and left it alone. Today was Saturday, and she'd taken my last two clients so I could cut out early enough to get ready for the formal dinner at his parents'. I hurried upstairs. He followed. I felt his negative energy building, growing, festering, like some big, freakish reverse orgasm. The moment we stepped into the apartment, I shot a puzzled Seth a glance and stormed into my bedroom. I walked to the window and rounded on Eli. Ooh. I was fuming.

"What is wrong with you?" I asked angrily. "Jesus, Eli," I said for lack of a better choice of words. "All week long, something's been eating at you. What is up?"

Eli's stare bore into me, his brows furrowed. "Nothing."

I blinked. Did he really just say nothing? "You're

freaking kidding me, right? You know—never mind."
No way would I be able to force Eligius Dupré into
telling me anything he didn't want to tell me. Stubborn-
headed vampire. I stepped toward him, nearly nose to
nose. "Whatever it is that has you so pissed off, deal."
I poked his chest. "Chill out, come to grips with it, and
don't ever show your ass in my shop again. You got a
problem with me, no matter what it is, talk to me. Pri-
vately. Don't just . . . piss and pout about it all week. I can
handle whatever, so don't hold it in and get your balls in
a twist stewin' over it all day. Got it?" I gave him a final
glare. "I freakin' mean that, Eli."

The expression on Eli's face changed very little;
but it did change. Subtly. The angry lines between his
dark brows . . . softened, and the dark flash in his eyes
dimmed—somewhat. Yet I knew he wouldn't budge.
Since we were due at his parents' house, I narrowed my
eyes, walked past him, blew it off and got ready. I didn't
like arguing, and I especially didn't like arguing and then
attending a family function where I'd have to pretend I
didn't want to strangle the hosts' eldest son until his pale
face turned blue. (Not that it'd matter—they all took liberties in my head, anyway. They'd probably figure it out
soon enough.) So a bad mood now shaded my usually
chipper persona. Thanks, Eli. I flung open my closet, dug
through the dresses hanging there, and grabbed a long,
slinky black halter made of rayon that clung deliciously
to my skin. I threw it across the bed and stomped into
the bathroom. Eli still stood in the same place I'd left
him, staring at me as though I had a friggin' horn growing out of my forehead. I wished I did. I'd have gorged
him with it. As I turned on the hot water, I swore in hot,
heated, emotional Romanian—several times. I thought

I'd heard a laugh in the bedroom, but I wasn't sure. I dried my hair and dressed. After choosing a kick-ass choker of black velvet with a green-beaded butterfly in the center made in the 1920's, a pair of silver hoop earrings, a set of silver bangles, and six-inch-high black pumps, I walked out; Eli's icy eyes were on me again, and I was pretty positive they remained on me the entire time after that.

"Whoa, Sis," Seth said, giving me an appreciative look as I walked into the living room,. "You look sweet."

I smiled at my brother. "Thanks." I checked out his black suit and tie. "You look pretty delicious yourself."

Seth glanced down at himself and grinned. "Right? Totally *Casino Royale*–ish, huh?"

"Yeah—and Josie will dig it for sure," I said, raising my eyebrows. Seth's cheeks turned pink, and I laughed. Then, I glanced at Eli. Yep, still glowering. I shook my head, made sure Chaz had food and water (Seth had taken him out), and we left in the Jeep. I'd thought the brisk drive through the squares with the top off would chill out the glowering Dupré. We pulled up to the light and sat, and I glanced over. Nope. Still pouting. We drove on to Monterey Square, and I parked in silence. Inside, Eli disappeared to get ready. I chatted awhile with Elise and Gilles. Elise, in a gorgeous long red strapless dress, silver strappy heels, and her hair coiffed in a smooth ponytail and secured with a gorgeous silver clasp, was completely delighted to have dinner guests. Gilles, in a dark suit, regarded me as he usually did, with depth and precision. The rest of the Duprés were pretty impressive. Luc and Phin, both wearing black Armani suits and ties, looked, as Seth had said, very *Casino Royale*–ish. Freaking hot was more like it. One with longer hair; the other with short-clipped hair—I was surprised girls weren't hanging around the gates of the mansion, twenty-four seven.

"Hey, Riley," Josie said, suddenly appearing behind me. I turned around and, to my surprise, found a stunning young woman in a tie-dyed, floor-length rayon gown with spaghetti straps, her long, loose waves pulled back in a clasp. The purple pumps made her a little taller. Seth stood next to her, his cheeks flushed.

Josie glanced at Seth. "I hadn't noticed," she said, then turned back to me. Her expression, always unreadable, fixed directly on me. "You like it?"

"Totally," I answered with a nod. "Makes you look at least . . . eighteen."

The smallest of smiles tipped Josie's mouth. Her blue eyes regarded me. "You think so?"

"Absolutely," I said, and I meant it. "Especially with the way you lined your eyes, sort of sweeping up at the outer corners." I nodded. "Cool. Very Cleopatra-like. I'm gonna have to try that."

Pride flashed Josie's face. "Thanks, Riley." She glanced at Seth. "Wanna go play Xbox until dinner?"

"Sure," he said, then looked at me and wagged his dark brows. "Later, Sis."

I watched my brother hurry off into the game room with a two-hundred-plus-year-old vampiress. Would I ever get used to it?

"You look sick, girl," Luc said, suddenly at my side. "Is there anything you look sucky in?"

I thought a moment. "Square dancing dresses?"

Luc laughed. "I'm picturing it in my head. You still look pretty hot—ruffles and all."

"Looks hot in what?" Phin said, walking up.

"Square dancing dresses," Luc said, his eyes twinkling.

"Totally," Phin agreed. I just shook my head.

As I said, Eli's siblings were laid-back and easygoing.

"They don't have someone to protect," Eli's voice said, suddenly against my ear. "I do."

I met his gaze without words. He rounded on me and stood with his brothers. I promise you, a more striking group of guys did not exist. All three glanced at me. All three—even Eli—smugged up. It was ego city, with testosterone overflowing, even with overly confident, somewhat arrogant vampires.

It didn't take Eli long, though, to resume his edgy attitude. All through dinner I could feel his tension. Even as I gawked at how absolutely freaking hot he was in a black Armani suit and tie, his unnamed irritation boiled inside him—freaking baby. Men, whether mortal or otherworldly, were just freaking babies. More than once I'd wanted to pick up a jumbo coconut shrimp by its fan tail and knock the holy hell out of Eli with it. Or grab a stalk of pickled asparagus and just . . . slap him with it. Every food item became artillery, and if I hadn't been so pissed at him, I would have laughed at myself. What an idiot I could be. But damn, I couldn't help it. I hated issues.

By the end of dinner, I'd actually thought Eli had chillaxed; he carried on a conversation in French with his father (in retrospect I should have suspected something was up with this, because, afterward, Gilles stared at me—a lot) and somewhat joked around with Luc and Phin. In between, though, he gave me deep, intense looks that left me breathless—and wanting to dot his eyes out at the same time. He'd grinned after that thought, and I'd really hoped he'd relax. I should have known better.

It was just after nine p.m. when we finished. Seth and

Josie wanted to jump the buildings on Bay Street, and, since Luc and Phin agreed to go with them, I didn't see a problem with it. Seth's tendencies had grown, and I mean fast. He was nearly as quick on his feet as Luc. I'd even thought it might be a good negative energy release for myself and mentioned going, but Eli grasped me by the elbow and leaned close to my ear. "Not tonight," he said. It was all he said before leading me in hurried silence, past the amused expressions of his parents, his siblings, and mine, to his private apartment upstairs. Had I not possessed a freakish amount of self-confidence, I might have been a little scared. I mean, seriously. Running through my body was scrumptious, mouthwatering although strigoi-tainted, grade-A crack-blood that was highly addictive to vampires, and a vampire, who'd been giving me fiery looks all night, was leading me upstairs to his totally private apartment with one helluva purpose. One would think I'd lost my friggin' mind.

I was totally turned on.

We never made it to his actual apartment.

Once we were down his wing, the lights dimmed, shadows flickered against the aged brick walls, and Eli's powerful presence and built-up tension all but suffocated me, closed in on me, wrapped around me like an invisible silky cloak. The farther we walked down the corridor, the darker it became, the more stifling the air, the subtle light diffusing to less than that of a candle. We were in another place, another time. At the end of the hall were the wide double doors leading into Eli's apartment. The tension overwhelmed me. I jerked to a stop.

"Eli," I said, the sound not as strong as I'd planned.

In a flash-second, his hands grasped me by the hips and pushed me hard against the wall; he followed me, leaning in close, crowding me. My breath caught in my throat on impact, and I stared into Eli's icy, angry cerulean eyes. They searched mine with ferocity.

"What?" I demanded, trying to shove him. It was like pushing on a concrete wall.

"I," he began, his voice way too steady, "don't like sharing. What's mine is mine alone. And I don't like being helpless or out of control. Lately I'm both, and, as far as I can see, only two things need to happen: Victorian has to die, and whoever else has crawled inside you has to die." His fingers dug into my hips, his body pressed against mine. Although his face was cast in gray distorted shadows, his eyes all but glowed as they searched mine; intense, radiant, and livid. "I fucking mean it."

I looked at him, not so stunned. I'd learned a while back that Eli was more than possessive when it came to me. He was a hothead on top of it. "You know, anger management class might do you some good, or a little Xanax—"

Eli's mouth covered mine, quickly silencing any further words of psychiatric or medical wisdom I might have offered. I didn't care. My desire for him had been building all night, just as much as his tension had. I grasped his neck and threaded my fingers through his hair, and kissed him back—hard. Our tongues grazed, tangled, and the sensation ignited an intensity of raw need that all but lit the room on fire. I groaned, sucked his bottom lip, kissed him hard again, and shoved Eli around. His back hit the brick wall as hard as mine had. Anger and passion drove me.

We both struggled for control; it became an involuntary game.

Neither of us won.

Our mouths fused. My fingers clawed at Eli's coat, pushed it off his shoulders, and it dropped to the floor. Blindly, I fumbled with his tie, and, finally, I loosened it enough to get it off his neck without strangling him. Our breathless moans and desperate kissing filled the otherwise silent corridor like a porn movie, and at the back of my barely reasoning brain I could hear it loudly. It turned me on, and I found myself seeking Eli's bare skin, almost insane to touch him. I unfastened the buttons on his shirt, pulled the hem from his pants, and dropped it, only to find an undershirt.

"Shit," I muttered in frustration, and I felt Eli's smile against my mouth. He broke from our kiss long enough to snatch the thin ribbed shirt over his head and fling it somewhere; then he pulled me against him. As his mouth sought mine again, he dragged his lips slowly, erotically, using his tongue against my bottom lip, then against my teeth; it drugged me. He tasted sweet, like coconut, and that other indescribable, irresistible vampiric thing that was alluring and uniquely Eli. As my hands grazed his flawless skin, over the muscles etched into his chest and lower, into his abdomen, I shuddered at the sensation the friction caused within me. I straddled his leg, mine on either side, and leaned into him, inhaling, tasting, devouring, and he pulled me hard against his thigh. I moaned and ground into him. When his hands left my hips and grasped the length of my dress and slowly lifted it, my breath caught. Finally, we were skin-to-skin. His hands raked over my bare thighs, cupped my ass, and pulled me hard against him. Our bodies fit perfectly, touching in all the right places, and my craving for him reached a level of desperation that shocked even me. My mouth moved to his throat, nipping and tasting as my hands pushed between us, grasping his belt and loosening it enough so my hand would fit down the front of his Armani slacks. The bare shaft of hard muscle I found, covered by nothing but velvety skin, made me groan against Eli's neck. He let out a low chuckle.

I found myself suddenly flung around, my bare back now digging into the wall, scraping against the rough aged brick, allowing Eli complete control. My mind became total gravy as his hands brushed my skin, over my hips, until his fingers slipped beneath the silky triangle of material that was my thong. Wedging his leg between mine, he shoved my thighs apart and scraped the highly sensitive flesh that throbbed with need. I arched against Eli's hand, my mind momentarily going blank. *Fuck me now, dammit!* my inner, primitive, craving-nasty-sex voice screamed without my permission. Maybe that sounds trashy, but good God—I couldn't help it. Eli makes me mindless-crazy. If I'd had any inhibitions before, they would have been swiftly bludgeoned with Eli's powerful, sensual touch. He was that potent. I moved my mouth to his ear. "Now," I half begged, half threatened.

With both hands on my hips, Eli lifted me to his waist; I wrapped my legs around him and, kissing me, he began to move. I didn't know where we were going; nor did I care. One second we we're in the corridor; the next, in his bedroom. He loosened his hold, I slid down his front slowly, and Eli grasped my face, lowered his head, and tasted every inch of my mouth, and when the angle didn't suit him, he tilted my head. Then his hands left me, found the clasp at my halter strap, and unfastened it. My dress pooled around my ankles, and Eli's hands covered my breasts. I moaned as pleasure shot through me.

His lips left mine and moved to my ear, the sensation of his mouth dragging against my skin making me shudder and my cravings increasing to a painful pitch. My fingers dug into his back, my eyes closed, and my head dropped to the side, weightless.

"I hope I'm more than a good fuck to you, Riley," he whispered against the shell of my ear. His hands moved to my lower back, then slid over my ass and pulled me tightly against him.

The words froze me, and my head snapped up. Amidst the haze of horniness, I stared into Eli's eyes. I'd regained my senses; yet I could say nothing. We simply stared at each other. I had no way of answering him convincingly, except with my mouth, my body. Words meant nothing. I lifted both of my hands and grasped Eli's jaw, and I kept my eyes trained on his as I pressed my lips against his. He stood statuelike still as I kissed him, gently, slowly, pouring all of my unstated feelings for him into that one act. Then, I wrapped my arms around his neck and simply hugged him. I buried my face in his neck and snuggled against him. His arms went around me, wrapped completely around me, and pulled me close, just as gently.

Now will you fuck me?

Damn. I couldn't help it. I'm telling you. I. Could. Not. Help. It. The dirty request slipped out of the restraints deep in my brain and into open, vampiric-readable gray matter. Dammit!

Eli's body shook against mine, and it was a few seconds before I realized he was laughing. I pulled back and stared into his shadowy face, peered into the depths of his ancient, disturbing eyes, and I knew then he understood me—fully. Then, he lowered his head, pressed his lips to mine, and kissed me.

"I love you, too," he said softly. It was the first time he'd said it. I'll never forget it, although I couldn't say the words back. Not then, anyway. Hopefully later. He then kissed me deeply as he backed me up until we reached his massive bed. Eli lifted me, kicked off his shoes and the pants that had dropped below his hips, then followed me down into the softness of a white down comforter. Not once taking his gaze from mine, with his forearms, he braced his weight, his body above mine.. Lifting one hand, he smoothed my hair back, traced my brows, the bridge of my nose, and with his thumb, grazed my lips. I saw nothing more than half his face; the other half was swallowed in darkness. The image was intimate, sexy, and Eli exploring my facial features like a blind man became the single most erotic experience I've ever had. It sank to my soul, and I felt my insides flutter with excitement. I couldn't believe someone like Eli belonged to me.

Slowly, he lowered his head, grazed my lips with his, then moved to my ear. "Watch me," he whispered erotically, and I felt myself grow wet at his seductive words. "Watch what you do to me, Riley." He pulled back and stared into my eyes; the possessiveness, the intense longing I saw there rocked me. Without another word, he moved, pushing his hard length fully into me. I was wet and ready and about to absolutely die with need, and his eyes grew dark with desire at contact. I wrapped my legs around his waist and moved with Eli, our bodies and rhythm becoming one, my heart beating enough for the both of us, and the whole while I kept my gaze trained on his. I held on as the orgasm built, strong, intense, until it erupted deep inside me. Its strength finally forced my eyes to close, and my body arched with pleasure against Eli's as waves crashed over me; over him. Finally, the climax began to descend. As it came to a rest, Eli wrapped his arms and legs around me and encased me completely, and I let him. It was as submissive as I'd ever get—with anyone. Eli wasn't after submissive, though. I knew what he wanted—the L-word—but I couldn't give it to him right now. Not that I didn't feel it, but . . . it's hard to explain. He knew, though, and patiently waited. My feelings for him were greater than for anyone I'd ever encountered, and it scared me. He knew it scared me. I hoped one day it wouldn't.

How long we lay there, our bodies wrapped and melded, I had no idea. I'm not even sure when I fell asleep. One minute I was completely relaxed, content, being drugged by the sensation of Eli's fingers dragging up and down my spine, his intense intimacy unlike anything I'd ever experienced. The next minute, or hour, or however long, I sat up, looked around, dazed and confused. Eli was nowhere, and I was in a strange, unfamiliar place. A church? An old Spanish mission? In ruins, the brick and mortar were covered in vegetation, something wild and out of control like wisteria or ivy, and surrounded by a dense wood. It wasn't Savannah but somewhere . . . else. I was alone. The heavy scent of rain and damp, along with ripened plant life, permeated the ruin, and overhead, the roof was almost completely gone. Nothing but a few old rotted rafters remained, the rest of the gap spindled and webbed with aged vines. It was night, and shots of moonlight breached the porous roof, illuminating the floor in splotchy, distorted, uneven patches. And although I was alone, several lit candles sat clustered together near the front of the ruin, and their flames caused shadows to skip across the brick. In the corner, beneath the only remaining stained glass arch, a long, wide stone bench stretched invitingly. After glancing around and seeing nothing or no one, I noticed how weary my body was, and I picked my way across bracken, sharp-hulled acorns, and scattered pine straw to the bench and sat down. One lone candle flickered in a ruby-colored glass holder on the sill. I pulled up my feet, which were bare, and wrapped my arms around my knees. It was then I noticed I wore nothing more than a white silky slip with satin straps, and it glided smoothly over my bare skin as I moved. I could have been completely naked, the slip was so skimpy, and as it was, I had nothing beneath it, anyway—no panties, no bra. No wonder I was so cold. . . .

"Riley," a voice said.

I jerked my head toward the voice but saw no one. Adrenaline raced through me; yet my heart pounded slowly. My eyes searched every inch of the ruin, but found nothing.

Then, the whispers began.

Riley, Riley, Riley, Riley . . .

Over and over, my name fell from unseen lips, harsh and intimate at the same time, and I gripped the brick sill of the window and scanned the room. Whispers were everywhere; yet there was no body, no physical voice to connect them. A gnawing sensation of panic crept upon me, and I hated the feeling. I wasn't scared of anything or anybody, but I'd rather see what was coming at me than cower like some fool by a window. The sense of dread grew, and I knew someone was about to die a horrible death.

Then, suddenly, as if those particular thoughts beckoned, in the time it took me to involuntarily blink my eyes, he was there—Victorian Arcos.

"Riley," he said, smiling, and I immediately knew the whispering voice I'd heard seconds before did not belong to him. "You came to me."

"Not a willing participant," I assured him. "You brought me here."

"Are you sure?" he said, still smiling.

"Dead positive," I answered. He moved slowly toward me, and I watched his every step as he seemingly glided over the bracken. His hair, dark and wavy, fell loose to his shoulders, and brown eyes regarded me without blinking. He wore dark jeans and a dark shirt, loosened at the collar. His skin was young and flawless, his lips perfectly shaped, the cut of his jaw that of a vibrant twenty-one-year-old man. A thick vein ran from the side of his neck and disappeared beneath his collar—another sign of youth, vitality. He smiled then, white teeth flashing against an olive complexion, and I knew having me inspect him so thoroughly thrilled him. "Don't get your hopes up, sunshine," I offered. "I just like to know my enemies inside and out."

Victorian squatted beside the bench I sat on and traced my jaw with his forefinger. "I am not your enemy," he said gently. "I am your destiny. And you will know me inside and out. I promise."

I flinched. "Sorry," I said, and shifted so my face wasn't so easily accessible. "I'm not into younger dudes." I glanced around, hoping to change the subject. "Where am I and how in hell did I get here?"

"Like it or not, my love, this is your fantasy. Your dream," he said in a heady Romanian accent, and without my permission, moved closer. I was thrilled and appalled at the same time. "I am honored to be in it. And for the record, you are much, much younger than I."

"You're a killer," I accused. "I saw what you did to that girl, in the parking lot, and the one at the bar," I said, knowing he wasn't the killer, but I had to know who was. I darkened my expression. "You make me sick. And don't kid yourself. You force your way into my dream, just as you force my reactions. I damn sure don't have them willingly."

A look of puzzlement crossed his features. "What are you talking about?"

I smiled. "Don't fuck with me, Victorian. I'm not an idiot. Like you repeatedly say, your venom is inside me forever. I can see, feel your moves, your kills, feeds, how you terrorize innocents." I glared at him. "You're a monster."

His puzzlement grew; his brows furrowed into an expression I'd not witnessed before. It was almost believable.

"I never terrorize, my love," he said. "And I'm anything but a monster. I adore women. I control my feeds, and my victims live." He shrugged. "With tendencies, of course." His eyes penetrated me, intense and sincere. "I have mercy, Riley Poe. I swear it. And of course I force my way into your dreams. You're a hardheaded mortal." He smiled. "I like that about you. And the chase gives me a hard-on like no other."

I ignored his confession and perversion. "The Duprés paint a very different picture of you and your brother, and I tend to believe them. Not you. I mean, seriously. You did try to suck all my blood out at Bonaventure, or did you forget that?"

Victorian's eyes darkened. "I could not forget if I

tried," he said gently, his voice even, controlled, seductive, and if I wasn't mistaken, somewhat remorseful.
"But you are mistaken. I would never have killed you. I
would have turned you, yes, and then you'd be mine forever. I am selfish, but I am nothing like my brother." His
eyes scanned my body, regarding me closely, intensely,
like a lover's caress. "I know what you need, what you
want and desire, Riley Poe."

"Yeah, I desire for you to stop calling me Riley Poe,"
I said sarcastically.

Victorian laughed softly, his eyes trained on mine.
"I've watched you for far longer than you think, Riley.
Since you were a young girl, I've known you, desired
you." The muscles in his jaws clenched; then, without
warning, a hot, seductive sensation washed over me, uncontrolled, unwanted, insatiable. Victorian didn't move
an inch; yet I felt his hands on me, everywhere, his voice
an erotic brush of air against my skin. I wanted to scream
in protest. I struggled not to writhe with desire. He easily controlled me with his mind. "You want my hands on
your body, tracing every curve and bit of softness you
have," he said, his words drugging me, and at the same
time I felt the sensation of his hands trailing my arm,
skimming my collarbone, pushing the satin strap aside,
letting it fall over my shoulder. "You want my mouth
on you, my lips following my fingertips," he whispered. I
felt his lips in the hollow of my neck, then across my collarbone, my jaw. I sat, totally frozen, powerless to move
as Victorian awakened every sexual sensation he had no
right to awaken. Invisible manacles held me hostage as I
sat in the window seat, and although I struggled, I could
not break free.

"You want me, Riley," he said, and though he sat

stone-still, my slip eased down my breasts as if invisible fingers grasped the silky material and pulled. "I am only obeying your silent command," he whispered, and warm breath brushed the sensitive peaks as though teasing with his lips. The slide of silk against my thighs as the hem of the slip rose slowly made my insides rush with excitement. I hated it. I wanted it. I tried squeezing my thighs together, but they wouldn't budge.

"Don't fight it, Riley," Victorian said smoothly. "It is me you desire, me you long for, me you want to feel deep inside you. Open . . . for me." Invisible fingers dragged over my skin as my slip rose above my hips, and sensations of unwanted pleasure darted my body like needle pricks. I gasped as hot breath brushed between my thighs. "Open," he demanded seductively. "You are so unique, so beautiful."

"No," I said, the sound barely above a whisper. I wanted to cry, shout, kick out; I wanted to hurt. . . .

I wanted to come.

Warmth, wet and delicious, delved inside me, again and again; I gasped. I lost my breath. "No!" I sobbed, louder, just before the intensity of climax crashed over me.

"Riley!"

My eyes fluttered open and stared into Eli's angry, flashing eyes. Confusion webbed my conscious thought, pleasure made my body shudder, and I had to blink several times and look around before I remembered where I was and what was happening. Eli, his arms braced on either side of my hips, stared up from between my thighs. He moved over me, and with his hands he held my head still, forcing me to look at him. We were naked, in his bed, his body covering mine, my senses and nerve endings humming from the sensual caresses from his mouth and his tongue.

A split second before it hadn't been Eli.

All at once, and so fast I didn't see him move, Eli pushed off me. Looking at him as he stood beside the bed, his face angered, his body rigid, I had a crazy moment of raw adoration. I thought I'd never seen a more beautiful soul than Eligius Dupré.

I hated that he was angry with me. Shame flooded me; ire built, and at that moment I didn't think I could hate anyone—rather, anything—more than I hated Victorian Arcos, and I was damn tired of his screwing with me. I pulled the sheet up to cover my naked body.

"I'm not angry with you," he said quietly, his voice controlled, totally on edge. He knelt down and grasped my chin, then turned my face toward his, almost painfully. A dangerous fierceness took over his features; gently, he grasped the sheet from my fingers and released the sheet. "Never feel shame," he said. "You are powerless, and he is powerful and obsessed with you; you cannot fight him. You will not win, and you will never rid your mind of him. He won't let it happen."

I stared in disbelief. "What?" I said incredulously. I pushed up on my elbows, and, unable to say anything, I gaped. No way was he right. "I don't believe it."

Holding my chin, Eli crept closer, covered my lips with his, and kissed me. It was more than a kiss; it was a brand, a memory of possessiveness I was surely meant to carry until death. The firmness of his lips, the drag of his mouth as he claimed mine, the slow tease with his tongue, made my body quiver, my nerve endings fire, my skin flush with heat. Suddenly, he pulled back and regarded me.

"You're mine, Riley Poe," he said, his voice dark, determined. "And while you may not be able to stop Victorian, I can." His eyes searched mine. "I don't share. Remember? He has' to be stopped."

Eli moved so fast, my vision saw nothing more than a hazy streak. I leapt from the bed, allowing the sheet to fall to the floor. "Eli, wait!" I cried, and I knew panic was close. "What are you going to do?"

At the door, Eli stopped, and I noticed he'd already changed. Dressed exactly as he had been the first day I saw him through Inksomnia's storefront window, in worn jeans, a white tee and boots, with a shouldered backpack, he looked like any average badass guy on the street; mysterious, dangerous, not to be messed with. I knew he was all that and much, much more. I also knew his answer before it left his mouth.

With a look of longing that will haunt me for the rest of my days, I watched Eli's face change from loving to one of pure determined hatred. "I'm going to fucking kill him." He turned and moved through the double doors, then stopped. His back remained to me, his posture unyielding, still as death. "Wait for me," he requested quietly.

Then, he was gone. Within minutes, the rumble of his silverback sounded, idled, and then roared up the street. I stood and listened until the motor faded completely away.

Eli was going after Victorian. Just like that, up and gone. Really? How would he even know where to look for him? I wanted to beat the hell out of Eli, and it was a helluva lot easier to stay pissed than it was to mope about his leaving. I didn't have time for that, so pissed seemed the better route for me. After climbing in and out of the shower, I pulled on the dress Eli had so sexily discarded hours before, then grabbed my purse and pumps. At the double doors I paused and glanced over my shoulder at the rumpled bed. The clock read 4:58 a.m. With what seemed an involuntary muscular action, I drew in a deep, long breath, taking in Eli's scent to litter my lungs, my taste buds, my memory. I knew what he did, he did for me. I also knew, somehow, he wouldn't find Victorian. Not easily, anyway. The other invading my mind? How could Eli find him if we didn't even know who he was? Eli had an explosive character. His emotions ran high in everything he did. When he was pissed, he was pissed. When he was happy, he was elated. And when he loved, man, he seriously loved. So it really didn't surprise me that he'd taken off in an angry cloud of dust to find the two things causing me misery. It didn't console or take away the edge I already felt inside. Within my rib cage, my heart ached—my fucking heart—and a hole had begun to tear, ragged inside my chest. Who knew what would happen? I hated that it all mattered enough to me that I felt pain. Angry, I closed my eyes briefly, breathed, then shut the doors and started down the corridor.

Philippe Moreau, the Duprés' butler, stood in the kitchen, a white cup and saucer in his hand, and a kettle on the stovetop. Dressed in a long navy robe and slippers, he turned at my entrance. Aged eyes regarded the dragons inked into my arms, the angel wing at the corner of my eye, and then, met my gaze full on. "Will you have tea, Ms. Poe?" he asked, in a very proper and French manner.

"No, thanks, Philippe," I answered, and headed to the door, where I paused. "Eli's gone," I said, not really knowing why I did.

"He will return," Philippe said comfortingly, as though he knew.

I nodded. "My brother?" I asked.

"He is in the game room with the others," Philippe answered. "Shall I call for him?"

I shook my head. "That's all right. I'll call later." No sense in dragging Seth home on a Sunday morning and making him suffer my badass mood. I had supplies to order for Inksomnia, some designs to go over with Nyx later, and a few things to pick up from the store—a typical Sunday. Seth might as well stay with Josie and the guys and have a little fun. "Later, Philippe," I said, then pushed out of the kitchen's screen door and into Savannah's early morning.

The sun wasn't up yet, but a dim, hazy glow hung in the air as I made my way to the Jeep. Thick fog wafted over Monterey Square and slipped through the live oaks, swallowing the black iron streetlamps along the walkway. Barefoot, I tossed my pumps and purse into the passenger side of the Jeep.

And into the lap of a body that wasn't there a half breath ago.

"Where ya goin'?"

I jumped and sucked in a breath. Luc grinned, and I glared at him. "Don't do that, Dupré. God. You're gonna give me a freaking heart attack." I slipped behind the wheel.

He grinned wider. "I know CPR. I'd save you. So? Where?"

I looked straight ahead. "Home. I got a business to run, you know."

"At five a.m.?"

I jammed the keys into the ignition, but before I

could start the Jeep, Luc's hand stilled mine. I sighed. "He left." I glanced at him.

A slight breeze caught his crazy hair and tossed it across his forehead. He pushed it back and met my gaze in the dim light. "Yeah," he said gently. "I know. He asked me to ride along."

"No," I said. "I don't need a babysitter anymore." I turned the Jeep's engine over. "I'm not a helpless mortal, Luc. I can take care of myself."

Luc grinned. "He said you'd say that."

"Well," I answered, glancing at him, "Seth will be with me this time. And as far as we can tell, there is no threat close by, right? The newlings have moved on."

"Seth is here. And the newlings have moved on. For now."

I frowned. "Preacher is right next door. I'll be fine." I pointed. "Get out."

Luc didn't budge.

"Don't you have a girlfriend or something?" I asked, knowing full well he did not. "Seriously dude—you've gotta move out of your parents' house, or no decent chick will have anything to do with you."

He grinned. "That reminds me. I've been meaning to talk to you about Nyx. Is she involved?"

I put the Jeep in reverse. "No way, Dupré. I wouldn't want her mixed up in all of this."

Luc leapt out and was at my door before I could blink. He met my gaze with a sincere one. "Would you have held back from Eli, had you known what you know now?"

"No." I didn't even have to think about it.

Luc smiled and pushed off the door. The yard lamp cast a yellow glow down on him, and I studied the severe similarities between Luc and Eli. Other than the dark blond, crazy hair, they looked very much alike—same disturbing eyes, same cut of jaw, same mouth. Well, almost the same mouth. "Your mind, then, is open game for me. That way I'll know if you're in trouble," he said, grinning, and gave a confident nod. "Yeah. I think I like this plan better, anyway."

I shook my head and glanced over my shoulder to back out. "I hate this plan. I think this plan sucks."

Luc laughed. "It's either this plan, or the one where I come babysit you full-time."

I scowled. "Fine."

"Excellent," he said, grinning. I'll drop by later. And don't worry about Seth. He's cool. And Riley," he said, his face serious. "He'll be back. Soon."

Turning the Jeep, I rounded the graveled circle drive by the kitchen entrance and pulled up next to Luc. "I know he will. And seriously, thanks. I mean it."

"No prob." He leaned over and tapped my temple with a forefinger. "I'll be right here."

"That's such a comfort," I said, gave a half-forced grin, and pulled out into the square. Deciding to get myself together and grab a coffee, I headed to Skidaway to the original Krispy Kreme, where I got in a fairly short line of die-hard Kremers who wanted that first, fresh, hot batch of doughnuts of the morning. Being the JFJ (junk food junkie) that I am, I ordered a dozen regular glazed (they melt in your mouth) and a large coffee with cream and sugar, then headed back home. I listened to the relative silence of early Sunday morning in Savannah as I made my way back to Inksomnia. Eli had started teaching me how to concentrate, to filter out all the extra sounds I could now hear, and hone in on just my immediate surroundings by focusing on one single sound. I wasn't totally good at it yet, but at least now I wasn't going nuts. When he first taught me, I had to close my eyes, breathe deeply, and concentrate so hard that my brain hurt. It was like being in a large convention room with two thousand people, all of them droning. Finally, I did it, and it was a relief. It wasn't easy to turn on and off, and sometimes it took me a few minutes to achieve control, but I was getting better, and I could now do it without squeezing my eyes shut. I mean, Jesus. It was kinda funny at first, but I quickly grew sick of hearing people humping and moaning all the friggin' time. God, they were having sex everywhere. I felt trapped in a porn dream. So this morning, after I shut out the other unwanted noises, I found everything was pretty calm, as it used to be before I had two strigoi bloodsuckers try to drain my life force. Light traffic; somewhere, a dog barking its head off, and, in the distance, a semitruck grinding its gears and chugging along the bypass—these were normal sounds.

I should have realized this was the beginning of a so-not-normal day.

By the time I pulled onto the merchant's drive and parked the Jeep behind Inksomnia, it was a few minutes after six a.m. Preacher and Estelle's light in the kitchen flickered on, so I crossed the cobbles to their back door. The haze was brighter outside now, but the sun still hadn't cracked over the city. I knocked lightly, and in seconds Preacher came to the door. The beam of light that shined behind him revealed his usual long-sleeved plaid shirt tucked neatly into a pair of worn dungarees and a big smile. He and Estelle always got up early, so I knew I wasn't intruding. When his gaze lit on the Krispy Kreme box, the smile grew.

"Oh yeah, dat's my girl right dere," he said, then kissed my cheek and pulled me into the small foyer. "Was cravin' dem tings earlier. Almost went out myself to get dem." He lifted a brow. "Don't let your grandmodder see 'em. She says da sugar makes me act all crazy." He chuckled softly.

"I heard dat, ole man," Estelle hollered from the kitchen. "Riley Poe, you git in here and bring dem tings wit you. Dat ole man acts crazy widdout da sugar, dat's right. Sugar makes him crazier."

I smiled at Preacher. "Yes, ma'am." I flipped open the box. Preacher lifted a doughnut out and in two bites had it gone. I shook my head, grabbed one myself, took a bite, and headed for the kitchen while my surrogate grandfather licked his fingers. I set the box on the table and sat down.

"I hope you left room in dat bottomless pit of a stomach for some magic," Estelle said with a fake scowl, inclining her head toward the simmering pot of tea on the burner. She grinned and glanced at the doughnut box. "You save me one now, dat's right."

"Absolutely," I said. "And yes, ma'am, I have plenty of room."

Estelle bustled over, wearing a hot pink Da Plat Eye T-shirt and a multicolored brush skirt, with a knotted head wrap to match. She smelled fresh, like Dove soap and something . . . herbal from the shop. Satin ebony skin shined in stark contrast to her white smile. "Drink up, Riley Poe. Don't want dem Duprés lookin' at you like you was a pork chop."

I shook my head and smiled. "I don't think they like me as much anymore," I said, and shrugged at the questioning look on my surrogate grandmother's face. "Tough meat."

Estelle stared for a second, then burst into laughter, shaking her head. "You crazy white painted girl, dat's right."

I grinned at Preacher.

He did not return the cheer.

When Estelle left the kitchen, he leaned over the table and looked hard at me. "What's wrong wit you, girl?"

I met his stare. I could never get anything past Preacher. "Eli left. He's going to kill Victorian. And I guess try to find the other one."

Preacher took a sip of steaming coffee and stared at me over the rim of his cup. "If he can find him, anyway. Dat Arcos boy is slippery." He set the cup down. "And I ain't too sure he's as bad as his brodder was." With a long, bony forefinger, he rubbed his jaw. "Sometimes, family makes a person do crazy tings, yeah? And he sure has it bad for you, Riley Poe."

The memory of Victorian's recent words rushed through my head. "He . . . said he's known me for a long time, Preacher. As in from when I was a kid." I looked hard at him. "How can that be?"

Preacher flicked something from his sleeve, rubbed his gnarled knuckle, then raised his head to look at me. "Maybe he been watchin' you from da hell stone all dis time," he said slowly. "I know dat when dey was entombed, dere powers was stripped, and dey was cursed. Dey couldn't smell your blood, couldn't crave. But maybe dey could see, hear. He must've picked up on you somehow, dat's right." He shook his head. "Might be why he wants you so powerful. Maybe he's been knowin' you for a long time, girl."

Victorian Arcos really did love me? "That's . . . weird."

Preacher laughed softly. "Only you would say dat, Grandchild." He grasped my hands between his dark leathery ones. "You watch yourself, baby, and I mean dat. Make sure your brodder stays wit you. And if you want Jack and Tuba to stay—"

I smiled and shook my head. "No, Preach—it's fine. Really," I assured him. "But if things get crazy, I'll let you know. Okay?"

"Hrumph," he grumbled. "You always did have dat hard head on ya. Don't be shamed to ask for help, Riley Poe." He rose and kissed my cheek. "I'll take a stick to dat backside, and I mean dat."

"I know, and I promise," I said, thinking it funny that Preacher had never taken a stick to my backside. "I love you," I said, rose, and hugged him.

"I love you, girl," he said, and pushed a small sachet into my hand. I glanced down. It was coarse burlap, the size of a golf ball, and filled with . . . something. He looked at me gravely. "Sprinkle it outside your apartment door and all da windows," he said quietly. "Do it tonight, before you go to bed."

I nodded. "Okay." Hell only knew what was in the sachet.

Estelle bustled back into the kitchen as I was leaving. "You want some crabs, Riley Poe? Capote bringin' dem later on. He an' Buck out dere on da Vernon right now pullin' traps, dat's right. I'm makin' some hush puppies, too."

I grinned. The Vernon was a brackish saltwater river that ran close to Skidaway Island and emptied into the sound, and Capote, when not' playing his sax, was out in the mouth of one of hundreds of creeks, crabbing with old Buck. And Estelle made the best hush puppies on the East Coast. "Definitely. I'll come by later." I kissed my dark grandmother good-bye, left several doughnuts on a plate for them, grabbed the remainder of the box, and left.

At the time, I didn't realize it, but soon I'd learn that nothing as simple as Savannah blue crabs, Gullah hush puppies, and Krispy Kreme doughnuts would ever grace my life again. But it took the rest of the afternoon to figure it out. The whole while, Eligius Dupré remained in my head. I'd be willing to bet a month's pay he did it on purpose. Of course, he wasn't the easiest guy to forget. I already missed him.

After taking Chaz for a walk, I loaded my iPod into the home unit, selected Sevendust, and spent my morning cleaning the apartment, tidying up the shop, and ordering supplies online while jammin' to "Unraveling" and "Ride Insane." It was a cool freaking band, and for a while it put out of my head Eli Dupré and the heat and emotions he stirred within me. I cranked up the volume, hoped Bhing from SoHo Boutique next door wasn't too irritated with the music, and rocked out. She was usually pretty cool about things like that, and for the most part, I didn't abuse it. Like, I didn't crank the music if it was too early or too late. This was the middle of the day, so I felt okay about it. The pounding hummed through my body, soothed, settled me. That was what fantastic tunes did to me. The music put me into the groove, and soon my bad mood had evaporated.

I checked my business e-mail and discovered a special on Skin Candy ink. Since it was my favorite brand, I stocked up. I also ordered another load of Inksomnia tourist T-shirts. I confirmed my appearance and temporary shop at a tattoo convention in November, went over my scheduled appointments, and studied the descriptions I'd drawn on plastic wrap (I hold it to the client's desired body part chosen for the person's art and then draw a rough sketch to the contour of the person's shape) of requests the clients had left. One girl, a nurse at St. Joseph's, had asked for a dragon/flower combination. She wanted a feminine yet traditional dragon. I sketched the head of a dragon whose body wound around and turned into swirly vines and flowers. By the time Nyx arrived at four p.m., I'd settled onto the floor with my sketch pad. Nyx joined me, and together we hammered out some pretty sick designs. Several hours passed. Seth called to say he, Riggs, the Duprés, and Zetty were doing a little training and would be home around ten p.m. or so. I said fine. So after Nyx and I ran next door for crabs and hush puppies at Preacher's, we settled back down with our designs. It was after eight p.m. Chevelle's "Sleep Apnea" played quietly (as quietly as Chevelle could play) in the home unit, and Nyx and I slipped into artist mode.

"That one is going to take at least two sittings," Nyx finally said, leaning over the design I'd drawn for a girl of a Japanese cherry tree, with different-sized blossoms sprouting all over the spindly branches. It was a pretty large project that stretched from the thigh, up the rib cage, and over one shoulder.

I glanced at my friend. Nyx wore her pigtails stuffed through side holes of a black and white striped skully, a black Iron Maiden T-shirt, and a pair of black jeggings and clunky Mary Janes. She scrunched her nose and peered at me with those huge, blue expressive Nyx eyes. "Don't ya think?"

I nodded, then froze. First, the fine hairs on the back

of my neck rose. Chaz's frantic yelp broke through my subconscious, and I leapt up. Second, a cold, frigid sensation crept over me. Third, my body jerked, totally on alert, and I scanned the living room. I'd toned my superhearing down so much that I'd not been paying attention as I should have. I'd definitely have to work on that.

"What's wrong?" Nyx asked, then followed my actions and glanced nervously around the living room. "Did you hear something?"

Chaz's growl, then high-pitched yelp met my ears.

"She definitely heard something," a voice said from the darkened hallway, coming from my bedroom. "Didn't ya, babe?"

I blinked, and three young male vampires stood in my apartment.

I hadn't even heard them enter.

Too bad I hadn't thought to sprinkle Preacher's magic dust.

I jumped up. As I stared at the speaker's youthful face, positive I didn't recognize him, my hand eased down the front of my baggy jeans to the concealed silver blade strapped neatly against my thigh. "What'd you do to my fuckin' dog, asshole?"

And in the very next split second, Nyx's scream reverberated off my apartment walls as one of them grabbed my best friend by the throat.

Part Five

MERCILESS

"Dark, dark! The horror of darkness, like a shroud, wraps me and bears me on through mist and cloud."

—Sophocles, *Oedipus Rex*

> *"I'm pissed now. It's one thing to fuck with me,
> but fuck with my loved ones? My best friend?
> My dog? Hell and no. I might be more arro-
> gant than what's good for me, but arrogance
> might be what's keeping me strong. Either that
> or I'm just freaking ignorant. Whichever one
> it is, I don't care. I can kick serious ass now,
> and I can do it without Eli's help. Good thing,
> too, because he's long gone. Like it or not, I'm
> not fully mortal anymore, so why not use my
> tendencies to the fullest? You can bet your ass
> I won't sit around waiting to be rescued like
> some weak little somethin'-somethin'. I got
> shit to do, people to see, and vamps to slay—
> all while running a goddamn business. Yeah,
> I'm pissed."*

—Riley Poe

Pure silver blades do nasty things to vampires.

After this was over, I'd stash them all around my apartment.

Nyx's scream died in her throat as the newling—a stocky blond guy about twenty-three years old—released her and dropped her to the ground. The blade I'd thrown at him lay buried to the hilt, straight through the pleather jacket he wore, directly into his heart. His opaque stare dulled as his body seized and contracted, and a painful gurgling emerged from his throat. Slowly, his fangs began to retract, and some white gooey stuff began to leak from his eyes and mouth. That was all I noticed, because the other two newlings dove toward me. I reacted.

In one leap, I fell onto the dying vampire, yanked the blade from his chest, crouched and leapt high, right at the two rushing me. In midair, I pulled my knees up to my chest, planted my feet against the rib cage of one, and pushed hard; he flew across the room and landed on an end table, shattering my favorite stain glass frame and falling against the wall. I plunged the blade into the other's heart. He fell to the floor, writhing and seizing. I didn't want to yank the blade out too soon, so I landed in a crouched position, my weight resting on my thighs, and faced the remaining vampire. He'd leapt to his feet and now crouched, waiting to pounce on me. He was older, about my age. I could tell he was not a new vamp; while his eyes were cloudy, insanely crazed, and vicious, I knew he was more experienced than the others. He wanted blood—mine or Nyx's; it didn't matter. And he had the patience to get it. I could hear my own heart, slow, sluggish, and Nyx's beating a million times per minute like a hummingbird's. She was terrified—so intensely that I could smell the scent of fear rolling off her body in the form of sweat.

"Riley," Nyx said, as if she'd heard me thinking about her, lightly, barely audible, just a whisper, petrified.

I glanced at her; a fraction of a second. It was the distraction the vamp was waiting for.

He leapt and had me on my back in less time than it took to blink. The air whooshed from my lungs, and Nyx screamed again. With my arms pinned to my sides, I could do little more than stare up at my captor's face. With distorted, gross, white skin with an exaggerated wide mouth and sharp fangs dropping from his gums, he was . . . horrifying, and barely recognizable as ever being human. His opaque gaze was fixed on the pulse at my throat. "Ready to die, bitch?" he said, his voice low, not human, determined.

"Grab the knife, Nyx," I commanded gently, slowly, "from the other one. Now."

So entranced was the bloodsucker straddling me that he didn't even realize what I was trying to do. But Nyx was in shock and terrified. I knew before the words left my mouth that she wouldn't be able to do it. I couldn't blame her. She must be freaked out as hell.

"What?" she whispered, then sobbed.

I couldn't wait. I inched my fingers to the pocket of my jeans, reaching for the sachet Preacher had given me earlier. Maybe the hoodoo powder would burn him enough that I could get him off me. The newling cocked his head, narrowed his milky eyes, and lunged at my throat.

My mouth opened; I sucked in a breath. I didn't even have time to scream.

A silver blade whipped by my face and was just . . . suddenly there, buried in the vampire's chest; a worn black Conversed foot shoved him backward off me. He landed with a thud against the wall and began to seize, gurgle, convulse. I turned away and stared up and into the troubled green eyes of my baby brother. He extended a hand. I grasped it, and he pulled me up.

"Why didn't you call? From inside your head? Luc would've heard." he said. Worry and anger sat etched into the lines on his forehead. "Why, Riley?" He pulled me into an embrace and squeezed me really hard. "They could have killed you and Nyx."

Nyx.

I glanced over Seth's shoulder and found her staring dead at me; blue eyes wide, horrified, her face drawn, even paler than usual. She'd backed against the wall, far from the dead/dying vampires, far from Seth, from the Duprés.

Far from me.

"Nyx," I said, pushing out of Seth's arms.

"No," Nyx said, and held up a hand. "You ... stay away," she said, sobbing and trying to back up farther. "All of you stay away." She glanced hesitantly around the room, her face revealing absolute horror, and she began to inch along the wall, looking for a way out. "I' have to go," she mumbled, her voice trembling, to no one in particular. She sounded in the early stages of good old-fashioned hysteria. I totally didn't blame her, but it saddened me just the same. I so badly didn't want her involved in this hell. I knew she'd come around, and that we'd have to tell what had happened, what was going on, etc. But I hated to. It was then I noticed Riggs and Zetty in the room. They both regarded me. Zetty gave a curt nod.

"You okay, Riley?" he asked.

"Yeah, Zetty. I'm fine."

He nodded again.

"Come with me," Luc said to Nyx, gently but firmly, grasping her arm when she resisted. Nyx stared up at him, and I'm not sure if he put the vampire whammy on her or what, but she nodded and allowed him to guide her to the door. Thankfully, Luc steered her way around what little was left of the corpses on my living room floor. At the door, he looked over his shoulder at me. "I've got this, Riley," he said, and I nodded. He walked a trembling Nyx out of my apartment. Her trembling and fast-beating heart resonated inside my ears. Pushing my thumb and forefinger into my temples, I swore in Romanian. This freaking sucked. Suddenly, noises infiltrated my brain, and the murmurings and shouts and cries and horns blasting bounded within me. I concentrated, hard. Some of the sounds retracted, at least enough for me to think. That unusual, unnamed feeling began to grow inside me again. I wished to hell I knew what it was. It made me anxious. Edgy. Angry.

And as Nyx and Luc walked out, Preacher walked in. He stood in the doorway, glaring. He reminded me slightly of Eli.

"Ri, are you okay?" Seth said again, holding my arms in his firm grip. "You don't look so good."

I turned to him. His green eyes were rimmed with worry. "Yeah, Bro, I'm fine." I hugged him tight. "Chaz—I think he's hurt. Off my balcony—"

Seth ran out of the apartment, Josie fast on his heels.

"I can't believe you took out the other two alone," Phin said, squatting beside one of the now-shriveled bodies—barely more than a little pile of skeletal dust— and shaking his head. He rubbed his jaw and muttered his favorite slang. "Sack ray blue." He looked at me. "Do you recognize them?"

"No," I answered, and gave the piles a furtive glance. "Please tell me you're going to help me get that junk out of my apartment."

Phin gave me a smile. "Absolutely. Riggs, Zetty, you guys come with me," he said, and turned to Preacher. "I'll be right back."

Seth and Josie walked in. Seth had Chaz in his arms. My heart stopped, and I moved to him. He lifted his head and whined the moment my hand touched him.

"He's okay," Seth said, looking at me. "He was walking in the grass by the river when I found him. Wasn't limping or anything. Probably just shaken up. I'll feed him," he said, and he set Chaz down. His backside wagged and he licked my hand. I squatted down and ran my hand over his body, and he licked my face. Relief washed over me. He didn't flinch with pain or anything.

"You gonna be okay, boy?" I asked in doggy talk. Chaz licked me again and looked hard at me with his all-knowing doggy eyes. Such a stoic guy—even if he was hurt, he probably wouldn't show it. I'd get him checked out in the morning, just in case.

"Come on, boy, let's eat," Seth said, and more slowly than usual, Chaz walked to the kitchen, wagging.

"You got sick moves for a mostly mortal," Josie said, suddenly at my side. Her expressions never swayed severely one way or the other; but you always knew she spoke the truth. With wide cerulean eyes and long light brown waves naturally streaked with blond, she studied me, weighed and evaluated me, all in the span of about three seconds. She looked like an average teen, but the wisdom in the depths of her gaze said otherwise. The very corner of her mouth lifted into what most wouldn't recognize as a grin. I did. It was a complimentary grin. "I'm wicked glad you made it."

"Thanks," I replied, and slid a glance to Preacher. "So am I." Crossing my arms over my chest, I moved toward my grandfather. He stared down at me, emotions evident only in his dark eyes.

"How come you didn't sense dem?" Preacher said quietly.

I shook my head and shoved my hands through my hair. "I don't know. I wonder how Ned didn't sense them."

"He did," Josie offered. "That's why we came."

"Almost too late," said my brother, who'd moved to stand close to me again. "I don't like it, Ri. Something's up."

"Ned's on his way," Josie said, pushing her cell into the back pocket of her skinny jeans. I hadn't even noticed her calling him. "He thinks something's up, too. Says he didn't sense them until they were already here. Totally unlike Ned."

My heart jumped. "That doesn't sound good," I said, then looked at Preacher. "What am I going to do about Nyx?"

"She saw everyting den?" he asked.

"Yes, sir, and it wasn't pretty," I answered, and shoved my hands into my pockets. Inside one I felt the sachet Preacher had given me earlier, and I wrapped my fingers around it. "She was in total shock. One of them had her by the throat and lifted her off the floor." I shook my head. "Her eyes, Preacher—I've never seen someone so totally freaked out and scared. She looked at me as if I were a monster." I looked at him. "Don't you have some sort of . . . something you can give her? Make her forget?" Certainly my Gullah-hoodoo-root doctor-conjuring grandfather could concoct some sort of hocus-pocus to brainwash my best friend.

One of Preacher's brows lifted as he looked at me.

"Guess not," I muttered, then looked up as Phin, Riggs, and Zetty came through the door. Zetty, wearing long baggy black shorts, a black T-shirt, and a gold and red braided traditional Nepal vest, stared hard at me. His long black braid hung to his waist.

"I didn't have time to call for help," I said, addressing his silent scolding. "I was just as surprised by them as Ned. Plus I had my hearing turned way down. Won't happen again. So chill." I gave the big Tibetan a slight smile. "And thanks."

"That's some good ass-kickin', though," Riggs said as he passed by. "Pretty decent for a babe."

I could do little more than roll my eyes.

"Once dese boys git rid of dat stuff," Preacher said, inclining his head to the piles of vamp dust on my floor, "bring it to me. Den you and dat long-haired Dupré boy bring Nyx over to da house. Togedder we will talk to her. Make tings right."

I nodded. "What are you going to do until?"

"Fix my house right so my woman is safe. Den I'll do yours and your brodder's."

I hugged my grandfather. "I'll see you in a little while."

Preacher patted my back. "Dat's right, child. In a while." Without another word, he left. I knew that "fix my house right" meant Preacher was about to do some major conjuring and hoodooing to safeguard his house and mine against sneaky vampires. Preacher held his emotions well; I could tell how it had worried him to know three newlings had waltzed right into my apartment and attacked without warning. It scared him.

It pissed me off.

I watched Phin, Zetty, Riggs, and Seth sweep the piles of vamp remains into, no lie, ziplock freezer bags, take some cleaner to the spot beneath the dust, and then sprinkle something over the whole area. No doubt Preacher had given it to them, and I was glad for it. I couldn't tell you what in hell Preacher was going to do with newling dust, and I wasn't convinced I wanted to know myself. I was not positive I'd ever sit on my living room floor again and not think about the gruesome death the vamps had died. I shuddered. Yeah, so I guess in the end, it freaks me out a little. Go figure. What doesn't kill you makes you stronger.

Phin rose, his blue gaze seeking mine. "Eli isn't going to be happy."

I shrugged, walked to the broom closet, retrieved my small broom and dustpan, and walked to the stained glass frame shattered on my floor. I knelt and picked it up, the picture bent inside. Running a thumb over the surface, I smoothed the aged photo paper, the smiling face of my mother with me leaning against her and baby Seth in her arms staring back at me. Emotion caught in my throat, and I shook my head to clear it away. "Eli's not here, so I guess it doesn't really matter, does it?"

"Why are you so angry at him?" Phin asked, crouching and ducking his head to hold my gaze.

I met it with fury. "I'm not angry, Phin. I'm pissed. He left, not because my life was in danger but because he is jealous of Victorian, which is really stupid since he isn't anywhere near me. He comes into my dreams and that's all he has. It's fake. Phony. Not really happening. I didn't ask Eli to leave, and I think it sucks that he did so on his own." I picked up a broken shard of frame. I was freaking sick of people in my life just . . . leaving me. I felt like the only person I'd ever be able to fully count on was Preacher.

A small smile tipped the corner of Phin's mouth. "Trust me, Riley," he said gently. "You can't imagine what you mean to Eli. Hell yeah, you can count on him. And hell yeah, all this does suck, but you know my brother. Noggin of steel. No one, save Papa, tells him what to do. Besides, you've no idea what Victorian

Arcos is capable of. He may seem harmless, but trust me. He's not. And Eli takes no chances on what's his." His gaze leveled. "None."

On what's his.

I nodded. "I understand. Still pisses me off, though. You can see now that I can take care of myself."

"Mostly," he added, and then he rose. I watched him walk the room with his plain black tee, jeans, boots . . . He moved intently through the apartment, the muscle in his jaw flexing. I knew he was ticked about the whole thing, too. But Phin handled things way differently than Eli did. They looked a lot alike but had totally different personalities.

I finished sweeping the broken frame, stood, and tossed it into the trash. "Are you in contact with him?" I glanced over at Chaz, who lay curled up by the window, dozing.

Phin nodded. "Of course. He's on his way back." He grinned. "And yeah, he found Victorian. Found out something interesting. I'll catch you up in a few."

Somehow, all of that surprised me. But my thoughts and surprise were interrupted by the Geek Patrol.

"Whoa, dudes, dudettes—gnarly business goin' on," Ned Gillespie said from the doorway. Chaz lifted his head and let out a bark.

"It's okay, boy," I soothed, and Chaz laid his head back down.

Dressed in skinny jeans, Converses, and a white T-shirt with SUGAR SHACK printed in red across the front, Ned held his hand to his forehead as he stepped into the living room and looked around. His crazy brown hair, tipped with blond stood every which way. His gaze lit on Josie, and his cheeks turned red. "Hey, Josephine.

Lookin' sweet." I'd almost forgotten they used to be superclose.

She grinned. "Thanks, Ned. You, too."

He nodded and glanced at Phin. "Thought the bloodsucker radar in my noggin was goin' out or something, but it's not that."

"What is it?" Phin asked.

Ned's expression turned serious. "Romanian hocuspocus, dude. Serious weirdicus." He glanced at me. "Glad you made it out okay, Riley."

I couldn't help but smile. "Thanks, Ned. So what kind of magic? Like a spell?" Even knowing what I knew about hoodoo and vampires, the question sounded stupid when said aloud. I wondered if I'd ever get used to things.

"Not sure, babe. Definitely Romanian, though. After I made the vamp alert 911 to Phin here, I was like, blown away." He gave a short laugh of uncertainty. "I mean, damn—how'd they shimmy under my radar? I should've picked them off long before their soulless selves hit the streets of Savannah." He shook his head. "Could've been bad, man. Could've been really bad."

"So what'd you find?" Phin asked, leaning against the counter.

"In one of my old tomes I read that some bloodsuckers can slip past detectors"—he glanced at me, pressing his fingertips to his chest—"that'd be me"—he turned back to Phin—"and attack without warning. Depending on their point of vampiric origin, it could be a spell, or maybe a wicked ingestion, or something they spread on their skin." He shrugged. "Impossible to tell."

"What makes you think Romanian?" Phin asked.

Ned nodded and rubbed his jaw thoughtfully. "It's

nothing concrete. It was more my . . . uncanny sense of knowing," he replied. "As soon as I picked up their scent, I thought, Damn. Romanian. I guess I smelled them."

"Why? Do Romanian vamps smell worse than other vamps?" asked Riggs.

Ned narrowed his eyes. "No, dude. Just different." He tapped Riggs' nose. "One of my special powers, capiche?"

I glanced at Phin. He smiled. "That's good enough for me, Ned. Romanian it is, although it makes little sense." I knew what he meant; Victorian was the only one alive. I guessed he was still alive, anyway.

Ned grinned. "Yeah, and I'm a hundred and twelve years old. Talk about making sense, huh dude? There could be dozens of Romanian bloodsuckers in the States—not just the Arcoses."

Phin chuckled. "Guess you're right."

"Wait. There's more," Ned said, holding up a hand. "There's a lot of bloodsucking activity going on in Charleston. Been picking it up in doses, but the dose just grew. Now it's like . . . a large blip on the sonar, if you know what I mean."

Phin nodded. "Thanks, Ned."

"No prob. Well, I gotta dip on out. I'm headed to a big gamer convention in Portland tomorrow. Should be sweet," he said, and turned to look at me. "You take care, babe. Watch your back."

I grinned. "I always do."

Ned smiled. "Righteous." He nodded to Phin, then glanced at Riggs, Seth, and Zetty. "Later, dudes." His gaze turned softer when he looked at Josie. "Later, Josephine."

Collectively, they all said, "Later"; Ned saluted and left.

As I always felt after any amount of time spent with Ned Gillespie, I thought I'd just left one of Bill and Ted's Excellent Adventures. Smart guy, though, and he knew his shit to the nth degree. And the Duprés trusted him indefinitely. And, I confess, he was cute in a goofy, nerdy sort of way.

"Okay," Phin said, running a hand over his close-cut hair. He glanced down at the ziplocks filled with undead dead-dust on the floor. "Let's get this stuff to Preacher. And Riley?"

"Yeah?" I said, regarding Phin.

"You know what this means, right?" A small smile tipped his mouth.

I rolled my eyes. "Hell yes, I know. It means you're staying here to babysit me until Eli gets back. Again."

"Or you could stay at the house, if you want," he offered, meaning the Dupré mansion.

I shook my head. "No, thanks. I have a business to run and all my stuff's here."

Phin shrugged. "Suit yourself. But if you change your mind . . ."

I smiled. "Thanks. I'll keep it in mind." I looked at Phin. "Did Eli kill Victorian? Luc didn't say." I felt like I'd know, and even though Victorian hadn't contacted me further, I didn't feel he was gone. I briefly wondered why I cared.

"No," Phin said. "Victorian got away. Details later, though."

Well, that answered that.

By the time we'd gathered at Preacher's, it was nearly midnight. My head had begun a slow throb, nearly as slow as my heartbeat, and when we stepped inside Da Plat Eye, my noggin was splitting into halves. Estelle gave me four ibuprofen (yeah, go figure—regular FDA-approved medicine) and a glass of water, and I downed them. Phin said it was kickback adrenaline from killing vamps. I believed it.

What I didn't believe was Nyx's reaction to me.

The moment I stepped into Preacher' and Estelle's small, tidy living room, Nyx leapt from the sofa and hurled herself at me, full speed. She wrapped me in the largest, tightest bear hug she'd ever given, I was sure of it. I hugged her back, and she sobbed.

"Oh, Riley," she said against my shoulder. "I'm sorry! I—" She pulled back and looked at me. "Oh my God, I had no idea. Luc"—she glanced at him, then set her gaze on mine—"took me to his house. I . . . met his parents." Large blue eyes stared at me and blinked. She dropped her voice to almost a whisper. "You know, I *saw* them."

"She hugged them, too," Luc said jokingly.

I stared at my best friend, at her pigtails poking through the sides of her white and black striped skully, at her dark red lipstick, her pale skin. She blinked. "I know, Riley." She leaned close to me. "Preacher told me. Creatures of the afterlight," she whispered. "Vampires."

I could do little more than stare at my friend.

"Gilles explained some things, and Preacher, he took care of the rest—including yours and Seth's tendencies," Nyx continued. "He wanted to wait for you, but I . . . I insisted. After I'd met Luc's parents, I had to know."

It hit me then, and I grasped Nyx's forearms. "I'm sorry I lied to you before about Seth," I said. "It . . . was the only way. At least, I thought." I looked hard at her. "I didn't think you'd understand, and I didn't want to drag you into all of this."

Luc was suddenly at Nyx's side. "She handled it all

pretty good," he said, and I noticed a protective hand move to Nyx's back. "Even when Papa changed."

"I fainted, but Luc stayed right beside me," Nyx confessed, then narrowed her eyes at me. "No more secrets, huh Riley?" Seth walked over and put his arm around Nyx.

I held my hand up. "No more, I swear it."

Nyx glanced up at Seth. "I always felt it was something more," she said, and I knew she meant Seth hadn't been on drugs. "Never thought it was something like this, though."

Seth pulled Nyx against him and kissed the top of her head through the skully. "Love ya, other sis."

Nyx's closed-eyed smile spoke way more than her words. "Love you, too, little bro."

"Dere's more to be done, dat's right," said Preacher, rising from his recliner and glancing at all gathered. It was late, and the lamp in the corner cast a very dim amber glow over the room, the haint blue ceiling mixing and casting a unique, surreal metallic color against the newsprint on the walls (to keep the *wudus* busy). I knew he and Estelle had to be exhausted. "You, Nyxinnia, will stay wit Riley and Seth—for a few nights, right? Until we know what's out dere, we want you safe. You don't have tendencies like she and her brodder do. Deys have powers now, and dem Duprés taught 'em to fight. You don't know dat stuff, and I don't want you gittin' hurt, girl. Luc will go wit you to your house and git your stuff, dat's right. Den you come back here."

Nyx nodded without question. "Yes, sir."

"After a few days, when we know what's out dere, we'll git your house right and den you can go back," Preacher said.

Nyx again nodded.

"Séraphin," Preacher said.

"Yes, sir," Phin responded.

"You and dose boys dere help me with dis stuff, right." He crossed the room and lifted an aged, hand-carved wooden box from the mantel. I knew it well. It usually contained conjuring herbs, crushed bones, body parts of various creatures—sort of a tackle box full of hoodoo stuff. He reached in and lifted three balls of burlap, larger than what he'd given me earlier. It was more like the size of a baseball. "I want you boys to shake dis around da building's foundation, inside each doorway, window, and da balcony." He handed the sachets to Phin.

"Come on," Phin said to the others. "Josie, you stay with Riley until we finish."

Josie, seated on the floor in front of Estelle's feet, looked up at me. "Sure."

Phin and the guys left.

Luc's cell rang then, and when he answered it, he looked directly at me. "Yeah, Bro, everything's cool," he said, then quietly slipped out into the foyer.

It was Eli. And somehow, as childish and immature as it sounded, it pissed me off that he'd call Luc and not me. Inwardly, I fumed. I'm talking frickin' frackin' fumed.

I immediately turned on my acute-hearing ability and eavesdropped.

"You should tell her, dude," Luc said.

"I don't need you telling me what to do, Jean-Luc," Eli replied, his French thick. "And I damn-fuck sure don't need her knowing anything. If I wanted to talk to her about it, I would. I don't. End of story. It would just freak her out more. I was just checking in. Papa wouldn't answer his cell. I'll be home later."

"Wait," Luc said. "She had visitors today."

"Who?" Eli's voice grew eerily controlled.

"Three newlings. Somehow they got under Ned's radar. Riley and Nyx were alone; Riley killed two of them. Seth came in with us and took out the last one," Luc said. "She's okay. They're both okay. I took Nyx to Papa. She knows."

The line was deadly silent for several seconds, then a burst of French expletives filled the air—so loud I almost covered my ears. "What the fuck did I leave you there for, huh? She's not capable of taking care of herself. Tendencies or not—goddamn, Luc—she's still a fucking mortal. She could have been ripped apart!"

"Riley?"

I jumped at Phin's voice, and quickly turned my attention to him. "Yeah?"

He grinned. "Shame on you." He inclined his head. "Finished. Let's go." It cracked me up, every once in a while, to catch the silver ball pierced through his tongue. He'd kept it, even after the disturbances in Savannah. But now I had another distraction. What was it Eli didn't want me to know? I guessed I'd find out soon enough. Poor Luc had really caught hell from his older brother. It was my fault totally. I shouldn't have turned my hearing so far down. Lesson learned.

I quickly hugged Preacher and Estelle, then wrapped my arms around Nyx's neck. "Everything will be okay," I assured her, trying to assure myself as well. I pulled back and looked at her. "I'll wait up for you."

"Okay," she said, smiling. "Luc—he's really nice."

I knew it. They liked each other. "Yeah, he is," I agreed. "He'll take good care of you."

"You be careful over dere, girl," said Estelle, who'd

been uncharacteristically quiet the whole time. "I don't like all dis stuff goin' on and will feel better once dat Eli Dupré gets his carcass home and watches my baby good, dat's right."

"Yes, ma'am. Me, too." I kissed my surrogate grand-parents.

With all that said and done, we left.

Riggs and Zetty headed home; Luc took Nyx to get her stuff to stay at my place for a few nights; the rest of us stayed at my apartment. While Phin, Seth, and Josie flipped through the channels, got hooked, and fell into watching *The Breakfast Club*, I decided to take a long, hot shower. Too many thoughts and feelings ran through me at top speed; I was sure I'd need a beer afterward. I craved a friggin' cigarette, but I'd promised Seth I'd lay off and stay off, so I excused myself, grabbed some comfy jammies, and headed to my bathroom. Having turned on the hot water, stripped, and climbed into the tiled stall, I let the steaming water soak through my hair and run over my body. My thoughts ran likewise.

I'd agreed, at the insistence of Elise Duprés, to allow her to homeschool Seth. I'd been hesitant at first; I wanted him to have as normal an upbringing as possible, and that meant a normal school, with normal interaction with other kids. Soccer. Baseball. Prom. Graduation. I'd finally realized none of that was possible. Not only had our mother been murdered, but our father was a loser deadbeat criminal who had abandoned us and was then imprisoned. Seth had nearly succumbed to vampirism in the worst possible way. Homeschooling under Elise's su-pervision and instruction could only be a positive. She'd schooled all of her children, and, I'd eventually discov-ered, all but Josie had attended college. She'd looked and been too young to attend, but had obtained degrees just the same. Before computers, she was homeschooled by Elise and was fluent in English, Latin, and Spanish, as well as her native French tongue. Eli had a law degree from the University of Glasgow in Scotland (the prick never even told me). Phin had a master's degree in biology from the University of Georgia, and Luc had earned his degree in astrology from Edinburgh. Astrology! Jean-Luc and Séraphin were frickin' scientists. Talk about kick-ass undead Myth Busters. All in all, I felt confident in Elise's teachings, and Seth was all for it. Of course, I think it may have had something to do with spending more time with Josie, but that was just my astute sisterly observation. Anyway, I was okay with the decision, and Elise would start classes with Seth tomorrow—as long as no other vampires showed up to attack us. Gilles had pulled me to the side to say how absolutely thrilled his wife was to have another pupil to instruct. He'd said his Elise had spent hours gathering teaching supplies and information from the Internet, so it was a fantastic dual-purpose decision, in my book.

The steaming water carried the scent of pomegranate as it mixed with the soap I'd just picked up, and as I lathered my body, my thoughts returned to Eli, and what I'd heard him say. I won't lie—it'd stung. Try as I might to be a tough-ass through and through, I was still a woman. I did have feelings and I could be hurt. I hated that Eli had that power over me. I'd sworn nobody—no man—would ever have it over me again. Not after what that insane fuck did to my mother. I could still see her sopping wet hair clinging to her pale face. I could still feel her body in my arms, limp; her eyes wide and fixed, a pair of lifeless orbs that used to look upon me with such love but that could no longer look at all. Those last few years of her life I'd been nothing but heartache to her; I regretted so much. Tears built behind my lids, and I allowed myself to cry. God, I missed my mom. Every day, I saw her face, and I wished like hell she hadn't died.

I plopped a glob of shampoo in my palm and scrubbed my head and my hair; then I rinsed and did the same with conditioner. Finally, and only when I felt the water start to run lukewarm, did I turn the knobs to Off and step out of the shower. I wrapped one towel around my hair, another around my body, and in the next second I collapsed, exhausted on my bed. My eyes grew heavy; for some reason, I fought sleep. Finally, I lost the battle.

I have no idea how long I lay there. I could hear Emilio Estevez's laughter spilling from the TV in the living room. It was the last thing I heard before falling into darkness.

When next my eyes fluttered open, I was walking through a park; live oaks, moss; a large pineapple fountain with water spraying sparkled beneath the tall black iron lamps posted along the walkway. It was dark and too late to be out alone. The air was damp, humid, heavy with brine. Palms mixed with live oaks. Leaning against the fountain was a woman: late twenties, maybe, average height, very curvy, with black hair pulled into a high ponytail, tight jeans, T-shirt, sneakers. She had a cell phone cradled between her chin and shoulder as she talked to . . . someone. Angry. Upset. Crying. She did not know I was behind her.

I was not me.

I was him.

The monster.

I could feel his anticipation within me as I stood

directly behind her, watching her, smelling her. I tried to scream, to warn her to run. I drew in air; it died in my throat. I tried to reach with my hands, to shove her, make her realize she was in danger; they weren't my hands that appeared before me. They were male arms, male hands, not young, not gentle. Inside, I felt as though I'd combust; no matter how hard I struggled, I was imprisoned in his body; my pleas, my screams were nothing more than ghosts. They didn't exist, and she'd never hear them.

I now felt what the monster felt; adrenaline raged within me, a mixture of sexual headiness and dark, ravaging hunger. Every thump of her heart reverberated inside me; with every beat I imagined the hot rush of her blood pulsing into my throat. My excitement grew; my patience ran out. She turned. Her eyes widened.

Her scream died in my mouth.

With one hand I yanked her cell from her hand and threw it into the fountain; with the other I tore off her T-shirt, her bra, and tossed them aside, all while holding her still with my fangs locked into her bottom jaw. I, not the monster, even knowing she'd never hear me, tried to scream, to warn, but nothing happened. His actions were now mine, as if I were the one controlling the actions. I sobbed hysterically, wanting to at least escape what I knew was about to happen; I could do neither. I could do nothing but accept, be his fucking puppet. With both hands free now, he palmed her breasts; heavy, soft, scraping his thumbs over her nipples. It made his cock throb. As I stared so close into her widened, horror-stricken, pain-filled eyes, I knew she was paralyzed. He'd known exactly where to inject his fangs to keep her quiet; to keep her still. Yet mentally, she was all there. She knew what was happening. Just like I did. Both of us were victims. Both of us could do nothing to escape.

In the next instant, his fangs retracted from her jaw, her head fell to the side, and he plunged his teeth into her heart; ripped into her chest cavity, tearing at her flesh, seeking the organ he craved. He was like a ravaged wolf. He found it and sank his fangs deep into its center. She didn't scream; she didn't move. He'd paralyzed her, but her heart still thumped erratically, and with every wild beat, her warm blood pumped just as fiercely into his mouth, his throat, like an ejaculation. It was a sexual rush as well as a frenzied, necessary feed. It got him off, and, as he drained her blood, he came, hard, fast. Nausea crashed over me.

Then, it slowed; her life left her with each slow beat, until it was over. When he lifted his head, I looked down at her ripped, bloodied flesh, her bare breasts, her pale skin, and her wide, lifeless eyes. He lifted her as though she were nothing more than a rag doll and tossed her limp body into the fountain. Her head hit the pineapple statue with a hard crack, then slid into the water. Facedown, she saw no more. He wiped his mouth with the back of his arm and walked away.

As if a bolt had rushed my body, I shot up.

Phin knelt beside my bed, staring at me, his hand on my shoulder.

"Why'd you wake me?" I asked suddenly, angered, adrenaline still pumping. "I could have followed him!" I glanced down and was glad my towel was still intact.

"What'd you see this time?" he asked. "What, Riley?"

I told him. I told him everything. He watched me closely the whole time, not once taking his eyes off mine. "Jesus, Phin—it's . . . horrible. I can't even describe what it feels like to be there and be . . . helpless. To feel his disgusting desires within me." Anger raged within me, and I looked at him hard. "I want to kill that prick, Phin. I want to kill him myself. I want him out of me!"

Phin grazed my jaw with his knuckle. "I know," he said softly. "I can't promise we'll let you kill him alone, but we'll get him. We'll kill him, Riley. Collectively." He looked at me. "Swear to God, we will."

My gaze was locked on his, so much like Eli's. For a split second, I wanted Eli so badly, it hurt. I missed him. "Phin, the monster's out of control. I've never felt such rage, hatred—such sickness. It's like something out of a horror movie." I pinched the bridge of my nose, then peered at him again. "How did you know?" I asked. "What was happening?"

He tapped my temple. "I could hear it. Hear it, but not see it."

I nodded. "Thanks. Luc and Nyx aren't back yet?"

Phin rose. "No, but they're on their way. Why don't you get some sleep? Some real sleep?"

"Yeah, good idea," I said, and rose. "Thanks again. For staying with me. I hope I didn't do anything weird."

Phin smiled. "Nothing weirder than usual."

"Asshole."

Phin laughed and left the room. I changed into a pair of loose boxers and a black cami. Then I brushed my teeth, pulled my damp hair into a ponytail, and crept back to bed.

I shouldn't have.

For a moment, I cranked my acute hearing to wide-open. Sounds came at me in a whispered rush, as if a faucet had been turned on high: people talking all over the city, phones ringing, laughter, dogs barking, horns blasting, music playing, people screwing, moaning, crying, fighting, TV's flipping ninety thousand channels at a time. Sweat gathered at my forehead and dripped down my temples. I squeezed my eyes tightly shut, grasped the bedsheets in my fists, and breathed—in and out; in and out. Slowly, rhythmically, easily. I chose one sound, dug one single sound out of a million—a priest, praying—and honed in. It seemed the safest. It seemed the wisest. The priest's voice, deep, even, consoling, filled my ears, and all the other sounds of the city fell away. I had no idea what he said; he spoke mostly in Latin, and every once in a while he'd say an English amen. It soothed me, so much that my body relaxed, the throbbing in my head eased, and my breathing returned to normal. I don't know why, but I felt safe. It struck me that I hadn't been to church in years.

I listened for Nyx and Luc to come back, listened to an occasional giggle from Josie, the familiar chuckle of my brother, and the low hum of *CSI: Miami* on the TV. My lids grew heavy, I grew tired, the noises became more distant, and before I knew it, I'd drifted again.

I found myself wandering the corridors of an enormous castle, one of ancient stone, wooden rafters, antique tapestries. A gray cat sat perched upon a window seat, napping, its purrs thrumming within me. No one was about—not at first. Soon, though, I heard laughter, and I followed the sound to a distant chamber, upstairs. A chill coursed through me, and when I glanced down at myself I saw why. I wore nothing more than a garnet silk robe, a pair of black spiked boots that laced in the back and rose to my thighs, my hair curled and piled loosely on my head. A garnet silk choker graced my throat. Why was I dressed like this? Where was I?

I continued on, but the more I sought the others, the farther away the voices seemed to get. Then, I was lost, deep in the bowels of the castle, where lights were dimmer, shadows stretched long, and the chill set into my bones. I pulled the edges of the robe closer together, but the robe was tight, barely fitting. Finally, I saw a light flickering beneath a closed door, and I pressed my cheek to the aged wood. There was warmth inside.

"Come in," a familiar voice called from inside. "I've something to show you."

As though I had no control of my actions, my palms flattened against the door and I pushed. It swung on creaky hinges, and, as I peered inside, I saw, standing beside a roaring fire, Victorian Arcos. He was dressed in head-to-toe black Armani, right down to his leather boots. His hair remained long, pulled loosely in a queue. My body tensed immediately with fear; I backed out and closed the door.

"Don't run," he said.

Victorian stood behind me, in the corridor. His breath brushed the shell of my ear. "Turn around."

As if it were someone else, my body turned to face him. I had no control. With my back to the door, I stared up into his beauty, breathless, speechless. "Eli spared your life. Why? What did you two discuss?"

"Ah, yes. Eligius had no choice but to spare my life. And I will leave it to him to explain why. Things are much more complicated than you or he can even imagine. Now, enough of this chatter. I cherish these times with you, and I don't want any other interference." He looked deeply into my eyes. "I know you want me to touch you, Riley," he said, his exotic accent washing over me as he abruptly ended any further questions. They're on my tongue, but

I'm unable to speak. "Just as badly as I want you to touch me." He lifted a knuckle and grazed first my jaw, then dragged it down the column of my throat, catching the material of my robe and pushing it off my shoulder. "Your body art fascinates me," he said. As he leaned close to inspect my inked skin, his breath brushed, whispered, enticed. "Just as you fascinate me," he continued, his brown eyes locked on mine as his hand, skimming my shoulder, lowered to the sash tying the silky material together. He pulled the sash slowly, until the loose knot fell free and the robe gaped open, revealing a clear path of skin between my breasts, all the way to the small triangle of silk that was my panties. Victorian's eyes grew darker.

"You can't continue to torment me like this, in my subconscious," I said, my gaze holding his. "You may be able to control me, but it's not really me you're getting your way with, is it? It's not really me you're touching, or me you're getting off on. I'm being forced, with no say-so, no control. You might as well have a fucking blow-up doll, Victorian."

For a moment, his eyes rolled back, the look of pure satisfaction on his face. He then looked at me. "Just the way you say my name—the way Victorian falls from your tongue and past your lips makes me hard," he whispered against my ear, pressing his body closer to mine. "Feel for yourself, Riley." With the back of his knuckles, he trailed the exposed skin of my abdomen, letting it linger against the silk of my panties. I wanted him so badly to stop; I thought I'd come if he moved a fraction lower. I hated him for it.

"Why do you insist on pulling reactions from me?" I asked furiously, and moved my hand to knock his. It was then I felt exactly what he'd been talking about. The

hardness wasn't him; it was the silver blade strapped to my thigh.

"See?" he said, his eyes growing warm. "I make you do nothing. You've had the power to kill me all along." His voice was a whisper against my skin. "You have the power now."

"How can I kill a dream figment?" I asked, my fingers brushing the blade.

"I am not a figment," he returned, brushing his lips across my cheek. "I interject myself here; you keep me here. Everything we share is real."

"You make me keep you here, just like you make me feel," I said. "Just like you keep me from prodding you further about what you told Eli. Mind control's a bitch when put to you like that, right? Sort of takes the romance out of things. So, to change the subject, what do you know of the ones who attacked me? What did you tell Eli?"

Victorian's body stilled; he grasped my chin and lifted my face. "What do you mean by 'attacked' you?"

I blinked, surprised at his animosity for whoever attempted to hurt me. It seemed . . . genuine. I guess it had happened after Eli had left him. "Three vampires, two of them newlings, made it inside my apartment and attacked my friend and me. I took two of them out. Luckily, my brother came in and took out the last one. That one nearly got me." I tilted my head in question. "You know nothing about it?"

Anger, and maybe even a little hurt, flashed over Victorian's features. "Of course I didn't know anything about it. Why would I want to hurt you?"

I stared at him. "One of our friends with tendencies has the ability to sense vampires miles and miles away— yet he didn't sense these until they were literally at my apartment. He thinks it had something to do with Romanian magic."

Victorian stared down at me, hurt. "I am not the only Romanian vampire in existence, Riley," he said quietly. "And I'd never hurt you. I wish you'd believe me."

I stared, not knowing what to say.

He leaned down then and brushed his lips over mine. "To convince you, I'll release you from this dream, instead of your Eligius rescuing you from it, like always." His mouth lingered against mine, before whispering, "I shall see you soon. . . .

With a start, I sat up.

Lamplight filtered in through my balcony window, and the TV's low hum met my ears. I glanced at the clock.

No more than five minutes had passed since the last time I'd checked.

With a heavy sigh, I lay back down and stared up at the ceiling. Confusion webbed my brain. I knew I didn't want Victorian. Yet despite what the Duprés thought, I felt he wasn't evil—not like his brother.

As I closed my eyes for the third and hopefully final time, I saw the hurt etched in Victorian's face behind my lids.

I knew then I'd made my mind up about him.

And it wasn't the same opinion the Duprés had. I wasn't sure how I felt about that yet.

Three more thoughts crossed my mind before slumber claimed me—even if for only a few hours. One, the murder I'd witnessed had taken place in Charleston. I'd visited Savannah's sister city only a few times, mostly for art conventions, and I hadn't strolled the gardens while there. But I did remember the pineapple fountain. It was a city landmark. It was also that girl's grave. We'd be going there soon, I was sure of it.

Two, I was feeling drained. I don't mean I'm-having-my-period-with-no-energy drained. It was more like an every-time-I-witness-a-murder-it-saps-life-out-of-me drained. It made me feel . . . weird. Angry. Edgy. It was taking me longer to recover after each vision, and I wasn't sure what to do about it.

Three, a fight was coming—another war, and this one was way different than the one in Bonaventure. There'd be more vampires. There'd be more bloodshed.

Don't ask me how I knew; I just did. And I really hated that.

Part Six

POSSESSIVE

"Terror made me cruel."

—Emily Brontë

"I'm pretty sure you're not going to get this—I don't get it myself. But I'm brutally honest to a fault, so why hide a confession? I'm attracted to Victorian. Now, don't get your panties all wadded up. I don't mean boom-chick-a-wow-wow attracted. He's beautiful and sexy as damn friggin' hell—I'll give him that. But no—that's not how I mean. I mean . . . shit. I don't know what I mean. It's hard to explain. Don't misunderstand me, please—Eli is my heart, my soul, even though I can't admit it out loud yet, and the more he's away from me, the more pissy I become, which equals, in my book anyway, the more I care about him. Despite the sexual dreams I always seem to be involved in with Victorian, that's not how I feel about him. A kindred spirit—that's it! I feel sort of a kindred spirit with him. Does that make sense? Probably not. It doesn't, even to me. And I'm pretty sure Victorian would hate it. He's made no qualms about his intentions with me; he wants in my pants. Probably more, but it ain't happening. All I know is that, while it irritates me to the point of wanting to hit someone that Victorian intrudes his kinky self into my dreams, I don't want him dead anymore. I just don't feel that he's evil. As a matter of fact, I'm positive he'd help me, if times called for his help. And I'm pretty sure all that sets Eli's ass on fire."

—Riley Poe

"A woman's mutilated body was found in the city's pineapple fountain early this morning by city workers. An autopsy is being performed. Next, a new cannon for the battery? No, says Charleston's historical society. More details at six."

I shook my head and glanced at Phin, who sat perched on the kitchen counter, watching me eat a bowl of Cap'n Crunch. Sunlight streamed in from the window, making his short buzzed hair glow golden at the tips. "I hate being right," I said. "I knew I recognized that fountain." I was on edge, pissed, and uncertain . . . about everything. "Does Eli know what's going on here? Victorian is not the threat—it's him. That monster. Whoever he is."

Phin's gaze softened. "Yeah, he knows, and he trusts us to keep you safe until he returns—which should be very soon. And he thinks otherwise, Riley. He believes Victorian is a full threat. I'm not positive why you feel otherwise, but please, don't be fooled."

It wasn't as if I wanted to jump up and leave Savannah. I had a business to run, and I'd more than once dumped my share of work onto Nyx's shoulders. No offense to Nyx, and pardon my arrogance, but people sought me out. The ones who made an appointment with me wanted art by me in particular. Not all, but some. Okay, most. It'd be like having gone to OCC to have a custom chopper made and you didn't get Pauly Sr. or Pauly Jr., or even Mikey. You got a fine craftsman, but not the one you wanted. It was my job, my career, and I enjoyed giving people one-of-a-kind body art. I hated ditching my customers again. Yet one thing I knew for damn sure was that I couldn't bear the thought of innocents dying at the hand of that motherfucker. I couldn't bear watching it—damn, almost participating in it. Something had to freaking give.

"It will give," Phin said, his gaze direct, assured. "And we have a contact in Charleston. A small group of guardians, if you will. They're not ready for us yet. When they are, we'll go. Until then, I watch your ass, you carry on your business, Seth gets tutored by Mama. Period."

I narrowed my gaze. "You could have just asked me. You don't have to go fishing inside my noggin, ya know."

He wagged his blond brows. "What fun would that be?"

"A group of guardians?" I asked, curious. "This sit-around-and-wait crap is sounding a lot like what happened here. Why can't we just pack silver, rush Charleston, hook up with the gang, and kick ass?"

Phin sighed, frustration etched in his forehead. "It's never that easy. First, we don't step on each other's toes. They're a prideful street gang, and some of the members have been guardians of Charleston for centuries. Very rough around the edges and prefer to handle their own problems. Still governed by Preacher's family, though. They watch over the city. Like Savannah, they haven't had trouble in a long, long time. And I'm not frustrated."

I narrowed my gaze. "They're not doing such a hot job lately," I said. I knew Preacher had kin in Charleston, and some in Buford and Edisto. I did not know he had a rough gang of vampiric guardians acting in the same manner as the Duprés.

"All had been calm until the Arcoses were released," Phin said, rubbing his hand over his hair. "I'm pretty sure the trouble's being caused by newlings created by the brothers. And the ones they've created. It's a snow-ball now."

"I guess you're right," I said, although I didn't agree with him on one brother. "Well, if they don't get a grip soon, we'll have to go whether they call us or not." I

stared hard at him. "I don't like what I'm seeing, Phin.
I don't. And for the sake of sounding selfish, I'd really
rather not be the eyeballs of a vicious killer. Know what
I mean?"

Phin slipped off the counter and placed a hand on my
shoulder. "I know, Ri. Hang in there. We'll get through
this."

After dumping a few cups of Gullah tea in my system, I pulled on a pair of faded jeans, an Inksomnia T-
shirt, and Vans, and I ran Chaz to the vet. The sweet dog
was acting normal, but moving a little more slowly than
usual. The vet checked him out and assured me he was
okay, probably just a little sore, and to let Chaz monitor his own activity. I felt sure the main thought that
ran through Chaz's head as he whizzed through the air
was *What the hell?* Since it was an old building, the drop
hadn't been as drastic as it could've been, but it made
me sick to think of that bloodsucker throwing Chaz off
the balcony.

When I got back home, Nyx was in the kitchen
making scrambled eggs and toast. She was dressed for
work, wearing a black 1940's-themed pencil dress with
a sweetheart neckline, stockings with the seam up the
back of the leg, and peep-toe pumps. Her hair was
pulled into a pair of curled pigtails, and she wore bright
red lipstick and a black choker with a silver spiderweb
dangling from the throat. She reminded me of an ador-
ably Goth version of *I Love Lucy*. Luc, of course, was
perched on the counter beside her. Phin was on the sofa
watching *MythBusters*, and Josie and Seth were already
at the Dupré House for Seth's first day of school. All in
all, I guessed this was as relatively normal as it was going
to get for us.

Eli was still gone. It still hurt.

It pissed me off even more.

I felt as if I were having an out-of-body experience the whole day; I was there, but it wasn't really me. It was more as if I were looking down and watching myself. Nothing felt real. Everything felt surreal, as if I were trapped in a dream, in an old black-and-white movie.

That was the story of my life lately.

Even with Jimi Hendrix's "Valleys of Neptune" thumping in the shop, I couldn't be pulled into that zone I loved. I managed good work, but my heart wasn't in it like usual, and that pissed me off.

The early part of the day rolled by; I'd inked that flower dragon on the lower back of a skinny biology major. Without the cushion of a little fat, she said it felt as if I was inking her backbone, and honestly I thought she was going to pass out. I hadn't had a passer-outer in quite some time . I had to stop, give her some water, let her catch her breath. I was impressed, though; she was a trouper and wanted to continue. We finally finished the outline, and I made her appointment for six weeks to come by for the fill-in. By the time she left Inksomnia, her color had returned. All I could think was that I probably was not going to be here.

"Thanks," she said, then jumped as Gene, the stuffed black raven, cawed at her exit.

"Later," I said, then decided to grab some lunch. Luc offered to go get it, but I needed some air, needed to be alone, and needed to just . . . release my thoughts, I guess, or maybe my bad mood. It was four p.m. and daylight; there was no fear of vampires lurking in the shadows, so the Duprés didn't push. My next appointment wasn't until five fifteen, so I grabbed my backpack and left.

Stifling, humid air hit me the moment I stepped out of Inksomnia, and I drew in a deep breath of the ever-present brine rolling off the Savannah River directly across the cobbles from my shop. I turned left. The tourists had thinned but hadn't completely disappeared, and I dodged bodies of all types and ages, wearing everything from plaid Bermuda shorts and T-shirts to long pull-over beach dresses and flip-flops; smiling, unwary people pointing in windows, snapping photos of the river walk and riverboats, and walking out of shops with bags of goodies from historic Savannah.

All I could think about was that dark-haired girl, her ripped-open chest, and her head cracking against the pineapple fountain in Charleston.

I stopped in at Kevin Barry's Irish Pub, ordered a corned beef Reuben on pumpernickel with double fries and malt vinegar, a large sweet tea, and headed out to the river walk to park on a bench and chow down. The September sun beat against my skin. I pulled a long swig of tea from the white Styrofoam cup, unwrapped the sandwich, and bit into the warm, crunchy, toasted dark bread. Corned beef and sauerkraut gushed out the sides. I closed my eyes and chewed. Yes, it was delicious. Yes, I ate every crumb. Yes, I know I'm a hog.

No, it did not relieve my mind of the problems at hand.

I wanted a smoke. A friggin' cigarette. Seth would kill me if I did, but man, the stress was piling up and a long drag on a cig would be heaven. But I'd promised, so I didn't cave. And, I admit, I did feel better without them. I'm surprised I hadn't gained any weight, but maybe my extensive Tendie workouts were enough to keep off the extra calories.

I smelled him long before I heard his voice.

A shiver coursed through my body.

Eli slid onto the bench beside me. He said nothing, but I felt his eyes boring into me. Slowly, I turned my gaze to his. Behind a pair of shades he stared at me; a black T-shirt clung to his chest, and a pair of low-slung jeans hugged his hips. My eyes were glued to his lips; perfectly shaped, full, and memories of how those lips caressed my body, devoured my mouth, filled my head. Again, I shivered.

"Do you have to keep your last appointment?" he said silkily.

I didn't answer. Instead, I slowly poked a French fry into my mouth and chewed; another followed. After I'd drained every drop of tea and eaten every single French fry, in total silence and extreme scrutiny, I inhaled deeply.

Eli reached over, grabbed my cup and wrappers, tossed them into the trash can beside the bench, then pulled me into a crushing hug. With strong arms, he embraced me.

"It's been less than forty-eight hours, but I missed the hell out of you," he said, his mouth against my temple. My arms went around him, and he pulled me closer.

"Forty-eight hours? I hadn't even noticed you were gone," I said against his throat, my voice muffled.

I felt his chest rumble as he laughed. He pulled back, took off his shades, and stared down at me. The shocking blue intensity caused another shiver within me. "We've things to discuss."

I nodded. "After my appointment. I can't get into the habit of ducking out on my clients, Eli."

With a heavy-lidded gaze, he regarded me. "Is it a big tat, or a little one?"

I grinned. "Medium. Shouldn't take longer than an hour."

In silence, he lowered his head to kiss me, but I covered my mouth. "Stop! Reuben with slaw. Gross."

Eli merely smiled.

"Hey, Riley. Eli, right? What's up?"

I turned and shaded my eyes. Mullet Morrison stood, grinning, his hands stuffed into his jeans pockets. I smiled. "Hey, Mullet-Man. What's up?"

Eli stuck his hand out and the two shook. "Mullet."

Mullet shrugged, glanced over his shoulder, and looked back at me. "Just hangin' out until Tiff finishes shoppin' in the SoHo. She's in there picking out a dress or something. So how's life?"

I nodded. "Interesting as always. You?" Eli sat silent beside me, his arm possessively around my shoulders.

Mullet nodded. "Sweet, sweet. Hey—Tiff wants some ink. I told her we'd come by next week maybe. Is that cool?"

Before vampires, I could have said yes with assuredness. Now? I had no freaking idea what I'd be doing next week. Hopefully, all the chaos in Charleston would be over. "Yeah, sure. Just have her call the shop and I'll work her in. Does she know what she wants?"

Mullet scratched his jaw. "Yeah, I think she wants a Japanese koi fish along here." He stretched and pointed to his side. "Pretty sick, huh?"

I grinned. "Sounds cool. Tell her to give me a call."

He stuck his fist out and bumped mine. "Sweet. Later, Riley. Eli. Oh, hey—did you hear about the murders in Charleston?"

My insides froze at the mention of them. "Heard

something about a body being found at the pineapple fountain. Why?"

Mullet peered at me. "You know, my cousin's on the police force, and he says there's been like, nine murders there over the past few weeks. Some pretty sick shit, from what Kelly says. Freaky, huh? They think it might be a serial killer or some crazy psychopath. I hope to hell they don't come south."

"Yeah," I answered. "Me, too."

"Right—later then," he said, and turned to leave. "Lock your doors, Riley."

"Yep," I answered, and watched him saunter off. "Cool guy, Mullet. I hope he never has to know the things I know—especially that it doesn't matter how many cops are on the Charleston case, they won't catch the killer; rather, killers." I looked at Eli. "There has to be more than one vampire working the streets. Nine murders, Eli."

Eli's expression was tight. "And those are only the ones they've discovered."

Pulling the cell out of my pack, I glanced at the time. I still had thirty minutes until my next appointment.

"I have to speak with Papa," Eli said, rising. I followed. "We've apparently got visitors. I'll meet you back here in a couple of hours to pick you up, *oui*?"

I loved it when Eli occasionally threw in an unexpected French word. It was sexy as hell.

He grinned.

"Yeah, that's cool," I said. And before I could stop him, he grasped my jaw with one hand and pulled my mouth to his. He kissed me, Reuben, slaw, fries, and all, and it left me breathless and wanting to peel his clothes off right there on the riverfront to have my way with him.

He kissed my ear and whispered, "Later. I promise."

I watched him slide his shades back onto his face and saunter away. He disappeared between two buildings. Shading my eyes with my hand, I glanced in the direction of Inksomnia, gauged the distance of walk time, and took off at a brisk pace. It still amazed me how fast a speed I could manage in a pair of spiked heels.

Eli was home! God Almighty, I'd missed him. Yeah, in less than forty-eight hours, I'd missed him. I was anxious to hear what he'd found out, and anxious for other things, too. I crossed the cobbles to the storefront side, cut up and through the steep stairway alley between two stores, and emerged onto Factors Walk. Crossing the parking lane, I managed my way through relatively few tourists to Bay Street, and turned right. I'd just passed the Cotton Exchange building when the smell hit me. It was so strong, pungent, that I stopped and looked around. There was nothing but tourists, cars, parking meters, and locals walking the sidewalk—nothing out of the ordinary. A young guy wearing a dark gray suit and carrying a briefcase bumped into me.

"Sorry," he said, then stared at my arms, then my breasts. He smiled and turned back up the walk.

I felt unsettled. I didn't like it.

Drawing in a deep breath, I caught the scent again, and, concentrating, closing out all other scents of the city, I zeroed in on this one in particular. It was sharp, almost spicy-hot, reminding me of wasabi sauce, and something else undefined. It was a scent unlike anything I'd ever inhaled, and I'd inhaled a lot of stuff in my youth. I could almost taste it in my mouth. I turned and followed it,

slightly amused by my weird, wolfish tendency. I crossed
Bay Street onto Drayton and continued up the sidewalk.
I weaved in and out of passersby, the scent drawing me
into, of course, an empty alley. I stood there, staring at
the aged brick walls, the ferns growing between the mortar, the rusty drainpipes running from the rooftop to the
lane. I opened my hearing, just a fraction, and listened
closely to the abundance of sounds around me, trying to
pick through to see if anything felt stranger than usual.
It wasn't easy. So many sounds—voices, a toilet flushing, car stereos, a rapid-fire heartbeat that was so fast it
could be nothing else but a mouse. I moved toward the
single door in the alley, the scent growing stronger.

I never made it.

My body was slammed, face-first, into the brick wall,
my arms grabbed and jacked halfway up my back. Unknown hands—they felt male—patted me down the
length of my legs and back up, between my thighs. In
the next second, one of those hands slipped inside my
low waistband, retrieving the blade I had stashed there
against my hip. I jerked, struggled; I was again slammed.

"Fuck!" I growled, wondering why in hell my
strength didn't seem very strong at all. "What do you
want?" I said, finding it difficult to speak since my face
was shoved against brick.

"That all the silver you're packin'?" the voice said behind me, close to my ear. "Or you got it hidden in places
I can't find without a little diggin'?" He laughed. "Not
that I'd mind, babe. Your call."

"That's it—that's all I got," I ground out. I gathered
my strength; I felt it growing inside me from my toes
upward. I elbowed my attacker, spun around, kneed his
groin, and as he staggered back I swept his ankles. He

hit the pavement with a thud. I pressed the heel of my boot at his throat.

He grinned. Sexy. Smug. "Not bad. Luc told me you were good."

I looked at him. He gently lifted a hand and moved my heel from his throat, then leapt up. He regarded me closely, as I did him.

Standing at approximately my height, my attacker wore skinny ripped jeans, chunky boots, a black ripped T-shirt, and had a headful of light brown and sun-bleached dreads, pulled back at the nape of his neck. He wasn't overly muscular, but he was lean and strong as shit. Porcelain skin—all except for a silver scar that shot out of one eyebrow—full lips, and the strangest mercury-colored eyes I'd ever seen. I stiffened. Realization kicked me in the gut.

Vampire.

A slow smile, revealing perfect, blindingly white teeth, stretched across his perfect face. "Ah, got a brain to go with the beauty, I see," he drawled, and it was then I noticed the defined Charleston drawl. "Sweet. Eli's one lucky fuck." Well, minus the gang slang.

I frowned. This guy—vamp—knew Eli. "Who are you and what the hell do you want?" I said, and rubbed my forehead. Luckily, there was no blood. "And what's that smell?" I glanced at his hand wrapped around my blade. "Give me my silver back."

"Uh, that'd be a no, babe," he said, then inclined his head toward Drayton. "No matter how fine you are, or how much Dupré swears how trustworthy you are, I'll make that judgment call myself." He nodded again and pulled on a pair of dark shades. "Come on. We walk. I'll talk." He peered at me over the tops of his glasses. "I didn't hurt ya, did I? Eli said you were tough. He'd kick my ass if he thought I hurt you."

The image of me, kneeing Eli in the nuts for putting me through a test, made me almost smile. "Name."

The dreadlocked vampire laughed. "Yeah. Right." He stuck out his hand. "Noah Miles."

I was totally confused, but I grabbed his hand and squeezed hard. "Well, Noah Miles, what the hell is this all about?"

Noah rubbed his chin, laughed, and shook his head. We left the alley and started up Drayton. "I called Eli a few hours ago. Shit's hittin' the fan in Charles Town, and he said you and the Duprés, and some others, are headed that way to help out." He glanced at me over the tops of his shades again, those silver eyes boring into mine. "He wanted me to check you out, make sure you were up to it."

"Well, I didn't do such a good job with my face smashed into the bricks and mortar," I said. This was the company Eli was referring to, apparently.

He laughed. "You did fine. And yeah, we're the company. Me and a few of my guys."

I walked without looking at him. "You had my blade in seconds."

Noah leaned close and bumped my shoulder. "That's because I'm good, sweetheart. Besides, you had only one blade stashed on you. You probably would have stuck me, had you had another one. Besides, you had me on the ground and at your mercy in seconds. Pretty impressive." He regarded my arms, then my cheek. "Sweet tats, by the way. I've heard about you."

"Oh, really? You've heard of my artistic talents as well as my ass-kicking talents? That's great." I glowered at him. Although I hated to admit it—I liked him. "So, Noah. How long have you been dead?"

He looked at me as we walked, and a somber expression crossed his features for a split second. "A long time, babe. Since the war."

"Which war?" I asked.

"England vs. America, darlin'."

I considered that. It was a long damn time to walk the earth. We walked up behind a small crowd waiting to cross Bay Street, and I looked at my new companion. "So, Eli sent you all the way to Savannah just for you to shove my face into a brick wall, feel me up, shove your hand down my pants, and pinch my blade? That's it? I passed the test?" The fact that Eli knew all that while kissing me senseless irritated me.

In front of us, an elderly woman wearing a floppy straw hat turned around and regarded us over the tops of her very large white plastic sunglasses. I smiled. She glanced at my arms, her silver brows shot up, and she turned back around.

Noah grinned at me. "Nope. That was my own test. And yeah—you passed," he said. "After talking with Eli this morning, I was told I had to bring a small group of my guys with me, ask permission from Preacher, as well as Monsieur Dupré, then set a game plan." We started to move with the crowd. "You must be pretty freaking important, darlin'."

I didn't answer. How could I? I didn't understand any of it myself. We stepped onto the sidewalk on the other side of Bay, hit Factors Walk, and walked the cobbles down to the riverfront. I stopped. Noah stopped and regarded me. "You already know I have potent blood?" I asked. I didn't want to look like the cartoon pork chop running around on legs any more than I had to.

"Hell yeah. We all do." He grinned. "Always have. We're governed by the Gullah-Gullah, too, don't forget. Pact and all, just like Savannah." He leaned over and sniffed me. "Barely noticeable at all anymore, babe. No worries. Although there is something else funky in there." He sniffed again, and I swatted him away.

"Two strigoi," I offered. "So don't piss me off."

"Day-yamn," he said, dragging the word out with his drawl, admiration noticeably in his voice. "Must have some wicked-ass tendencies." His grin was wide and bright white. "This I gotta see, babe."

"Riley," I offered. "My name's Riley."

Noah barked out a laugh. "Sorry 'bout that—habit." He lowered his shades and openly oogled me. "But I gotta tell you. You are a babe, babe."

At the riverfront, I stopped and rounded on Noah. "So there's some big meeting at the Duprés' tonight? Permission slips and all that to be signed? That's all fine with me, but first I have clients to finish and a business to settle." I shook my head. "Nyx is gonna kill me."

"Sweet. I'll hang with you till tonight, then," Noah said.

I stared at him as we headed up the sidewalk toward Inksomnia. "Behave yourself until Eli gets here."

He grinned. "Don't worry. I was raised a Southern gentleman, darlin'."

I shook my head and led him up the walk. Just before we reached the shop, I stopped and met Noah's shaded gaze. "Okay, first, what was that smell? Second, why this, all of a sudden? Phin just told me you guys would contact us when you needed help. He even said your group and ours don't exactly get along."

Sincerity sank deep into Noah's features, surprising me. "First"—he withdrew a sachet of something and dropped it into my hand—"my mask. Most vampires, creatures of the afterlight, whatever, have a certain special something about them that makes them distinct from all others." He grinned. "Mine is my scent. If I didn't carry this around, I'd have chicks—of all species—chasing me down. It was pretty enticing for the first twenty or so years, but then"—he shrugged— "wore my ass slap out, keeping up with all the women." He winked. "Not to mention all the poodles named Fee Fee I had to chase off. Second"—his face grew serious— "one of ours was destroyed last night."

"What happened?" I asked.

Noah shrugged. "Simply, we were outnumbered." He shook his head. "Never seen so many newlings gathered before. Freakin' out of control. We knew then we needed help."

I stuck out my hand and took his in a sincere shake. "I'm not a kick-ass vampire, but I promise to kick some vampire ass."

Noah grinned. "I totally believe you."

We started up the walk again, and, at Inksomnia's storefront window, I stopped once more. I still had his sachet in my hand. "Okay, so wait a minute. Are you telling me that if you didn't have your magic anti-want-me powder, I would be all over you?"

Noah's smile was pure raw male seduction, and, for a quick second, my insides pinged with lust. He reached slowly down and pried the sachet out of my fingers, his face, those eyes, mere inches from mine. I shuddered. "That's exactly what I'm tellin' ya, darlin'."

"Whoa," I muttered, amazed, still feeling as if I were

in a slight horny haze. I shook my head again, and he grinned. "I hope my dog doesn't start humpin' your leg, Noah." I hoped I didn't start humpin' Noah's leg. God-*damn*.

Noah burst out laughing.

"Miles, sup my man?" Luc's voice said, suddenly beside us, grabbing Noah's hand and the two bumping shoulders in a man-hug. Luc glanced at me, his brow raised in puzzlement. "Ri, you okay? Ah, dude—you didn't?"

"Sorry," Noah said, smirking. "She asked."

I shook my head, my gaze still transfixed on Noah. His smile was subtle but still seductive. Shithead. I shook my head again and moved between Luc and Noah, grabbed the black iron door handle of my shop, and opened it. "Yeah," I muttered to Luc, my head still a web of lust and confusion. "Fine."

Before the door closed behind me, I heard both vampires laugh.

By the time I wrapped up my last client—a sick freehand tribal tat of a raven inked onto the chest of a visiting RAF pilot from Northumberland, England—it was six thirty p.m. Noah had hung out in Inksomnia, watching me work, watching Nyx work, and catching up with Luc and Phin. Seth and Josie had wandered in around six, and had left right back out to the downtown branch library to check out books. Then, Eli arrived. We'd all planned to meet up at the Dupré House by nine thirty. Permission slips. Game plan. Proving one's abilities. Stuff like that. Luc had taken Nyx home. After treating her house adequately with Preacher's special sauce, he'd felt she was safe to return. She now knew all she had to do to have Luc there in an instant was to think it. She was cool with that—probably cooler than cool. The two had been staring googly-eyed at each other all day long.

The moment Eli walked in, he headed straight for Noah. They did that guy thing, slapping hands and then doing a man-hug. "I heard my woman kicked your ass to the ground," Eli said with pride. "Guess I shoulda warned you."

Noah grinned over Eli's shoulder at me. "She's a wildcat, man. She can definitely hold her own."

That, as I smiled at Noah, I sincerely appreciated.

"So let's get out of here," Luc said. "Papa's waiting for us." He glanced at Noah. "You ride with me."

Eli's gaze found mine. "You ride with me."

I met his gaze. "No. You ride with me."

The guys all laughed, and they left us alone. I locked the shop behind them, and before I could turn around, Eli was there. His arms encircled my waist; his mouth nuzzled against my neck. "Riley?"

"Yeah?" I said, my eyes closing from the intoxicating feel of Eli's closeness.

He turned me in his arms and looked down at me. "I want to tell you something. Alone. Not in front of my family."

I nodded. "Okay."

"I tracked Victorian to Richmond. I could've killed him." His eyes bore into mine. "I wanted to kill him."

"Why didn't you?" I asked.

"Because his mother begged me not to."

My eyes stretched wider. "His mother?"

"Yes. In my head. She swore Victorian was innocent— has always been innocent." He shook his head. "But that's not the reason why."

I continued to stare, waiting for the answer.

Eli inhaled. "She also told me that by killing Victorian, you in turn would be harmed, in some form. Because you have his blood. His DNA. You are part of him."

I blinked. "I have Valerian's DNA, too. You killed him, and I'm still here."

"And that may be why you're experiencing kills," Eli said. "Victorian wasn't quite the asshole I expected him to be. He was a lot more humble. But he did tell me something."

"What?" I asked.

"He says Valerian isn't dead. That we may have destroyed his physical body, but he's found another way to revive." Eli caressed my jaw with his thumb. "And I believe him."

The air in my lungs ceased. "No freaking way."

"We have to investigate it further, but I'm pretty sure Valerian, in whatever form, is the cause of the disruption in Charleston. I believe Victorian." He scrubbed my jaw. "Don't like the fucker, but I believe him."

I drew out of Eli's arms and paced the shop. I pressed the pads of my index fingers into my temples. "Well," I said, then turned on him. "I guess we'd better get to your parents'. We definitely need a game plan now." I moved to the stairs, but Eli stopped me, his hand firmly grasping my elbow.

"He won't get to you, Ri," he said, an edge to his voice. "I swear it."

"I believe you," I answered, and grazed his jaw with my fingertip. "Let's go see what your dad says."

We were silent on the ride to Monterey Square. The September air had finally grown a little cooler—not much, but a little, and it whipped at my skin as we drove through the streets. It was hard tonight, to concentrate; to block out the sounds, the smells. They assaulted me from every direction, and it was really starting to piss me off.

"It's because your mind is worrying about other things," Eli offered. "It's natural."

Nothing, I thought, was natural about any of this.

Philippe opened the door as we walked up the steps to the Dupré House, his face unreadable in the dim lamplight and shadows. He almost—almost—reminded me of that tall creepy guy from the old horror movie *Phantasm*. Tall, thin, with a long, structured face, gray hair, and constant expression of doom. He liked me, though—I could tell. I was going to make that man smile one day. "Hey, Phil," I said as I passed by. He glanced at me, and I nodded. "Sup?"

"At this late hour, nothing, young lady," he replied in his dry tone. "They're awaiting you in the parlor," he said. I smiled and shook my head. "Thanks."

We walked in to find Luc, Phin, Gilles and Elise, Preacher and Estelle, Jack and Tuba, Zetty, and four others I didn't recognize; three guys, one girl. I surmised they were with Noah. They all regarded me, expressions unreadable. I gave a slight nod and moved to stand beside Luc. Eli stood behind me, Gilles on my other side. Noah approached Gilles first, shook his hand, took Elise's and brushed a kiss to the top of it. Then, he surprised me further by moving to Preacher and Estelle and giving them both a hug.

I had to stop and wonder if Noah was in any way related to Nyx, what with the hug-a-thon I'd just witnessed.

"*Non*, we've just known Noah for a long time, *ma chérie*," whispered Gilles, leaning over me. "Nice boy, Noah."

Elise leaned around her husband and glanced at me, her elegantly coiffed ponytail barely bobbing with her movement. She nodded in agreement and smiled. "He truly is."

"Is that with or without his magic powder?" I muttered, and Elise's eyes glittered, her mouth tipped into a smile.

The horny devil had even gotten to Eli's mom!

Elise leaned close to me. "Only slightly, love."

I grinned at her.

Gilles rose. "Most of us know one another. Some of you I've known for a very long time," he said, and glanced at Noah. Noah gave him a respectful nod. "We are sorry to hear of your loss. Your loss, invariably, is our loss as well. While it's our nature to honor one another's boundaries, in this we bind together. We'll do all we can to help."

"The newling band in Charles Town is large, Monsieur," Noah said to Gilles. "Last night we were outnumbered."

Gilles nodded. "Spawns from the Arcoses, no doubt," he said. "As is our way, we'll attempt to gather as many in transition as possible. Some, undoubtedly, will be lost causes, I'm afraid. An unavoidable mission."

Noah nodded. "Of course. We appreciate any help you can offer, sir," he said, then glanced at me. "What about Eli's woman?"

Eli's woman?

"She's more powerful than even she knows," Gilles announced, and glanced at me. "You've only uncovered a fraction of your abilities, Riley dear. The rest will eventually surface, with experience."

"Until then?" Noah asked. "Will her present tendencies be able to withstand the danger? What of her brother? The newling band is led by an unknown. He has complete control over the newlings. They do any and everything that's asked of them." He shook his head. "I've searched and come up empty each time."

"I have a little insight on that now," Eli said, stepping forward. "Somehow, Valerian Arcos has a hand in this."

"A hand? We burned his *head*," Luc said. "How can he have anything to do with this?"

Eli glanced at everyone, then turned his attention to his father. "I spoke with their mother, who begged me not to kill Victorian. She said their DNA and Riley's are one. To kill Victorian could harm her."

"But Valerian is dead," Phin said. "We all had a hand in it."

Eli nodded. "Yes." He looked at me, then back to Gilles. "But not before he passed his DNA on to another."

Silence filled the room for several seconds. "He's been reborn in another," Gilles said, his voice stoic, deadly. "And to destroy either will possibly destroy Riley?"

Eli turned his gaze full-on to mine. "*Oui*. And I can't allow that to happen."

"Of course, darling," Elise said kindly. "We wouldn't even think of such."

My insides shook—literally, shook. Air squeaked through my windpipe, barely allowing enough oxygen in.

Eli's strong arms encircled me, holding me up.

"Only one ting to do, den," Preacher spoke up.

All eyes turned to the old Gullah.

"We gotta entomb dat boy. Dat Valerian. No mattah if he is inside anodder's body. We gotta find him. Curse him. And put him in da ground."

Gilles met Preacher's hard gaze. Then, he nodded. "You're right, old friend. Now 'tis the matter of finding him."

"Can you find the band of newlings?" Eli asked Noah.

Noah glanced at him. "Absolutely. Three times a week."

Phin cocked his head. "What are you talking about?"

Noah glanced at his group, then at Eli, then at Phin. "They gather at what used to be a church a couple of centuries ago. The bad part of the city grew around it, and it's been used as many things. Now? They conduct fights. Vampires against mortals. They're brutal." He glanced at Gilles. "They move around to different locations, but they've been at this one for a few weeks. It's how they're weeding out the weak mortals from the strong." Noah's gaze met mine. "It's why I have to know if Riley can handle herself."

Gilles gave a short nod, then glanced at Preacher.

He then began to speak in French. Preacher answered likewise.

Estelle shot me a look of worry.

This is when I knew things weren't looking all that sweet.

"Calm down, calm down," Luc said quietly as he leaned over. "They're simply discussing your abilities."

"Why am I not in the discussion, then?" I whispered. "Don't I have a say?"

"No," Eli answered. "Not at all."

I wasn't too surprised by his answer. "How's it looking?" I asked.

"Not too good," he replied.

Both Gilles and Preacher lifted their heads and glanced my way. Both studied, regarded, weighed. The longer they stared, the more I wanted to shout *What!* at the top of my lungs. Then, they put their heads together again. Discussed. Chatted. For several minutes. In French.

"You're in," Eli finally offered.

Gilles crossed the room to stand in the center. "Yes, Riley, you're in. But there are stipulations, of course," he said. "First, you will never be alone. Either Eli, Jean-Luc, Séraphin, or Noah will always be with you." He shot a glance at my brother. "Same with young Seth, and Zetty." Gilles' gaze lingered on Zetty. "You may be an intimidating mortal young man, but, after all, you are still a mortal. Even with your formidable tendencies, you can be destroyed."

Zetty nodded, silent.

"If there are any newlings or those in the quickening that can be spared, they must be gathered and brought to Da Island for rehabilitation. The fewer killings, the better. Understood?"

Multiple heads nodded.

The room tilted.

I blinked, shook my head, and blinked again. Gilles' voice became muffled, far away, until the words melded together, now meaningless. I staggered, leaned against Eli, and held my stomach as he whipped me around. As I stared up into his face, my eyes locked on his mouth; his lips moved frantically, speaking frantically and fast. No sound emerged. I understood nothing. Then, as if someone pulled a shade down in a bright room, shadows slipped over my lids, and I saw nothing but blackness.

I knew then *he* was about to kill again.

As the shadow slowly lifted, I blinked several times to clear my vision. The lights were dim—so dim I could still barely make out shapes. Music thumped hard all around me. I recognized it—"So What, I Lied" by Sick Puppies. People glanced my way, barely noticing me at all as they moved to the music. Lights flickered, flashed, and I continued through the thick throng of clubbers, to the bar near the back. I sat. I wasn't alone long.

"There you are," a girl said. She wore a short purple glittered minidress with a zipper pulled down the front, exposing a swell of pushed-up breasts. She wore tall spiked black heels, a lot of makeup, and had her bleached blond hair piled loosely atop her head. "Come on, baby. Let's dance."

Delicate hands tipped with red acrylic fingernails grasped my hand and pulled me back into the throng of dancing people. The hand she touched wasn't my hand; the ass she grabbed wasn't mine either. When I looked down, the hand holding her waist was large, big-knuckled, rough. We began to move; she seductively, brushing against me, her tongue darting out to lick her painted lips. Holding my gaze, she grasped the zipper and pulled lower, allowing more of her breasts to spill. She grinned, shimmied down my front, and slowly raised her body, dragging it against mine. All I could do was cringe in revulsion because, although the body wasn't mine, I felt his emotions. His cock was hard beneath the leather pants he wore. The girl's gaze lowered and she noticed, turned around, and pressed her ass close.

Hands not mine slipped around her rib cage, her hips, and pulled her against his hard cock. The girl squirmed and wiggled; then her head fell back and she laughed. She was wasted, her gaze hazy, dim. She looked up at me backward, her eyes squinted, concentrating, focused.

*   *   *

I lowered my head, said something in her ear, and no matter how hard I screamed, I was trapped, somewhere back at the Duprés', floating in some weird purgatory, and, helpless, all I could do was watch. Nothing I could do would change the situation. Smiling, laughing, the girl grabbed my hand and stumbled through the club. Then, everything began to slow; the noise in the club dulled to a low hum, a jumble of uttered words and muffled music that I didn't recognize or understand. She turned, smiling through her high, hazy and drug-induced, and although her lips moved, no words came out. She stumbled, laughed, but I heard nothing. As we pushed out into the night, no sounds greeted my ears, no smells infiltrated my senses, and although a streetlamp lit the path directly in front of the entrance, it dulled to darkness. I saw nothing; I heard nothing. The girl in front of me disappeared. Blackness engulfed me.

Like a burst of energy, a new sensation filled me; a craving I couldn't define, driven by lust and desire. In the darkness I groped hungrily for it, grew angry when I didn't find it, sighed and groaned when I finally did. My fingers sought and found skin; immediately I knew I had to have it. I pulled hard, wanting it now, wanting it fiercely, and when it resisted, my anger grew. I reached, found a solid chest, sank my fingers into rock shoulders and shoved, hard—and followed. With my hands I felt for lips, found them, and devoured them with my own, deepening the kiss, tasting with my tongue, my hand holding the body fast, hard; refusing escape. I grabbed a firm jaw and held it still as I continued to ravage with my mouth, a need so fierce building within me that I had to quench it. Quench it now. Quench it yester-freaking-day.

The body tried to leave; not happening! I reached,

grabbed, found a handful of thick . . . ropes? No, hair. Hair ropes? Whatever. I yanked hard, and the body emitted a low groan.

"Riley! Stop it!"

My eyes popped open, and as my foggy vision cleared, my consciousness regained. I don't know how long that took—several seconds. Maybe a full minute? Eventually it happened, though. Now, in the present, in the flesh, my faculties united, I stared around the room.

And then directly into the seductive, mercury eyes of Noah freaking Miles.

Eli stood, staring at me over Noah's shoulder, eyes flashing, brows furrowed.,

The scent of . . . something sharp caught my senses.

A few chuckles sounded in the room.

With a jerk, I let Noah's dreadlocks loose. *Dick*.

"Ow, babe," he said, holding his head and grinning. "Easy on the dreads."

"What . . . just happened?" I asked, fuming. Raising my fingers to my lips, I pressed against them. They felt numb. And they burned a little.

More chuckles sounded.

"Noah used his special powers and pulled you from that horrible vision you were in the middle of," Luc said, draping an arm over my shoulder and inclining his head in Noah's direction. "Eli tried first but was, surprisingly, unsuccessful. You should thank Noah for saving you."

I grabbed the silver hoop in Luc's lip and pulled. "Ow, ow, ow," he laughed/cried. I let go and elbowed him in the gut. I know it didn't hurt him, but he had the good grace to grunt and pretend anyway. He stood, grinning.

Then I turned to Gilles, then to Preacher. "Sorry for . . . whatever I just did." I knew what I just did. I'd almost fornicated with freaking Noah, right in the Duprés' freaking parlor, with everyone, including Eli, freaking watching—including Seth. I turned to him quickly. "Sorry you had to see that, Bro."

He exaggerated a shudder. "Scarred for life."

I shook my head and looked hard at Noah. He shrugged. I sought Eli's gaze. I mouthed, *I'm sorry*. With a quick snap, he punched Noah in the jaw. Then, satisfied, he gave me a surprise reaction. He grinned. Noah merely rubbed his jaw and smiled.

"What did you see, *ma chérie*?" Gilles asked, gracefully drawing the conversation to more important things.

Eli stood behind me again, his hand on my lower back. I rubbed my forehead, ran my hand to the back of my neck, and remembered. "When my vision cleared, I was in a club—I didn't recognize it. Packed with people, though, and the girl . . ." I stood in the center of the parlor, squeezing my eyes shut but seeing. "She was typical of his kills—young, midtwenties maybe, bleached blond hair, super short dress, super high heels, and super, super wasted." I shook my head. "She had no clue at all about who or what he was. She was leading him out of the club when"—I glanced at Noah and narrowed my eyes—"Noah rescued me."

Noah simply shrugged and smiled.

"Unfortunately, she has met her fate by now," Gilles said. He clasped his hands behind his back and glanced around the room. "There is nothing we can do from here. You leave collectively in the morning, unless some of you wish to go tonight."

Noah gave Gilles a short nod. "My group will head back tonight, but we thank you for the invitation."

"My cousin Garr, he will have somethin' for you dis

night, right?" Preacher said. "You know where to meet him? Pick it up, yeah?"

"We do," Noah said.

Preacher met his gaze. "Good, den. You take it and keep it wit you."

Noah nodded. "Thanks, Preach. We will."

Preacher turned to Eli. "Jack and Tuba, dey go wit you in da morning, dat's right. Dey stays wit Riley along wit da rest of you fellas. I don want her near dat fightin' by herself. Seth neider. Zetty goes, too."

Eli nodded. "Yes, sir."

With his hand to the back of his neck, Preacher looked at me. "Don you be actin' crazy, girl. Dat boy Eli, he'll be wit you. You got dese boys here, too, and Jack and Tuba. You don go actin' foolish."

"Yes, sir, I won't," I promised, and turned to Gilles. "Will it be okay here? With all of us gone?"

Gilles smiled and crossed the room, took my hands in his, and pressed his lips to my knuckles. I found it strange how it hardly even crossed my mind that a vampire's fangs slipped so close to my skin. "Young lady, I may be older, but I have a few good fights still in me, as does my Elise. We have your Preacher and his kin here, as well as their magic. We'll be more than fine."

I nodded. "Okay. I believe you," I said, smiling. "And I don't think you're old at all."

Gilles' eyes twinkled.

I suddenly remembered what he could turn into. Any doubts were immediately stricken from my mind.

"*Bon*," he said, with a slight nod. "I'm glad you see it my way."

I narrowed my gaze and gave him a mock frown. He chuckled.

"And now that Nyx knows of us," Gilles continued, "we'll take care of her and help with your business."

I again nodded. "Thank you."

Before we left, I hugged Preacher, then pulled a still-worried Estelle into a hug. "I'll be fine, Grandma," I said, crooning into her shoulder. "I have the best guardians in the world right beside me, dat's right."

Estelle's face, darker than usual in the dimmed parlor, gleamed perfect ebony. Her eyes widened, her teeth shined in a large, comforting smile. "I know dat, baby." She grasped my face between her aged hands. She gave a firm shake, squishing my cheeks. All at once I thought of how I would now outlive her by God only knew how many years. "You listen to dem Dupré boys and dat Josie, and dat odder one dere, Noah. Dey will keep you and your brodder safe. Come back to me, girl. I mean dat ting. You my baby."

I smiled, my cheeks squishing even more. "I will. Promise."

Estelle hugged Seth. "You, too, boy. Keep a good eye on your sister. She got dat hard head, yeah."

"Yes, ma'am," Seth said, and kissed her cheek. "I love you, Grandmodder."

"I love you, boy." She swatted his backside. "Now git on dere. You got work to do."

After good-byes, we all left.

The ride back to my place felt shorter than usual. "Eli—"

"No need to say a word, Riley," he said, then slipped his hand over my thigh. "Noah pulled you out. I couldn't." He smiled, his eyes dark orbs in the shadows. "Besides, I got mine in. We're cool."

He was referring to that pop he gave Noah on the

jaw. "Okay," I answered, and downshifted as we came to a light. I stopped the Jeep. "But—"

Eli leaned over and covered my mouth with his. I instantly melted into his kiss, and only the honk of the car's horn behind us pulled me back to the present. He smiled seductively. "Drive."

If the air hadn't cooled my skin, I would've had to fan myself.

Once back at Inksomnia, I glanced around my living room and marveled at how many vampires could fill a small historic building-turned-apartment. I was introduced to Noah's people—Saul, Tate, Cafrey, and Jenna—and they left for Charleston. I figured I'd get to know them all better once there. Also crammed into my apartment were Zetty, Jack, and Tuba, along with all the Duprés; .a lot of big guys taking up a lot of space.

On the way out, Noah stopped at the door, turned, and looked at me. "For the record," he said, his smile crooked, arrogant, his strange silver eyes twinkling. "You're a helluva kisser. Ever get tired of Dupré? . . ."

I shook my head. "Whatever. Get out. I'll see you tomorrow."

As I closed and locked the door, his laugh sounded in the merchant's drive.

Upstairs, I made plans with Eli, his siblings, Seth, and Zetty, and Jack and Tuba. We'd leave for Charleston at daybreak. We were staying in a house on the battery belonging to a friend of Eli's, although, according to Phin, we probably wouldn't see much of it.

Apparently, we'd be spending a lot of time running the streets.

I hoped we'd be gone only a few days. I wanted to

stop the monster and break up the newling band, and I wanted to do it yesterday.

"I gotta get a little sleep," I said, and said good night. Eli moved with me.

The others whistled. I ignored them.

I threw some stuff into two backpacks. One was for clothes and a few necessities; the other was for my sheaths and blades. Eli leaned against the wall, watching in silence. When I finished, he pulled me against him. "Slow down, *chérie*," he said. "You're shaking."

"I just want this to be over," I answered, and leaned against him. "I have to make a call."

I made a quick call to Nyx; she was, as I knew she'd be, totally cool with taking on the business until we wrapped things up in Charleston. She'd take Chaz home with her after work and keep him at her place. I assured her I'd be careful.

Zetty, Jack, and Tuba went next door to stay with Preacher and Estelle. Seth and Josie took Chaz out for a walk, and I showered. Exhaustion overcame me, and I hoped like hell I wouldn't have any more dreams or murderous visions. I was simply too tired. I showered, changed, and when I finished, Eli was waiting for me. I crossed the room, my towel loosely wrapped around my body, and when Eli pulled me to him, I went willingly. I forgot my exhaustion when Eli's touch seared me, awakening my desires. He tugged at the towel, and it dropped. His hands found my waist, moved up along my ribs, cupped my breasts, and kissed with silent passion. Shadows played across his face in the darkness of my room, and slowly, I undressed him. Taut muscles covered by silky flawless skin played beneath my palms, and when I traced the lines of his abdomen, he scooped me up and laid me against the pillows stacked on my bed. Without a word, without a sound, he made love to me, his eyes never leaving mine. When he entered me, I gasped, and he covered the sound with his mouth in an erotic kiss that sent me soaring. We moved together, exquisite friction, until the orgasm built with such ferocity, I lost my breath. Slowly, we both came down; his lips dragged across mine in a possessive, delicious brand. We settled in, slumber once again pulling at me, and with Eli wrapped around me, I drifted into a peaceful state. His fingers stroked the skin of my stomach, traced the dragons on my arms, the wings at my cheek. He murmured words in French; I had no idea what they were. I didn't care.

"I'll keep you safe, love," he said against my throat. "Sleep."

The urge to tell Eli how I felt about him overwhelmed me. But sleep came too fast. Soon, I thought. I'd tell him soon.

Once asleep, I did dream, but thankfully, it was just of something out of the blue and bizarre, with no meaning. At least, I thought it had no meaning. It was a dark and stormy night—literally—and for some reason I was lying on the ground, in tall, wet grass—a forest maybe? It was winter, the trees bare and stark, the forest bleak, the air cold, the moon huge and round, like a harvest moon. Thunder boomed, lightning flashed, and rain splattered down. Staring up at the spindly, leafless branches that weaved and stretched above me, I saw in the moonlight a single bird, crawling across the branch.

Crawling? Birds didn't crawl. How retarded. What did that even mean? I guess anything was better than watching a vampire rip into a victim's heart.

After that, I slept. And while I slept I must have done some serious soul-searching, a little dwelling on certain things that pissed me off, and nursed a lot of hatred toward whoever—whatever—was behind the Charleston kills. I slept all the way until my alarm went off at five a.m. When it did go off, I awoke refreshed, edgy, determined.

And ready to kick some dirty nasty vampire ass.

Part Seven

✦━◆━✦

BLOODLUST

"All the ways you wish you could be, that's me. I look the way you wanna look, I fuck the way you wanna fuck, I am smart, capable, and most importantly, I am free in all the ways you are not."

—Tyler Durden, *Fight Club*

"The word *monster* means something a little different for everyone, I guess, but let me tell ya—to me, it defines every vile, fanatic, horrific dark evil you could possibly ever conjure up. It's the thing that wracks your body with unstoppable quivers, terrors so mind-numbing you pee your pants just thinking about it. That's him—the monster whose feeds I've been witnessing. I haven't peed my pants yet, but I damn sure almost did. Never has something petrified me so badly. I'm now not only hesitant to fall asleep, but to not fall asleep, because that bastard shows up at any given time, day or night. It's dragged bad memories of my past out of the dusty recesses of my once-juvenile mind and pushed them to the surface. I'm seeing my mother's death all over again; feeling her lifeless body limp in my arms, her wide dull stare fixed but not seeing. I'm scared I'm losing my friggin' mind, and to top it off, I'm faced with fighting a fuck-load of newlings in some sadistic fight club. Bullshit, man. Simply put, bullshit."

—Riley Poe

The TV was on in the living room; I knew the Duprés were just chillin' while the mortals rested. I rose, worked out on the bag for thirty minutes, showered, and dressed. As I stood in my bra and panties, I adjusted my blade straps; one on each upper thigh, inner and outer; one on each calf, inner and outer; one at my lower back, one on each hip. I stared at myself in the full-length mirror, satisfied that the lightweight sheaths Preacher had had made for me out of moleskin were adjusted just right, the weight of the blades perfect, easily retractable. Turning halfway, I stared at the reflection of my back; the dragon tattooed up my spine, down my arms, the black angel wing at the corner of my eye, and me, standing in black bra and a black thong with eleven pure silver knives strapped to various body parts. I had fifty more in my bag.

I confess, I looked badass—Marvel badass.

I prayed I could be Marvel badass when faced with a dozen vampires.

"You can," Eli said, studying me from the doorway through my mirrored reflection. "And you're definitely Marvel badass."

I grinned. "Thanks." Seeing him there shot a thrill through my insides.

Eli smiled wider. Sexy as hell, that one.

I pulled on a pair of loose knees-blown-out boyfriend jeans that sat low on my hips, a black tank, and a lightweight black Adidas jacket. No need for a trip to Mullet's this go-round. I was dressed for comfort, movement, jumping, stabbing, throwing. Pulling my hair into a ponytail, my feet into my worn black Vans, I grabbed my bags and we left the room.

Zetty, Jack, and Tuba seemed to be waiting for me to appear around the corner; they were already staring at me as I entered the living room. All gave a nod.

"Hey guys," I offered, then found Seth, seated on the floor with Josie playing Burnout 3 on Xbox 360. Phin and Luc were at the kitchen table, both with their special

V8', and Luc inclined his head for me to join. I walked over and set my bags on the floor.

"We ready or what?" I asked. Chaz walked over, nuzzled my hand, and I scrubbed the fur on his noggin. He'd been fed, watered, and walked, but the old guy just needed a little reassurance. Moving to the fridge, I opened it, pushed past the Duprés' bag-o-meals, grabbed the OJ, and swigged from the carton. Sweet juice and pulp filled my mouth and slid down my throat.

"How're the sheaths Preach made for your blades?" Phin asked.

I nodded. "Feels great. I barely even know they're there." I took another swig of juice. I knew Zetty carried silver; was pretty sure Jack and Tuba did, too, amongst other Gullah stuffs.

"Yeah, mine, too," said Seth, never even glancing away from his game.

"Good," Phin said. "Jack brought his truck. Tuba will ride with him. Josie and Seth can ride with me. We'll split the bikes and gear between the two trucks. Luc and Zetty can ride with you and Eli," he said to me. I nodded.

"We'll drive straight there and set up," Eli said. "Then a quick tour of the city." He regarded me. "Maybe not so quick. How long has it been since you were in Charleston?"

I thought. "A while. Maybe last June? Even then, I didn't know my way around town, except how to get to the battery, and city market."

Eli regarded me. "You'll know it well by tonight."

"Yes, I guess I will," I said. I squatted down to say good-bye to Chaz, holding his fuzzy face between my hands. "I promise you some quality time when I get home. In the meanwhile, you be good for Nyx. Go take a nap; she'll be here before you wake up," I said to the dog, and allowed his big, slobbery lick across my cheek. I kissed his muzzle, scrubbed him between the ears, and stood. I grabbed my bags and said, "Let's go." Eli quickly relieved me of them. "I got these," he said. Even when going to fight vamps, he was a gentleman.

We hit the lights and left. Outside, a thick, muggy fog hung over the city and wrapped around us. I had the top off the Jeep; I preferred it that way. Within fifteen minutes we had both Phin's and Luc's bikes and gear loaded and were pulling out onto Bay Street. Phin led the way in his black Ford F-150, both bikes strapped in the bed, followed by Jack in his wicked-restored blue '59 Chevrolet, and trailed by me.

"Nice creepy morning, huh?" Luc said from behind me as we sat at the red light. "Reminds me of the old days, before electricity. Nothing but gas lamps throughout the city." He looked at me in the rearview mirror. "You could hear them hissing as you passed by. Remember that, Eli? Ahh, the clop-clop of the horse's hooves on the cobbles, the hissing gas lights." He leaned his head on the seat rest and sighed. He turned and looked at me. "Not that I'd give up cell phones and hot water for it."

I grinned. "Don't blame ya."

Zetty remained silent.

"The hissing gas lights were pretty cool," Eli offered.

The light changed, I eased off the clutch, built up speed, and shifted into second gear. It wasn't light out yet, and a filmy haze hung over the city. I felt irritable, anxious, and edgy. I wanted this to be over. I missed . . . normalcy. And it was time for my period.

*   *   *

"Oh," Luc said, nodding, apparently reading my thoughts. "Gotcha."

I shot him a glare. "Put your seat belt on." I shot Zetty a similar one. "You, too." A final one I shot at Eli, who'd already started to pull his on. "That's better." He merely grinned.

I glared at Luc in the rearview mirror. In the early-morning light, his skin nearly blended with the fog. He smiled and did as I asked. "Sure thing, babe." Zetty also complied, but silently. I learned that most of the time the Tibetan didn't have a whole lot to say.

Once we pulled out onto Interstate 16, I flipped the stereo on, shoved in a Drowning Pool CD, and cranked the volume to rise over the wind. "More Than Worthless" rocked us all the way to the Interstate 95 exit where we headed north. More than once I glanced at Eli, who silently returned my look. His hand rested on my thigh. We didn't talk. Luc was pretending to be asleep; I suppose he was simply enjoying the ride. His crazy long hair blew all over the place, a content, peaceful look settling into his flawless features. And as the morning light grew stronger, it winked off the silver hoop in his lip.

"Flawless, huh?" he hollered over the wind. "Thanks, babe."

"Stay out of my noggin," I yelled back. He smiled. We continued on.

Ten miles later, my fuel light flashed. "Wanna call Phin and Jack? I need gas," I said. Luc pulled his cell from the pocket of his baggy cargo shorts and called his brother. At the next exit, I pulled into a Sunoco and stopped at one of the empty pumps. Phin, Jack, and Tuba pulled in and parked near the exit. Eli unbuckled his belt to get out. "I got it," I said, and waved him down.

"Won't take but a sec." Eli stared at me for a moment, then gave a nod, and I slid from my seat. Only then did I notice the debit card feature wasn't working. "Please see manager inside" was written on little white pieces of paper, on all the pumps. "Damn," I muttered, tempted to drive off and choose another gas station. Instead, I started across the parking lot. One pickup truck and a semitruck, parked in the back, were the only other vehicles around. I pushed inside and walked up to the counter where a middle-aged woman, rail-thin with hard life written all over her, gave me a nod.

"Mornin'," she said in a smoker's raspy voice. Her gaze went to my dragon-inked arms.

I handed her my debit card. "Forty on number three," I said, then thought better of it. "Wait." My ravenous appetite kicked in, and I suddenly wanted junk. Turning up the candy aisle, I grabbed a handful of Chick-O-Sticks, a bag of salt and vinegar chips, and a package of those cupcakes with waxy icing on top and gooey white cream in the middle. While debating on a pouch of spicy roasted peanuts, I felt a presence behind me. I glanced; a pair of big, dirty knobby-toed boots stood close. Too close.

It happened all too fast.

"Drop the shit and get up. Nice and slow," the voice belonging to the nasty boots said. His hand grasped my ponytail and pulled, slowly but firmly. "And don't cause a scene. I know you got boys outside."

I momentarily closed my eyes. "Are you freaking kidding me?" I said under my breath. I left my junk food in a pile on the floor and slowly rose. "Dude, you really don't want—"

"Shut up," the voice commanded. "To the back of the store. Exit door by the head. Do it now, bitch." I felt the cold press of steel against my ribs through my shirt. "I'll stick you if you make a sound."

Even before I'd been introduced to my new tendencies, or to the vampiric world, humans hadn't scared me. This guy, with his knife that he'd stick me with, damn sure didn't scare me. He was a loser punk who hung out at gas stations robbing people on the interstate. He was the very least of my problems. But something wasn't right. It wasn't three o'clock in the morning. It wasn't the middle of the night. It was like when you noticed a nocturnal animal, like a raccoon, out in the middle of the day, you knew something was wrong. That raccoon had to be sick. This guy had to be sick. Not wanting to cause the cashier any stress, I did as he asked; I'd take care of him out back, get my junk food, gas, and leave.

I eased out the exit door, and a second later, the idiot followed.

Before the door closed, I swung my leg high and around, knocked the knife from his hand, and shoved him hard against the concrete wall. It was the first look I'd had at him, other than his booted feet. My height, stocky, and appearing to be late twenties, he wore an Atlanta Braves baseball cap pulled down over a burred head of sandy hair. He wore shades.

Just that fast, he turned and knocked me to the ground. I managed to sweep him with my leg before I hit. I landed on my backside. He landed on his backside. His shades fell off. Opaque eyes stared hard and angry back at me.

Well damn. Didn't see that one coming. Frickin' frackin' newling at the Sunoco. Go figure. He must've gotten loose from whatever changed him. Great. Free-roaming newlings.

I leapt up just as he lunged; we met head-on. He was wild, uncontrolled, unaware of his powers. I was not. Just as his fangs dropped, I reached for the blade sheathed at my back. The silver flashed in the early-morning light, and the newling's eyes widened. A nasty snarl curled his inhuman lips.

"You're her," he murmured, and shoved me.

Just then Eli appeared, Luc and Zetty right behind him.

The newling's eyes grazed both, then back to me. "Later," he said, his voice not matching the newling face. With a fierce shove, he flung me against the wall. By the time I scrambled up, he was across the parking lot and disappearing into the dense copse of tall planted pines behind the Sunoco.

Grasping my knees, I breathed hard, catching my breath. First, I kept my eyes trained at the tree line. Then, the silence drew my attention to my parking lot companions.

Luc stood, frowning. Zetty stood, frowning more.

Eli took off after the newling.

"What the freak is wrong with you, Riley?" Luc said. He shoved his fingers through his hair, staring hard at me. "Do you honestly think you can handle everything by yourself?"

I rose and met his gaze. "Sure. Why not?"

Luc continued to stare for several seconds, as though trying to see something, then blinked. "Unbelievable."

I jammed the blade back in its sheath. "What?" I asked.

Luc shook his head. "Never thought I'd see a head harder than Eli's. Do you have a problem asking anyone for help, or just from me? Or Eli?"

I shrugged. "I had him, Luc. If I'd needed help, I would have definitely asked." I scratched my jaw. "He said, 'You're her.' What's that supposed to mean? And why was he out here in the early morning, alone? Don't newlings usually run in groups? At least, for a while?"

"Usually," Luc said, and led the way into the store. "But we're dealing with Romanian magic—or so Ned says, and I tend to believe him. There's no telling what we're up against anymore." He rounded on me as we stopped at the pile of junk food sitting on the floor where I left it. "Which is why you freaking need to call for help"—he tapped my temple—"when something's going down. Got it? Or do you really want to see Eli kick my ass?"

I glanced at Zetty, whose dark gaze remained fixed on mine. He merely shrugged.

A cynical laugh slipped from my throat. "Whatever, Dupré." I bent down and gathered my junk food, then headed to the cooler. "I gotta tell ya—I'm pretty sick of hearing how Eli's going to kick everyone's asses for me getting into trouble." I flung open the cooler, grabbed a Yoo-hoo, and let the door slam shut. "Where is he, anyway? It's been too long."

Eli walked through the front door. He shook his head. "He's fast. Got away."

Luc and Zetty followed me up to the front. The cashier, who'd stepped out the front to smoke, was just making her way back behind the counter. I set my junk food on the counter. "You can add this stuff to the gas," I said. She rang it up, looking at me uncertainly the whole time.

"Receipt?" she asked.

"No, thanks, "I responded, scooped up my stuff, and left.

My cell vibrated. I dumped my junk food in my driver's seat and grasped the phone from my back pocket. I glanced at the screen and rolled my eyes when I saw Phin's name. I answered. "Hey." Eli glared at me.

"The next time you pull something like that, Riley I will personally kick your ass," Phin said.

I hung the phone up and flashed him the bird.

I was really, really getting tired of all the ass-kicking threats.

Already, I was getting irritated, and it wasn't even eight o'clock in the morning yet. I opened my gas cap, lifted the fuel nozzle, and jammed it in. "Aren't we going to go after him?" I asked about the newling. "He's pretty close to Savannah."

"No," Eli said, leaning against the Jeep's fender. "I told Papa. He and my mother will take care of it. Just like I will take care of you."

I eyed Luc in the rearview; his grin spoke volumes. Finished pumping, I stuck the nozzle back in the pump, screwed the gas cap back on, and looked at all three of my Jeep occupants. "Let's get out of here."

I'd already had enough newling excitement for one morning.

Twenty-seven miles later we merged onto US 17 North. I'd shucked out of my jacket, and cars filed down both lanes. Palm trees and live oaks dripping with Spanish moss gathered along the highway, along with the occasional Gullah woman, sitting out beneath a pitched half tent, or a beach umbrella, in a plastic and metal lawn chair with a quilt spread on the ground and dozens of sweetgrass baskets for sale. Small country stores advertising homemade peach preserves and boiled peanuts, along with fruit stands, gathered at the edge of the highway. In between those fruit stands were pieces of plywood nailed to trees: PEACHES, WATERMELONS, PECANS, FIVE MILES. It was all unique, very South Carolina. Very Charleston.

"You like it here," Eli said, peering at me behind a pair of aviators.

I regarded him behind my own pair of shades and smiled. "I remember my mom taking Seth and me here, to Folly Beach, when we were very young," I said. "We'd stay at the Holiday Inn, and Seth and I would hang out at the ice machine, eating it by the handfuls. Nice memories."

"They're good to have," he answered. "Hold on to them."

It was the best piece of advice I'd been given in a while.

By the time we drove the sixty-plus miles to Charleston, the sun drove harshly into the open top of my Jeep. Overhead, white fluffy clouds drifted in a sky of pure blue, and the breeze that whipped at my face and my ponytail, felt warm, at times smoldering—typical dog days of summer. One would never think such ease and beauty would lead to immortal monsters jabbing their fangs into the hearts of humans, or crazy vampire cult fight clubs taking place while the city slept. Or worse— newlings hanging out at the Sunoco, waiting for victims. Fucked up, I tell ya.

More palms and mossy oaks stood along old neighborhood streets as we hit the historic district. Spearing the sky was the tall, spindly spire of St. Michael's, and farther along Church Street, the well-known and aged French Huguenot Church. I downshifted with the slower traffic along Market Street, glancing over at the Gullah women and their wares in the city market. Sweetgrass baskets of all shapes and sizes and strip quilts covered the market stands, filled with goods varying from fruit preserves to handmade jewelry. We didn't stop; instead, we continued toward the harbor, following Phin, east of the Ashley River and all the way to South Battery. We pulled in behind the two trucks Phin and Jack were driving. We were parked on the driveway of a large, white, three-story historic home. It looked like something out of *Southern Living* magazine. I'm talking full-front verandas, large-paddled ceiling fans, white rocking chairs, and dozens of huge green Boston ferns, and flanked by tall palms, crepe myrtle trees, and aged magnolias with large, waxy green leaves. It sat in the famous line of battery houses overlooking Charleston Harbor. We pulled around back and parked in the shade. I threw the Jeep into neutral and yanked the emergency brake.

I looked at the battery mansion before us. "Whose place is this?"

Eli looked at me over his shades. "Belongs to Jake Andorra, but he won't be here. It'll just be us."

"So where's Jake Andorra if he's not here?" I asked, unfastening my seat belt and sliding out the Jeep's door.

Luc grinned and answered. "London."

"And . . . how long has Jake Andorra been dead?" I continued.

"About four hundred and sixty years," Eli said with a laugh. "Good thing he's not here."

"Why?" I asked, pushing my shades up into my hair.

Eli stared at me for a moment, his grin widening. "He'd like you too much."

I shook my head. Eli grabbed my bags and his from the backseat and rounded the Jeep; Luc did the same, as did the ever-silent Zetty. We walked toward the others. I glanced at Luc. "And does he drink V8' like the Duprés, or—"

"Don't ask," Luc replied. I couldn't tell by his expression what that meant exactly, so I dropped it.

Phin, Josie, and Seth, loaded down with backpacks, and Jack and Tuba, loaded down with . . . something, turned to us as we walked up.

"We'll get our gear inside. Zetty, Jack, Tuba, and Josie will make the place safe while you and Seth learn the city," Phin said. He stared at me. "Ready?"

"Have been," I answered.

"Me, too," Seth answered. He glanced at me and smiled. I can't say I was happy at all to have my baby brother facing fight club vamps, not to mention be in the same city as the monster in my visions. All I can say is that his tendencies were smack-daddy kick-ass, and to have him backing me up made me feel a helluva lot better.

With a nod, Phin led the way into Jake Andorra's mansion.

Inside, everything was spotless. Yet empty. Vaulted ceilings and an open plan made it look even emptier. Just at first glance, as Seth and I walked through to the second level, I noticed no photographs; very little home décor—a vase here, a plant there, probably fake—and everything squeaky clean. Yet empty. It was a fully stocked home with no personal touches. Upstairs, the rooms were massive. Phin led us past a mammoth library that I barely glimpsed. Then, into my room; our room, rather—mine and Eli's.

"Home sweet home, Riley," he said, then inclined his head to Seth. "Come on. Yours is across and down the hall." Seth grinned and wagged his brows at me, adjusted both packs on his shoulders, and followed Phin out.

Any woman would just melt in a house like this. I glanced around, only slightly miffed that this was no vacay but instead, a vamp hunt. But day-yum, it should be. In another life, maybe. The room held an enormous king bed piled high with pillows and topped with a down comforter, fireplace, ceiling fan, and various pieces of antique furniture. A wicker love seat sat close to the white-painted French doors leading to the veranda outside the room. I dumped my stuff on the floor next to the bed. I wasn't an indulger, but I couldn't help opening the door and taking a step out. The air smelled like home, heavy and tinged with brine. I breathed it in and took in the view. Charleston Harbor was just across the way, and, in the distance, boats dotted the water. Nice. It was . . . nice. With a deep inhalation and slow exhalation, I resigned myself to doing what I did, being who I was.

"You like it?" Eli asked.

I nodded. "Definitely."

"Ready, guys?" Seth asked from the door.

"Yeah, Bro," I said. "We're ready."

After a quick trip to the bathroom, we headed downstairs and rounded the corner just in time to see Luc lift a small vial to his mouth. I sidled up next to him. "What's that stuff?"

Luc grinned. "Preacher gave it to us. It masks our origins to other vampires and allows us to slip into their zone without being detected." He slurped the last drop and set the vial on the counter. "Lasts for about three days," he said. He handed Eli a vial.

"You have more, right?" I asked. Three days wasn't a long time.

Phin walked up, Luc tossed him a vial, and he and Eli downed theirs in one sip. "Yes, we have more. Preacher gave us a decent supply." He wiped his mouth and set his vial next to Luc's. "And this is our second vial. Took the first one a few days ago. You two ready to learn the city?" He glanced at Seth and me.

I looked at my brother, who seemed overly eager. "Yep," I answered, and we headed outside.

"I'm sitting this one out," Eli said. "I have some things to get in order with Noah." He kissed me, and the others made goofy noises. "See ya in a bit."

"Okay," I answered, and gave him a saucy smile.

Jack and Tuba had unloaded the bikes. I rode with Luc; Seth with Phin. Before Seth slung a leg over Phin's bike seat, I stopped him with a quick pat-down. Seth's green gaze, slightly humored, met mine.

"Yeah, I got my silver, Sis. Don't worry so much," he said, then kissed my nose, pushed my glasses down and in front of my eyes, and slid his shades on. Phin handed him a half helmet, despite the no-helmet law of South Carolina, and Seth snugged it in place.

My brother looked and acted way older than fifteen these days.

"Just checking," I answered, then threw my leg over Luc's bike seat. He turned, handed me my half helmet, and grinned. "Law or not, I'm not taking any chances with yours or your brother's noggins." He looked at me over his shades. "Ready?"

I pulled my helmet on. "Been."

With a laugh, Luc jumped and kick-started the bike; Phin did the same, and we pulled down the driveway, past two tall palms, and onto the street.

For several hours after, we rode every street and alley

of historic Charleston; from Market Street, to Church Street, past the white exterior of the French Huguenot Church, the unique salmon-colored Unitarian Church in Charleston with its square-topped steeple, up to Marion Square, and then down again. We learned King Street, Queen Street, Meeting Street, the open market, the historic district. The church district lent tall spires that stabbed the sky, and the French district had cafés and shops. That was all pretty easy to get the hang of. It reminded me a lot of Savannah, although we had more squares. Still, it was pretty easy to get, and simple to get the feel for. For a couple more hours, we rode; no alley, no side street next to a tourist shop, no restaurant, went unsearched. Late afternoon approached fast.

Then we rode out a ways, to the industrial part of the city, where the scenery wasn't so picturesque. Compared to the clean-lined historic district, with its palms and white buildings and pristine parks, this part of the city had an underground, postapocalyptic feel to it. These streets and barred-windowed businesses were purposely kept out of the travel mags and tourist brochures. Everything looked . . . dirtier. Rather, forgotten. We pulled up to what appeared to be an old brick warehouse. In faded red letters against a gray metal sign, the words MALLORY'S FISH MARKET stretched in an arch. The moment Luc killed the motor, a single door opened and Noah Miles stepped out.

He looked dead at me.

"Know the city now, do you?" he asked.

"Yeah," I said, and glanced around. "Where's Eli?" I asked.

"He left about an hour ago. Had to go make arrangements with Garr, Preacher's cousin."

Luc braced the weight of the bike with his legs, and I stayed on the bike. "So where's the fight club?"

Noah rubbed his jaw and grinned. "Not anxious, are you? Already packin' silver?"

"I'm ready to get this over with," I answered. And dammit, I was.

He nodded, and the others we'd met at the Dupré House the night before filed out and stood behind Noah. Street tough and ready to fight as they were, one would have a hard time believing they were actually vampires. Jenna, no more than nineteen, was of medium build and had long blond dreads she wore pulled back, similar to Noah's. Saul was Asian, early twenties, and had zero readable expression on his face. Cafrey and Tate, I'd learned, were brothers from Arkansas, both with buzzed hair with a sturdy, kick-ass build.

"So," Noah said, "screw the pleasantries, yeah? Welcome to Charles Town. Now, before we get dirty, which only happens after the sun dips, there's someone we gotta see."

Getting dirty meant free running, which I'd later discover, Noah and his guys were totally sick at. But we had a few hours of daylight left, and apparently, someone wanted to see us. "Who?" I asked. "And why?"

"Garr," Noah said. "He's waiting for us just a ways out of town." He grinned at me. "Eli's there, too. And not only do you mortals need to eat, but he wants to see da crazy painted white girl Preacher man been talkin' bout, dat's right."

"Well," I said, unable to stop the grin from tipping my mouth upward. Noah sort of had that effect on people—on me. He had that cocky, quick-witted, smart-ass attitude that, I don't know, I thought was pretty funny, I guess. I met his gaze. "I'm starved, so let's go meet him."

I gave my brother a glance; he grinned. Then, Noah and the others disappeared back into the building. Minutes later, one of the garage doors lifted and Noah backed out in a kick-ass blue restored muscle car. I had no idea what it was, but I had to say it was totally Noah.

"It's a 'sixty-nine Camaro Z28 RS with hooker headers, four-speed mucie, 373 psi, and four-wheel disc brakes," Luc offered. He turned and looked at me, the sun glinting off his silver hoop. "In original Leman's blue with a black leather interior. Saved it from the junkyard and restored it himself. Pretty sick, huh?"

Noah pulled the car alongside Luc's bike and gave me a smile any other woman would have fainted dead over.

I merely shook my head and grinned.

"Boys and their toys," I said. "Dead, undead—you're all the same."

Noah flashed his white teeth. "Follow me." He pulled out, his exhaust rumbling, and we fell in behind him.

Heading north on Highway 17, we eased out of Charleston following Noah. Approximately twenty-eight miles later, we hit the small town of Awendaw and turned east toward the river. I held on to Luc as we turned down a narrow gravel lane that led back into the wood. The sun was beginning to drop lower in the sky, and shadows fell long and jagged from aged live oaks across the palm fronds and sweetgrass hugging either side of the lane. I knew we grew closer to the river; the pungent smell of sea life clung to the humid air like fog. Up ahead, Noah's taillights lit up as he pulled in front of a small, older river house; painted green several years before, it had a screened-in porch and a single yard lamp. Luc pulled next to the Camaro and killed the engine. I swung my leg over and off the bike.

"Come on," Noah said, grinning, suddenly at my side and grasping my elbow. A deep, singsong voice that sounded strikingly familiar broke through the night air.

"Awe, now, dere she is, den," a tall, wiry black man said from the top step of the screened-in porch. "You come on over here, Riley Poe, and bring your brodder; dat's right. Let me take a look at you two."

I threw one more glance at Luc, whose back was to me as he spoke, and for a second I thought to crank up my strigoi hearing and eavesdrop. I didn't get the chance. Garr, Preacher's cousin, stopped me. No—I mean literally. He stopped me—with a lot more strength than an old man should have had. I stared at him.

Garr flashed me a gap-toothed smile.

Then, it hit me. He had tendencies.

A little something Preacher had left out.

As Garr led me up the steps into his river cabin, Noah, Phin, and Seth on my heels, he let out a deep, amused chuckle.

"Well, baby," he said, and we stepped into the cabin. "We got some catchin' up to do, me and you." All of six feet five inches, he looked down at me. The ceiling fan whirring in the living room seemed about to take his head off. "Now, we ain't stoppin' in here, no, sir." He inclined his head, adorned with a faded Awendaw Blue Crabs cap, perched slightly crookedly. "Straight out da back door, to da pavilion. Your Eli is waitin' for you out dere." He narrowed his eyes at me. "You like crabs, don you, girl?"

I smiled. "Yes, sir. I do."

"Good, den. Let's get out dere before dey all get eaten."

Garr left no chance for me to discuss anything with Noah or Phin. He continued to pull me through the little river house, straight out the back door, and down a long wooden dock over the marsh. A slight breeze kicked up and blew briny air across my cheeks, and the rustle of saw grass blades scraping against one another nearly soothed me.

Nearly, but not quite.

Once at the end, three other Gullah standing by Eli raised their heads and grinned. Two were older, maybe in their late fifties, and one was younger, midtwenties. The barefoot younger guy, bare-chested and wearing cut-offs to his knees, was dumping a basket of live crabs into a large pot of boiling water. Metal crab baskets lined the dock, and two long metal, green-netted scoop nets rested against a lawn chair in the middle. Two large coolers sat beside them. The boy nodded, keeping his gaze trained on me. Eli walked toward us.

"Come on in here, girl," Garr said, and led us into the screened-in boathouse. A long, well-used wooden table and benches took the length of the small house; covered in newspaper, a large pile of boiled crabs, red from cooking, sat heaped in the center.

"Sit," he said, and crossed in front of me to sit on the other side. "Eat." Old gnarled hands picked up a crab, pulled off the claw, and pulled the pincers apart. He sucked the juice from the claw, then cracked into the meat with a tiny hammer.

Eli stepped inside and found a seat beside me. Seth slid in next to me, on the other side; Noah and Phin crossed over and sat on the other side, next to Garr. A few minutes later, Luc wandered in and sat next to Seth. We all ate. The young Gullah brought in plastic cups and a cold gallon milk jug filled with sweet tea, then poured our glasses and left.

"You see, girl," Garr started, in between bites of white claw meat, "Charles Town in a bad way, dat's right. Just like Savannah. Maybe worse," he said. "Dat Preacher, he told me what happened over dere, with da hell stone." He shook his head. "Dat's bad stuff, dem Arcoses. But dem Duprés, dey handled it good, wit your help." He glanced at Seth. "You all right, boy?"

Seth nodded. "Yes, sir."

Garr nodded. "Well, we glad to have your help here in Charles Town. Been a long time since we had much trouble here, dat's right, Noah?"

Noah gave me a quick glance. "Yes, sir."

Garr leaned forward, crab meat sticking to his fingers. "Well, we got it now, doh. Dem Arcoses, dey turned some, dey left some wit tendencies, dey killed some. No tellin' how many runnin' round now, doh."

"Preacher says we have to entomb them again," Eli offered. "Maybe just one of them."

Garr nodded. "Probly so." Eli had already explained to Garr Victorian's explanation, and about me. The whole while, Garr said nothing more. But he watched me with ancient, wise eyes.

We finished eating; I don't think I'd ever eaten so many crabs at once. They were good, with just the right amount of seasoning. Some of it I recognized as normal, regular, everyday spicy crab boil seasoning; some I did not.

"To keep up your strength," Noah said, staring at me from across the table. He wagged his brows.

By the time we finished, the sun had nearly set; the gloaming, Noah had called it, with no sun, no moon, and the eerie glow of afterlight. Usually, the gloaming was filled with bugs and birds and frogs, calling, mating, singing—not so much anymore. Funny how nature knew what was going on, but humans didn't.

We left the dock, and the afterlight, behind.

Inside Garr's river house, he pulled something from the pocket of his white T-shirt and stopped us one more time. He handed a vial each to Seth and me. "Drink up, Brodder and Sister," he said. "Dis will let dem newlin's tink you mortal all de way. Might help for a spell, dat's right."

Neither Seth nor I hesitated; we unscrewed the small little lid and turned the bottle upright. We drained every drop. It tasted a mixture of sweet and tang, but with no aftertaste. We handed the vials back to Garr.

"Dere now. You go and take care of stuff. I'm here if you need me," he said.

"Thank you," I returned, and before I could go, he grasped both of my hands. With aged fingers he trailed the dragons on my arms, scraping the wings at my cheek.

"You mind dem Duprés, girl," he said. "And dis Noah, too. Dey keep you and your brodder safe, and Preachers boys and dat odder big dark fella." He narrowed his eyes. "Don be a hardhead, girl. You can't take dem all on by yourself."

"Yes, sir," I answered, and could only wonder what sort of conversations he and Preacher' had had about me.

Garr grinned. "Wasn't no Preacher, girl. Was Eli Dupré. Now git."

I could do nothing more than stare.

Garr laughed and shooed us out of his little old green river house. Eli grasped my arm and pulled me close.

As we crossed the yard, the lamplight cast an amber half circle around the house. Beyond the circle, fire-flies blinked in the night. It felt surreal here, on the Awendaw; almost disjointed from the hell in Charleston. I knew better, though, and by the time we left and headed south on US 17, complete darkness had fallen. This time, I rode back with Eli on his bike.

Just as we hit the city limits, I felt Eli's hand grasp mine, wrapped around his waist, and squeeze. He said nothing. He didn't have to, and I wasn't going to ask.

No sooner had Eli stopped the bike than Victorian's voice fill my head.

Please, Riley—you don't have to do this. It is a fight you will never win, love. Don't you see? There're too many of them, and I cannot stand the thought of your putting yourself in danger. I'm begging you—leave now. Please? And yes—you can answer me in your head. Another strigoi quality. Just think to me. . . .

"*What is it that you can't stand the thought of? My killing your kind? I'm in constant danger, Victorian. Whether I'm in the fight or not. You know me by now—I will not sit idly by and watch others die. Maybe you can live with that, but I can't,*" I thought.

"*Ah, see? Just that easy. You'll find more abilities as time goes by. And this—it's one of the many qualities I adore about you, Riley. I so wish I could just take you away. You and I, completely alone somewhere, far away from the melee you're about to subject yourself to. I dream of nothing, day and night, but you; the smell of your skin, the taste of your lips, the feel of your hands on me. It's . . . almost painful.*"

"I'm not getting into that with you right now, Victorian. You know where my heart lies," I thought to myself.

"I know where you think your heart lies. I aim to prove otherwise. For now, love, I beg you; listen to those around you. Let them keep you safe. My existence would be no longer if you perish."

"I can't make promises, other than I will be careful. Now, go away. You're distracting me."

Ah, a promising gesture indeed. Distraction. I have more hope now than before. I shall see you soon, love. Stay safe.

"Ri, what's wrong?"

I blinked, and just that fast, the conversation was over. I focused on Eli's face. I could tell he couldn't hear my conversation with Victorian. "I just carried on a conversation with Victorian. In my head," I said, closing my eyes briefly. I looked at him. Eli's eyes were harder than usual, but he said nothing. "He says it's my strigoi blood that gives me the ability, and no," I said, meeting his angry gaze, "I don't want it. But I'm stuck with it. And he was begging me not to fight." I wasn't lying—Victorian was a distraction. Eli was a distraction. Anything right now was a distraction. I had to get my mind in the game and erase all other distractions from my thoughts. It was bad enough my little brother ran beside me in all this; I had to do things right the first time and get this shit over with.

"Thank you for telling me," Eli said. "No more secrets, Riley."

My stomach turned. "No more secrets."

"We ready to get dirty?" Noah said, walking from the garage and standing before me in the beam of street light.

I glanced at Luc, who rolled up and pushed his bike in next to the Camaro.

"Yep," I said. "Let's go." Noah's guys appeared from the building; Zetty with them. Phin, Luc, Seth, Eli, and I gathered.

"This way," Noah said, and took off running. His team followed.

"Ladies first," Luc said, but Eli grabbed my arm when I started off. "Riley," he said. "Be careful. I mean it."

"I always am," I said, and hoped he could detect the sincerity in my gaze. He gave a short nod—meaning he understood—and we took off after the group.

Jenna, in her baggy jeans, T-back, and black high-tops, could just about outrun Noah. We moved through the city's industrial section on foot, bounding off rooftops, treetops, cars and awnings; there wasn't a flat surface we couldn't use. Zetty, whom I hadn't done any free-running with, surprised the hell out of me. That big guy could haul ass and jump just as high as Phin. He wasn't quite as nimble, maybe, and obviously not as experienced; Phin had been doing it a lot longer. Still, he was impressive.

The brine of the city, mixed with the dirt and trash and urine of downtown industrial Charleston, hung thick in the air, trapped in the same fog of humidity as Savannah. Dark clouds had formed, just before dark, and a slight rumble sounded in the darkened distance. Every once in a while, heat lightning would flash across the sky.

It brought back heated memories of Eli and me on the barrier island, not too long ago, and he must have remembered, too, because our gazes met frequently and there was always something there, heated, between us. It thrilled me and urged me on.

As we ran and leapt, my anger, anxiety, fear, propelled me. I pumped my arms, used my thigh muscles to spring from ledges, and moved with all my energy until I burned. It felt good; the weight of my blades, sheathed in moleskin made by my surrogate grandfather, felt more familiar; adrenaline built up. By the time Noah led us to a dilapidated redbrick building in a row of other old buildings in the very slums of Charleston, I barely recognized it as an old church; after I noticed the double wooden archways, I wondered if it'd once been a carriage house. Graffiti in white paint marked the double doors—two large *M*'s, whatever that meant. Crouched atop the roof across the street, we peered at the row. I could hear the roar inside. With my sense of smell I detected sweat, piss, and the metallic scent of blood. I struggled to keep the exaggerated oscillatory sounds of the city out, and after a few moments of concentration, I filtered out most. I glanced upward. One small oval window, near the top, flickered with light. Noah moved next to me. Eli stood protectively on my other side.

"No cops wander this side of town," he said. "They skirt it, avoid it, and it's always been bad, and I don't mean vampire bad." He glanced at me. "That's a new development. I mean street gangs, drugs, whores—you name it. It's just easier for the cops to let what happens, happen. Not enough room in the prison for all this."

I looked at him.

He pointed up the street. "See that convenience store?" I looked. "Whatever kind of shit you want, you can get out back next to the Dumpster, right along with a loaf of bread, a bag of Chick-O-Sticks, and a six-pack of beer."

"Sweet place to raise a family," I offered. "Now, are

we headed in or what? I don't want to be in the middle of a fight when a vision comes over me again. I go totally out."

"I know," Noah said, his mercury eyes regarding me, then shifting to Eli. "I can always pull you out of it."

"The hell you will," Eli said, his voice dark and threatening.

I narrowed my gaze at them both.

He laughed. "Okay, Riley Poe. Bro. Chill." He inclined his head. "Once we're in, we separate. If any of the newlings notice us all together, they'll get suspicious and come after us, despite the Gullah potion we all drank. You wanna try and save a few in the quickening, right?"

"Yeah," Phin answered. "As many as possible. Garr's ready for them, right?"

Noah nodded. "Yep. They're waiting at our place. One call and his guys are here to haul them off."

Phin nodded. "Good deal."

Noah continued. "All right. Eli, Luc, stay with Riley. If she goes out, get her out. Josie, I'll be with you and Seth." Noah gave my brother a hard look. "And don't zone in on your sister. She's our concern tonight, not yours. You watch your own neck. We'll watch hers."

"You can use Luc on someone else. I got Riley," Eli said, moving close.

Noah grinned. "Luc's for you, man, in case you get out of control."

I looked at Eli's face. It darkened. "I'll be okay," I assured. It didn't seem to help much.

Seth threw a glance my way. The wind caught his dark brown hair and tossed it into his eyes. I could tell he hated this, and for a second I wished like hell we could go back, to before the Arcoses were released. I missed his innocence. *Love you*, he mouthed to me. I mouthed it back, then nodded to Noah. "Okay."

Noah gave him a return nod, then turned to the others. "Phin, you're on Zetty. My guys, scatter. Keep your eyes peeled and stay close—but not too close. We don't want them knowing we're all together." He glanced down at the street and pointed. A group of four guys had turned the corner and were headed to the entrance. "Mortals. Perfect. Let's follow them in. And hey—we're not here to cause shit tonight. The killings won't happen until the end of the week, anyway, so keep your head on straight." He looked at me and smiled. "Follow me, darlin'."

I looked back at Eli, who inclined his head to follow Noah, and I did. Luc stayed behind us. We swung down, bounded, and leapt, until we dropped to the sidewalk. In the distance, a siren blasted over the city, and close by, a baby's unhappy scream seeped out of an open window and ripped through the night. It gave me chills to think of a baby being raised in this environment. I knew there were thousands more I'd managed to tune out.

I followed Noah to the front entrance, and we filed in behind the mortals. Inside, the fanatic boom of heavy metal music thumped against the walls, joined by the muffled rumble of hollering, objects being slammed against surfaces, swearing, cheering.

Screams.

We found more graffiti inside. The whole place was dim, with a few candles lighting the interior of the shelled-out church, with a fading charred outline of Christ on the cross where it used to hang on the wall, obviously before a fire took it out. Charred rafters overhead and a set of narrow steps leading upward near the back made up the room. We headed to the stairs. The mortals had already started up. Hurrying across the floor littered with cans, trash, liquor bottles and cigarette butts, we followed them up and pushed into a crowded room above. Our group instantly separated. The scent of kerosene burned my nostrils as I followed Luc around a ring of spectators. Inside were two fighters; bare to the waist, wearing ripped jeans, and barefoot. Both were mortal. As I squeezed through the crowd, I glanced around and noticed several guys wearing dark shades.

"Newlings trying to hide their freaked-out eyes," Luc offered. "Keep up."

I pushed closer to Luc. "Why is it mortal against mortal?" I said into his ear.

He looked at me. "To weed out the weak," he offered.

Just like Noah had said, the newlings were looking for the strongest of the mortals to lure into their band. It made sense.

"Let's get in here," Eli said, and pushed in next to a pair of guys at ringside. Two guys fought, their faces cut and bloodied. I could literally sense the bloodlust accumulating in the room, vying with an immense overload of testosterone. How the newlings were keeping their cool, I had no friggin' clue.

"Whoever created them is controlling them—that's how," Eli said against my ear. "With one thought he could tell them to maul and devour everyone in this room. That's why I want you to watch your mouth, your ass, and not to do anything stupid."

I looked at him hard. "Yeah, I got that, Dupré. Stop worrying so much." The guy next to me jumped, and I fell hard into Eli's side. "Does that mean he's here?" I asked.

Luc pushed beside me and shook his head. "He's not here."

The crowd cheered as one of the fighters roundhouse kicked the other in the face and knocked him down. One of the newlings, dressed in dark jeans, a dark tee, and a black skully with dark shades, walked the perimeter of the man-made ring, watching everything—including what went on in the crowd. Across the way, I noticed Noah and Seth. My stomach lurched at the thought of watching my brother fight. He normally wasn't a fighter. He was sweet, and he had a kind, cheerful soul.

"Now he has a kick-ass soul," Luc offered. "Pay attention, Riley. Head in the game."

I swore in Romanian. Eli pressed against me, probably to make sure I knew he wasn't going to put up with my being pig-headed, and continued to watch the fight.

The guy beating the holy crap out of the other thought he was one tough bastard. Even when the other guy was on the floor, he stomped and kicked him in the ribs. The more the crowd cheered, the more brutal he became. We watched him fight one more guy, nearly beating him to death, before I could take no more. The weaker one kept trying to get up, would make it on one knee, and the other would smash into his face with his elbow, then his heel. I pushed the guy in front of me, heard Eli swear as I rushed the floor, and I knew Luc had restrained him, because he didn't follow. Just as big bully badass was about to drop his half-dead opponent, I roundhouse kicked him in the ribs. I heard Eli behind me say, "Fuck!" just as my new opponent dropped to one knee.

The crowd roared.

From the corner of my eye, I noticed the newling

moderator move toward me. I challenged him. "What?" I threw my hands up. "You got a fuckin' rule says I can't fight him?"

A slow smile spread across his face. I couldn't see his eyes, but I knew they were weird and opaque behind his shades. His skin was pale—almost a blue hue. Funny how no one else seemed to notice. His gaze raked over my inked skin. "There are no rules, bitch. Go for it."

The moment he said it, the crowd roared, and my opponent, jumping up, lunged toward me. I dodged and swept a leg out. He tripped and hit the floor.

I really, really didn't want to fight a mortal.

I didn't dare look behind me, back into the crowd. Eli's anger hit me like a wave, and I could only imagine Luc was having a helluva time restraining him.

It was like fighting a toddler—unfair; no sport—and it wasn't accomplishing anything. I wanted to kill vampires. I wanted to kill *him*, the monster.

I let my opponent land a few hits, just for show. They hurt. I dealt. I made sure no blood was spilled.

Unavoidably, my gaze hit the crowd. Twice I found Eli glaring at me. Luc grinned. I'd caught Noah's stare as well, but his was a slight smile instead. He was diggin' it, I could tell—freakazoid.

His smile broke wider, and I shook my head.

Finally, I grew tired of playing around with the mortal dude. I'd made my point—to the crowd and to the newlings. With an elbow to the gut, and a double fist to the nose, I sent him to la-la land. The crowd roared. I feigned slight exhaustion, grabbed my knees, and breathed. I lifted my head slightly; Luc's expression had softened. Eli's had not. But a slight nod assured me to keep going.

Next, I fought a girl: early twenties, solid as stone,

mean as shit, and high as a friggin' kite—high, but not wasted. She was totally pissed at me for some odd reason, and once we got the go-ahead nod from the newling ref, she threw herself at me like some crazed banshee, squalling and screeching. She scared the holy hell out of me.

"Come on, whore," she said, dancing around me and taking pokes with her balled-up fists. I didn't even flinch, her marks were that off. "You scared or somethin'? What'cha waitin' for, huh, bitch?"

Bap. I took her down, just on principle. One punch and she was out cold. I still hadn't broken a sweat. Again, the crowd cheered.

Somebody dragged her off the floor.

I noticed two newlings standing together; something I hadn't seen all night. They were talking, and once I honed in on them, I realized they were talking about me. I wasn't exactly sure if that was a bad thing or not.

I fought two more guys before I noticed Eli in the sidelines waving me out. After I took the last one out, I once again pretended exhaustion, and I staggered from the fight floor. It was covered in blood, spit, and something else I dared not to try and identify. Disgusting. At least it wasn't my blood—or any other body fluid.

"Hey," the one newling who'd been watching me closely for the past two hours said, grabbing my arm. "You wanna come back Friday night?"

I glared at him. "I don't know. You got somethin' more than a bunch of pussies and druggies for me to fight?"

I heard Eli hiss behind me.

A slow smile spread across his pale face, and I noticed his brows were so blond, they blended in with his undead skin. The black skully he wore stood in stark contrast to his pastiness. Some would be scared. I wanted to beat his arrogant ass. And it suddenly struck me how well the potion Garr gave the guys—the vampire guys—worked. They paid them no attention. Cool. "Yeah. Come back Friday night and find out."

I gave him a hard glare and knocked his shoulder with mine as I passed. He smiled, knowing I'd be back, and I bet he was looking to try and whip me himself.

"What about you?" he asked Eli. "You here to watch your woman fight? You a pussy or somethin'?"

The air around us stilled. "What you got for me?" Eli said, his voice deadly.

The newling's mouth lifted at the corner, and he inclined his head to the ring. "Come on and find out."

Eli didn't even spare me a glance. He followed the newling.

At the ring, the newling nodded at another, and in seconds, a big, heavily muscled guy in his midtwenties stepped up. He had to be all of six feet seven—taller than Eli. I could tell he was on something. Eli shrugged out of his shirt and stepped into the ring. The big mortal came at him like a truck.

Eli gave a good show. He toned his strength way down and let the guy get in several good punches. I watched in fascination the movement of muscles across Eli's back, his biceps, and the raw power he managed to restrain as he fought. Finally, he popped the guy in the jaw and the mortal hit the floor, out cold. Eli spit on the floor beside him and stepped out of the ring. The newling moved, said something to him, and Eli made his way back to me.

His firm grasp on my arm was almost painful. Eli's mouth pushed to my ear. "Let's get the fuck out of here before you do something else stupid and get pulled back into the ring."

I glanced over my shoulder as we moved through the crowd. I limped for good measure. "Yeah? It seemed like the right thing to do, Dupré. That first guy was gonna kill that kid."

"And what do you think's been happening all along? What's going to happen tonight? We can't stay and baby-sit them all."

I rounded on him the moment the crowd thinned. "I didn't come here to fight mortals. I thought we were here to take care of a bloodsucking problem."

"You fightin' again, Bro?" Luc asked.

Eli nodded. "Yeah. So it seems. Luc's head lifted, and he gave a short nod. "Let's go. We're meeting the others outside, rooftop."

I felt the newlings' eyes on me the whole way out.

Luc, Eli, and I were first out the door, so we free-ran to the rooftop across the street and down a ways, and waited for the others.

I paced.

"Why couldn't we just round up all the newlings inside? Trap them in? Gather the ones in the quickening phase, destroy the newlings, and take the freaking hell off?"

Luc shook his head. "Riley, Riley, Riley. No patience, huh? Just like before, there are reasons you can't just rush in and do." He tapped my temple. "Think, smarty-pants. Remember how the Arcoses could control the boys from before with a single thought? Well, whoever is controlling this band—Valerian reborn—can do the same thing. He gets one whiff of interference and things could turn really, really ugly. They outnumber us."

"And they're mixed in a building filled with mortals," Noah said, leaping up beside us. The others joined him. He grinned at me. "No matter how much of a dick some of them are." He punched my arm. "Crack shootin', Poe. I'm impressed."

Eli glowered and moved closer.

Seth interrupted, angry. "Riley, you didn't have to jump in like that."

I looked at my brother. Worry etched his green eyes, and the muscles in his jaws clenched, dark brows slashed into a frown. "I could've done it."

"Hey," I said, and hugged him. "You know I'm unpredictable. I couldn't stand seeing that one guy log into the other one. He'd have killed him. It was instinct, not a plan. I promise."

Seth pulled back and met my gaze. The wind caught and pushed his hair to the side. "You gonna do it again?"

"Yes," I answered. "But you are all going to be there to back me up. I have the newlings' attention. We're getting somewhere."

Seth frowned. "I don't like it, Ri. But okay."

Noah walked over and draped his arms over each of us. "You two are just so darn cute," he said, mercury eyes twinkling. He glanced at Eli. "But let's go. That is, if you want to save a few souls."

Seth threw me a *whatever* glance. I couldn't help but grin at Noah's ridiculousness, and we followed him and his roof jumpers over the ancient city of Charleston. Eli ran close to me—so close I could feel the air he moved.

One major difference between vampires and mortals with tendencies I'd like to quickly point out is mortals have to pee. "Guys, no way can I leap from one more rooftop with a full bladder," I said as we stopped to inspect the area. I glanced down. "There's a Denny's. Open twenty-four hours. I'll be right back." I turned to descend.

"Whoa," Eli said. "Wait up."

I quickly stopped. "Oh come on, Eli. Gimme a friggin' break. It's right down there." I bent down, rested the heels of my palms on my knees, and peered down and into the restaurant. I pointed. "Look. You can see the bathrooms from here. Straight in the back." I rose and glared at Luc. "I pee alone. Got it?"

"Got it," Eli said. "I'll be right outside the bathroom door. Waiting. While you pee alone."

I rolled my eyes. "Whatever. Let's go."

In a flash, as I praised God I did regular Kegels, we descended the building, leapt against the trunk of a magnolia, and fell to the sidewalk in a crouch. I glanced around and ran across the street and into Denny's. Eli ran beside me.

"Ma'am, this isn't a public restroom," an older waitress said.

I hurried past her. "Honey, will you order me a burger to go? Rare," I said to Eli. He growled. Seriously—what was she gonna do? Drag me off the toilet? I all but skipped to the back and pushed into the women's restroom while Eli stayed behind to deal with Mrs. Denny's. I hit the end stall, made fast but careful business of taking care of business (eleven blades strapped to my body, don't forget) and, relieved, finished. Flushing the toilet with my foot, I moved out of the stall and to the sink to wash my hands. I splashed water on my face, rubbed my eyes, and when I opened them, *she* stood behind me—a girl, dressed in black destroyed jeans, clunky black biker boots, a black and red ribbed tank with spiked studs along the collar and arms, and a headful of black dreads. Gaze fixed, she stared at me through the mirror, un-blinking, at the pulse near the base of my throat. She licked her lips.

I knew then what she was.

In the next second her face contorted, her jaw un-hinged unnaturally, and jagged fangs dropped. Her eyes went white, the pupils pinpoint red, and she lunged.

Part Eight

MELEE

"You know that person you said there's no such person? I think he's in there. In person."

—Lou Costello, *Abbot and Costello
Meet Frankenstein*

> *"Oh my freaking God, when will this end? I'm tired, my body aches, my language has gotten worse, and I'm dying for a smoke. Charleston is crawling with the undead, and they're mean little fresh fuckers trying to earn their place in the vampiric world by hunting down me—and others like me. Hello?! No, thank you! I'm ready to rock and roll, do the hokie pokie, do a little dance, make a little love, and get down tonight. In other words, wrap this shit up and take a goddamn vacation."*

> —Riley Poe

"Whoa!" I barely shouted. Then I ducked, lunged, pushed with my feet, and bounded off the sink, then the wall, and landed across the bathroom in a low crouch.

The she-vamp crashed into the mirror. Glass shards fell into the porcelain sink.

It didn't make her very happy.

A strangled, pissed-off, inhuman sound emerged from her throat, and she lunged at me again—damn, she was fast—with fangs long and face weirdly distorted, some gross juicy stuff dripping from the corner of her mouth, her dreads flying all over like so many Medusa snakes; she wanted me and wanted me bad. I wasn't wasting any time with her. I ducked and dodged again, bounded off the far wall, ran the length of all five sinks, broke a few faucets;

reached down the back of my pants, drew my blade, and, the moment I landed, turned, aimed, and released.

The look of shock as my silver buried to the hilt in her heart was picture-worthy.

Dropping to the floor as though every bone in her body had melted, she immediately began to convulse.

The bathroom door flung open and crashed against the wall. Eli stood there. Luc and Noah ran up behind him, staring. Luc's face showed concern. Noah, well, he was smiling, as usual. Eli looked pissed.

"Sick, sick!" Noah said, like a proud daddy. "You just nailed your first Charles Town bloodsucker, babe." He slapped my shoulder. "Sweet."

"Riley, what the hell?" Eli said, as if something were my fault. I had to freaking pee! That was it! He read my thoughts, and his gaze softened a little.

"Sir, excuse me," the waitress from out front said behind the door. She was trying to look over Luc's shoulder. "What's going on in there?"

Luc turned and backed out. "Oh, my sister, ma'am. She's sick. Threw up all over the floor. Flu, I think. You gotta mop? I'll take care of it."

"Just a minute," I heard her say. "You'll clean that up, right?"

Luc glanced at me over his shoulder. "Sure, no problem."

I watched yet another vamp turn to dust, this time right in the freaking Denny's women's restroom. What a way to go.

"Let's get out of here," Eli said, grasping my elbow. He did a lot of that lately, and I couldn't decide if it was endearing or annoying.

"I need to clean it up," I said.

Luc cleaned up the mess; he literally swept the dust into a ziplock and pocketed it. Then we left.

"Ever see her before?" Luc asked Noah, behind us.

He shook his head. "She was a totally random rogue; I didn't recognize her, and apparently she'd been lying in wait in the bathroom for her next victim." He grinned at me. "Bet she wasn't expecting a vampire slayer strapped with pure silver to have to pee."

I looked at him. "Vampire slayer with tendencies, dude." I shook my head. "I'm just glad she at least let me finish peeing first."

Back on the rooftop across from Denny's, Seth paced. The moment I swung up, he rushed at me. "Ri! What's freaking wrong with you?" he said, anger burning in his eyes. "Why do you have to keep doing that?"

"Whoa, whoa," I said, gently. "I didn't do anything. Had to go to the bathroom."

He shoved his hand in his hair. "You can't seem to do much of anything anymore, without getting into trouble. Next time take Josie. Into the restroom. Please?"

I hugged my brother. "Okay. Promise." I glanced at Josie. She simply shrugged and grinned. "Now, let's go."

We ran into the city and hit a club called Meter 59, a hole-in-the-wall punk club just on the edge of the historic district. We filed in, and the music, the lights, thumped through my body. The place was packed with more black leather, black lace, spiked hair and severe piercings than I'd seen in years. This was a rough bunch. We spread out. Eli, of course, stayed on my tail.

Eli grabbed me by the hips and pushed me into the crowd of dancers; we moved to the music. His hooded gaze locked on mine, and I almost forgot we were there to scout newlings, or those in their quickening. We brushed, not touching but seductively close, and as he turned me, his hand trailing down my back to my ass, I spotted them—three in all; two guys, one girl.

"I see them," Eli said, his mouth brushing my ear, making me shiver and making it hard to concentrate. His hands skimmed my ribs. "I've told the others. They're looking for more. We'll keep our eyes on these three."

I nodded, and, keeping with the blasting tunes of the Yeah Yeah Yeahs, I moved my backside against Eli's front. To others we looked like a normal, average horny couple dancing and enjoying the music. Well . . . we were all that. But we also had our sites locked on almost-vampires. I knew from experience they were mean little fuckers. They wouldn't be easy to take down.

"You're driving me crazy," he said against my ear. His hand settled seductively over my stomach, then slipped lower over my hip. "Jesus, Ri."

I smiled at that. My insides quivered. I wanted him. And from the hardness pressing against my back, he wanted me, too.

A low growl rumbled in Eli's chest.

Then, the three started to move to the back. They had two mortals with them. "Let's go," I said, and began to weave through the crowd.

We followed them through the dancers, to the back exit. They'd already managed to get out into the alley by the time we hit the door. The moment I stepped out, the scent of old trash, urine, and brine mixed in my senses. I could have easily barfed, it was so pungent. One of the guys had a knife and was ready to use it on the kid they'd convinced to follow them. The three almost-newlings looked up. The biggest one glared at me.

"Get the fuck outta here," he warned.

I sighed. "I don't think so."

Eli lunged before I did as all three came at me. The girl skirted Eli, hit the ground, rolled, and shot up running. Crazed and out of control, I braced myself for her. Summoning all of my strength, I clotheslined her as she lunged. She snapped back and hit the concrete flat on her back. She leapt right back up in one motion, teeth gnashing and gnarling. I didn't have time to see what Eli was doing. The one I had was a handful.

We fought. She was strong as hell, but I swept her legs out from under her and she fell again. This time, I pinned her throat with my foot, retrieved one of my blades, and held it to her face. "Chill," I instructed.

Opaque eyes stared crazed up at me. She didn't move. I glanced over at Eli. His face had contorted. Both almost-newlings were out cold.

Noah and Phin burst out of the exit door and ran to us. "I've already called Garr's guys," Noah said. They're on their way."

Eli, his face returned to normal—well, at least my normal—locked his gaze on mine. "You okay?"

I glanced down at the girl, whose face looked murderous, inhuman. I pressed my foot a little harder into her throat. "Yeah. I'm fine."

By the time the ruckus finally wrapped up, it was close to four a.m. Garr's guys came to collect the three, and we ran the roofs till nearly dawn before heading back to the battery. We encountered no further rogue vampires, no further newlings or those in the quickening, and although I wanted them off the streets, I was glad. Exhaustion began its descent, and I wanted nothing more than to crash. We said good-bye to Noah and his group, split, and headed to Jake's.

Inside, my brother grabbed my arm. "Are you okay, Ri? Seriously?" Seth asked. "You don't look so good."

"Sure, squirt. I'm cool. Just tired. See ya in a bit, huh?"

He nodded. "I'm not tired yet, so I'll hang with Josie down here. Call me if you need me, though." He glanced at Eli, who stood directly behind me. "Take care of my sister."

"I will," Eli said gently. "I got her."

I gave my sweet brother a smile and trudged up the stairs, Eli's hand resting possessively against the small of my back the whole way up. With each step I wondered how in hell I'd made it through the night, jumping from buildings like a freaking monkey, fight after fight. Adrenaline had obviously kept me going. Well, that had worn off now, and I felt like Indiana Jones after one of his big fights. I hurt everywhere. Now that the action was over, I felt like a wet noodle. I needed a shower, then rest. I made it to my room and pushed inside.

"I'll be right back," Eli said. "I need a word with my brothers. For just a few minutes."

"Okay," I answered, my tongue feeling heavy in my mouth. Eli left out, and I scanned my room—Jake's room.

Lamplight from the riverfront streamed in through my balcony door, casting a narrow beam across the floor. I eased to the bench at the foot of the bed and sat down softly, pushed my Vans off with each opposite foot, peeled my socks off, and just . . . sat for a second. Every muscle, every joint, even my skin ached. Slowly, I shrugged out of my tank, stood and peeled off my jeans, and dropped them on the floor. With my blades still sheathed to my various body parts, and in only my bra and panties, I hobbled to the balcony door, opened it, and stepped out onto the veranda. A slight breeze lifted my ponytail, and I reached up, pulled off the elastic band holding it together, and let my hair down. Overhead, thunder boomed; a few seconds later, a streak of lightning lit the sky. Red blinking lights flashed in the harbor as shrimp boats and fishing boats headed out to sea. As the briny breeze caught the palm fronds, they crackled, rubbing against one another. I let the sounds and smells and sights of normalcy wash over me. I leaned against the veranda's railing and closed my eyes. I stood there for a while; how long, I didn't know.

"Riley."

My eyes flashed open, and my heart leapt at the voice. A dream. Of Eli. In my head. I'd fallen asleep standing up on the veranda.

"No," Eli said against my ear with a soft laugh. "Not a dream."

Gently, with both hands, Eli grasped my face and tilted my head up. He looked down at me, his eyes searching mine. The lamplight gleamed in their blue depths, and a small smile tipped his sexy mouth. "I missed you, Riley Poe."

"Ow," I said as he pressed closer. "Easy, easy. Not so hard." My body ached everywhere.

"I'll be gentle," he whispered against my lips.

"Ah," I said, flinching. Even my damn lips hurt. I wanted him inside me. I wanted to taste his skin. I wanted him to kiss me. But I freaking hurt.

Eli's gaze searched mine. He kissed me gently; yet I felt the power he used to restrain himself. He pulled back, searching my eyes. "I'll stop if you hurt too much."

I looked at him, puzzled. "Are you crazy?"

In his eyes shined possession, fierce longing, and

something way deeper I had no desire to dwell on at the moment. "Come in here," he said, grasping my hand and pulling me into the room. I followed.

Inside, he stood me next to the long antique dresser facing one wall. "Stand still."

I did as he asked.

Slowly, and one by one, Eli's deft fingers moved over my skin to the blades I had sheathed against my body. Loosening each one, he removed them and set them on the dresser. My eyes closed as his fingers trailed down each hip, unclasped the sheath, moved to the next ones, lower on my thighs, then on my shins. When they were all removed, he stood there, simply staring. He grasped my hand. "Come with me."

Leading me across the floor, my gasped breath hitching with each step as the pain in my body shot through me, Eli drew me into the massive bathroom. A large, walk-in tiled shower with multiple water jets faced one wall; a claw-footed bathtub faced the other. Eli walked to the shower, turned on the jets, adjusted the water temperature, then dimmed the lights. When he returned to me, he stood there, staring down, his eyes devouring me. I felt it; I craved it. I craved him.

A small smile lifted his mouth at the corner. "I love how unshy you are."

Steam quickly filled the room; Eli grasped his shirt at the hem and yanked it over his head. In fascination I watched the muscles pull and grow taut with movement. His eyes never left mine. In less than five seconds he had his jeans and boots off and shoved against the wall. My vampire stood there, looking at me with wild hunger and desire in his eyes and not wearing a stitch of clothing.

My body involuntarily shook.

He came to me, then; close, his body brushed mine. His fingers eased over my shoulders, across my collarbone, down the front where my bra clasped between my breasts. He released it, eased the straps down, and, as I held my arms straight, I winced. With a gentleness that no longer surprised me, he pushed the silky material off my body and dropped it to the floor.

Inside, I was dying; outside, my body raged with pain.

"I know, baby," he said, slipping his fingers through the waistband of my panties and easing them to the floor. "I'm going to fix that."

My heart leapt.

Slowly, Eli grasped my shoulders and walked me into the shower. Although it was equipped with pulsating, massaging jets, he'd adjusted the water stream to a soft, soothing, and very, very hot waterfall. Guiding me beneath it, he followed. "Close your eyes," he whispered. I did.

With gentle fingers, Eli tilted my head back, and soothing hot water glided over my head and my face; it soaked my hair and drenched my body. His hands smoothed my wet hair back; his fingers traced my nose, my jaw, the column of my throat. Already, the tension in my body began to seep out.

An aroma of jasmine and verbena filled the air; I realized quickly it was the shampoo that filled Eli's palms. Gently, he lathered my hair; blunt, strong fingers dug into my scalp, massaged it, and I thought I'd fall asleep standing there.

"No, don't do that," he whispered. "Stay with me, Riley."

I sighed. "I'm trying."

His seductive mouth against my wet skin made my nerves leap. "Try harder."

"Rinse." He pushed me beneath the cascade of water and rinsed my hair. Next, the air filled with the same aroma as he lathered his hands. "Now be still. Don't move."

Then, he lathered my body.

I stood and allowed it for a little while.

Eli's hands, slick with water and soap, glided over my shoulders, down my arms, intertwined his fingers with mine, and drew me close. His wet body pressed close to me, his lips sought the top of my shoulder, my throat, my ear, jaw, and slid to my mouth. In a slow, erotic kiss, his tongue grazed mine, his teeth scraped my lips, captured the bottom one, suckled gently.

Inside, I grew heavy with desire; my knees weakened, and I lifted my arms to his chest, trailed the muscles there; his breath caught in his throat; he captured my hands in his hands and lowered them.

"Not yet, Riley," he said, his voice strained, his accent more prominent, his breath brushing against my ear. "You touch me, I'll explode. Just . . . be still."

"Then don't kiss me like that," I said.

I felt his smile against my skin. "No promises there."

I sighed.

"Turn around," he said against my cheek.

I did, and he pushed my hair over one shoulder and lathered my back, his fingers kneading deep into the sore muscles. I gasped with pleasure and pain, and it took every ounce of strength I had to remain upright. It took even more not to touch Eli.

There was a wet, sexy, naked vampire in the shower with me.

Eli's low chuckle as he read my thoughts resonated against the tile, and his fingers continued to work magic. For now, I didn't think of carnage, vampiric attacks, monsters, or fight clubs; I thought of nothing but Eli, his touch, and the craving he stirred within me. His hands glided over my body, every inch passed made my eyes roll back in bliss; I wanted him everywhere, inside, out, and I never, ever wanted him to leave me again.

His hands moved over my hips, encircled my stomach, and pulled my body against his. I felt his muscles pressing into my spine; his hardness pressing against the small of my back. His arms tightened around me, his mouth at my jaw. "I swear, I'll never leave you again," he whispered, his voice strained, somewhat painful.

I turned in his arms, and together we stepped out of the mainstream waterfall; steam rose all around us, and I locked my gaze on his. His dark, wet hair fell across his eyes, and I reached up and pushed it aside; I grazed his jaw and ran my thumb over his sexy lips. "Don't," I said quietly. "Don't ever again, Eli."

His mouth sought mine. "I promise," he whispered, his tongue tasting mine.

I pushed him back. "Now you be still."

A small smile tilted his mouth. "Yes, ma'am."

I gathered a handful of liquid soap. "Sorry." I ran my hands over his chest, his shoulders, down his arms, over his stomach. "You're gonna smell like a girl."

He ducked his head and captured my mouth. "I don't care," he said, in between sensual kisses and nips. I lost myself in his drugging kiss; my hands glided over the muscles in his back, over his tight ass, his hips. The feel of his tongue against mine, his teeth scraping my lips, made me hot, wet, crazy. Blind with need, the pain of my battered body forgotten, I moved my soap-slickened hands over the cut ridges of his abdomen, lower, and grasped his slick hardness. He gasped in my mouth, groaned, kissed me deeper.

"Jesus, Riley," he said, pained. "Control's slipping." He pushed me against the tiled wall, his hands roaming all over me.

"Don't care," I muttered against his throat, my hands stroking him. "Need you," I panted, pressing my body to his. "Now, Eli."

Without words, he lifted me; as I wrapped my legs around his hips, I slid over his hard length until Eli filled me completely. My head dropped back, drugged, weightless. Beneath the waterfall, Eli's mouth tasted my skin, his tongue teased the hardened, sensitive peaks of my breasts; first one, then the other. With his fingers digging into my hips, he moved me effortlessly, the feel of his hardness sliding inside me making me crazy high. His mouth caressed me as his cock moved within me.

"Eli," I gasped, and held on, our rhythm matching, and somewhere deep within me, an intense orgasm began like a faraway storm. We moved beneath the steaming water, fast, out of control, until the storm grew in strength and finally crashed. Wave after wave of climax claimed us both. I lost my breath, and spasms wracked my body. Eli held me close, his mouth pressed to my throat. The world tilted still; Eli's lovemaking had that effect on me. I could do nothing more than hold on to him. I knew if he wasn't holding on to me so tightly, I'd slip to the tiles below.

"I'd never let that happen," he whispered against me.

"I know," I answered, and ran my fingers through his soft, slick hair, tracing the shell of his ear.

Without words, Eli reached down with one hand and turned off the waterfall. Through the steam, his eyes searched mine. Slowly, he lowered his head, captured my mouth, and kissed me. Now, his control had returned, and he used it to savor my lips and my tongue, speaking to me with just his mouth; they were actions that spoke volumes over any words he could have whispered.

Still wet from the shower, and with me still clinging to him, Eli walked to the bed and followed me down into the softness of the down comforter. We shifted, and he pulled me close against him, my head resting on his chest, his arm completely around me and holding me to his body. He pulled back, just enough so that I could see his face without it being blurry.

Serious, cerulean eyes bore into mine. "I love you, Riley Poe." He brushed a thumb over my lips. "Don't forget that." He kissed me, slowly, erotically, then looked at me again. "Ever."

I opened my mouth to tell Eli how I felt, but his fingers over my lips stopped me.

"No, Riley," he said gently. "Another time. When you're really ready."

Before I could respond, he pulled me against him again; resting his chin on top of my head. "Go to sleep, mostly mortal woman. We have a busy few days ahead of us."

Prick, I said in my head.

Eli laughed, squeezing me a little tighter, and I closed my eyes, smiling.

Finally, I fought the exhaustion no more. I was content. I mean, how could I not be? Eli was naked. I was naked. We'd just had mind-blowing, soul-searching sex. The only thing better right now would be . . . I don't know. Some corn dogs, maybe. Or a bag from Krystal.

"God, you've become such a hog," Eli said, shaking with laughter. "Go to sleep, girl. I'll get you food after you've rested."

I laughed. "Okay." I snuggled against him. His body temperature was perfect—not too warm, and definitely not too cool.

"Thank you," he whispered. "Sleep."

Just before sleep claimed me, I felt relief that the monster hadn't killed again; it was nearly daybreak, anyway.

How very wrong I was.

I experienced two kills, back-to-back. It was almost too much for me to handle.

I'd just felt that wave of exhaustion and contentedness wash over me.

I found myself walking along the city market. In the harbor, a tugboat blasted its horn, but I paid little attention and continued up the walk. Most of the stores hadn't opened yet, but in the French Quarter a little café opened its doors to early risers; they weren't about yet, but I slipped along the wall, to the back entrance of François Patisserie. Silently, I eased inside. The scent of fresh-baked bread and pastries filled the café, but that wasn't what made my stomach ache with need. In the back, near the double ovens and beside a long stainless steel counter, stood a plump, middle-aged woman, pulling a fresh batch of croissants from the oven. She had no idea I was in the kitchen with her. Rising on pudgy tiptoes, she reached for the top shelf over the sink, grasped a plate, then slid a hot croissant onto it. She smiled, moved to the counter, and removed the lid from a ceramic butter tray. With a knife she buttered her already-buttery croissant and took a big bite. She groaned with pleasure.

A feeling of impatience came over me, and I knew it was his feeling, not mine. I did the usual—scream, holler, but nothing came out, nothing worked, and I could not warn the plump baker that her death was coming.

No sooner had the baker woman swallowed her bite of croissant than I moved directly behind her. She must have sensed a presence, for slowly, she turned.

Her scream died in her throat.

The monster wasted no time. He lunged, held his hand over the woman's mouth, and ripped right through her white cotton blouse. He sank his fangs into the flesh of her chest before finding the pulse of her heart. As he pierced the pumping organ, her warm blood gushed into his mouth and slid down his throat; fast at first, then slower, slower until her life force was no more. He dropped her on the floor, wiped his mouth with a rag left on the counter, and left.

The moment he stepped outside and noticed the jogger heading toward the river, I knew he'd kill again. I don't know how, but I did. I thrashed, bile rising in my throat at the memory of the poor woman in the bakery, her blouse doused with blood, her dead face contorted in shock and terror.

Thankfully, the next kill was swift. The shirtless man jogging along the river was young, extremely fit, his chest cut with muscle, a six-pack to die for. He wore a Gamecocks ball cap as he ran, his iPod jamming in his ears. The moment he turned off the river and down an alley to cut through to another street, the monster was there. He stepped out, bumping into the man. The jogger stumbled, his blue eyes shocked to see someone else along his path. The monster waited for nothing. He changed; I knew this because of the horror on the jogger's face. The monster

*ripped into him just as he'd ripped into the baker woman,
nearly snatching the man's heart out with his fangs. But
the moment the hot metallic fluid pumped into him, he relaxed; he drank fully, and, when he was finished, he threw
the jogger against the brick wall and walked away.*

*The last thing I remember before waking and separat-
ing from the monster, was his laugh.*

It was oddly familiar. . . .

I bolted up in bed, my surroundings unfamiliar for
a split second. Only then did I notice Eli was gone. I
looked around, noticing how dim it still was outside.
Eli must have slipped out the moment I'd drifted off.
The exhaustion I felt was too real, too thick, and no way
could I get out of bed right now. I must have closed my
eyes at the exact moment the monster decided to feed;
unless he knew me and was torturing me on purpose.
If Eli was right, and Valerian, despite how Eli and his
brothers had destroyed him, had manifested himself
into one of his newlings, then he was the monster. He
did know me. And I was pretty fucking sure he wanted
to torment me to the fullest. He was succeeding.

There was nothing else I could do; no one I could
save. I needed sleep. As selfish as it sounds, I lay back
down, pulled the sheet up to my chest, and closed my
eyes, allowing slumber to take me. Hopefully, Eli would
return and pull me into his arms. I slept so much better with him wrapped around me. My eyes grew heavy;
Sleep claimed me again.

I slept for some time; I don't know how long.

When I woke, I emerged in yet another dream state.
*I was sitting in the dark. A dark room, a closet; I was on
the floor, my back against . . . something. I felt a presence,
though; someone was with me. Immediately, I knew who.*

"Where have you been?" I asked angrily.

Victorian's low, sexy soft laugh filled the dark empty space. "Why? Have you missed me?"

I thought about it. "Yes. And no."

"Please, tell me why yes first."

"I have no freaking idea, other than you're my connection to why I behave and feel the way I do, since it's your DNA clinging to mine. Yours and Valerian's. And I sort of like you. When you're not being so pervy. And I'm glad Eli didn't kill you." His soft sigh filled the shadowy space we occupied together. "And that pleases you?"

"Well, I don't exactly want you dead," I said. "Not sure why, but somehow . . . it doesn't seem right."

He laughed. "I'll take that as a compliment, I suppose."

"If you want," I said. "But believe me, I'm the only one who feels that way."

"No doubt. And why not?" he continued.

His presence seemed closer; I can't explain it, since we were in total darkness, but I felt as though his body was very close to mine. I shrugged, even though we were in total blackness. "Because it seems whenever I experience a terrible vision of the monster making a kill, it's not long after that you appear. That concerns me."

I felt the brush of his whisper against the column of my neck when he spoke. "Do you still think he and I are one and the same?"

I shook my head. "No, not at all. I've seen his skin, his arms—they're not yours. But they're Valerian's, aren't they? Manifested in another newling he created?"

"That you've paid such close attention to my physical detail makes me happy," Victorian said, and that warm breath brushed my cheek. "Very happy. And to agree, yes.

*I fear your monster is my brother. He's even more power-
ful than I ever was."*

"Well, hold on there, Tonto," I said. "Don't get too
wound up. It's kinda noticeable that you have youthful
pale skin. The monster has older, tanned-like-leather skin.
Didn't take a rocket scientist to figure it out."

He laughed. "You wound me."

"Whatever," I said, resting my head against whatever
hard thing was behind me. "Where are you?"

"Here, with you," he answered. "And see what a good
boy I'm being? Not once have I asked you to grope me."

"Freaking miracle," I answered, and he laughed again.

"It should hopefully win me points," he said.

"I didn't know we were working on a points system."

"I'd work on anything to get in your good graces," he
said somberly. "If only you knew how much so."

"Well, Vick, you're not too difficult to read," I answered.
"How is it you're able to totally block Eli from reading
my thoughts, or yours, when we have these rendezvous?"

"Hmm. Is that what you consider our encounters? I
think that turns me on, Riley."

I chuckled. "What doesn't turn you on, Vick? Now answer the question please."

Victorian sighed. "Very well. It's my strigoi nature.
That part of my DNA is more potent than you can possibly imagine. You, Riley, have powers that have simply
not manifested yet. When they do, you will ... Let's just
say you will be amazed. Anyway, I am able to implant my
thoughts, myself, into your thoughts and mind and keep
any and all intruders out. I'm selfish that way."

"That doesn't surprise me," I said. "And it also leads
me to know that you have complete control over me. You
can make me do whatever you want, can't you?"

"I confess, it's true. But because I'm a gentleman, I restrain."

I chuckled. "You get another point, then, I guess."

"Something's bothering you," he said next. "I can tell. What is it?"

I sighed. "You mean besides my being linked in a killer's body while he feeds?" I asked.

With a soft chuckle, Victorian answered. "Yes."

"I killed a vampire tonight," I said. "She was young, and it bothers me."

"Why?" he asked. "It was either you or her, and I for one am more than glad you emerged the victor."

I laughed. "God, Victorian, you've got to brush up on your modern lingo. You sound like an old fart talking that way. Sometimes I forget you're so old."

Victorian laughed. "Perhaps I do. Maybe you should teach me your modern lingo? Now, finish telling this old fart why killing the female vampire bothered you."

I thought for a second. "Because she was young. Before she was a vampire, a killer, she was a human. Someone's sister, someone's daughter. Someone's loved one. It just makes me sad."

"We all were, Riley Poe."

I sighed again. "I know that."

"Well, as much as I'd love to use my wiles to win your heart, or better yet," he said seductively, "just do as I want with you, I shall not. To show you my restraint, I will leave you now, untouched, unkissed, and without orgasm—although it pains me to do so. You are a breathtaking beauty while in the throes of passion. It's a vision I see inside my head all the time. A true vision of beauty. Good night, Riley Poe."

"Later, Vick," I said. "I'm impressed."

"Aren't you going to stop me?" he pressed.

I laughed. *"No. Get out of here—wherever here is."*

"It's wherever you want it to be. . . ."

The week passed—flew by actually. We worked well as a newling/vamp/quickening victim recovery team. We hit every seedy club after hours we could find and rounded up at least a dozen and a half newlings and almost-newlings. Only two were destroyed, but it was unavoidable. They were freaking everywhere, and not all were being ruled by the monster. I call him the monster, even though I know he was a newly manifested Valerian. We still haven't tracked him, but we will. He's here. We all feel it.

We hit the fight club on the appointed night. The newlings were looking for me. Why I had impressed them so much, I had no clue. There were some pretty badass chicks in the club; none with the same DNA as me, I guess, and that made a difference. I quickly rose to the top as a club favorite. Seth hated it. Eli hated it. Noah and Luc loved it. I wouldn't be surprised if they were taking bets on the side. Phin and Zetty were unreadable. I'd be in the ring, fighting a guy, a girl—didn't matter. My gaze would scan, catch either of theirs, and I'd see pride mixed with a hooded scolding look that nearly cracked me up.

Zetty—now that was a fighter right there. I'm pretty sure his unique tats across his forehead and his sheer size made him a ringside favorite, just like mine did. He was a silent fighter, though. His expression hardly changed at all, even when some crazy ass high on crack would slug him in the jaw. I swear, he was probably exactly the same even before he had tendencies. Zet-Man was cool as shit, and I was damn glad he was on our side.

Eli's fighting fascinated me. I know, that sounds sick. But he's, well, a sick fighter. What can I say? Maybe it's the fact that I know he's holding back, and using a fuck-load of restraint to do so. The newlings wanted him to fight. They didn't suspect he was anything other than a cocky mortal, but because of his beauty, I imagine, they wanted him in that ring. I even think they wanted some-one to take him out. And I was pretty damn sure they wanted that someone to be me.

I wasn't surprised when they had us fight each other. They didn't give us any time to dispute it.

The crowd roared. Eli frowned.

I glanced out at the spectators and found Noah. A smile lifted his mouth. *Dick.*

Inside my head, I spoke to Eli. *"Don't worry. Land a few on me for show. It won't hurt too much. But ob-viously, I have to win. So be ready to hit the floor."* I grinned.

By the look on Eli's face, I knew he hated this.

Not one punch landed on me. His knuckles grazed the air next to my chin, enough to make my head snap back out of reflex. But mine landed. We danced and played for several minutes as if we were killing each other. Then, Eli hit the ground. He stayed. I won.

The newlings, despite their sunglasses, zeroed in on me. We were to come back for the final rally in two more nights. Meanwhile, we ran the city.

And I, unfortunately, witnessed three more kills.

We'd been in Charleston more than a week now, and, after the last run, I hit the bed, exhausted. Eli was always there, attentive, seductive, sexy as hell. He awakened my tired body, making me feel more alive than ever. Just the brush of his lips over my skin aroused me. He was one drug I never wanted rehab from. Finally, spent from mind-blowing sex, I fell into a deep slumber. No dreams awakened me. Even Victorian left me alone.

When I finally did rise, I was surprised to find it was nearly one p.m. I was also surprised to find Eli gone.

Deciding he must be out with his brothers, I yawned, content.

I'd thought mortals with tendencies didn't require as much sleep as regular Joe Schmoe mortals. Guess I was the exception. I showered; memories of last night with Eli swamped me, and, as corny as it sounds, they made me feel whole. Then, I wrapped a towel around my wet body and wandered out onto the veranda. A large leaf-shaped paddle fan whirred in the breeze above my head, and the long fronds of the Boston ferns swayed in white wicker baskets. I leaned over the balcony as though I weren't here with a load of vampires hunting evil newling vampires and one sadistic vampire, and I peered at the harbor, the sparkling water of the Atlantic, the palm-lined walk of the battery. For a solid second, I closed my eyes and indulged, pretending to be on a weekend getaway with—

"Mornin', sunshine."

I jumped and turned to find Noah standing directly behind me. I narrowed my eyes. Only then did I inhale that weird spicy scent of his that kept me from humping his leg. "What are you doing here?"

Noah laughed, then pushed a stray dread behind his ear. I always had the perception that dreads were gross—stinky clumps of unwashed hair. Noah's were anything but. They actually smelled good.

He grinned. "Thank you. I try to take care of myself. And to answer your other question, nothin', babe. Just chillin'." He gave my toweled body the once-over—a long once-over. "You got any silver hidden under all that fluff?" he asked, inclining his head toward my over-sized white towel. His silver eyes winked in the daylight.

"Piss me off and find out," I answered.

He laughed again. "Always a tough ass, huh?"

"Pretty much."

"Turn around."

I glanced at him. "What?"

He rolled his eyes. Yes—the dead-sexy vampire with dreads rolled his freaking eyes. "Oh, dead sexy, yeah?" He chuckled. "I said, turn around. I want to see the dragon on your back."

I laughed but dropped my towel a bit in the back and turned around. "Dude, that line is lame. I get twenty re-quests a day to check out my dragon." I shook my head. "Vampires, dudes, undead, humans—all the same."

Noah's breath and fingertips brushed my bare back as he inspected—cough cough—my dragon tattoo. "What do you mean?"

I turned back around and met his mercury gaze. "Weenies! You all think with your weenies!"

Noah's eyes softened and held mine. A slight smile lifted the corner of his mouth. He shook his head and turned away. "Like I said"—he glanced back over his shoulder at me—"Eli's one lucky fuck. It's too bad he found you first."

I lifted a brow.

His grin spread to full-on, white-teeth-bared bright-ness. He laughed.

And then he walked away.

I stared after him.

"There's a sack full of Krystal's down here," he called over his shoulder.

"Yes!" I said happily, flung my towel off, and got dressed. Quickly fishing out a pair of loose green khaki hipsters with a wide leather belt and a burgundy halter, I left my hair down to dry, pulled on a pair of socks and my Vans, and hurried downstairs. Led by my growling stomach, I found the kitchen. By now it was two p.m. Seth sat at the table, chowing down. I glanced around.

"Where's Eli?" I asked Phin, who was propped against the counter. I must have had a worried expression on my face.

"Calm down, Poe," he said. "He tried to tell you this morning, but you were too sacked out." He rubbed a hand over his head. "He ran out to Garr's with Jack and Tuba. There were a few things they needed before tonight."

I crammed nearly half the burger into my mouth. Yes, hoggish, but I didn't care. Hot, squishy greasy bread— heaven. I was starving. "What's tonight?" I mumbled.

Noah dropped into the chair beside me and flung an arm over my shoulder. "Well, darlin', a lot of things," he said, his mercury eyes all but glowing. "First, a little dirty runnin'. Then, a little bit of Gullah-Gullah." He grinned. "Hoodoo."

I chewed. I only halfway understood.

I decided I'd know when it came.

Noah threw back his head and laughed.

The afternoon passed relatively fast. I dropped a call to Preacher and Estelle. They'd already spoken to Eli and knew of our plans. I promised my surrogate grandparents we'd stay safe and return soon.

"So," I said, finally full. I wiped my mouth on a napkin and swigged down several gulps of Coke. "What sort of Gullah-Gullah are we up to tonight?"

Noah grinned. "You'll see."

By the time the sun began to set, Eli, Jack, and Tuba returned. Eli walked in through the kitchen, spied me, and strode purposefully straight to me. Without missing a beat, he pulled me into his arms, and, despite my Krystal breath, kissed me full-on in front of everyone. Several whistles and yells filled the kitchen; all of which I imagined were everyone's except Noah's. When I looked at him, his gaze held mine, and he simply shook his head and mouthed, *Lucky fuck*. I laughed.

With Eli's arms like steel bands around me, I leaned back and looked into his eyes. "What sort of hoodoo are we about tonight?" I asked.

A slow grin spread across his sexy features. "A little grave robbing is all."

I lifted a brow. He laughed. "The only way to end Valerian's reign is to entomb him again. That's not going to be easy. But there are things we will need."

I nodded, accepting.

Soon, night fell.

Everyone except Jack and Tuba left Jake's on foot and free-ran the city. Oddly enough, we encountered nothing—no vamps, not even a mugging. Even stranger was that I didn't have a vision of Valerian the monster. I referred to it as a monster now because there were obvious character differences in vampires. At present I was living under the same roof with four, and at night kept company with eight in all. I trusted them all with Seth's and my life. Even the monster's own brother, to me, was safe. I fully believed he loved me, and although I didn't return the sentiment, I did like him. I knew he wouldn't hurt me despite what Eli and his family thought. And Eli and his kin, Noah and the others? They were Gullah-

vamps, as I started referring to them; Preacher's cousin
Garr treated Noah and his bunch just as Preacher
treated the Duprés. A pact to keep the city safe meant
keeping the vampires safe. Not only did their centuries-
old traditions of hoodoo magic keep their cravings to
a controlled minimum, but it made them . . . more like
their true human characters, I believe. Take Noah. I
can't imagine he was much different in life as he is now,
as an undead. Crazy fuck. I liked him, though—freaking
fine as all double hell, with or without his weird anti-
hump-me powder. He was a helluva free-runner, and an
even better fighter—a regular Tyler Durden with dreads
if you ask me. I loved having the secret that he was a
vamp concealed by some special hoodoo juice. As was
the truth about Seth's and Zetty's and my tendencies. It
was all pretty fantastic if you asked me.

We finished running the streets, and it was well past
two a.m. when we descended the buildings and entered
the Circular Church Cemetery in the historic district.
Any cemetery, in my book, was creepy at night; the Circular had to top the list as most creepy. A mist had sidled
in from the harbor and sifted through the aged trunks of
the live oaks, between the marble and slate headstones
covered in black decay and draped with moss. Swear to
God, it looked like something out of a freaking movie.
We closed the front gate behind us and eased deeper
into hallowed ground.

"Why is it you guys can come in here?" I asked.

Eli glanced at me, his hand tightly holding mine.
"What do you mean?"

"You know. Hallowed ground and all that," I answered in a whisper.

He grinned. "We're not evil spirits, Riley. Besides,

Garr fixed the cemeteries here a long, long time ago. Just like Preacher did the ones in Savannah."

"Gotcha," I said.

We continued on.

At one particular grave, Luc, who was leading, stopped. Jack and Tuba knelt beside it, murmuring Gullah words I couldn't understand. With a pocket knife, Jack scraped some of the headstone into a plastic cup with a screw lid; Tuba, with his hands, pulled at some of the sod until he reached dirt. Retrieving a bag from his back pocket, he opened it and sprinkled the contents all around the grave; then dug a few handfuls of dirt, dropping them into a ziplock.

I was beginning to see the value of a ziplock.

Moonlight shined down through the canopy of trees and shot darts of illuminated glow throughout the gravestones. Seth elbowed me, and pointed; I followed his finger to a Gothic-y square-sided spire, jutting into the sky.

"The Unitarian Church of Charleston," Noah said beside me. "Sort of reminds me of Notre Dame."

I had to agree.

"Whose grave is that?" I asked Noah.

He glanced down at me. His face grew somber in the moonlight. "Elizabeth Mont Frey. Once, a very beautiful, highly respected woman of Charles Towne." He glanced at the headstone. "She didn't make it through her quickening before she was killed. Garr was saved by his daddy," Noah looked at me. "They were taken at the same time, by the same vampire. You can imagine back then, a Gullah man and a prominent white woman, together." He sighed. "They were crazy in love, those two. Things haven't changed all that much, I'm afraid.

Anyway, despite her blood being tainted by a vampire, Garr insisted she have a Christian burial. Even in death, her body exudes mystics only Garr knows how to use." Noah's eyes bore into mine. "Almost as if she knows his desires, and allows only him to utilize her gifts."

I stared into the silver depths of Noah's gaze. I nodded in understanding.

We'd only just stepped out of the Circular Cemetery when Eli's back stiffened. Phin, Luc, Josie, and Noah glanced around, peering through the darkness. Saul, Jenna, Cafrey, and Tate, also on alert, began to move around the rest of us in a circle.

Then, they descended from the trees above us—six newlings; all punks, all rogues, all ravenous.

Eli shoved me—hard. "Get down, Riley!" he ground out. I flew several feet away and landed on my backside. I jumped right back up and ran to stand beside the one person I knew would let me fight—Noah.

Eli growled. It almost made me laugh, how protective he was. Even after seeing me fight, he still wanted me out of the fray. The newlings lunged, Eli swore in French, and the fight began.

I quickly learned why Eli was so concerned; they all seemed to hone in on *me*. I'm talking long-jawed, fangs dropped, faces grossly distorted, hideousness. Slobbering and rabid, they all lunged straight for me. Eli grabbed one by the throat and threw him against a tree. His body hit hard, but in a split second he was up, eyes seeking me out.

It gave me just the time I needed to grasp the blade from my back sheath, aim, and fling it at him. I threw hard. The blade hit its mark and pinned him to the tree.

He screamed in agony; I ignored him and turned to the others.

All of my vamps had changed. I tried not to focus on that.

I found Seth and we stayed back-to-back; Jack, Tuba, and Zetty formed a circle and did the same. Rogue vamps fell from the trees like flies. Where they all came from, I had no clue. I didn't recognize even one of them from the fight club. They were rabid, out of control, and lunging almost faster than my vamps could catch them.

Seth whipped a blade directly at one I swear was no more than three feet away. My brother was strong, and the blade hit hard, knocking the she-vamp back at least ten feet. Another blade flew by; Zetty had thrown that one and damn, he was one strong man. The vamp he nailed flew back and over the wrought-iron fence of the cemetery. It lay there, writhing, screaming, gurgling, until finally, it was silent.

Some of the rogues looked barely older than Seth. It made me sick; I'd puke later. Now, we had to survive. I nailed four more with blades, one rapid-fire shot after another. I no longer waited to see if I'd hit my mark; I knew I had.

I glanced to my left; Noah, whose beautiful face had contorted into something I'd rather not remember, grabbed a rogue just as it lunged past him, headed directly for me. In one shake he'd snapped its head off—clean freaking off, like a dandelion head. He dropped the body and turned to me, eyes white, red pupil dead center.

I could've sworn his lips curled into a smile.

The count had lowered, and although the remaining newlings continued to lunge toward me, my vamps took them all. Jenna and Saul had a pair; Cafrey and Tate had another. Although it felt like hours, only minutes had passed.

Before I knew it, the fight was over.

Garr's men came and collected the writhing, pawing, scratching newlings. That was a sight all its own. I had a hard time believing they could be detoxed. But with Preacher and Garr, anything was possible. They left in a van, leaving us with the mess.

Eli was suddenly at my side, his flawless face returned to normal. His hands searched my body for injury; his eyes followed. When he was satisfied I wasn't hurt, he pulled me into his arms and pressed his mouth to my temple. "You scared the shit outta me," he murmured against my hairline. "Such a badass, huh?"

"Survivalist," I corrected, but slipped my arms around his waist. His arms went around me, tightly, protectively. I confess I enjoyed it.

Luc approached. "All mostly mortals accounted for?"

Seth chuckled, and he, Jack, Tuba, and even Zetty murmured, "Yeah."

"Good," Luc said, and glanced around. "Let's clean this mess up and make like a tree and get outta here."

One more thing I hated about killing vamps: cleanup. You did not leave vampire waste lying around. It was a valuable hoodoo ingredient, and we salvaged every dust bit possible. Not to mention, Preacher and Garr now both believed that even a small fraction of a vamp left behind would be potential for resurrection later on.

To that I say, *No, thank you, Monster.*

Cleanup took longer than the kill. By the time we finished, the first church bell tolled from St. Michael's. It was six a.m., nearly light outside, and the group of us were toting around dusty vampire guts in ziplocks.

We hurriedly departed.

As we left the historic district, Eli ran on one side of

me; Noah, on the other. Noah glanced over at me. "So," the Charleston vampire said, mercury eyes catching the first rays of daybreak, "beautiful, huh?" He was referring to my earlier thought.

I shook my head and looked straight ahead. "Oh my God, the ego."

Eli laughed beside me, grabbed my hand, and pulled me faster.

Noah's voice trailed behind us. "You'd better keep a good grip on that hand, Dupré!"

He didn't have to finish. I knew exactly what was on Eli's mind.

Noah's laughter followed us to the battery, where he turned and departed with his crew, back to the dregs of the city.

I later learned he preferred it there so to keep a closer eye on things.

Apparently, Noah Miles took care of disobedient humans just as much as rogue vampires.

As we entered Jake's, we all filed in through the kitchen. Eli led me straight upstairs.

"I'm not going to ravage you this morning," he said, smiling. "But only because we've business at Garr's this morning."

I looked at him. "Who's staying here with us?"

"Josie will be here. Noah's only a head-shout away," he said, then frowned. "But I doubt you'll need him."

I gave Eli a slow smile. "Okay. Hurry back, then."

He pulled me against him and kissed me long, slow, and just when my hands crept up his neck and into his hair, he pushed me gently away. "I'll see you later," he said, with another quick kiss and an even quicker exit.

I looked at the door he'd just left through and smiled.

Quickly, I showered and fell into bed. I slept. I needed it. Late afternoon arrived too soon. Once we all were ready and the mortals had eaten, we headed out to the city. This time, we walked the historic district before it grew dark. We strolled through the city market, and Eli and his brothers and sister visited with some of the Gullah women selling baskets. They all knew the Duprés; I could tell they thought fondly of them.

Soon, darkness settled over the city, and we headed out of the historic district.

Atop the city, we ascended the buildings; Noah and his group met us close to the old burned-out church where the fights took place.

Eli grabbed me and spun me around. His expression tight, he looked . . . angry. "You can't imagine how I hate your going in here," he said, his eyes searching mine. "Stay close, Riley. And watch yourself. I mean it. I don't want to have to kill someone."

"Don't worry, Eli," I said, and grazed his jaw. His eyes darkened at my touch. "I don't exactly have a death wish, you know."

"You guys ready?" Noah asked.

"Yep," Phin answered, and he and Jack and Tuba pushed in ahead of us. Music thumped from inside the hollowed walls, and I knew tonight would be way different from the other night.

Apparently, they sparred at the fight club three nights a week and, after that third night, they chose—chose, and then fed. I was ready for it.

At least, I thought I was.

Noah suggested that Eli take Seth and Josie, Luc stay with me, Phin with Zetty, Noah with Jack and Tuba, and the rest scatter. Eli hesitantly agreed. We filed into the crowd, and I spotted the shade-wearing newlings immediately. They spotted me, too. I moved slightly away from Luc; I didn't want them thinking I had backup in any form. Immediately, the one newling from two days earlier approached.

"I see you made it back," he said, his lips curling into a grin that caused a shiver. "Jump in whenever you see opportunity."

"You know I will," I said, chin lifted.

I waited; I watched a few fights; I watched Eli over the crowd. Every time I looked at him, he was looking at me. How he kept his thoughts trained on the club, I had no idea. I tried not to dwell on it.

The fights were more vicious this night than the others.

The weak had indeed been weeded out.

Luc and I were standing close but not together. We'd all managed not to be linked and had stayed apart while at the club. It had taken some convincing, but Eli finally conceded and didn't stand glued to my side. I guess he was sort of starting to trust my abilities.

Victorian, though, did not. He suddenly interrupted my concentration.

"Honestly, Riley. I don't understand why you have to fight. Let the others do it. You're too delicate, and I couldn't stand the thought of your getting hurt."

In my head, I answered. "You've apparently not seen me fight, Vick. I got it. No sweat. Besides, Eli wouldn't let anything happen to me."

"He's good for something, I suppose. Still. Be careful."

"Later, Vick."

"I love that you have a nickname for me now. Makes me feel special."

Victorian finally left me alone, and my concentration zoned back to the fights. Some kid hadn't liked the way Seth had looked and had challenged him. We watched them spar now.

If that was what you wanted to call it.

I watched my baby brother take it all easy, slow, not show-offy like me. He reflected and ducked more than he fought; but when it came down to dirty business, Seth fought, and fought hard. I could feel his restraint with each punch, so much so that the ridges in his abdomen were flexing. He knew the force of his power, his tendencies, and no matter how much of a prick his opponent was, he didn't want them too badly hurt.

I was proud of him for that.

Seth roundhouse kicked the guy, who was at least a foot taller than he was, right in the chest and sent him sprawling. The movement knocked several spectators back. Seth followed him down, choked him with one leg, and dared him to move. No rules meant no rules, and when the kid tried to buck Seth off, Seth popped him in the nose. I heard the bone break from where I was standing.

Seth won that fight, but it was his last.

I saw opportunity in the form of another Billy Badass, and I jumped in. I heard Eli's hiss of disapproval from across the ring.

Too bad. This was why we were here. I wanted it to end—tonight. We'd rounded up dozens of newlings and those in the quickening. We needed to take the main vein of threat out—now.

Pushing through the crowd, who recognized me from the before, I shoved the weaker fighter out. The crowd roared. My opponent was a big, burly, helluva guy; midthirties, shaven head, muscles on top of muscles. He stood no less than six feet six inches.

He slowly rounded on me, the roar of the spectators so loud, I couldn't think. I kept my eyes trained on him. He grinned.

"Fightin' you is gonna be more fun than fuckin' you," he said in a thick, country-fried drawl. "Maybe I'll do both." He cracked his neck.

I simply grinned. What a big, brainless dick. "If you think you can," I egged him, "come on."

The big idiot circled me. He wore a dingy-white wife beater, cheap jeans, big leather boots. He wore chunky gold—probably fake—rings on four fingers, on each hand. He stuck out his tongue. It was extra long, extra gross, and he must've thought extra sexy, with the gold ball pierced through it. Inwardly, I cringed. He probably had a little pecker.

I saw Eli in my peripheral. Noah stood beside him, probably to restrain him.

A punch flew my way and I ducked; he missed me, and I dipped and popped up behind him. With a round-house I kicked him in the shoulder blades, and he stumbled forward. The crowd laughed.

He did not.

Foul words flew from his mouth, along with a disgusting amount of spit; I did not entertain him with some of my own. I watched him close. For a big guy, he moved with more grace than I'd have given him credit for. He swung a few more times, and I nimbly dodged his fists. The last thing I wanted was my juicy delicious blood, tainted though it might be, spilled on the fight club floor with newlings all around. I let him get close, then swung upward with both fists clenched, landed it into his nose, two elbows to the gut, and once he was bent over at the waist, I kicked his knees out. He hit the mat with a yelp and a curse.

He tried to get up.

I landed a solid punch to his jaw. He teetered, swayed, then fell back. Out cold.

With the crowd cheering, I left the ring.

Across the ring, I saw Eli's face. Mad was not the term I'd use to describe his expression. He was . . . more like a half inch away from changing. Tee-total pissed off—at me or the dickhead, I couldn't say.

"You are so sexy when you kick ass," Luc said in my ear. "Too bad my big brother wants to wring your neck for it."

"Whatever," I said. We watched a few more fights. I got in a few of them. Despite how good I was at it, I really, really hated it. I wanted it to end, the night to be over, the newlings put in their places, the monster caught—not necessarily in that order.

Eventually, the familiar newling—who I guessed was a leader of sorts—approached me.

"So, how have the pussies managed?" he asked over the roaring crowd.

I shrugged. "I'm still here."

The smile he gave me chilled me. "And you've only fought one decent opponent. Come to ringside."

I glanced at Luc, and he nodded forward. I glanced upward, at the next level, and met gazes first with Eli, Phin, Seth, then Noah. Zetty and Josie were on our level and in the corner.

They all had my back.

I shrugged and followed the newling.

And then stepped into the ring with a newling.

The moment I saw her, I knew it'd be a challenge; she was lithe, young, and obviously had contacts in to mask her opaque eyes. But I knew. I could sense her undeadliness. She wore head-to-toe black leather, like some freakish postapocalyptic catwoman, and the look of sheer confidence in her face could have chilled me, had I allowed it. I did not.

I'd learned a while back not to wear restrictive clothing to fight in; it was easier to withdraw my silver in baggy clothes. And since they were all hidden below the waist, I stripped off my tank, to the roar and whistles and cries of the mostly male crowd, leaving me to fight in a black sports bra. My opponent's eyes were nailed to mine as she circled me; I circled her. When she attacked, I held back not one ounce of strength.

She was a fury of fists and long-legged kicks; so fast I almost had a difficult time keeping up. Her abilities challenged me, provoking my adrenaline to rush through me, and I gave back just as good as she offered. She roundhouse kicked me in the jaw; I'd almost managed to duck, but she caught me with the heel of her foot and it sent me reeling. The moment I landed on the floor, she was on me. I bucked her off and straddled her; she did the same. We both landed on our feet again. I lunged this time, not waiting for her. I came down, both fists clenched, and smashed into her jaw. She yanked me by my ponytail and brought my face close to hers.

"I know what you are, bitch," she said. "You know what I am?"

"Oh yeah," I muttered, and elbowed her in the gut. She dropped me.

"We'll fight, then," she said. "Like mortals."

Our fight continued over the cheers of the crowd.

Suddenly, another joined in.

I now faced two female newlings.

With a quick glance, I found Eli. Noah physically had his hands on Eli's arms. He was holding him back. And Eli's face looked thunderous. I ignored it.

I took one helluva whipping, but I kept them both off me. At least, I kept their fangs from probing into my flesh. It was almost as if they dared me to make them morph; I have no idea if they knew I carried silver. But because of the number of mortals in the room, I wasn't about to drop them.

I could have, but I didn't.

My body was rushed by both; I leapt and cleared them. The crowd cheered.

Then, the crowd grew silent.

Then, they started to scream.

Only then did I notice why.

The newlings had begun their attacks on mortals. I guess my cover, and probably those of the others, were now officially blown. I didn't glance around; I didn't have time. The two newlings in the ring with me were now determined to make me one of them. They lunged, simultaneously, and I had to concentrate and zone the screams out, focusing just on *them* if I wanted to stay alive.

As a mortal with tendencies; not a newling.

I bounded off one of them—using her face as a springboard as I grasped the silver from my hip in mid-air and plunged it at the she-vamp lunging toward me. The moment she dropped, I did the same, crouched, grasped another blade from the other hip, and threw it at the other. She was ready for me, though, and caught it.

I grasped another, aimed, but before it left my hand,

she lunged; a body flew in front of me, directly at her. They collided. Chaos was all around me, and all I could do was stand there and stare, dumbfounded.

Eli.

He ripped the she-vamp's heart out, as it was the only way to instantly kill besides using a silver blade. When he turned and spared me a look, it truly frightened me.

It wasn't just that his face had contorted. I dare not even say what I really thought.

"Get out of here, Riley," he ordered, his voice a deep growl.

I set my jaw.

"Luc! Get her the *fuck* out of here!" he yelled over the crowd.

I turned and ran, but not away. Blood and killing were all around me; the metallic scent of human blood tainted the air, along with the screams. I was going to take out as many newlings as possible before I let any Dupré take me outside. I found one, his fangs about to pierce the throat of a boy no older than twenty. I was close. With Five Finger Death Punch's "Hard to See" slamming in some random boom box and mixing with mortal screams and blood gurgling, I lunged, plunging my silver blade directly into his heart, just before his fangs made contact. I didn't wait for reaction. I sought another.

Mentally counting my blades, I totaled nine left. In my peripheral, I saw Seth and Zetty, both with gleaming blades in their own hands. I glanced and saw Noah's beautiful face transformed once again; Phin's and Luc's as well. And Josie's. I didn't look for Eli; I knew he'd be one pissed-off vampire. I'd worry about it later. After this.

This was over in less than thirty minutes.

I knew it was over when all was quiet. Some mortals had escaped. The ones who'd been bitten remained inside; Garr's people would be here soon to collect them. I knew that because Noah had already morphed back into his human form and was talking on the cell phone. I zoned in and listened long enough to know that an ass-load of bitten mortals would be taken to Garr's version of Da Island this night. At least a lot would be saved. But this was still not over. Far from over—just . . . *this* was over. For now.

I glanced around at the ones who would never see life again. They lay in heaps of mangled flesh, blood, and bone; some with their chest cavities ripped wide open, their hearts pierced. Some even still pumped blood, and I had to wonder for a split second how Noah, his folks, and the Duprés could stand being in such close proximity of so much blood and not go . . . nuts. That was the power of hoodoo and the conjuring of Preacher and Garr, I suppose. Pretty cool shit.

Without my permission, my body gave out; I dropped to both knees and simply looked around. I'd used all of my blades; I was still covered in mortal blood and vamp goo. I felt as if I'd been in a medieval melee, as if I'd been fighting alongside William Wallace or something. This had to be close to what that'd been like.

Minus the vampire aspect, of course.

I was drained. My head throbbed. I no longer had the capability to filter out all of the exaggerated sounds and scents of the city. I resisted the urge to cover my ears.

"I wish someone—anyone—would turn that fucking boom box off," I yelled.

I waited; no one did, so I got up, pushed my way

through the bodies of mortals and dusty piles of vampire newlings, and found the music. I love some Five Finger Death Punch, don't get me wrong. But I was drained; irritable beyond belief, and ... something else I couldn't define. PMS? Who the fuck knows.

I picked the box up and threw it against the wall.

I felt my body falling then, completely out of gas.

Strong arms caught me before I hit the floor.

When I looked, it was Eli's painfully beautiful face I saw, and I inhaled deeply. He smiled down at me, lines of worry etched into his brow. "Hey, gorgeous," he said.

The beauty of his smile gave me energy.

A lot of energy.

I tilted, regained my footing, and Eli steadied me on my feet. He moved to wrap me in an embrace I knew—knew—I'd melt into. Unfortunately, I didn't get the chance.

I passed the hell out.

Part Nine

CAPTIVE

"Monsters are real, and ghosts are real too. They live inside us, and sometimes, they win."

—Stephen King

"What did I say before? Don't fuck with my loved ones. Sorry for the potty mouth of late, but Jesus and hot damn—a lot of shit's happening and, frankly, it's starting to overwhelm. I'm afraid it's going to consume me, all this evil; or at least turn me into some crazed, psycho, silver-totin', vampire-huntin' fool who says fuck way too much. It's like who the hell can you trust anymore? I keep finding that the ones you least likely thought you could trust are the most trustworthy of them all. How weird is that, huh? All I know is this: all the horror movies you watched as a teenager? Go back and watch them again. Make notes. Make lists from the notes. There are survival skills embedded in those wacky dacky fricky fracky slasher stories that will one day come in freaking handy. Start with Zombieland. Smart movie, that. Rule number four: the double tap."

—Riley Poe

My eyes fluttered open; it was daylight. I scrubbed my closed lids with my knuckles, then looked around, gathering my bearings; Jake's place in Charleston; king-sized bed; my own personal veranda. I glanced beside me.

One hot freaking naked vampire.

Eli Dupré, damn him and his birthday suit, lay

sprawled out beside me in the white down fluff of a gazillion-count comforter. I strained my eyes hard and searched the digital clock on the far side of the room— three forty-five p.m. Damn, I'd slept a long time. Eli seemed out cold, too. I didn't remember getting here, getting naked, or falling into bed. It made me wonder just what else I didn't recall.

For a moment, I permitted my eyes the pleasure of looking slowly over Eli's beautiful, flawless self. Dark lashes brushed his pale cheeks; tousled black hair fell over one eye. Muscles cut into his lean frame were covered by a layer of silky-smooth pale skin. Perfect lips, slightly parted, invited me. I was tempted.

I quickly glanced at myself again. Oh yeah, I was naked, too. I was totally tempted.

Oh my God! Had I had sex and didn't know it? What kind of freaking torture was that?

There was no way to tell until Eli woke up, I supposed.

I resumed my perusal, but hey—I was a girl in love. Yes, I admitted to myself, I loved Eli, and it seemed like a long freaking time since I'd just casually gandered. I did remember socking him the other night in the club, but as I inspected his perfect features, I saw no evidence of it.

I lay back, not wanting to get out of bed yet, and obviously not realizing how tired my body still was. One second, I was there, stroking Eli's skin with my fingertips, and in the next second I closed my eyes again, and I was walking along the riverfront, at a slow, leisurely pace. *As I looked around, I saw several things that disturbed me. One, was the* Savannah River Queen. *That riverboat worked singularly out of Savannah Harbor. I continued to walk, and my vision was his—the monster's—once more. I looked one way and saw River Street Sweets, and farther down, the Hyatt Regency Hotel. I glanced in the opposite direction and noticed the SoHo Boutique. Through the storefront window I saw little Bhing, rushing around in her fast-walking manner, helping several customers browsing through her clothes racks.*

My vision then moved with his, the monster's, and it settled on the storefront window next door.

Inksomnia.

Next to that, Da Plat Eye.

His eyes moved back to Inksomnia's storefront, peering directly at Nyx as she gathered her skull and crossbones shoulder bag and headed out the front door. She turned, locked the door, and started up the walk.

He stood and followed.

I began to thrash, to scream, "No! Nyx! Oh my God, please don't let this monster go after my best friend!" Inside, my adrenaline rushed as fiercely as if I ran hard; I mentally kicked and screamed. It did no good.

He crossed the cobbles, stepped up onto the sidewalk, politely stepped aside as a passerby moved by him. His gaze found Nyx again.

We then passed another storefront. He glanced in. I looked.

He stopped, staring.

Somehow, in the reflection, he saw me, too. He recognized me and mouthed, "Hello, Riley," in the glass so I'd see.

A slow smile spread across his unfamiliar face. He was just a random victim, midthirties, tanned leathery skin, menacing eyes. Valerian indeed knew me, and he'd manifested his DNA into this new victim. He had a different body, but he was the same monster. Slowly, he lifted one finger to his lips, mentally telling me to keep quiet. Then he crooked that same finger, mentally beckoning me.

His maniacal laugh woke me cold turkey out of the vision. And at the same time, another voice infiltrated my head.

"He wants you to come, love," Victorian said, his voice angry, heavy. "He cannot speak to you in your mind, as I can, but he has found me. He speaks to me. And he wants you to come back to Savannah. Alone."

"Really?" I said inside my head. "No shit. And why, Victorian? Have you known his plan all along? Have you known who he was, where he was, all this time?"

"No!" Victorian said with vehemence. "He's no longer my brother. My brother died a long time ago. He didn't resist the evil as I did. He's, as you say, a monster. Out of control."

I believed him. "So what do I do?" I said to him in my thoughts. "Why can't I at least bring Zetty and the guys?"

"He'll play only by his rules, love," Vick said. "He's in control. All I can do is tell you what he seeks. And that's you. He'll know if you bring anyone. He'll kill your friend if you do"

I gave a short laugh that was not a laugh at all. "I'm on my way."

"I'll do what I can to help, Riley. Never would I let you be harmed."

I ignored Vick's last statement. A wash of dread crashed over me.

I sat up, still nude, still beside my naked vampire, who was still totally out cold. I'd been warned by Preacher never to awaken slumbering vampires. Not that they'd purposely harm me, or any other mortal, but being roused out of their vampiric slumber might cause a reaction they'd not like. Or I'd not like.

Much like the crazy-ass bird in my dream had crawled across the branch, I crawled from bed, doing my very best to keep quiet.

Valerian was alive—manifested in another's body, but still alive. I wasn't sure exactly how but what I did know was that the bastard was using Nyx as bait. In my heart I knew he'd kill her just for spite, and I had to get to her in time. It was all coming to an end. Valerian Arcos was the monster. And I was going to kill him. He wanted to throw rules at me? Don't bring my guys? Don't wake Eli? Fine. He'd be in for a big-ass surprise when I rolled into town.

I strapped on every sheath I owned and stuffed each one with every silver blade I could find. I pulled on a loose gauzy skirt, a ribbed tank, pulled my hair into a ponytail, and found my shades, Jeep keys, and backpack. I slipped into my Vans.

As I made my way through Jake's mansion, I noticed everyone else was out cold, too—all except Jack and Tuba; I didn't see them anywhere. I took a solid five seconds to look at my baby brother's face; his smooth skin, his dark hair and brows, his relaxed expression. It was a very real possibility I wouldn't see him again.

I left before I bawled.

I eased out of the kitchen door, crept to my Jeep, popped the emergency brake, and made sure it was in neutral; I pushed it down the drive and out into the street. Thinking better of it, I pushed it a little more, away from Jake's, then jumped in, started it up, and tore up the street. Soon I was headed south on US 17, toward Savannah.

Hopefully, to save my best friend's life

And kill someone—something—that was supposed to be already freaking dead.

I grabbed my cell and dialed Nyx's number. Maybe at least I could warn her; tell her to get her ass to the Duprés'. It rang and rang.

"Pick up, dammit!" I yelled over the wind. "Freaking pick up, Nyx!"

She didn't.

It went to voice mail.

"Get your ass to the Duprés' and stay there," I said. "Do it!"

Then I dialed the Duprés. Thankfully, Elise picked up. Valerian didn't want me bringing help? Well I damn sure would call for some.

"Riley darling, what's wrong?" she said.

"Nyx is in trouble and she won't pick up her cell," I said frantically. "It's Valerian, Elise. He's the monster. He's manifested himself into another of his victims who carries his DNA. He ... saw me in a vision and has threatened to kill Nyx if I bring anyone. I'm on my way home, but I'd hoped you could—"

"Gilles and I will go look for her," Elise said. "You calm down, sweetheart, and drive safely. Is Eli at least with you?"

"No, ma'am. They're all in slumber."

"You left alone?" she asked.

I sighed. "Yes, ma'am."

"Oh, dear, are you in big trouble."

"I know. I left a note."

"Hmm. Hurry. But drive safely, love."

"Yes, ma'am."

We disconnected and I raced up the highway. My ponytail all but beat me to death, but I didn't care. I hit Nyx's speed dial a gazillion times, but she never would pick up. Not until the last time, that is.

My cell phone vibrated against my thigh. I picked it up and looked at the screen. Nyx. I answered. "Nyx!"

"Riley," an unfamiliar voice said. I could hear the smirk in his tone and it made me want to throw up. It was Valerian, but not Valerian.

"Don't touch her," I warned. "I fucking mean it, Valerian. Do not."

He laughed then—laughed hard. "So you've discovered my little secret, yes? Impressive. Unfortunately, I had to trade in my youthful body for this older one, but it'll do for now. You meet me at Tunnel Nine, just off Washington, an hour after dusk. If you're a good little bitch, you'll do exactly as I say. I'm sure you don't want to watch your friend here die."

"Riley," I heard Nyx whimper in the background. "Hurry. Please."

"Can I—"

The line went dead. I knew what kind of monster he was; I'd watched him feed multiple times. He had no mercy. Which meant I had no time.

If Nyx made it through this, it'd be a miracle. My stomach lurched, my insides raged with fear for her.

The only thing that could save her was the possibility he'd want me worse than he'd want Nyx. I prayed that was the case. Nyx would not be a challenge to him. She'd be an easy, effortless kill. I, on the other hand, would be anything but.

Thankful the traffic was thin, I raced toward Savannah. Once I hit Interstate 95 South, I threw the Jeep into fifth gear and tore up the road.

I made it to Inksomnia, and I ran in through the back door. I'm not sure what I searched for; I knew everything would be exactly where it needed to be. The monster—Valerian—hadn't come inside. He'd waited for Nyx outside. She was with him now, terrified, and it made anger boil inside me. Out of control, I screamed, and punched the wall. My fist broke through the sheetrock. I sagged against the wall and sank to the floor, sobbing.

I knew I was being useless right now; crying and whining, doing the wall-slide while my best friend sat, prisoner of a vicious killer. What the freak was wrong with me? Why couldn't I find him myself? Why couldn't freaking Victorian help me find him?

Preacher would know what to do. Maybe there was something he could give me, I didn't know. To help me find Nyx? I concentrated—hard—on my new senses. Maybe I could hear her, if she was close enough? I strained my ears, and a flood of sounds fell in. None of them was distinctively Nyx. I sighed and dropped my head against the wall.

The thought lingered in my brain, and lingered a fraction too long. Just when I'd made my mind up to run next door, heaviness settled over my body, weighed me down, nailed me to the very spot I'd fallen to the floor. I tried to speak; I tried to move. My arms, legs were like anvils, and I could move neither. My insides wretched because I knew what was coming. Even in my paralyzed state, I knew.

My eyelids fell, and darkness fell behind them, a menacing shadow that no matter how hard I tried to lift, it wouldn't. Finally, it did, and *I found myself looking through his eyes once again; I tried closing mine, fearful of what I'd see. I couldn't. I felt the pleasure he took in knowing me now, in knowing I unwillingly watched, partially participated, and it made me wonder if he hated me that much; that he'd kill Nyx just so I'd have no choice but to be a part of it. Nausea swept over me, but I couldn't even relieve the sick sensation myself by vomiting. He moved. I moved with him.*

We were downtown, on the other side of Bay Street and over the bridge; an old apartment building, dark, a bad neighborhood. He pushed into a side door and entered the building, taking the first set of stairs to the right. Climbing three flights effortlessly, he passed no one. On the third floor, he opened the door and stepped into the corridor. A small dog barked its head off in some random apartment close by. Otherwise, no one was about. He walked to the end, to the very last room. The apartment number was 340. He knocked. The door opened, and relief washed over me as a woman, not Nyx, stood there. She stood in the doorway, in a short blue skirt that barely covered her ass, a thin black vest that laced up the front, barely containing the extraordinarily large, perfectly round fake breasts, and high leather boots that reached her thighs. A stripper, maybe? A hooker? A cigarette dangled from her mouth, and without touching it, she pulled on it, inhaled, then blew a plume of smoke in his face. Early thirties, she wore heavy makeup, thick black eye liner, electric blue shadow. Her hair, several shades of blond, was braided back from her face, then left to fall in dreads halfway down her back.

She removed the cigarette from her lips. Her nails were painted the same blue as her eye shadow. "I have to work in an hour," she said, her voice low, husky from years of smoking. She knew him. And he knew her. He liked her.

She reached down then, grabbed my hand—his hand,

and pulled him into her apartment. Seductively, she leaned into him, locked the door, pulled the chain latch. She let her hand trail down his chest, down his stomach, to his belt where she loosened it and slid her hand down the front of his pants.

"Oooh," she crooned, her eyes growing dark with lust. "Cock's already hard for me, huh baby?" She rubbed her thumb over it, squeezed, then let go. "Wanna show first? Like always?" Crooking her finger, she beckoned him. "This way."

She sauntered backward, then turned and moved seductively through the small apartment. He followed, with me, trapped in his filth. The girl leaned over the kitchen counter where she already had a line of coke, snorted it, then rose up, wiping her nose and sniffing. A glass with amber liquid sat nearby. She grabbed it, downed it, and licked her lips. Setting the glass down, she kept her eyes trained on him.

I fully understood her; the only way she could stand being in Valerian's presence was to first do a line of coke and down some liquor. Didn't blame her for that.

The woman moved toward him, then led him by the hand to an overstuffed chair in the living room. She playfully pushed him into it, then backed away, keeping her eyes on his. She began to sway seductively; her fingers grasping the laces holding her vest together and tugging slowly until her breasts spilled out. Wasted now, she licked her fingers, one by one; groped her breasts; grazed her nipples and moaned.

His cock stiffened, and nausea swept me as I felt his excitement grow to a fever. He knew I hated this; he did it on purpose to torment me.

The woman continued her seduction; it worked on

him. She moved toward him, slowly lifting her skirt, revealing nothing below, all hair shaven. She touched herself, moaned again, and as she grew close, draped one long, booted leg over one arm of the chair, the other leg over the other arm. She wiggled her bareness into his lap, and his adrenaline pumped hard.

With haze-filled, high-as-a-kite eyes, she stared into his. Her fingers fumbled in his jeans and freed his hardness. Taking it in her hands, she stroked it, and just when she was about to straddle it, he pushed her back.

"Suck me," he instructed.

With a slow smile, she slid off his lap and knelt between his legs.

The moment her mouth encased him and she drew him in, he came. He grabbed her by the hair hard and held her mouth in place. At first, she moaned in pleasure. I never wanted to throw up so badly in my entire life. I bucked and writhed inside, and still, I could do nothing. I couldn't even close my fucking eyes.

He knew it, too. The sick, sick bastard knew it. I'm pretty sure that turned him on as much as the woman had.

I knew the exact moment he decided to kill her.

He thrust once more, yanked her up by her hair, and stared into her eyes for a split second. Her large breasts dangled. She threw a leg over his arm, hoping there'd be more.

There was, but not what she'd imagined.

He changed; I saw nothing but the look of terror in her eyes.

Then, he covered her mouth with his hand and plunged his fangs into her chest, ripped into the cavity, and entered her heart. It pumped for nearly a full minute, warm blood squirting deep into his throat. Before the last beat, he *flung her from him. Her body crumpled to the floor, her face turned just enough to stare lifelessly at him.*

At me.

He rose, belted his pants, lifted his zipper. Without another glance he walked right past her body.

In the small foyer, he stopped, looked left, and stared directly into a mirror.

"That was for you, Riley Poe," he said, his voice making me physically shake inside. "I thought of you while I came."

In my dark purgatory, I screamed, kicked, swore, cried.

He laughed.

"Dusk, girl. Don't be late. And don't goddamn bring anyone with you, or your little friend will die way worse than this one did today."

"Riley!"

My eyes fluttered open, and I stared into the dark brown orbs of Preacher's worried gaze. "Girl, what you doin' on the floor? Git up now," he said, grasping my arm and helping me to stand. He peered at me. "You seen somethin' bad, right? I could tell on your face, baby. You seen somethin' bad."

I nodded. "I did, Preach." I hugged him. "I hate this. It's got to end," I said, holding back tears.

He pulled away and looked at me for several seconds. "It's goin' to, baby girl," he said. "I promise you dat. But you gonna have to pull some strength from down there," he said, tapping my heart. "I talked to Gilles. I know dat Valerian monster has Nyx." He stared hard at me. "Dem Duprés, and dat Noah—dey on dere way now. You watch yourself till dey git here, dat's right. Now I gotta go back to your grandmodder. I don wanna leave her alone wit all dis goin' on today. Might take her to da Dupré House."

I hugged Preacher again—maybe for the last time. "You go take her there. I'll keep my cell on me, and I'll call Gilles if anything goes on. Promise."

"Okay, baby," he said. "I trust you, and I know you been trained good. Be careful." And with a final glance, he left my apartment.

With a silent prayer, I begged whomever to keep my surrogate grandparents alive and well.

For a second, I could do nothing more than stand in the center of my apartment and try to think. Not an easy task when your best friend was being held hostage. But I had to clear my mind. Quickly, I strapped on my sheaths and blades. Then, I sat, but for only a few minutes. I put my head down on my kitchen table, my mind a jumble of wires. *Then I found myself at the top of a castle wall walk, peering over into the trees and forest beyond. My palms gripped cool stone, and, as I looked down, I noticed the dragons winding around both of my arms. I wore a bejeweled shift; if I didn't know better, I'd think it some sort of a medieval wedding gown. It was the first piece of clothing from my dreams that wasn't sexual. Amazing.*

Why would I be wearing a medieval wedding gown?

"Ah," Victorian's voice said, softly, sexily, "because it is what you secretly dream of. Marriage"—he leaned over my shoulder, brushing his mouth against my ear—"with me."

"No, I do not," I insisted. "Why am I here?" I asked. "This is not the time for one of our visits. What is this, your home? In Romania?"

He now stood beside me, looking out over the landscape. "Yes, it is. Beautiful, isn't it?" He was silent for a few moments, scouring the land before us. "As beautiful as you, I imagine."

"*Victorian,*" I began, "*don't.*"

"*Don't what, love?*" he asked, then chuckled lightly. "*Don't for a second think I'll give up my pursuit of you, Riley Poe. Never have I wanted another so fiercely. And I am used to getting everything I want.*"

Now I chuckled. "*Yeah well, you can't always have everything you want, Vick.*"

"*Why not?*"

With a heavy sigh, I turned to him. "*Because you just can't. That's why.*" The present returned to me, and I looked hard at him. "*Why can't you help me? You know what sort of trouble Nyx is into now, and yet you've made yourself scarce at the most crucial of times. Why is that?*"

He looked down at me, his dark, liquid eyes troubled. "*I am in transit; it is difficult for me to connect. I am sorry.*"

I nodded and rubbed a rough patch of stone beneath my fingertip. "*Everything is fucked up. Valerian recognizes me. He has even seen me in a storefront reflection, and in a mirror. He's captured Nyx and is tormenting me, threatening to kill her. I can't stand another second of it. If anything were to happen to her—*" I sobbed. I hadn't meant to, but it escaped.

"*Christ, Riley. Don't weep. Please,*" he said, and grazed my wet cheek with his knuckle. "*I am trying my best to get to you. Please, hold on just a little longer.*" He leaned close to me and sniffed my hair. "*What else has my brother said to you?*"

"*He wants me to meet him at dusk, at this club,*" I answered. "*I'm pretty sure he wants to trade Nyx for me. I'll do it; he has no idea what sort of a fight I can put up.*"

"*Do the others know?*" he asked, worry lines etched deep into his face. "*Are they aware of matters?*"

I shrugged. "Probably by now they are. I've turned my phone off to rejuv myself before the big fight tonight.

"That comforts me little." He put his hands on my shoulders and turned me around to face him. "Don't do anything foolish, Riley. I'll be there, and I'll make it better. Do you understand?" he asked.

I nodded. "Yes, Vick, I understand. Seriously. I got this."

Victorian then leaned his head close to me, and brushed his lips against mine—not kissing, just very, very close. "No, Riley," he whispered, "I do not think you do. But I will make sure you obey my every command this night. " 'Tis the only way."

I jerked awake. Immediately, I glanced at the clock.

An hour before dusk.

Hurriedly, I got ready.

This time, the hunt, the evil, would end.

Part Ten

—◆◆—◆◆—

TORMENTED

"No man knows till he experiences it, what it is like to feel his own life-blood drawn away into the woman he loves."

—Bram Stoker, *Dracula*

"I never thought it'd end this way. Oh my God! I didn't. Inside, my heart feels like it's being ripped out, just like one of the monster's victims. The pain is so great I can barely breathe, and I feel like it hardly even beats anymore. I don't know how things are going to turn out, or if I'll ever see the ones I love again, but I will never, ever give up. I know I'm rough around the edges, I've got a sailor mouth, but when I love, I love, you know? I took a fucking beating as a kid; I deserve happiness as an adult. I've worked hard for it. My loved ones deserve happiness. I used to want nothing more than to have my mother back. I miss her! But she's in a good place—a place only angels like her go to. What I want now are my live loved ones. I want Nyx. I want Seth. I want Eli. My grandparents. I want them all. But I'm not sure I'll get what I want after all, in the end. You can bet your sweet ass I'll die trying, though."

—Riley Poe

I'd ignored all calls from all acquaintances. It didn't matter what they knew or where they could go. I knew whom Nyx was with, and he wanted me. I knew that now. I figured Eli and the others would talk to his parents and they'd all head this way. I'd told Elise and Gilles exactly where I'd be going, and what time. For now, though, it was he and I—Monster vs. Bitch. No more newling puppets.

I prayed I would win.

I didn't change clothes; I didn't need to. I had eleven silver blades tucked away beneath my skirt, and if it took every single one to take Valerian down, I'd do it.

For spite, I wanted to plunge one of my silver blades into each of his eyes, just for making me watch the filth and horrors of his desires.

The streets were busy for a Thursday night; the humidity heavy; the brine heavier. As I pulled into the parking area for Tunnel 9, the scent of stale urine assaulted me. I choked back a gag, slipped out, and looked around. Several cars filled the parking lot; heavy metal thumped against the walls from inside, and I could hear people pissing in the toilets near the back of the buildings. I'd turned on all my senses and wasn't about to go unarmed. My best friend was in there. My worst enemy held her against her will. He had the ability to rip her heart out.

I'd rip his out first.

I filed in behind a group of people walking in; young twenties, dressed to the hilt, completely unaware of what sort of monsters really exist. I know most people don't believe in monsters; I didn't for a while. I damn sure as hell believed now. I believed in a lot of things now.

Inside, smoke filled the room; smoking was against the law, but somehow, places still got away with it. The place, newly opened, reminded me a lot of the Panic Room. As the crowd jumped and moved to the music, I weaved in and out, keeping a low pro, and inching my way to a place that seemed all-too familiar. I was drawn to the back, just like at the Panic Room.

Riley! Please help me!

I heard Nyx's voice and glanced frantically around. "Where are you?" I shouted.

The couple next to me glanced at me as if I were nuts. *In the back! Please! I'm so scared!*

I wanted to run—I couldn't. People were crammed

into the club like friggin' sardines. I pushed my way to the back, elbowing, squeezing, and just when I thought I would cut through to the back, I felt a vision creeping up on me. Oh God! No! Please don't let it be, please don't let it be . . .

Near the back wall, I sank to the floor, shadows filled my eyes, and I saw nothing. Then, slowly, light filtered in. Dead silence surrounded me. A familiar scent rose to my nostrils—Downy fabric softener. I glanced around. I was standing inside my old apartment, in the foyer, by the front door.

It was the apartment Seth and I had shared with Mom.

I blinked; in the very next second I slammed the door behind me. "Mom! Are you even freaking here?" Irritated, I sighed and moved to the kitchen, opened the fridge, and drank from the orange juice carton. When I was finished, I put an empty carton back. "Hey—Mom! Come on, dammit! I need some money!" I waited, my irritation growing at why in hell she wasn't answering. Angry now, I stomped to the back, pausing long enough in the hall to stare at myself in the mirror. Thick black liner rimmed my eyes and swept outward, like Cleopatra, and grazed my angel wing tattoo. It looked fucking wicked if you asked me. Mom hated it, though. "Hey!" I shouted, angrier. It pulled me away from the mirror, and I stomped to Mom's room and looked around. The bed was unmade, clothes strewn on the floor, the lamp broken on the floor beside the nightstand. What the hell? "Mom!" I yelled, and noticed the bathroom door ajar. I hurried to it and flung open the door. I froze as my eyes locked on to my mother's. Hers were unseeing, lifeless. She lay in a half-filled tub of water, naked. My heart leapt to my throat. "Mom!" I hollered, in a totally different tone now.

My heart slammed inside me; fear choked me. "Mom, Mom!" I continued to shout. I grabbed her by her shoulders and tried to drag her out of the tub. Her body was cold; wet, and a little stiff. Her body slipped, and she sank back into the water. "No!" I cried, and grabbed her again, this time more tightly, under the arms. I pulled, sank all of my weight onto my heels, and heaved until her body slid, over the rim of the tub, and fully onto me. We both fell back onto the tile floor.

It was then I noticed the blood.

The blood, and the rip in her chest where her heart should have been.

I shook her then, hard. "Mom!" I yelled into her ear. "Mom!"

Nothing. My mother was dead, already starting to stiffen, cold.

Sobs wracked my body, and I held her tightly, crying her name, over and over and over. I don't know how long I lay there, soaked, my mother's dead body on top of mine, cradled in my arms. It must have been a long time, because my teeth chattered, and my insides shook continuously and uncontrollably until the black-as-night man—my mother's employer—pulled me away from her. My fingers wrapped around her now-dried skin and refused to let go.

"She's in shock," I heard a slightly accented voice say. "If she's lucky, she won't remember any of this, Preacher."

"I hope she don remember, dat's right," the black man said. "Dat poor baby girl."

"Riley! Get up!"

I heard a faint laugh, somewhere deep, somewhere far, far away. It was Valerian's laugh.

I turned. My eyes widened in shock at the person

whose tight grip on my forearms was pulling me off the floor.

Victorian.

He pulled me close, his hands on my elbows; he brought his mouth to my ear. "He is here, love," he said, his breath brushing my skin. "Please, come with me. I swear to you I'll get your friend to safety."

I pulled back and sought Victorian's eyes.

"You will come with me, Riley. Now," he said, his voice alluring, pulling at my mind, into some unfamiliar zone. "Hurry."

My mind was a ball of tangled barbed wire. I'd just had a vision of the day when I'd found my mother's body, and here before me stood a vampire whom I'd known mostly in my dreams. In my heart, I didn't want to go with him. Somehow, though, he made me—against my will. My actions were no longer mine. I couldn't help it; I reached out and grazed his jaw with my fingertips, just to see if he was real. He was real, and this was real—not a dream; not a vision. Confusion made my brain ache. "Nyx."

"I know," Victorian urged. "Please. There's not much time."

"What do you mean?" I asked.

"There's no time," he insisted.

Everyone started screaming at once.

Several newlings swung from the lights, bounded off the counters, the bar, the stools, and descended upon the clubbers in a rabid feast. I moved away from Victorian. My confusion erased, I shook my head of the intoxicating fog and I kicked into action. I knew what needed to be done, and I wouldn't leave here without my friend; with all these mortals helplessly falling victim to their bloodsucking prey. I blinked, my hand going beneath my skirt before my brain really registered what was happening.

"Please, Riley," Victorian begged, moving closer. "Come with me. I promise to get your friend to safety."

"Fine!" I yelled, "but you'd better get her now!" I ducked and flipped a blade from my thigh. Just as a newling lunged at me, I plunged it into his heart. He began to jerk. "Get her now, Victorian!" I yelled. "In the back!"

Victorian disappeared.

No sooner had he vanished into the melee than Eli, Luc, Phin, Josie, Seth, Zetty, Noah and his guys, stormed through the door.

A second full-scale melee ensued.

Eli made his way toward me, his face livid, etched with terror and fury. He grabbed me by the arm and shook me. Anger and confusion mapped lines into his face. "Are you okay?" he asked.

"I'm fine!" I shouted.

He didn't glare at me long. He took off. He trusted me. He shouldn't have.

I took as many out as I could. Every once in a while I saw Seth. He was alive and kicking ass. Relief washed over me as he stayed, back-to-back, with Noah.

Just as I flung another blade, hitting my mark and turning another vamp newling to dust, my arm was grabbed again. This time when I turned, it was Nyx. She threw her arms around me. "Oh, Riley!" she yelled, and squeezed me hard. "I was so scared!"

Relief flooded me at the sight of Nyx unharmed. I didn't have time to revel in it. "Go to Luc!" I said, dragged her by the arm, and gave her a push in his direction. *"Luc!"* I yelled in my mind. He turned, faced me, saw Nyx, and ran directly toward her. Once his hands were on her, I knew she'd be safe.

I had one undead left to kill. I pushed my way to the back of the melee. I was shoved, pushed, grabbed.

I was abruptly stopped by Victorian, his hands vices on my shoulders.

His gaze bore into mine. "You promised."

I yanked against him. "I'm not leaving with you! There's one more that needs to die first," I yelled. "My life is here! I love Eli, my brother, my family. You know me, Victorian! I can't let your brother live! He's a monster!"

"I know, but you must!" he yelled back, and dragged me effortlessly through the horrified mortals. He turned when we were in a thinner crowd. I fought him, pulled, yanked, beat him in the back with my fists. "No," he pleaded, ducking further swings from my fists. "You cannot, Riley. Please." He grabbed my hands in his, stilling me. His drugging dark gaze pinned mine. "You will come with me. Now. Away from this."

My actions were once more no longer under my control. My adrenaline pumped, and my inhuman-like heart slammed slowly, methodically. I didn't want to go. Victorian left me no choice.

"Come now, Riley," Victorian said slowly; it became the only sound inside my head. "It's the only way any of this can be resolved."

I couldn't leave. Valerian had to die.

"He can't die, love," he said, close to my face. "He cannot."

I didn't exactly understand it, but somehow I knew Victorian spoke the truth.

"I'll tell you on the way," he said. "I promise—this is the only way to stop him. To stop all of this."

"This way," he said, and pulled me effortlessly through the crowd. My mind and body were powerless to stop him; to resist him. We'd muddled through a lot of people, and at the last second, perhaps because Victorian had eased up on his mind power over me, I yanked free and ran.

"Riley!" he yelled after me.

I ignored him and sought Eli. I had to tell him; I had to explain. I ran up behind him, just as he shoved a mortal to safety, yanked him by the arm, and spun him around.

Eli glared at me with opaque eyes and pinpoint red pupils. "Get out of here, Riley," he threatened. "Go now!"

With that, he shoved me, and with so much force I flew back—far.

I landed at Victorian's feet. Without another word, he lifted me. "You'll come now." Once again I was powerless. He helped me to the back and out the door into Savannah's sultry, dark night. I knew Eli hadn't shoved me for any other reason other than he wanted me safe. I knew that in my heart. He was angry because I was in danger, plain and simple. Yet the thought of leaving him, like this, burned a hole in me, made my chest hurt, and made it ache. I didn't want to go!

Near the back entrance was a stone silver convertible Jag. Victorian opened the driver's side door. "Get in, Riley."

Almost as if stuck in the weird, crawlin'-bird-across-the-branch dream, I did as the powerful strigoi vampire commanded, and I crawled my ass straight over to the passenger's side.

He followed me in and jammed the keys into the ignition; the engine roared, and the dual exhaust rumbled. Gravel crunched beneath the tires as he threw the car into gear and slammed on the gas.

As we peeled out of the parking lot, I felt a heavy presence behind me. It was so thick, it nearly choked me. I turned my head, pushed the fuchsia bangs from my eyes, and peered through the wind and darkness.

Two figures stood, side by side.

Eli's gaze bore straight into me, staring hard after me as I drove away with an enemy vampire. Seemingly, to them, I went willingly. They didn't know Victorian had me under some sort of mind control.

Noah Miles stood next to him, his mercury gaze glowing. He said nothing. He didn't have to. Neither of them did.

Eli, though, didn't hold back.

"Ri-ley!" he yelled, his voice hurt, in deep pain, reverberating inside my chest, inside my bones.

I looked until I saw him no more. We turned onto Martin Luther King Boulevard, then Interstate 16. We were headed north. Where to, I had no idea. I couldn't think; my mind was a myriad of emotions.

"All will be well soon," Victorian said, and put his hand on my knee. He wiped a smudge of . . . something off me, then grasped my chin and forced my stare to meet his. "I promise, Riley Poe. I vow it. I will make this right. You'll suffer no more, love."

As we headed out into the night, the ever-familiar brine of Savannah's salt encased me. I wasn't in my own body; I was in another's—or so it felt similar. I laid my head back on the headrest, the hum of Victorian's Jag and the ever-pressing sadness of leaving my loved ones, making my lids grow heavy. I closed my eyes, only for a second. In that fraction of time, Eli's voice filled my mind, so much that I reached out, just to see if he was there beside me. It was desperate; it was tormented, filled with so much agony, it hurt for me to hear it. Yet I craved it, as I craved air to breathe, to fill my lungs, to live.

As vampires irrevocably craved human blood.

Neither vampires nor humans could help their cravings. I know that now. Both needed a vital something to remain alive. For vampire's, that something was more gruesome, and at the cost of human life, but still—it was their sustenance, and they could help it no more than I could help drawing in a lungful of air. I know that now. I understand it a little more.

Eli's voice sounded in my head. He spoke to me, and only to me.

I'll cherish the sound, pained as it was, forever.

I will come for you, Riley. I love you, and I know you love me. I'll find you. Until I do, be strong. Do what you have to to survive. You're mine. You always have been and you always will be. I will come for you. . . .

Read ahead for a sneak peek of the next book in
Elle Jasper's Dark Ink Chronicles,

EVENTIDE

Available in 2012 from Signet Eclipse.

I'm on my back, a weight not my own pressing me down. I now smell pine, fresh-cut grass. Slowly, I open my eyes. A weight presses into me. I can't move.

Only then do the sounds around me waft through and bring me back to the present. Cars and semitrucks whizzing by, unevenly, at various speeds. A can dispenses through a soft-drink machine. Laughter in the distance. A stereo system blasts Twisted Sister, one speaker blown in the back. Victorian is straddling me. He has my arms pinned above my head, holding me still. My eyes scan past him. We're at a rest stop.

I find my voice, and I struggle against him. "What are you doing?"

Victorian studies me. His grip on me tightens. "You don't remember?"

For a second, my brain races. I don't remember, and I don't stick around to try to make myself remember, either. I buck hard and Victorian's grip breaks; I leap up and take off. A slice of light from several tall lamps illuminates the side of the concrete building of the rest area; I avoid it and run straight for the shadows and the trees beyond. With arms and legs pumping, I fly through the darkness. I don't care who sees me. It's not like there are a lot of people out at the rest stop at two a.m. In seconds I'm sifting through dense pines, and because I'm still wearing the same gauzy skirt, tank, and Vans I had on at Tunnel 9, brambles grab my bare legs and scratch the holy hell out of them. I don't care. I have to get away. Ease the craving now gnawing at my insides—

I jerk to a sudden stop. Confusion webs through my mind, and my memory races wildly. Craving? I only crave Krystal burgers and Krispy Kremes. What—

A body rushes mine, and I am once again flung to the ground. Without looking, I know it's Victorian. Sharp pine needles and cones littering the wood dig into my skin as his weight presses against me. My face is smashed into the damp leaves and moss.

Quickly, my hands are tethered together.

"Sorry, love," Victorian apologizes. He binds my ankles together, too. "You can't imagine how I hate this, but somehow"—he helps me stand, then looks at me—"you broke free of my suggestion." His head cocks to the side as he studies me, and the moonlight shooting a slender beam through the trees glances off his face. "Intriguing. I've never met another who can break free of my suggestion."

Rage fills behind my eyes, pounds in my chest. "Well, now you have. So now what? What are you gonna do now, Vic? Throw me over your shoulder like a sack of dog food and haul me to the car?"

The slightest of smiles tips his sensual lips upward. "That's exactly what I'm going to do." In one move, Victorian ducks and over his shoulder I go. He keeps his hands secured around my calves. My skirt is probably up around my waist. We move out of the wood and start across the lawn of the rest stop, past the concrete picnic tables and restrooms. No one was about. Only a few semitrucks parked, their drivers more than likely sleeping. It wouldn't do any good for me to scream; Victorian would simply suggest to anyone who heard that I was really okay, and they'd believe. So I keep quiet.

Until I hear the lock click, and the Jag's trunk open.

"No freaking way," I say evenly. "Victorian, do not put me in there."

Victorian puts me in there. Lays me gently on a soft down comforter. Warm brown eyes look down at me with obvious regret. "I apologize. I truly hate this. But for you to break free from my suggestion?" He shook his head. "You're stronger than I thought—than you even think you are. You're a danger to yourself, Riley. I can't let anything happen to you." The trunk starts to close.

"Wait!" I say frantically. He waits. "Where are you taking me?"

Lowering his hand, Vic grazes my jaw with his knuckles. "Somewhere safe. Somewhere I can help you."

Without another word, he closes me in. The moment he does, another voice rises.

"What the fuck are you doing, man?" a deep voice grumbles. "Open the goddamn trunk."

"Perhaps you'd be better off minding your own business," Victorian warns evenly, gentlemanly.

A heavy thump hits the back of the car. "Perhaps you'd be better off shutting the fuck up and opening the motherfucking trunk," the stranger says. "Now."

Silence.

"What the fuck—"

The only noise I hear is a choked gurgle.

A car door slams, and in seconds, the purr of the Jag's engine rumbles around me. I know without having seen what just happened. Victorian fed. In his defense, he tried to warn the guy. In the guy's defense, he was trying to save me. It's all so messed up. Victorian shifts gears and roars up the interstate. We're on the move. To where, I have no clue.

The one question I have right now is, where the hell did a centuries-old vampire get friggin' tie-wraps? I jerk my ankles and wrists—no go. That thick, hard plastic won't budge even a fraction. In fact, they tighten. So I relax and try to forget I'm in the back of a trunk, bound. And that back at the rest stop, a man lay dead in the parking lot, his blood drained. I close my eyes, the sound of the road and the Jag's engine a respite.

A vision of Eli crowds my mind: his face, his jaw, his eyes. The way he touches me; his lips against my skin. More than that, the last words he spoke to me as we drove away from Tunnel 9 resonates inside my memory.

I will come for you.

How would he know where we are headed? The look on his face as I'd driven off with Victorian had been that of anguish, betrayal, then of determination. All in about five seconds. It was not in Eli's nature to give up. I think he probably was that way, even as a human. Before vampirism. It's definitely a quality I like.

Time flies by. I drift in and out of slumber. The back of my legs and back are sweaty atop the down comforter, and I wish I could get a small breath of fresh air. I don't know how long we drive for; but I've reached my limit.

With the flat of my Vans, I start kicking the side of the Jag's trunk interior. I kick for maybe five minutes before the car comes to a stop. Victorian's door opens and closes; the trunk pops. The scents of car tire, motor oil, fill the cool air. We're in a large area—one that echoes.

"Are you okay?" he asks, pushing my long, choppy bangs from my face. He traces my sooty angel-wing ink on my cheek. Concern is etched in his face.

"You mean besides not having any air to breathe and being hot as hell? Not to mention I've had to pee for the last hour. Sure. I'm great, Vic." I glower at him. "Get me out of here."

Victorian freezes, glances around. "We've got to hurry." He easily lifts me from the trunk and sets me on my feet. "Are you going to make me carry you in the same way I put you in the trunk?" he asks.

"Nope," I say. "But as soon as we get to where we're going, you're telling me everything."

He nods, and produces a pair of wire cutters from his pocket. In a few quick snaps, my ankles, wrists are free.

"Let's go," he says, slams the trunk and grasps my elbow; he leads me through a parking garage that is slightly lit and mostly empty. We make it to the elevator, and Victorian pulls me inside. I know he's using all of his suggestion to keep me restrained because I try to break free; this time, I can't. He pushes the L. Just as the doors begin to slide together, I catch a scent. A familiar scent.

With my next breath I am literally snatched out of the elevator by my arm and flung. I land with a grunt on the concrete floor of the parking garage, ten, twelve feet away, on my side. Phin is there when I stand.

"Are you okay?" he asks. His hands are everywhere, checking me for injury. As I knock him away, my eyes search for Eli. The moment I see him, I leap for the elevator.

"Riley, stop!" Phin yells, makes a grab for me, but misses.

I don't listen. I can't listen. Because I know Eli.

He'll kill Victorian.

Just as I hurl myself at the elevator, Eli and Victorian fall out of it. In a mass of growls, grunts, French expletives and Romanian curses, we all hit the ground. Eli is completely changed—fangs dropped, face contorted, eyes white with a pinpoint scarlet pupil. Victorian's appearance has totally morphed; it's unlike anything I've yet seen. His skin is ashen, almost dead looking. His eyes are bloodred, his fangs long and jagged. Eli shoves me away, and I once more hit the ground. With a violent curse, I jump up, but Eli and Victorian are already thirty feet away. They're tangled, snarling, throwing each other. I run up, despite Phin trying to grab me. Just as I reach them, I stop. With one hand around Victorian's throat, Eli takes his other hand and makes to fling me again. I slap his hand away.

"Eli! Stop it!" I yell, and throw myself between them. It's like being in the middle of a pair of fighting pit bulls. "Now!"

"Move, Riley," Eli growls, his voice inhuman, nearly inaudible. He once more tries to hurl me.

I cling to Victorian, but my eyes are fastened onto Eli's. "No, dammit! Stop and listen to me!"

"Phin!" Eli shouts. "Get her the fuck out of here!"

With as much emotion as I can summon, I hold Eli's gaze. "Please, Eli, don't kill him." I'm not used to begging, and it doesn't sit well with me. But in this, I have no choice. "Please."

Phin's hand is on my shoulder, and he pulls. I resist.

Eli's inhuman white glare freezes onto mine. "Why?" he asks, his voice deadly smooth, even, quiet. I can tell he is confused, hurt. Angry is a given. I don't blame him.

Behind me, Victorian's body shudders, but I keep my eyes trained on Eli's. "I don't know," I answer honestly. "It . . . just doesn't feel right."

Eli's sharp gaze flicks to Victorian. It's filled with hate. "Doesn't feel right, Riley? He abducted you." His grip tightens on Victorian's throat. "He almost killed you."

Yeah, I already know all that. It doesn't matter. "He isn't the monster his brother is," I say. "Please. Trust me."

Eli literally shakes with rage. The scarlet pupils widen, like a cat's adjusting to darkness.

"Eligius," I say calmly, and he looks at me. "Move."

Pure white eyes stare at me in silent debate for what seems forever. Without looking at Victorian, he manages, "Not until he tells me what the *fuck* is going on."

Moving from between them, I turn to Victorian. Bloodred eyes seek mine. I keep my hand on Eli's arm for support, and give Victorian a nod. My stomach churns with anticipation.

Victorian simply breathes for several seconds, head bowed, collecting himself. His shoulders, broad but slim, rise and fall with air I'm certain does not circulate within his lungs. When he lifts his head, the only remnants of his vampiric morphing are his eyes. They remain crimson and fixed on me. "Riley has too much of my brother's strigoi DNA. It's . . . changing her." He glances at Eli. "Changing her in ways even her dark brethren cannot cure." His Romanian accent is heavier at times, like now. "She is beginning to crave. I've seen it." His voice lowers. "She will kill."

"I will what?" I ask, shocked, staring back at Vic. "Are you friggin' crazy?"

"Bullshit," Phin says, and his angry voice echoes off the concrete walls of the parking garage. "She went through weeks of cleansing."

"You underestimate the power of a strigoi," Victorian replies.

"We underestimate nothing," Eli says quietly, deadly. Threatening. "You're wrong, Arcos."

"She broke my power of suggestion," Victorian argues, flashing me a glimpse. "Started growling, convulsing." He glances at me, then to Eli. "Nearly jumped from my car going eighty-five. I had to pull over and restrain her physically, and even then she briefly overpowered me."

"So where were you taking her?" Phin said. His voice sounded not his own; he was getting impatient. Out of character for Séraphin Dupré.

Then again, the flashes I'd had while running through the wood behind the rest stop had been out of character for me. What the hell was that? I settle it within myself to believe it was nothing more than backlash from the trauma at Tunnel 9.

"Where?" Eli states. His patience is going fast, too.

Victorian's unholy gaze settles on mine. "To my family home in Kudzsir. To my father."

I blink, and Eli's body flies in front of me. By the time my vision finds them, Eli has Victorian crushed against a wall. "So you can turn her? Have her for yourself?"

"Eli!" I yell.

With his face close to Victorian's, Eli growls, "I'll fucking tear your limbs from your body and burn them myself before I let that happen. And I'll start with your goddamn head."

"No!" I run now, because Eli's looking like he's about to start dismembering Victorian right where they stand. My arm is grabbed and I jerk to a jolting halt. I turn and glare at Phin. "You'd better turn me loose."

Phin just looks at me. Tightens his grip.

Just then, a beam of light arcs over the gray concrete walls of the garage; an SUV pulls in.

"Eli, let's go," I plead. "Now. Just forget about this. I'm all right."

At first, he ignores me—nothing new there. Then he flings Victorian several feet and storms toward me. As he passes, he grabs my hand. He doesn't say a word.

Victorian has more balls than I give him credit for. He's leapt up and now stands directly in Eli's path. With an assured look, he speaks. "Know this, Eligius. Only a powerful strigoi like my father can cast out the evil growing inside Riley. And you will soon see—it is definitely there."

Eli stares at Victorian for a split second, then takes his hand and shoves him out of the way. We continue on through the parking garage. I turn and watch Victorian.

"You will soon see," he says, standing in place. "You'll bring her back to me. I will be here, waiting."

We round a corner, and Victorian is no longer in my sight.

His voice resonates through the garage.

"You fool!" he yells. "You'll soon see, Dupré. When you do, and the evil overtakes her and she becomes unstoppable, I will be here, waiting. Do you hear me, Riley? Whatever it takes, I will wait for you!"

We reach Phin's black Ford F-150 in tense silence. In the distance, I hear a door slam and an engine start up. It's not Victorian's Jag. Phin hits the lock-release button on his key chain, and Eli opens my door. As I put my foot on the side step to climb in, he stops me.

With both hands on my face, he kisses me, long, ungentle, desperate. I breathe in his scent and return the kiss. His lukewarm lips are full, sensual as they devour mine. Then he pulls back. With startling blue eyes, he inspects me from head to toe; at my bare thigh, he lingers, lowers his hand, and grazes a large scrape.

"Must've gotten that at the rest area," I say, and although his features are cast in shadow, I know he studies me with ferocious intensity.

"Let's go home," he says, and climbs in beside me.

Phin starts up the truck and exit the parking garage. It's not until we hit Peachtree Street that I realize Victorian and I had made it all the way to Atlanta.

It's close to four a.m.; traffic is nonexistent as we weave through downtown Atlanta and make our way back to Savannah. Before we hit the Interstate, Phin pulls in to a BP and fuels up. I run inside, Eli right behind me, and use the bathroom, grab some drinks and a bag of Chic-O-Stix, and settle in for the drive home.

Even with Eli's body crowding mine in the cab of Phin's truck, his hand protectively on my thigh, one thought pounds through my brain; one thing needles me and doesn't let go.

Am I truly turning evil? Am I going to kill?

Will I crave blood?

Goddamn, I hope to hell not.

I'm sleepy again—why, I don't know, but I feel like I haven't slept in days. I close my eyes and slumber soon takes over.